Can't wait
for you to see
what I got
next coming
for you
LOVE YOU

PORTER

WILLIAM CHASE

BOOK II

N. M. BOBOK

This book is dedicated to my beautiful Nana, Dulcilea, both she and Marcus' grandma, Maria share the same Astrological Sign: Leo. Thank you for always taking care of every single one of us, our family is forever thankful,

Com amor, seu netinho.

CHAPTERS

I

SÓLFAR

There aren't many places like this.

Even though I've been here countless times before, it's always a great place to get a break from the world, or worlds if you're a Porter like myself. From where I'm sitting, I can see Sólfar – the Sun Voyager, a sculpture by Jón Gunnar Árnason; it is a dreamboat, an ode to the Sun. Intrinsically, it contains within itself the promise of undiscovered territory, a dream of hope, progress, and freedom; here is where tourists come to watch the midnight Sunset which happens during summertime in Reykjavík, Iceland.

It is 11:55 P.M. local time.

I have a local porter in my hand - a beer that is - and I'm enjoying the Sunset in a place where young weekenders are just about getting ready to enjoy the nice warm night of fifty-eight degrees. I've been there before. I've had my nights of fun somewhere in the 1900's, even though it was centuries ago; my looks, however, says otherwise. At the age of eighteen, I've become a Porter. Porters are people who can transform themselves into their constellation, in my case, the Lyre.

The Lyre is a constellation outside of the twelve known astrological signs which are also known as Wonderers, because of that I'm part of the other less known constellations known as the Wanderers. The difference is almost minimal: Wonderers, also known as The Twelve Chosen Ones, have a set home planet and were handpicked by the Queen of our Solar System, Mariah Stars. Wanderers don't have a set planet, making them truly wanderers from planet to planet and are picked mostly by other Wanderers.

I remember like it was yesterday: I walked in this dark cave with only the lights of the moons Titania and Ariel reflecting inside. Victor Tool, Wanderer Porter of the Pictor's Constellation, the Painter's Easel, walked in with my mentor and trainer Luke Horace, Porter of the Wanderer Constellation of Hercules, the Hero, and said calmly to me:

"Mr. Chase, are you ready to become a Wanderer, Porter of the Lyra Constellation, the Lyre?"

I nodded, somewhat nervous, afraid even, not because of becoming a Wanderer but because it was my first tattoo ever.

"Sit over here," he pointed to a stool nearby. I sat facing a calm, peaceful lake. Miranda, the moon we were on, was quiet and beautiful with small caves and low mountains. Its planet, the prominent, pale-blue Uranus, was right in front of us with two of its many moons, Titania and Ariel, still there, side by side, brightly in the sky. As he began tattooing my arm, I felt no pain. If it weren't for the weird noise coming out of his equally weird tool, I wouldn't even know I was getting tattooed.

The stars became brighter than they were. Some even seem to appear in the sky. The moons got more vivid and defined as if my eyes somehow got higher resolution. I could see the remaining Uranusians moons, over twenty-something, revolving around the planet, to which now I could see the faint rings. It was then I realized my eyesight was heightened more than that of a regular human, or as we call it, an Unportable. Every Porter's Constellation manifests itself differently according to who you are as an individual. Your personality defines how a Constellation reveals on you, meaning two Porters of the same Constellation could manifest completely different abilities.

When I first transformed into a lyrebird, I was both surprised and pleased about it. Apparently, before me, there was no one else like me, none of the previous Porters of the Lyra Constellation had ever become a lyrebird.

"All done William. Now go make your name proud and chase the stars while Luke and I'll finish up," Victor told me as I took my first flight as a midnight-blue lyrebird.

A few years later, the Halley comet came by, and

I got its dust infused in my existent tattoo. Its effect stops the aging of a Porter's body. I was twenty-five years old then, just as I am twenty-five years old now.

I've seen many moons rise, many Sunrises, many Sunsets, but to me, there is no better place than here on this Earthian country of Iceland. Reykjavík to be more specific.

It's now 12:15 A.M.

The Sun was set.

In a couple of minutes, the Sun would rise again.

"Here, I got you another beer," he sat right next to me, replacing the empty beer bottle in my hand for a new one.

"Thanks, uh...?"

"Marcus. Name's Marcus. Did you forget it already, American?"

"Listen, Marcus; I gotta go," I got out of there with the beer in my hand, "and by the way, *ég er ekki Amerísk!*[1]"

"Really, man? Just gonna bounce outta here like this?"

I was already a few feet away from him when I heard him curse me in Icelandic. Took a few turns and disappeared inside of my Exotic Matter Sphere back into my house. Exotic Matter Sphere is a semi-sphere located in the belly button of all Wonderers and Wanderers only. Porters do not possess it. When any of us presses it, we are sucked inside of it in a va-

---

[1] *Ég er ekki Amerísk:* I'm not American (Icelandic)

cuum tunnel, commonly known as Wormhole, transporting us from the place we are to any other site we want. However, we are not allowed to go outside the Kuiper Belt, the circumstellar disc of small bodies asteroids revolving around our Sun's planetary system, the Solar System.

I reappeared back in Pluto's moon, Charon, a place I've been residing for the last few hundred years. Pluto is a Planet that, as of now, is outside of the Queen of our Solar System's jurisdiction. Pluto goes in and out of the Kuiper Belt, causing a very heated stir between the Queen herself and King Titus Vespasian, ruler of the galaxy where our Solar System resides, the Milky Way. Until they decide the future of Pluto and its moons, I'll live here indefinitely.

Besides my house and a few other houses here and there, Charon had a small village a few miles away from my home. The people here kept mostly to themselves, everyone knew each other, and they would gather in each other's houses every weekend only so they could rejoice in one of the biggest productions of crystals in the Solar System. If you look hard enough, you could see the tiny lights of the village from my living room, but I, instead, rather look at Pluto on the horizon, through my high ceiling windows.

"Were you on Earth again?" A beautiful young lady in her early twenties sitting on the bench outside of my house asked.

"Donna, to which do I owe you the surprise?" I made my way outside of the house in the middle of a cold evening here in Charon, a detail non-important for those who can't usually be bothered by the weather like myself and Donna Saihtam, Porter of the Virgo Constellation, a Wonderer and one of the Chosen Ones.

"William, when does a girl need a reason to surprise her best friend?" She handed me a tiny purple box wrapped with a silver ribbon.

"Fomjot's Chocolate? If I didn't know you better, I would be suspicious about this," I told her, unwrapping the silver ribbon sitting next to her on the bench in front of my house.

"Why, you don't like them?" She asked, knowing the answer.

"Oh, I do, Donna, but I doubt you've brought me chocolate from the farthest Saturn's moon, just because." I bit off one of the petite delicacies.

"Ugh, you're no fun," Donna got up and kneeled in front of me, holding both of my hands so I couldn't reach for any more chocolate, "Willie, we need to talk. Allison and I—"

"Nope, nope," I got up walking away from her, "whenever you and Allison have a conversation about me, is either to set me up on another stupid blind date or to go drinking in some forsaken moon in the Solar System, and I'm not in the mood for either."

"Actually, she suggested that would do you some good to get a job." She sat back on the bench.

"A job?" I asked, wondering if I heard her right.

"Yes, a job, you and I both know that once you're

done with your training, which you are, if you're not training anyone, or protecting anyone, then you should find a job in the Solar System."

"I don't know," I sat next to her, "You know I'm more of a free—"

"Free-spirited kind of guy, I know, that's why we think it's best for you to work for Mario Shwayze."

"The lunatic Italian guy who's been planning to take over Mariah Stars' place for centuries? No, thanks." I got up making my way back inside my house.

"Allison and I have been working with him for a while, and yes his ideas are a little bit out there, but the money is good," she offered me the box of chocolates before I could walk back in, "think about it, at least?"

"Alright, no promises, you know I'm not into politics," I grabbed the box of the assorted chocolates from Fomjot, "I'll make an appointment to see him sometime next week."

"Actually," she followed me inside of the house, "Allison already arranged an appointment for you to see him today."

"TODAY? What were you two thinking?"

"We both know if we leave you to it, you'll never do it," Donna sat on the couch across the high ceiling windows in the living room, "now go on, get ready and I'll go with you."

I left her in the living room, went up the stairs to be bedroom to take a shower, and change my clothes to something dressier. If I am to get a job, I have to impress the boss, right?

"Finally!" She exclaimed once she saw me coming back down the stairs, "did you brush your teeth?"

"My teeth? Is there something in my teeth?" I checked my teeth in a mirror near the mantel.

"No, but you had a beer breath before," she got up to fix my tie, "was he cute?"

"What are you talking about?"

"C'mon, you and I both know you love to spend time with those Icelandic boys," Donna joked around, "I honestly don't know what you see on them, I much rather the dark, tall, red-skinned men from Uranus."

"I wouldn't know," I activated the Stardust Dome around the house, "I have never been to Uranus."

"Maybe that's what you need, to spend some fun time in Uranus." Donna stretched out her hand, "shall we?"

"We shall," I held her hand as we both disappeared inside our Exotic Matter Sphere.

When a Porter wants to take another Porter to a place that only one of them have been before, they hold hands together. The Porter who knows the destination thinks about the location of where they are going while the other Porter keeps his mind clean so they can both go to the designated place that one of them is thinking; and the place that Donna thought before pressing her Exotic Matter Sphere was Jupiter.

"And here we are," Donna spoke once we materialized. "Welcome to Retip, the City of White Skies."

In the North Tropical Zone, in the eastern country of Üji, one of the three-thousand-five-hundred-and-sixty-seven nations in Jupiter is the southwestern city of Retip.

True to its name, Retip sky was white, not cloudy like on Earth, but genuinely white with pale-orange clouds here and there. The city itself had a vibe of old Indian culture, similar to the one on Earth, with small rustic houses everywhere, people of brown skin and colorful hair crossing in every direction, making it harder for me to blend in, a white complexion guy with midnight-blue eyes.

Donna, having olive tone skin and long dark-brown hair, would have blended in if it wasn't for her revealing red blouse and tight black pants, completely the opposite of the pale earthy tone clothes everyone here was wearing.

"Wish you'd told me to dress in more earthy tone clothes to blend in," I kept my gaze down as to not call attention upon myself. "I stand out like a polar bear in the middle of the desert."

"Of course, you do; your pale complexion and matching midnight-blue eyes and hair makes you look like you're from Rasa, the country in the South Temperate Belt, where mostly everyone is boring looking like yourself," Donna laughed obviously mocking me.

I followed her strutting her high heel boots throughout the way, up the stairs in the only big house around, so big that it resembled a mansion.

"*Ciao, benvenuti a*[2] Retip, the City of White Skies,"

---

[2] "*Ciao, benvenuti a:* Hi, welcome to (Italian)

a robust man in his fifties with short salt-and-pepper hair, dressed entirely in black and nice shining, polished shoes, greeted us by the door with a solid Italian accent.

"I'm Mario Shawyze, Wanderer Porter of the Orion Constellation, the Hunter and also future king of the Solar System, and you must be William,"

"William Chase, Wanderer Porter of the Lyra Constellation, the Lyre," I introduced myself. "It's nice to put a face on the name finally."

"Indeed, it is, Allison has told me quite a great deal about you, Mr. Chase," he walked back into his house, gesturing for us to follow him inside the wide-open room, "the first Lyrebird ever."

"It's no big deal; I'm sure there were others before me,"

"Mr. Chase, would you please demonstrate what your powers can do?" Although he asked, his tone made it sure that it was an order.

"Alright," I thought for a second, "Hello, Mr. Shawyze," I spoke with Donna's voice.

"HEY!" Donna shouted, creeped out, "I told you never to mimic me."

"Impressive," Mr. Shawyze complimented me, "However, I have a feeling you can do more with your voice than just mimic other people's voices."

"I could, but I'm afraid I might break something here," I told him looking around in the room.

"William, may I call you William?" I nodded as he continued, "There are only a few vases around the room for decoration. I can get them replaced before you can press your E.M.S. out of here."

"Okay, cover your ears," I let out a small sonic boom destroying the vase directly in front of me, a few feet away from us.

"That was good," Mr. Shawyze clapped his hands in excitement, "Now, direct it at me."

"Mr. Shwayze, his voice just shattered a vase in less than a couple of seconds, I don't think—"

"Hush, Donna, you're too young to understand this sort of things," Mr. Shawyze shushed her, "now, William, give me everything you've got, don't hold back."

Mario's eyes went from black to bright-white like stars, as did mine and Donna's, who had taken several steps away from me.

I took a deep breath, trying to calculate a sonic screech that would impress him without killing him, I stared at Donna who sent me a T.P., *'Please, don't kill him,'*

I look back at Mario, who had a big smile on his face just like frat boys do when they are dared to endure challenges to see who is the strongest of them all.

"*Andiamo[3]*, Willie," he encouraged me, "I don't have all day."

"HAAAAAAAAAAAAAAAAAAAA!"

My sonic screech has a very high pitch, shattering fragile objects like all the vases around the room, blowing Mario a few feet away from me, crashing on

---

[3] *Andiamo:* Let's go (Italian)

another vase behind him.

"ARGH!" Donna shouted as if trying to shake off the screech still echoing inside her head, getting up to her feet.

"Mr. Shawyze, are you okay?" I helped him up.

"That was *stupendo⁴!*" He hugged me in comradery, slapping my back a couple of times, "I wonder what else you can do."

"There aren't sounds that I can hear and not replicate them," I explained to him.

"If I train you well, you can even kill any Porter with just the power of your voice, turning them almost instantaneously into Stardust," he laughed maniacally, "can you imagine the damage you can do?"

"I can honestly say I haven't imagined killing anyone, Mr. Shawyze,"

"Mario, call me Mario, Willie," he put his right arms around my shoulders, "you're hired, by the way."

"King Shwayze, sorry to interrupt," a tall black man with long dreads, fully dressed in black as well, walked in the room,

"What, Midnight?" Mario's pleasant smile was gone as he barked back at the man.

"You asked us to inform you about any incidents evolving the Mathiases,"

"Yes, I did, what is it? Did Mr. Mathias finally decide to enroll his boy at C.H.E.P.?"

"Actually, it is Mr. Mathias' mom. She's gotten

---

⁴ *Stupendo:* Stupendous (Italian)

worse." He informed the room barely moving an inch.

"Oh, good, the old lioness is long overdue. If she hadn't have given her spot to Mr. Larkson, she wouldn't be in this position." Mario raised his left eyebrow as if asking for my approval, to which I ignored politely.

"Mr. Mathias is going to Rio de Janeiro, leaving the boy alone with his mom, sir."

"Oh, really?" Mr. Shwayze's eyes widened up in excitement again, "Get me the Twins, I have a mission for them."

"Yes, sir," the man called Midnight stepped out of the room.

"Mr. Chase, as you've noticed, I have important business to attend," Mr. Shawyze took my hand, shaking it. "I'll contact you soon. You may have a mission sooner than you think."

"Thank you, sir, I won't disappoint you."

Donna and I walked out of the house back in the City of the White Skies.

"Interesting character, isn't he?" I asked Donna once we were away from the ears of the crazy house.

"He's not as bad once you get to know him," Donna assured me. "What do you think he wants with the Mathiases?"

"Don't know, don't care." I lied to her. The Mathiases were once pretty close to me.

"Do you know them?" She asked me, surprised by the statement.

"Let's just say we grew apart."

"Oh, so I guess you wouldn't mind if Mario has

them killed?" Donna asked, casually.

"Killed? Why would Mario have them killed?" I have indeed grown apart from the Mathiases but, in no way would I want them murdered.

"I don't know. What I do know is that Mario would not have one of his Hounds to go for the Twins if he didn't want them killed."

Maybe Donna was right. I couldn't let Mario kill a family that was once my family as well.

'Marcus Mathias, where are you?
I know you're here somewhere.
I bring you wondrous news,
News to tell you that no one dares.
Where are you, Marcus, where?'

I sent Marcus a Thought Projection. If he's in danger, I have to help him, even if he's unaware of it.

"Donna, you might be right. I'm not sure what Mario has in mind, but I'll keep a close eye on them."

"Whatever it is you're planning to do; you better do soon. By the tone of Mario's voice, he's not playing around," Donna told me as she walked away in the middle of the crowd. "Send me a T.P. if you need me."

"Will do."

II

THE MATHIASES

I have to make a decision soon; I have to make a decision now. There are rumors that Roberto's kid may be a Natural, but no one is sure of it yet. If he is a Natural indeed than his powers might be manifest at random times, if he's not a Natural, then he hasn't gotten my T.P. which brings me back to the urgency of finding him.

In a blink of an eye, I pressed my Exotic Matter Sphere in place of where my belly button should be, and disappeared inside of it, reappearing on Earth, northern hemisphere, in the western country of the United States of America, in the state of Massachusetts, city of Everett where the Mathiases live.

Appearing outside of the house that I haven't been to in so long. A modest two-story-high house where Roberto Mathias and Katherine Mathias live along with their son, Marcus Mathias, who I haven't seen since he was five years old.

A blond, blue-eyed guy in his mid-teens passed by me completely unaware of me, thanks to the power of the Stardust Dome, an invisible bubble that protects us, Porters, to stay unseen by the Unportables.

"*Joyeux Anniversaire*[5], Marks!" he exclaimed loudly by the door before Marcus invited him in.

I allowed myself in as well, again invisible to the human eyes who don't have Stardust running in their bloodstream. It is a bizarre feeling to be back in this house. Everything is different; everything has changed. It has a story now. You could feel the warm family vibe around the whole house.

"PUT IT ON!" The blond kid, Jacques is his name, shouted making Marcus almost drop the gift box of the visual game he had given to him, Mirabilis.

To see Marcus, a young man now, celebrating his sixteenth birthday was somewhat surreal. He looks just like his father, Roberto, except for his eyes. Roberto's eyes are brown; Marcus' are green just like his mom, Katherine.

"Is this another zombie apocalypse video-game?" Mrs. Mathias walked in the living room, also unaware of my presence.

I haven't seen her in so long. Her brown hair up in a messy ponytail, in her everyday clothes, Katherine was still a beautiful sight to see. Her green eyes

---

[5] *Joyeux Anniversaire:* Happy Birthday (French)

standing out against her white skin complexion, with a beautiful smile on her face.

Not long ago, she, Roberto, and I were pretty close friends. Luke, my mentor, thought it would be a great idea to train them on how to be a Porter along with the guidance of Kent Hors, the mighty Wonderer of Earth, Porter of the Taurus Constellation, hand-picked by the Queen of our Solar System, Mariah Stars. Little did I know at the time that the three of us would become such good friends. Seeing Katherine walk in the room like that, it was easy to see why Roberto chose to marry her or did she choose him?

DING-DONG

The doorbell brought my attention to a different character.

"Hello, birthday boy, I hope you don't mind me stopping by before everyone else."

A young girl with almond-shaped and colored eyes, matching her wavy hair, walked in with a light, different accent than that of Marcus' and Jacques'. She walked in, ignoring the blond kid and handed Marcus his birthday gift. Was she Marcus' girl? Were they already dating? But they seem so young.

"Well, I'm very happy to see you, *ma belle princesse*[6]," I guess I was somewhat right, but the boy who is captivated by her was Jacques and not Marcus.

It's pretty nostalgic to see them acting their age. Not long ago, I was the same age as them. To see them like this, playing around, celebrating their best

---

[6] *Ma belle princesse:* My beauty princess (French)

friend's birthday with no worries, nothing to concern themselves with, just enjoying themselves, was refreshing. I have almost forgotten about it.

'William, I'd like to meet up with you soon, when can you stop by? Or would you like me to come to you?' Mario sent me a Thought Projection.

'I'll come to you.' I replied.

"YES! That's a great idea, right guys?"

Mario's voice was still echoing in my head when Marcus' voice brought my focus back to the living room.

"Let me go to my room to drop this game off and grab my jacket so we can head out," Marcus told his two friends before making his way upstairs to his room.

That was it. That was the moment I needed to talk to Marcus on a one-on-one. I was hoping to run into Roberto first, but I'm running out of time, so I teleported myself into his bedroom.

Marcus had the video-game projected on the wall through a device on his wrist. I decided to make myself visible for him, dissolving the Stardust Dome around me.

"Marcus, we need to talk," I spoke from behind the projection, making him jump startled, "I'm here in front of you."

"Whoa, this game is really good, he looks very real." Marcus leaned over to take a closer look at what he thought was a projection on the video-game. To see him so close with his bright-green eyes staring at me, just like his mom's; his skin complexion was similar to Roberto's own skin tone. I almost forgot where I was for a second.

"Marcus, I can assure you that I am real," I approached him, grabbing his forearms, making him fall backward in his bed.

"Who are you? How did you get in here?" He asked panicking.

"Listen to me! Your friends will be missing you soon so let me explain it before you panic any further," I tried to calm him down, but the touch of my own pale hands made him panic even more.

"Panic? I'm not panicking!" he lied, "Who are you?"

"Hey, Marks, is everything okay up there?" Marcus' friend, Jacques, shouted from downstairs.

"Marcus, don't tell him I'm here. I'll come back later to talk to you. Please, Marcus, don't!"

"Marcus, let's go, your mom is calling you," Jacques' voice was getting closer.

I couldn't take the chance of being exposed to his friend, but also, I needed to let Marcus know the existence of us, Porters.

"Happy Birthday, Marks," I smiled at him and let my eyes shine bright-white like stars, transforming myself fully into a lyrebird. I winked and flew out of his room, teleporting myself back to Jupiter once I was out of his sight.

I reappeared back in the City of White Skies, Retip, right in front of Mario Shawyze's house.

"What took you so long?" Midnight opened the front door, "Come in."

"Ah, our last guest has arrived!" Mario spoke after I had walked in.

Unlike before, the room now was full of people, full of Porters, with all the vases that I have shattered before replaced by brand new ones.

"Welcome, Mr. Chase, please have a seat."

I sat down at one of the chairs between Donna and Allison. Midnight sat across from us next to a much bigger guy compared to him. To our side were the Gemini Twins, Lynne and Lee Yang. Behind them were three other Porters that I haven't met before.

"Thank you, everyone, for coming in such short notice," Mario began speaking to the room, "to those who couldn't come, I will make sure I visit them myself. I'm not going to sugar coat this meeting. The time has come for us to elect a new reigner in our Solar System, a new Porter to take over the Throne, someone who's been alive longer than all of you here in this room combined. Someone who can create any weapon he desires just by thinking about it. Someone old and new at the same time. A Porter who is capable of making the Solar System great again. 'But how?' you would ask, I will tell you how, by opening the frontiers, abolishing the divisions between Porters, no more Wonderers, Wanderers or Formers who are all scattered, hidden in the farthest moons in our Solar System, under tunnels, domes, caves and coves in every planet."

"I'm sorry, your Eminency, but the Formers are gone. The Queen had their powers drained from them, vanished."

"So, you were told, Ms. Prior. Rumor has it that the Formers found a way to keep their powers even against the Queen's orders. They're hidden from the rest of us, and we need to find them, to join our cause. And, while they are not here to speak for themselves, we have to be their voices, we have to bring them out of hiding, we have to find our brothers and sisters, and bring them back to the Sunlight. No more confinement. Vanishers, how now Formers are known, deserve the right to come and go as they please, just like us, Wonderers and Wanderers alike. All of us deserve to have a planet of our own, an Exotic Matter Sphere to transport ourselves anywhere we want in the Solar System or any Sun system they desire."

"YEAH!" The big man next to Midnight shouted in agreement.

"So, my friends, my family, I hereby announce today that I'll be your new King, the King of the Solar System, the King who's going to reshape our System, our Galaxy even. I, Mario Shawyze will be the King that you and every Porter in the Universe deserve. Are you with me?"

"YEAH!" The whole room shouted in unison.

"Good, for your mission starts now. I have

assigned a planet in the Solar System to each one of you. You're to go there, and its moons, find every Porter you can, Wonderer, Wanderer and Vanishers alike, anyone who's ever been touched by the Stardust should hear the good news. First, Mr. Sean Rocks, Porter of the Centaurus Constellation, the Centaur,"

One of the three Porters sitting behind the Gemini Twins got up. "My king,"

"You'll go to Venus, address everyone there, leaving Josh Rogers for last. His loyalty to the Queen is admirable."

"Immediately, sir." Sean pressed his Exotic Matter Sphere, disappearing out of there.

"Mr. Eisehein Dawn, Porter of the Equuleus Constellation, the Horse, Mars is your location, be careful out there. Jennifer Lowell does not play, and her touch can drastically hurt you."

Eisehein disappeared out of there without saying a word but nodding his head in agreement with his new King.

"Mr. Nelson Aniston, Porter of the Monocerus Constellation, the Unicorn, will take over Mercury, the Speed Planet, you—"

"But, your majesty, Lynne and I are the Wonderers of that planet, why not send us there?"

"Mr. Yang don't ever interrupt me again. After the fiasco on your last assignment, I'm sending you and your sister back to Earth to—"

"We'll go immediately, sir." Lee and Lynne got up, about to press their Exotic Matter Sphere.

"DO NOT YOU INTERRUPT ME!" Mario shouted at them with his eyes bright-white like stars, "You'll go when I say so, now sit down."

They both did without speaking a word.

"Mr. Aniston, you may go," Mario told the slender, pale-green, tall man in the middle of the room.

"Mr. Isahul Blahq, also known as Midnight, Porter

of the Canis Minor Constellation, the Lesser Dog, you have faithfully followed me and my orders, and for that, you'll be assigned to Saturn and all of its moons. With your powers, there will be no one you can't find."

Isahul Blahq, the guy they call Midnight, exchanged a handshake with the much bigger guy next to him. Midnight is the lighter of the two, yet much darker than any of us in the room. On Earth, they would be considered of African ethnicity, but here, they could be from any planet, any continent throughout the Solar System. Calling them black would also be a mistake since there are actually black people in a lot of worlds, just like green, blue, pink, yellow, and every other existent color.

"Where do you want me, my king?" The guy next to where Midnight was, asked Mario.

"Mr. Ezra Sirius, Porter of the Canis Major, the Greater Dog, you'll go to our home star, the Sun, also known as Sol, there you have to befriend Leonard Larkson, but please be very careful, he's not the only Leo you're looking for. Now go, I need you two back as soon as possible. I have another mission for you upon your return."

"Yes, sir." They responded in unison as they both left inside of their own Exotic Matter Sphere.

"Now, back to the two of you," Mario addressed the Gemini Twins who got up instantaneously, "Mr. Lee and Ms. Lynne Yang, brother and sister, sharing both the same Constellation of Gemini, first Porters ever to do so. Wonderers of Mercury, as I said before, after the fiasco on your last assignment, I'm sending you both to Earth to redeem yourselves. Bring me the boy and his mom. With her on my side, it will be easy to convince him to join us before he can manifest his powers. Now, you can go."

"Yes, my king," They both disappeared inside their Exotic Matter Sphere simultaneously.

"My dear Allison Prior, Wonderer of Pluto, Porter of the Scorpius Constellation, the Scorpion, who brought me not long ago the young Donna Saihtam, also Wonderer of Pluto, Porter of the Virgo Constellation, the Virgin. The two of you stand in front of me with a new addition to the group, Mr. William Chase, Porter of the Lyra Constellation, the Lyre." Mario pulled up a chair, sitting in front of us, crossing his legs as if deep in thought.

"Donna, you will go to Uranus, Allison to Neptune, William, you'll go to Pluto while I'll stay here in Jupiter. I'll start with the moons and finish here on this planet, as I advise you to do the same."

"And once we find them, what is that you want us to do?" Allison asked him.

"Keep a tab on all of them, don't stop looking for the Vanishers, we need them by our side." Mario got up to his feet, pacing in front of us, "However, Ms. Prior, I need you to come back soon. I have a feeling I'll be needing you on Earth."

"Of course, my king."

"Now go, you three, I have business to attend with the Queen, see you soon,"

Mario disappeared inside of his E.M.S., leaving us

three alone in the big empty room.

"Wow, intense much?" Donna leaned back as if relieving some stress out of her body.

"You heard your mission, let's go!" Allison disappeared too.

"So, what did you think?" Donna asked as she and I got up, facing a window nearby.

"I think he's crazy. Rumors about the Formers being alive have been speculating throughout the Solar System. Don't you think Mariah would have found them by now?"

"I'm not sure, I've hardly spoken with the Queen herself. She's not the friendliest Queen, you know?"

"Yeah, I've barely exchanged a few words with her myself," I looked outside the window, gazing the orange clouds in the white skies of Retip.

"Do you think the Twins will get to Marcus in time?"

Marcus! I forgot the Gemini went after him. I have to find Marcus before they do.

"I'm not sure, but we better do what Mario asked of us," I jumped out of the window, "see you soon?"

"See ya,"

I flew for a couple of minutes in the white skies of Retip before disappearing out of there, back to Earth. Marcus' backyard, to be more specific. I could hear people inside shouting in happiness after singing "Happy Birthday" to Marcus. I approached the doorway invisible to everyone again.

Marcus began cutting his birthday cake shaped as a bleeding corpse. Marcus was passing by and giving away slices of the cake, and then the most unexpected thing happened: our eyes met. Our eyes couldn't have met. I was invisible, protected by my Stardust Dome, he couldn't have seen me.

I stepped outside back to his porch wondering how was that possible, but before I could make any sense of it, Marcus was there, looking around for me. Maybe I was not careful enough, allowing myself to be visible for a few seconds.

After realizing he was by himself, Marcus got closer to this mermaid statue they have in the middle of the backyard. A gift his father gave to his mom on their honeymoon.

"He's fine, Marcus," I told him, allowing myself to become visible again right behind him, making him drop the plate of cake he had in his hand.

"What a waste, that cake looked really good!" I told him once he faced me with his wide eyes completely startled, "Sorry, I didn't mean to startle you."

"Who are you, and how did you get here?!" He pretty much shouted at me.

"Marcus, I told you I'd see you later on, and this is later on..." I told him casually.

"WHAT DO YOU WANT FROM ME?"

I disappeared out of there once I noticed Jacques came outside to check on him. One thing is for sure; the Gemini Twins would not attempt anything right now in the middle of his birthday party.

I reappeared in Rio de Janeiro, in the city of Copacabana where Roberto's family was from. I have been here before, so I knew exactly where to look for Roberto. I kept my Stardust Dome around me all the time as I looked around the house.

"Hi," Roberto greeted me. I turned around only to realize that he was talking to one of his relatives. I sighed in relief. Being a Porter himself, Roberto could see right through my Stardust Dome. I'm happy that he did not see me.

Roberto was in the living room surround by family members, all wearing a somber smile on their faces. A sign that something mournful has happened.

Seeing him sad like this gave me to courage to talk to him, but somebody got to him first.

"I'm sorry, Roberto, but she's gone," the young lady hugged him as they both sobbed.

One of the perks of having Stardust running in your vein is, while everyone is speaking in a foreign language, your ears translate it naturally to your native tongue; otherwise, I would have no idea what they were talking about since the native tongue here is Portuguese.

It didn't take long for me to understand that Roberto's mother had passed away. Roberto and with the whole family were beside themselves; tears were falling freely everywhere; I decided to go outside and wait for when Roberto was alone to talk to him, to offer my condolences.

"Yeah, I know you don't like me using my Exotic Matter Sphere but I'll be inside of the airport, he won't even know," Roberto stepped outside talking on the phone in English which could only mean he was talking to his wife, "no, don't tell him, I want it to

27

be a surprise. I'll see you in thirty. Love you too. Bye."

I could have talked to him right then, but Roberto was already on his way home. I wrote down a note and left on top of his suitcase and disappeared out of there.

I reappeared back in my house in Charon. I took a shower and changed my clothes. The whole thing with Roberto's mother took a toll on me; while I was not close to her, I'd met her a few times before, and the passing of someone was never something easy to endure.

Roberto should have been teleporting himself to the airport, and I had to catch him before Marcus and Katherine got there. I appeared inside the airport by the gate Roberto is supposed to wait at for his family. But he was nowhere to be found; instead, I saw a boy with his bright-green eyes staring at a big screen hanging from the ceiling announcing flight deals. I decided to play with him. Roberto is planning a surprise to his son so, I got to stall him.

"Who goes to Iceland on vacation?" He thought out loud.

"Don't knock until you've tried it," I told him with one my many voices trying to disguise myself from him.

"What in the world?"

"I'm serious. In Reykjavík there's this place called Blue Lagoon which has naturally heated water, a great place for relaxation," I looked at Marcus who was still speechless looking at the big screen mouth-opened, "what's the matter, Marcus? Rather go to

Hawai'i instead?"

Marcus jumped to his feet by the sound of his name.

"What, don't recognize me?" I let my blue bangs down and my eyes to match its natural shade of blue.

"YOU!" He shouted once he recognized my face," WHAT DO YOU WANT FROM ME?"

"You? What makes you think I want something to do with you," I told him with a calm and eerie voice, "I'm merely stalling you."

"Dad..." He said under his breath.

"Attaboy," I congratulated him, allowing myself to become fully visible, giving him the impression that I jumped out of the screen in front of him.

"WHERE'S MY DAD?"

I could hear Marcus' anger in his voice, "Calm down, Dogie, you do not want to lose your temper. I'm here to help you," I tried to comfort him, though I only made things worse.

"Dogie? What in the world is 'Dogie' and why does everyone keep calling me thaargh!" Marcus shouted in pain, holding his head with both of his hands.

"Marcus, are you okay?" I asked concerned about him, but no response. Instead, Marcus was slowly turning into a bull. I used my Stardust Dome to block us from everyone's view, but he was getting out of control, and there was nothing I could do except to teleport him out of there.

I tried to get close to him, but he let out a loud cow-like *MOO*, knocking me out of the way as if I were a fly. I got up again, but this time, Marcus fell.

His hooves produced a mini earthquake, knocking everyone around him unconscious, including myself.

I woke up a little before everyone else did, except Marcus was nowhere else to be found. Knowing it would be a waste of time to look for him, I went for the only person I could think of until Roberto gets here: Kent Hors, the Wonderer of Earth, Porter of the Taurus Constellation and one of the Twelve Chosen Ones by the Queen herself.

I reappeared next to Kent's house. His house is located in the middle of an ocean bank, across from the Rowes Wharf Hotel in the center of the Sea District in Boston. I flew close by, knocking on the door, but no one answered. I wonder where he could be. I could send him a T.P., but I haven't talked to him in so long that I didn't want to worry him unnecessarily.

Unexpectedly, I saw the Gemini Twins back on the shore with two semi-unconscious people with them, a woman and a teenage guy. I tried to get a closer look from afar, but I couldn't identify them, and since they are Porters like myself, I couldn't hide under my Stardust Dome, just like every Porter, they would unquestionably see me.

Then, just like that, they disappeared right in front of the hotel. I flew over there, looking for them but again, nowhere to be found. I went inside the hotel to see if they had made a reservation, but nothing. At least nothing under the names Lee Yang, Lynne Yang or Mario Shwayze.

I went back outside looking around for them but found something else, or better, someone else. I saw it but couldn't believe it. Marcus Mathias was being dragged by the current, drowning underwater.

Under my Stardust Dome, I flew toward him, removing him from the icy-cold water, dropping him safely in front of the hotel.

"You okay there, buddy?" I asked him in a light tone, trying not to scare him, "You must be really hot to go swimming at this hour."

"I'm okay," he said, shivering with cold.

"Whoa, we should get you dried up. Are you staying at the Rowes Wharf as well?" The truth is, I wasn't staying at the Rowes Wharf, but I had to make a believable excuse. I remove my light jacket, putting around him, trying to warm him up.

"Where? Oh no, I'm from here. Everett, actually. I'm okay. I'll just walk home or take a bus or something. I will dry up along the way." He tried to get up but fell again, still shivering.

"Hold on there, buddy," I helped him up, putting one of his arms around my shoulders, "listen, I'm staying at the Rowes Wharf Hotel. I'll take you there, get you some towels, and make a phone call to your parents to pick you up, okay?"

He took a moment to think, finally agreeing with me after I pointed out the hotel was only a few feet away. Once inside the hotel, I left Marcus in the lobby and went to see an attendant to book a room. I came back with some towels and a cup of hot cocoa for him.

"Feeling better now?"

"Yeah, thank you again—" He stopped mid-sentence, staring at me expressionlessly.

"You sure you okay, there? Cause the way you're looking at me it's kinda weird," I joke with him, afraid that he might be recognizing me as a bad guy and not a guy who was trying to help him.

"I'm sorry, you look like someone I met a few days ago," he explained, taking a sip of his hot cocoa.

"Is his name William Chase?" I smiled at him, clearly joking with him.

"I should get going, thanks for the towels and saving me from that freezing water."

I offered him to use the phone in the lobby to call his parents or a cab, but he assured me he was okay, even though he hasn't moved for a while. We then realized that he had no money or cell phone to call anybody.

"Hey, no worries. I can give you a lift to where you need to go if you're okay with that. I mean, I'm technically not a stranger anymore, and I just saved you, it's not like I'm just gonna try to kill you or anything," I laughed, trying to break the ice, but Marcus just stood there looking at me.

I explained to him that Everett is not that far and that I would be willing to give him a ride home, but once again he assured me he was okay, and that his father was out there. All he needed to do was find him. I wasn't sure how much of lie that was, I knew Roberto should be already back in Boston, but I doubt he was nearby.

"Okay then, but be careful out there and don't go swimming again, okay?" I told him jokingly.

"Yeah, I'll try," he finally let out a laugh, "thank

you again for helping me get out of the water."

"Hey, sure. See you around, Marcus."

I let his name spill out of my lips, forgetting that Marcus had not introduced himself to me. I wondered if he had finally recognized me or not.

"Yeah, see ya." Was all he said before walking out of the lobby toward the water again. I, of course, decided to follow him.

I walked behind him, invisible to his eyes. Marcus was walking around, looking at the water as if reliving the moment he was inside of it not too long ago, probably thinking he would never try something like that before.

I was wrong.

Marcus, unexpectedly, jumped back into the water. I ran after him, pulling him out of the water within minutes.

"What the heck are you doing?" He yelled at me without even glancing back, "My friend's underwater, I need to help him."

"I leave you alone for a minute, and you jump right back in the water, again!" I told him looking at the water, trying to find whoever it was that Marcus was talking about.

"William, what were you thinking? My friend is underwater, trapped, or something. I gotta go help him," he pleaded with me almost jumping back in the water.

"What's up with you guys from Boston and this dirty water? Stay here!" I told him, jumping in the water. I looked underwater for a couple of minutes, but couldn't see anyone under this dirty, clouded water, "he's not here, Marcus,"

"He has to be; I just saw him… there!" He pointed to who I recognized to be his friend Jacques, unconscious, about fifty feet away from us.

I would never make it in time swimming, Jacques' life was hanging by a thread, I had to save him. So, I did what I had to do. I apologized to Marcus and flew out of the water toward Jacques.

Marcus yelled, screamed at me to not touch his friend, to leave him alone, afraid that I was going to hurt or kill him. By the time he was done cursing at me, I had Jacques already in front of him, laying on the floor, unconscious.

"Get away from him." He shouted, pushing me out of the way.

III

UNDER MY PROTECTION

That was the first time I showed myself fully transformed to Marcus, powers and all. To have him stare at me with his eyes bright-white like stars in anger, in pain, was heartbreaking.

I had a hard time convincing Marcus to let me help his friend Jacques, who was shivering with cold. Under Marcus' insults, I performed C.P.R. to try resuscitating the boy. After excruciating seconds, Jacques finally came back to it, coughing out all of the water he had swallowed, only to have him lose his consciousness again.

Afraid that he was suffering from hypothermia, I offered to take them to my room, where I could run a hot bath for the both of them, and that was what I did.

I flew us three through the window of the room I had booked.

Jacques, after the hot water bath, gained his senses back. I put him in the bed while Marcus rested in the lounge chair across from us. I let them both sleep while I sat in the windowpane, looking at the beautiful Waxing Crescent Moon over the city of Boston.

Marcus was sleeping soundly for a while; that was until he started to have a nightmare. I could hear him mumbling some words under his breath, pushing whatever it was out of his way, and finally letting out a loud cow-like ***MOO*** waking Jacques up.

"What was that?" Jacques asked, completely confused by what he'd just heard.

Before I could say anything, ***BANG***, Marcus fell out of his lounge chair, straight to the floor, waking himself up. I asked him if he was okay, but he brushed off the question embarrassedly, jumping in the bed where Jacques was, asking him a thousand questions about what had happened to him, but Jacques, to our surprise, was unaware of who had taken him and how he ended up in the water.

Honestly, neither did I know how either one of them had journeyed themselves into the water, but something tells me it has to do with the Gemini Twins, and for that reason alone, I will not leave Marcus alone. I will protect him until I can safely deliver him to his dad, Roberto Mathias, a Porter like myself.

After a lot of talking, I convinced them both to let

me give them a ride home. On the way, Marcus told us everything that had happened to him thus far, including his visions, the accident in the airport, the disappearance of his mom, how he met the Porters Kent Hors and Margaret Hills, and how he is the Natural Porter of the Taurus Constellation, the Bull.

Usually, I would interfere. Keeping Porters' businesses among Porters only is a secret we have to keep for the sake of our own. However, due to my Stardust Dome around the car, once Jacques was out of it, he would forget about it anyways. Marcus could use a good friend right now, and no one's better than his own best friend.

It didn't take long for us to arrive at Marcus' house, but to our shock, it was destroyed with nothing, but rumbles left behind. None of us could believe in what we were seeing. Some clothes scattered here and there, broken picture frames, pieces of furniture, one of the couches overly damaged. It looked like a scene from natural disasters we only see on television but now was here right in front of us.

Jacques, seeing all the mess around us, suggested we go to his house, where they could take a shower, change clothes, eat something, and finally get some much-needed sleep.

I made plans to meet up with them in the morning to help them find Roberto. I could send him a Thought Projection, but also, I'm pretty sure Roberto must be busy right about now, trying to find his wife, and possibly who destroyed his house, so yeah, I will keep an eye on Marcus for as long as I can.

In the morning, they both jumped into my car, where we drove off toward the Rowes Wharf, where Marcus believed his dad to be, at Kent's place. Right around the block from Jacques' house, we ran into another one of Marcus' friends: Mileena Watson, who Marcus introduced to me. Jacques made sure that I would never flirt with his mademoiselle, a risk he had not to worry about with me.

A few more blocks down, after leaving Mileena behind, we got interrupted again, this time by Lynne Yang and her twin brother Lee Yang, Porters of the Gemini Constellation, Wonderers of Mercury, who quickly took hold of myself and Marcus, thanks to their speed-of-sound movements.

"LET THEM GO!" A voice that I haven't heard in a while scared the Gemini Twins and us; it was Kent Hors, Porter of the Taurus Constellation, the Bull, Wonderer of Earth, fully transformed in a black bull, taller than my blue S.U.V. Right behind him was Margaret Hills, Porter of the Aries Constellation, the Ram, Former Wonderer of Mars, and Roberto Mathias, Porter of the Taurus Constellation as well, entirely changed into his brown bull shape.

That was when I hit my Exotic Matter Sphere and teleported myself out of there and back to my house in Charon, Pluto's moon. I knew I had a short period to talk to Mario before the Gemini Twins could get to him. I went upstairs to my room, took a warm shower, jumped in new clean clothes, and grabbed a quick bite to eat before teleporting myself out of my house, back to Retip, in Jupiter.

I walked down the pale streets of the City of the White Skies, making my way to the big, rustic, open house that is Mario's home. I was greeted at the door by the tall, muscular black man that is Eisehein Dawn, Porter of the Equuleus Constellation, the Horse.

"Welcome," he said, opening the door, allowing me in. "Mario is not in a perfect mood, so whatever it is, good luck to ya."

"WHAT DO YOU MEAN HE ESCAPED?" Mario shouted from inside.

"I can see that," I told Eisehein, as we both made our way into the open room.

Mario Shawyze was predominantly shouting at Lee and Lynne Yang, Porters of the Gemini Constellation, who were in the middle of the room surrounded by Sean Rocks and Nelson Aniston, as Eisehein and I sat on a couple of chairs around them.

"Mr. Shwayze, the cattle showed up and got in the way of us getting him," Lee explained.

"And, your point is?" Mario stared at him, waiting for an answer. "You can duplicate yourselves, move at the speed of sound, making you the fastest Porters out there, and you're telling me you couldn't get to Marcus Mathias?"

"Sir, I—"

"You, Lynne, you and your brother will press that little button inside of your belly button and disappear out of here and not return until you bring me the boy, and make sure it is the right boy this time." Mario increased his tone of voice with every single word he spoke between his teeth, with his eyes bright-white like stars.

"Yes, my King." Just like he told them, both Lynne and Lee pressed their Exotic Matter Sphere in their belly button, disappearing out of there, leaving nothing but a trail of Stardust in the air.

"My King,"

"WHAT, Mr. Dawn?" Mario shouted at him, not noting my presence there, till just now, "Mr. Chase, how are you?"

"I'm sorry to show up like this," I reached out my hand to shake Mario's hand. "I can come at a better time."

"What is it that you need, Willie?" Mario shook my hand firmly.

I despise when people that I'm not close with, call me Willie, but Mario is not in the right mind to be corrected right now, so I just went with it.

"I'm here to talk to you about Marcus Mathias," I began.

"Done!" He told me before I could even finish my thought. "Those twins are not getting the job done, they won't be able to catch Marcus, and I know you can with your eyes close without even having to hit a note, Mr. Chase. Is that it?"

"Yeah, thank you. I won't disappoint you, sir."

"I know you won't. New blood like you, is always ready to work and to show your worth. Mr. Chase, I believe you and I are going to get along just fine. Now go before the twins make a fool out of themselves again and, well, I would have to kill them, right?" Mario laughed loudly, followed by his three minions standing right behind him. "Now if you'll excuse me, we have other matters to attend to, Mr. Chase. See you next time with Marcus in your hands. Dead or alive, dealer's choice."

"Yes, sure. Bye for now." I pressed my Exotic Matter Sphere and was out of there in a blink of an eye, back to Boston, on Earth.

'If only he was here.' I received for the first time, Marcus' Thought Projection right after I manifested myself on Earth, so I flew to his exact position.

The thing about Thought Projection is, if you're having a conversation with the other Porter, they can sense your location if you allow it. Marcus is an untrained Natural Porter, with Stardust flowing already in his bloodstream. I don't think he realizes what he is capable of doing just yet.

'Marcus Mathias, Porter of Taurus Constellation, the new Wonderer of Earth,' I sent him a Thought Projection of my own, after landing on a tree in front of his room, in my full blue lyrebird form. *'You really can't see me, can you?'*

"No, I can't, and honestly, I think you're inside my head."

'Look again, hard enough to where my voice is coming from. Listen to it in your mind and find me.' I sent him another T.P.

Teaching Marcus how to hear Thought Projections and how to find Porters was not easy, but it was not impossible either, especially for a Natural like himself.

"Can it be?" He asked out loud, finally spotting me

at a branch of the tree across from his window.

'Good job, Marcus. I knew you could do it if you put your heart into it,' I flew toward him, transforming myself into my standard human shape just before landing right in front of him. "Surprised, Marcus?"

"William, huh, how did you do that? And how did you find me? Am I hallucinating again?" He mumbled out his words.

"You are never hallucinating, Marks, everything is real. You should be getting used to it by now. I can change my voice at will, it's one of my many talents," I explained to him.

"I have often watched over you whenever no one seemed to pay attention or notice all this craziness happening to you. I wanted to make sure that you were, well, portered." I landed on the parapet.

"Interesting choice of words, Will," Marcus went back to his room, still annoyed. I followed him inside, sitting on a lounge chair across from his bed.

"I know Marcus, how you're feeling right now about this whole 'Porter' thing. It's too crazy to believe but also too real to ignore, right?"

"Exactly, I don't even know if I want to become a Porter. It doesn't make sense to me. My father is a Porter and expects me to follow in his footsteps, as Mr. Hors and Ms. Hills do too. I just want to be a regular kid, you know?" Marcus sat on the bed across from me.

"I understand, but if your father is right, you don't have much of a choice, after all, you're a Natural."

"What do you mean?"

"Marcus, they kidnapped your best friend, who we rescued from the waters of the Rowes Wharf Hotel, your mom is missing, and no one seems to know where she is; also, your father destroyed his own house. So, why don't you just go along with it for now?" I suggested to him, summarizing all that has been happening in his life right now.

"I'm listening, and I think I get what you're saying. I do as I'm told just so I can get to my mom again, and then once everything is back to normal, I'll walk away from it all. There's no way they can keep me as Earth's Wonderer. I just want to be a football player."

"You got it, Marcus. See, you gotta give yourself more credit. You're young and have a lot to learn, and if you need anything, just say my name, and I'll be there," I assured him.

"William, you're not that much older than me,"

"Give or take a couple of hundred years." We shared a laughter.

"As much as it pains me, you're a cool guy, Will, besides all the frightening moments you gave me before," Marcus laughed, remembering all that we have been through so far. And so, did I.

Maybe having Marcus going at this with the wrong mindset might not be the best idea, but it is the best I could come up with. Once he's entirely in it, he'll understand his powers and precisely who he is and won't back out of it.

"Marcus, can I come in?" Marcus' friend, Jacques, knocked from outside of his bedroom door. I didn't stick around to hear Marcus' answer. I disappeared inside of my Exotic Matter Sphere before Marcus could open the door.

"There you are," I heard as soon as I reappeared back at my house. "I hope you don't mind that I let myself in."

I looked behind me and saw a now-known face sitting down comfortably in one of my couches, "Mr. Blahq, I wasn't expecting anyone here,"

"I would imagine. Your protective Stardust Dome around the house is quite efficient; it took me some time to find your place if it wasn't for my canine abilities..." He pointed to his own nose as if he had sniffed his way to my house, as I'm sure he did.

"To what do I owe you the pleasure, Mr. Blahq?" I sat opposite him on the other couch.

"Call me Midnight, Willie. Can I call you Willie?"

"Will, if you must."

"A man of short words. I like it." He got up and sat next to me. "You know, I was wondering what you've been up to. Mr. Shawyze told us to go sniff out the Formers around the Solar System, but you, what did he have you do?"

"I'm not sure if I understand the question, Midnight?"

"Let me rephrase that. Our future righteous king may have put his trust on you unequivocally, but that's not the case with me and some other Porters working for him. I'm not sure you're trustworthy."

I looked firmly into his eyes, not intimated by his accusations. "Mr. Blahq, you may have just met me, and your accusations are, as you put it, unequivocally false. I have been watching the Natural boy closely just to make sure he doesn't represent a threat to our future King."

"Oh yes, the Natural Wonderer Porter of the Taurus Constellation, Marcus Mathias," he got up again, walking around the rug in the middle of the room, "and how is he, Mr. Chase? Are you keeping an eye on him, or are you keeping him away from us?"

"What do you mean?"

"I mean, will you be okay knowing that while we are here, chatting, the Gemini Wonderers are right about now approaching the boy and his girlfriend?" He sat down again on the couch across from him with a smile on his face.

"Why wouldn't I? Less work for me, right?" I lied to him. The truth is, I know Marcus wouldn't be safe, but maybe if I can warn him, he can call his dad to come and protect him again against Lynne and Lee just like he did before.

'Marcus, Marcus, it's getting late. Danger Approaches as the Sun sets. Get your friend and run away before your enemies find their way... TO YOU!'

I know I wasn't clear enough, but the best I could come up with without scaring him was to send a T.P. For all I know, Midnight could be lying right now and the last thing I want is to scare him.

"Right, if you say so." Midnight just stared at me as if trying to read my thoughts, a gift I was thankful he didn't possess.

"Since you're staying for a while, can I get you a drink? A beer, maybe?" I got up to get us a drink in

45

the kitchen, but he stopped me, saying: "No need for you to move. Stay put, Mr. Chase."

'Marcus, Marcus, it's getting late. Danger Approaches as the Sun sets. Get your friend and run away before your enemies find their way... TO YOU!' I sent him another T.P.

"Am I a prisoner in my own house?" I got up to my feet with my eyes bright-white like stars.

Isahul Blahq got up, meeting my eyes with his own black eyes turned bright-white like stars, "Mr. Chase, don't make me do this in your own house."

"Give your best shot."

Isahul came charging against me, and just before he could lay his punch at me, he vanished into thin air, leaving nothing but a trail of Stardust behind.

'Boss called me over; they got the boy. Next time, Birdie.' Isahul sent me a T.P. just before I disappeared out of there inside of my own Exotic Matter Sphere, reappearing outside where Marcus was: Coffee & Books by Bella.

Through the window, I could see Lynne holding Marcus' friend, Mileena, against her will, while Lee was nearing in on Marcus. I had to do something.

'Marcus, cover your ears,' I sent him a T.P. before letting out a sonic screech, shattering the window in pieces, knocking everyone out of their feet, *'Are you okay?'*

But Marcus didn't reply to my Thought Projection; instead, he was just staring at me, completely frozen, so I woke him up from the trance by saying it out loud, "MARCUS, are you okay?"

After getting up to his feet, Marcus told me he was indeed okay. The Gemini Twins turned their attention to me now, but instead of me dwelling with them, I put them to sleep with a couple of notes played out of my tail. Not only them, but everyone in the library fell asleep too, including Mileena and lastly, Marcus.

I took them both out with me before any of them could wake up. Mileena woke up first and not long after did Marcus. We were all by a bench near the subway station. I couldn't fly them both to safety or teleport all of us inside of my Exotic Matter Sphere, so I told them to take the train back to Ms. Hills' house, the place Marcus was now staying after his dad destroyed their home. A thought Marcus unwillingly shared with me once he heard the news from his father himself.

I explained as much as I could to Marcus and Mileena on the train, but the ride wasn't as smooth as I had hoped. Allison Prior, Porter of the Scorpius Constellation, made an appearance for the first time in front of Marcus and Mileena, shredding the train in pieces before getting to us, sending all of the people in the train out of it in panic mode.

I put a protective Stardust Dome around the whole train, so they'll forget everything they saw once they crossed it over to the other side of it, returning to their normal lives, completely oblivious to what had just happened.

"Well, well, well, isn't this the so-called Earth's new Wonderer, Marcus Mathias?" Allison spoke in her velvet-smooth voice approaching Marcus slowly.

"You must be Mileena Watson, and of course, how are you, Mr. Chase?" Allison's scorpion-like piercers became her hand again, for me to shake it as she transformed herself back into the beautiful woman she is.

"Allison Prior, what a surprise to see you here on planet Earth all the way from Pluto." I greeted her without touching her hand.

Allison wasn't happy to be here either. She was sent after Marcus right after finding out the twins didn't bring him back to Mario Shawyze. I explained to her that Marcus was now under my protection, but she wasn't having it; she went for Marcus, nevertheless.

I grabbed Marcus with both of my talons, throwing him all the way to the back of the train, far away from Allison's grip, however, she was fast enough to get ahold of me with her scorpion's pierces before I could let out any note.

Everything was happening too fast. Allison was about to snatch me in half, sending me straight to the stars. I could feel my body flickering back and forth, losing the ability to transform myself, losing my consciousness. Then, all I heard was a loud crashing sound. Marcus, fully transformed in his bull shape, charged against Allison, knocking her unconscious with impact, as I, myself, lost my senses.

I woke up on a bench with Mileena next to me and Marcus nowhere to be found.

"Where is he?" I asked her, jumping out of the bench looking around for any sign of him.

"He went back. Allison told him she knows where his mom is."

"Let's go!"

Mileena and I went back in the tracks, up in the train where we were in not long ago. Marcus was outside of the train and so was Allison.

"Marcus, I think it's time for us to get going," I told him, but Marcus needed to know where his mom is.

Allison explained to Marcus that his mom was evil and was trying to get him, to kill him, to which Marcus lost his temper, but still wouldn't hurt her.

"Marcus, this is nonsense. She is just playing with your mind. Let's go before the police get here." When I lost my senses, the Stardust Dome that I had put around us had vanished as well, allowing the outside eyes to see everything that's going on, so in no doubt, the police would already have seen us through their security system and sent people our way.

"I'm not leaving until she tells me what I want to know. Where is my MOM?" Marcus' tone of voice didn't shake Allison. Instead, she just disappeared inside of her Exotic Matter Sphere, leaving nothing but a trail of Stardust behind.

After ditching the police, Marcus, Mileena, and I got out of the train station and made our way to Margaret Hills' house.

'William, I heard you had an encounter with the Gemini Porters and Allison Prior. Is everything okay?' I heard a T.P. in my head from someone I haven't talked to in a while: "Angela!"

We were above a bridge when I received a T.P.

from the Queen of the Moon, Angela Carey, Porter of the Cancer Constellation, the Crab.

"Marcus, I'd like you to meet a very good friend of mine. Come with me." I flew Marcus down to the water where Angela was standing in her beautiful dress, unbothered by the unsinkable water, thanks to her ability.

'Don't have time to explain everything right now, but can you watch over him for me. We need a place to hide.' I sent her a T.P. followed by a bow, "My Queen,"

I explained to Marcus who she was, telling him that she would be taking care of him for the next couple of hours while I took Mileena back to her house. I didn't tell him though that I was hiding him away from Mario or whoever was after him. I didn't want to worry him.

'Will, you and I have been friends for a long time now, do what you have to do. I do, however, need an explanation of everything that's going on.'

'I'll see you soon, my Queen,' I sent her one last T.P. before flying out of there with Mileena.

I dropped Mileena in front of her house and explained everything I could before disappearing inside of my Exotic Matter Sphere.

I reappeared in my living room.

MR. CHASE, YOU HAVE A HOLOCALL FROM MARIO SHWAYZE

S.T.A.R.S.S., the Service of Telecommunications Around Representatives of Sun Systems is a hologram projector very common throughout the Galaxy. Its female robotic voice broke the icy air of my house.

"Accept, S.T.A.R.S.S." If Mario wanted to talk, let's talk. I accepted the call, allowing a projection in the middle of my living room.

"CIAO WILLIAM, COME STAI?[7]" His voice was deep and raspy, yet with a hint of sarcasm and a false sense of care. His short gray hair didn't hide his age, to which I think he liked the look of being fifty-some-thing-years-old. His eyes were dark blue, almost black, much darker than mine.

"Sto bene, grazie e Vostra Maestà[8]?"

"WILLIE, CALL ME MARIO, WE ARE WAY PAST FORMALITIES."

"It's hard to lose the formalities with the future king of the Solar System, Mr. Shwayze." Mario hasn't heard from Allison yet, or if he did, he's playing cool.

"AND YOU NEVER LET ME FORGET IT. I KNEW THAT THERE WAS A REASON WHY I LIKE YOU, WILLIE,"

Usually, I would have corrected anyone by now, but Mario Shawyze was one of those people whom you can't correct. He will call you whatever pleases him, regardless if you like it or not.

"I'm flattered, Mr. Shwayze. How can I be of service?" I helped myself to a glass of yamahuie liquor: a very large, orange, bitter fruit, prevalent in the western side of Jupiter. It was similar to Earthians grapefruit; however, its liquor was very light and

---

[7] *Ciao William, come stai?:* Hi William, how are you? (Italian)

[8] *Sto bene, grazie e Vostra Maestà?:* I'm fine, thanks and Your Majesty? (Italian)

minty, perfect for a chilly evening drink.

"SIGNORINA[9] ALLISON TOLDE ME YOU GOT IN HER WAY WHE SHE WAS TRYING TO GET THE NATURAL TO ME. WHAT WAS THE PURPOSE OF THAT?"

So, he did know about my encounter with the Porter of the Scorpius Constellation.

"I was under the impression that the Gemini Porters, Lynne and Lee Yang were the ones assigned to bring the boy to you, sir." I sat in the lounge chair facing him.

"ARGH, *QUELLI IMCOMPETENTI!*[10] YOU AND I BOTH KNOW THAT THOSE TWO ARE INCAPABLE OF DOING ANYTHING I ASK. I HAD ALLISON ITER-VENE AND BRING THE BOY TO ME. BUT THESE ARE SMALL DEATAILS THAT ARE BEING DEALT WITH RIGHT NOW. TELL ME, HOW IS MARCUS?"

"I was with him for a couple of minutes. He is doing good, but I don't think he will be causing any problems any time soon. He's still having a hard time controlling his abilities."

"HUM," Mario's been worried about Marcus ever since he heard about him being a Natural. *"AS-COLTA,*[11] WILLIE, I DON'T WANT ANY PROBLREMS WITH THIS KID. IF HE GETS IN THE WAY OF ME BECOMING THE KING OF THE SOLAR SYSTEM,

---

[9] *Signorina:* Miss (Italian)

[10] *Quelli incompetenti:* Those incompetents (Italian)

[11] *Ascolta:* Listen (Italian)

YOU'LL HAVE TO ANSWER TO ME, *CERTO?*[12]"

"Mr. Shawyze, I gave you my word that I would keep an eye on him, and I'll do so. If he gets in the way of your plans, I'll make sure to take care of him myself."

"*BENISSIMO,*[13] WILLIE! I KNEW I COULD COUNT ON YOU. ONCE I DETHRONE MARIAH, I'LL MAKE SURE YOU HAVE A PLACE OF PRESTIGE IN MY COURT."

"That's unnecessary but welcomed. Thank you, sir."

"*ARRIVERDECI,*[14] MR. CHASE"

"My Lord." With a swift movement of my hand, I turned S.T.A.R.S.S. off.

Mario Shawyze was the Porter of the Orion Constellation, the Hunter. According to our history, he has been the only Porter since the Constellation was formed; longer than pretty much any of us, including the Queen Mariah Stars herself.

His obsession with becoming Mariah's successor was driving him insane. He has been waiting for her to pass on the title to him eventually, but lately, as of three hundred years or so, he's been plotting to dethrone her. He is tired of waiting, and he won't stop till he is sitting on the throne.

The whole division between Wonderers and

---

[12] *Certo:* Right (Italian)

[13] *Benissimo:* Great (Italian)

[14] *Arrivederci:* Goodbye (Italian)

Wanderers has gotten all of us unsatisfied with this situation. Mario is looking to assign a Porter to every planet in our Solar System, even if it means creating many more worlds. An idea that Queen Mariah herself is against merely because, according to her, not all Wanderers are Wonderers material. Whatever she meant by that.

I, being a Wanderer myself, agree with him. Lately, however, I'm not so sure about it. The whole idea of Marcus being able to stop him just because he's a Natural Wonderer doesn't make any sense to me. Whatever his reasons are, he is keeping an eye on him, or better yet, I am.

I poured myself another glass of yamahuie liquor.

IV

CHAMELEON

'*William.*' That was an involuntary and incomplete Thought Projection of Marcus Mathias. '*I'm always close by, Marcus. Don't you worry. If you need me, just call me.*' I sent him a T.P. of my own just to let him know that no matter how far I am, I'll be there in a blink of an eye.

'*I wanna talk to you, Will. See how you're doing.*' Marcus' Thought Projection was loud and clear, but also confused and sad, with a hint of guilt.

It took me a moment, but I finally decided to show up at Marcus' room. I'm not sure why Marcus is feeling the way he is, but I needed to talk to him and find out, personally.

There was no one in the room. Marcus was in the bathroom taking a shower. I connected my S.T.A.R.S. S. wrist device to his radio, playing one of my favorite

55

Earthian musicians. Marcus came out of the bath-room humming to it.

"It's Mozart! Do you like it?" I asked him, still observing his radio device.

"Whoa, don't you ever knock?" Marcus reached for his towel again, wrapping himself around it.

"What? You're somewhat decent," I smiled at him, sitting in the lounge chair, "and I've seen you in your underwear before, remember?" I reminded him of that night I pulled him and his friend Jacques out of the cold water of the Rowes Wharf.

"I'm never gonna get used to you appearing and disappearing like this. How are you?"

"I'm good. I heard you wanted to see me, so here I am."

"How do you do that?"

Marcus threw on a pair of jeans and his lucky green t-shirt while I explained to him about Thought Projections, a system that allows Porters to com-municate with each other by thoughts, reminding him that every time he was thinking of me, he was sending involuntary T.P. to me. The idea had never occurred to Marcus. I took him outside to explain the reason that he, being a Natural Porter, can send T.P.'s. Also, the difference between Wonderers and Wan-derers.

I spent a few hours explaining to Marcus how powers manifest differently in every Porter, how a Constellation chooses you. How Exotic Matter Sphere transport us from one place to another just by thought. I also demonstrated to him how the Stardust Dome works, showing him that even though I've met Mileena and Jacques before, they would not remem-ber me unless they were inside my Dome or became Porters themselves. The same could not be said about Jena, a friend of Marcus who I had just now met.

56

His father came over and took him to a baseball match. I followed them, invisible to their eyes just to make sure they were safe on the way there, but after talking to Marcus for a couple of minutes, he reminded me that if anything was to happen to him, his dad was there to protect him. He was right, Roberto Mathias is quite capable of protecting his son.

I left Fenway Park inside of my Exotic Matter Sphere, transporting myself all the way to Moon. I needed to talk to Angela Carey and explain Marcus and Mario to her.

"Mr. Chase," Indio Tao, Porter of the Indus Constellation, the Indian, greeted me as I manifested myself inside of the main hall in the Pearl Castle. "To what do we owe the pleasure?"

"I came to see the Queen of Moon, Ms. Angela Carey." We both exchanged a handshake.

"She has been expecting you." Indio showed me the way to where the queen was: The Overall Room, a room on the top of the highest tower where you can see the whole Queendom of Luna.

'William Chase, finally,' she greeted me as Indio and I made our way in the room, where she was sitting in a lounge chair near Afirina Keeygee, Porter of the Scutum Constellation, the Shield.

"Your Majesty," I bowed, "Afirina,"

Angela looked at Afirina, to which she replied with a "right away, my Queen."

'I asked Afirina to grab you a drink. If I'm not mistaken, yamahuie liquor is your favorite.' The queen gestured for me to take a seat next to her.

"Yes, it is. Thank you, my queen."

'There is no need for formalities between us. You should know that by now.' Angela and I have known each other for a while now, but something about her that doesn't let me forget that she is a powerful

queen. *'Now, would you please fill me in on your interest in Roberto's son, the Natural?'*

"You've met Mario Shawyze before, haven't you?" I began, accepting the glass of yamuhuie liquor that Afirina had just brought to me.

'That lunatic should have never been allowed to become a Porter in the first place, especially of the Orion Constellation, the Hunter, he has no control over his guns or himself,' she remarked.

"I wasn't sure about him until a while ago when Donna and Allison advised me that I should work for him, to get my mind off of things."

'And by off of things you mean off of your failed past relationships?' Angela took a sip from her own pearl cup, followed by Afirina and Indio's smile.

Angela can no longer speak due to injury on her throat while back on the battlefield; for this reason, she communicates through sign language. Indio and Afirina didn't hear her voice inside of their head like I am right now. However, I'm pretty sure they understood what she gestured.

"You didn't have to gesture that last part, you know?" I spoke out loud so everyone in the room could hear, slightly bothered by her comment.

She smiled at all of us, *'anyways, failed relationships are tough to recuperate, sometimes taking centuries to heal, depending on how long they've been together, but I must tell you, you gotta move on, let it go.'*

"It's easy for you to say. You and Afirina have been together even before I was made a Porter." Afirina didn't like the remark much, but Indio gave her a look agreeing with my statement.

'Back to Mario...'

"Yes, back to Mario. He told me to keep an eye on Marcus to see if the rumors of his being a Natural were true or not. Now I can assure you that Marcus is a Natural and Mario is not happy about it. He wants to bring Marcus to his side; otherwise, he'll kill him himself or have me kill him."

'Is it true that Mario is still plotting to dethrone Mariah Stars?'

"It is, but he's been planning on dethroning her for thousands of years, nothing new," I reminded her.

'True. What does Marcus say about all of this?'

"He doesn't know all of it. If he weren't born a Porter, he would never become one."

'Yet, he was born one; therefore, he has no choice but to become a Porter.' Angela went to one of the windows nearby. *'You have to talk to him, explain to him everything's that's been going on. If Mario truly wants Marcus dead, he will have it.'*

"You're right!" I stood up, approaching the queen, "I'll talk to him right now. We gotta make sure Marcus is ready to deal with Mario."

'William, go save the kid, but don't get involved.'

"How do you mean?"

'I remember that look when you first met Roberto.'

Angela has been my friend and confidant for a while, more than anyone else has been. She does know me better than I know myself. I pressed my E.M.S. and disappeared out of there without saying a word.

I appeared back at Margaret Hills' house, under the tree in her backyard where Marcus and his friends were having a conversation. I waited until they were done talking so I could speak alone to Marcus.

"Can I talk to you first?" I asked him before he could go inside to watch a movie with his friends, "Missed me, buddy?"

"Where have you been?"

"I was waiting for your dad to leave so we could

talk, you know, just us." I approached him.

"I still think my dad would be okay knowing that you're around when he is not. I mean, the more people on our side, the better, right?" Marcus sat in one of the chairs close by.

"True, but as we discussed before, all in its right time. Once your dad finds out what happened to your mom and figures out the connection with Jacques' unexplained quick kidnapping, I'll come forward and prove to him that I'm trustworthy."

"Well, clearly you're more trustworthy than the Wonderers. Did you forget about Lee and Lynne? How about Alison? All of them are Wonderers who tried to kill me or bring me to their 'king,' whoever he might be. I mean, this all has to be connected some-how, right?"

"Your dad doesn't know about Allison yet," I re-minded him.

"That's true. Everything is pretty weird, but I'm sure my dad will figure it out. I'm just curious to find out who would do this and why. I mean, what do they want with my mom?"

After a couple of hours debating about who could have taken Marcus' mom, our conversation got inter-rupted by a crashing sound coming from the kitchen.

"Did you hear that?" I got up with my eyes bright-white like stars.

"It's okay, Will, put those away. I'm sure Jacques got tired of waiting for me and went to the kitchen to get something to eat. He's always hungry. I better get back inside." He got up.

"Alright, Marcus. I'm gonna let you get back to your friends. If anything, just send a T.P., and I'll be right over, okay?" I popped up my wings open.

"They are beautiful, you know?" Marcus touched my wings.

"Thank you," I said, quite flattered and proud of my big midnight-blue wings.

"I'll see you later, Will." Marcus waved before I could fly away.

"Later, Marks."

Marcus went back inside of Ms. Hills' house, but I did not fly away; instead, I flew over the house, landing on the rooftop, in a place where I could still see him and whoever was making that noise, and to Marcus' surprise and mine, we found the clumsy person.

"Mom?" Marcus said in a very fainted voice that almost didn't come out. I flew from the rooftop to the floor, hiding out of their sight.

"Marcus, I was looking for a frying pan when I knocked a glass to the floor. Hopefully, Margaret won't kill me," she said apologetically, "sit down, honey, I'm making cheeseburgers for everybody. They would've been done sooner, but I had to go buy some beef, you know Marge has no meat in the house being vegan and all. Have some macadamia nuts white chocolate chip cookies, for now. I know they're your favorites."

I could see her but couldn't believe it. Marcus' mom was back, and yet she seemed somewhat differrent, including her hair, which was now dyed blonde.

"Is everything okay? You look like you've seen a ghost," she asked, realizing Marcus hadn't moved. After a few awkward silent seconds, Marcus sat down.

"Do you want some milk?" Marcus' mom was trying to act naturally, but something was off about her. I knew that couldn't be Marcus' mom; the Twins had taken her to Mario. Or at least that's what I heard.

"I'm sorry, honey, she only has almond milk. I should have bought milk also. I don't understand the point of someone being vegan. I mean what is—"

"Mom, where have you been?" Marcus interrupted her, "what happened?"

"What do you mean, honey?" She sat down on the chair next to him, pouring a glass of milk.

"Mom, you vanished without a trace, and now you are here in front of me like nothing happened, except that I haven't heard from you for over a week." Marcus' eyes went from green to bright-white like stars. "What happened?"

"Son, calm down. I know that look of yours. I'll explain everything to you, everything you need to know from the beginning. Now have some cookies while I finish up the burgers."

Marcus took a chunk out of the cookie and took a sip out of his almond milk almost at the same time. "So?" He asked his mom with his mouth still full.

"All right, where do I begin? Oh yeah. On the night that your grandma Maria passed away, your dad called me, and we spoke about him coming back to Boston to get us for the funeral. The next day I woke up and made some breakfast for us. When you came downstairs, I was on the phone with your dad. He was giving me all the details of his flight so I could pick him up that afternoon at the airport. I was going to tell you, but you left school before I could.

"Once I got back home from work, I realized you were not home yet, so I took a shower and was on my way to the airport when I heard on the radio about the little earthquake. I have never heard of such a thing here in Boston. Next thing I know, we'll be dealing with hurricanes and tsunamis," she paused and let out a laugh of disbelief, expecting him to laugh too, but he didn't.

"Anyway, so I decided to turn around and make my way back home which was a good thing, your dad's arrival date got postponed till the next day because of the earthquake."

That was a lie. Roberto did arrive that afternoon.

"I tried to call you on your cell, but it was off, so I called Margaret to see if you had gone to work, but she said she hadn't seen you at all that day."

"Yeah, I was out with Jacques." I could tell Marcus was not believing a word out of this impostor.

"I finally got home only to find our house destroyed, so I called your dad and told him what happened. I called the insurance company and went to Alexia's house hoping that you may have shown up there and stayed the night. I left you a message on your cell phone, but again, no answer."

"And where have you been all this time?" It seems like Marcus decided to go along with the lies.

"The next day, Alexia told me that Jacques called her saying that you had stayed over Mileena's and that later on, you would go meet up with Jena in the mall. Don't you remember, honey?"

"Yes, I do."

"Yeah, so I went to pick up your dad at the airport, and we came here. I kept missing you. I've been busy at work, as I'm sure you also have."

"Mom, how do you know Ms. Hills?"

"Sweetie, Margaret and I have been friends for a while. When I heard that you were working with her, I was delighted. She said only good things about you, you know?"

"What about Mr. Hors?"

"Oh, Kent is a very close friend of your dad. They've known each other since high school. He and Margaret have been together for a while, you know? Honey, can you help me with the buns?" She asked him, pointing out to the bag of buns by the countertop.

"Mom, why are you lying to me?" Marcus decided to confront his mom, making her drop a plate on the floor.

"Marcus, why would you think that I'm lying to you?" Marcus went to grab the broom and dustpan, but instead, his mom told him to leave it, taking outside to the backyard where I was hidden, sitting exactly where Marcus and I were not long ago.

"Marcus, your father and I have always loved each other very much, so don't ever think otherwise. But ever since this whole Porter-thing came into our lives..."

"You know about that?"

"Know about it? Honey, I lived through it. When I met your father in high school, he was always sick, or somebody else was sick, never showing up for classes, exams and all. Nobody seemed to notice that something was weird with him, but I knew. I knew that it was nothing related to sickness or anything that serious for that matter."

"I still can't believe you knew about all this and never told me, Mom. Why?"

"Marcus, you know very well about all the secrecy this is, and if I ever opened my mouth, they would make sure that I'd disappear somehow, either going to a new planet or worse, killing me if they had to."

"How did you find out about all this? Did Dad tell you?"

"Oh dear, no. Your dad never meant for me to know all this. You see, one day, I was late for class. I bumped into your dad when he was cutting class. Back then, we barely even knew each other, so he looked at me, apologized, and ran away to wherever he was going after. I saw in his face that expression that the world was ending or something like that, so I decided to follow him, without him seeing me.

He went on a few streets behind our school, your school, Everett High. He then met with a much younger Kent Hors and Margaret Hills, and this old bearded man. Then in a split of a second, they vanished. All four of them. I couldn't believe what I had just witnessed, so I decided to linger on a bit longer, hoping that your father would come back soon from wherever he was and tell me what was happening."

"Wait, I thought my dad grew up in Brazil," You could see Marcus' frustration on his face. He knew his mom was lying.

"Your dad was born in Brazil. He came to America when he was five and went to school here until he was nineteen. He and the rest of the family moved back to Brazil, but your dad could never stay there for long, he would come here for vacation and visit his old friends every time he could," she explained.

"So, what happened?"

"I stayed waiting all morning for your dad. The evening approached, and I didn't even notice when I fell asleep under a tree. And then I saw your dad alone, coming back with the happiest face I have ever seen. So, I had to ask what happened. Your dad at first was very skeptical about everything, but eventually, we became close friends, and he told me everything and how he became a Porter, Wonderer of Earth."

"But I thought Kent was," Marcus was right. Kent has always been the Wonderer of Earth.

Marcus' mom explained everything about how Kent has been looking for a new Porter of Taurus to take over his place so he could move on with his life along with his longtime girlfriend, Margaret Hills.

"So, I guess I should step into Kent's shoes and become a Porter, right, Mom?"

"Oh no, son, this is why I'm here. I'm here to tell

you not to become a Wonderer. You'll become immortal too, and you won't be able to have a normal
life like your friends. You'll see them all grow old and
die, and you will still be in the body of a twenty-something-year-old man. Think of Jacques, think of Jena.
Would you bear to see Mileena dying and you being
all alone, unable to fall in love, to get married, to have
kids?"

"But, Mom, it's in my blood. What happens if I
don't become a Wonderer?"

Atta boy! Marcus remembered what I told him.

"Marcus, I'm sure between your dad and Kent,
they will be able to find a new Porter, right? I mean,
how many kids are out there? You don't want to do
this, son."

*'Marcus, listen to me. Remember, the world needs
your protection. You're unique. It is in your blood.'* I
sent Marcus a T.P. to remind him that I was there.

"Son, what is it? Are you okay?" Katherine spoke
with a shaken voice, noticing Marcus' face.

"Yeah, I'm okay. Gimme just a second, Mom. Why
can't we talk to Dad when he gets here? He and
William mentioned that they need me and couldn't be
anyone else but me and—" Before Marcus could
finish his sentence, his mom jumped over him,
grabbing him by the arms.

"WILLIAM? As in William Chase?"

"Yeah, Mom. William Chase. He is a good friend of
mine, I—"

"HE IS NOT TO BE TRUSTED!" She screamed at
his face, and I knew that she was not his mom.

"DROP THE KID!" I flew over her, stopping midair
between them. "Do not harm the boy!"

"William, don't be stupid. This ends here and
now." The impostor took Marcus as a shield, pointing
a dagger on his neck with her eyes from brown to

bright-white like stars. "Fly any closer, and I will kill the boy."

"You should know that to kill you, I only need to SCREEEEEEEEEEEEEEAM!" I let out a high screech, destroying everything around us, making her drop Marcus to cover her ears, in vain.

'Duck!' I sent Marcus a T.P. just before diving over him, knocking his mom in the bushes of white roses behind her, landing on top of her, clawing her against the floor as she struggled to free herself.

"NO!" Marcus shouted right after she dodged my beak, leaving a scratch on her face. "Will, she's still my mom, please don't!"

Marcus' plea distracted me, giving her the opportunity she needed to kicked me off of her, this time climbing on top of me with her dagger pointing to my heart.

'I'm sorry, Marcus...' I sent him a T.P. apologizing for not having the time to explain that she was not his mom. I darted my beak on her neck, making her fall sideways. This impostor was not even igniting her Stardust anymore, making her pass as a human by allowing herself to bleed slowly from her neck down.

"I'm sorry I failed you, son..." She whispered to Marcus before losing her conscience. I knew I had no time to explain to him, whoever this impostor was I had to take her away and heal her. I need her alive.

"NOOOOOOO!" I could hear Marcus in the background as I flew away from there and back to my place in Charon, Pluto's moon, where I reside, a tranquil place to take care of this impostor.

V

My home is probably not the best place to bring a criminal, especially one who's purposely dying, but I had nowhere else to bring this woman posing as Katherine Mathias.

"Who are you?" I questioned the semi-conscious woman.

"Ha, ha, ha, ha, you are as gullible as they say," she laughed, coughing up blood out of her mouth.

"You and I both know you're a Porter, why don't you ignite your Stardust to heal, woman?"

"Because I'd rather die than betray our king, like you have, William." She spouted the words out on my face.

"You're working for Mario Shawyze as well?" If she is working for Mario, then it wouldn't be a bad idea to let her die. If Mario finds out I've betrayed him, he could have me killed easily.

"I am. You aren't, at least not anymore. Mario won't be happy when he finds out you got in the way of me killing the Natural Boy. And then it will be bye-bye, birdie." She let out another laugh, but this one was short, cut abruptly by her cough expelling out more blood.

Then, as if in a pass of magic, the woman in front of me who looked like Katherine Mathias, let her natural brown color take over the blonde hair. Her body was more prominent, more toned than that of her predecessor, and her skin tone was darker, just like Marcus'. Her eyes went from brown to bright-white like stars and then to a different shade of brown to a different shape of eyes in a whole different face.

"The Stardust in your body is barely keeping you alive. Ignite your powers, Ms. Liam."

"So, you do know who I am." The woman, who was still lying on the floor barely moving, looked at me, surprised at my deduction.

"I've never officially met you; however, the only Porters that can make their bodies take shapes of different Porters are the Porters of the Chameleon Constellation, and while I have never met you, I know that the actual Porter of the Chameleon Constellation is Camille Liam. Thanks to my studies at C.H.E.P. many years ago," I explained to her as she was going in and out of her senses.

"Here, have some water," I squatted next to her, helping her up to a sitting position, pouring the water into her mouth.

"Thanks," she said, unaware of her surroundings, "you know, I can almost feel it vanishing away, my powers, the Stardust in my system. No hard feelings, Will, I don't even know you, but I'm happy to be finally dying."

She stared at me with a half-smile on her face, as if she had succeeded in her mission. Her eyes squinted as if she was focusing on something next to me.

"What's that? Oh, by the stars in heaven," Camille let out a scream of fear and panic, wrapping her knees against her chest, "where did those snakes come from?"

"I can assure you my girls mean you no harm," a man next to me told her, recoiling his snakes back into his staff.

"William, who are these people, and how did they get here?"

"This is Dr. Octavio Ruer, Porter of the Ophiucus Constellation, the Serpent-Holder. To my left is the Queen of the Moon, Angela Carey, Porter of the Cancer Constellation, the Crab," I helped Camille up to her feet, "as you noticed by now, your powers are back, thanks to Dr. Ruer's snacks."

"Oh, you didn't—"

"Oh, but I did. Now, if you'll excuse me," I grabbed her arms behind her back, handcuffing them."

"You know these aren't gonna stop me, right, Birdie?"

"They are involved in Antimatter." I told her. "You won't be able to break out of them or to press your Exotic Matter Sphere, now if you behave, Angela might let you live."

"What? You're leaving me with them?" She shouted through her lungs as I stepped away from her, and Angela stepped closer to her.

"I gotta undo the mess you did. I'll be back soon." I disappeared inside of my Exotic Matter Sphere back to Ms. Hills' place, landing on the tree's branch across from Marcus' room.

'Marcus Mathias, where are you?
I know you're here somewhere,
I bring you wondrous news,
News to tell you that no one dares.
Where are you, Marcus, where?'

Once upon a time, I sent this T.P. to Marcus without a response; however, this time, I got an answer: *'William Chase.'*

"Have you gone completely crazy? Did you come here to kill me or perhaps to get killed by me, William?" Marcus shouted to the wind, unable to see me, a sign that Stardust has not yet manifested fully in his bloodstream.

'What's up with the anger issues? I'm here to help you, just like I did with your 'mom'.' I did help Camille Liam back to life, but I don't think Marcus understood that I meant his fake mom, the impostor.

"You are here to KILL ME TOO? SHOW YOURSELF!" Marcus demanded with his eyes bright-white like stars.

'If you insist,' I flew over to where Marcus was standing, knocking him out to the floor by the wind caused by my wings flapping vigorously, showing myself seconds later flying toward him with my whole body turned blue, showcasing my tail and wings.

"The nerve...," Marcus said getting up to his feet, I try to explain to him that indeed I am his friend, but Marcus didn't want to listen; instead he just charged after me. I flew quickly over him, avoiding his attempt to attack me.

"I like your spirit, but you're coming at the wrong guy. I'm not the bad guy here."

Again, I tried to explain to him that I was trying to protect him against Camille Liam, but, as usual, he didn't let me finish. He ran toward me inside his room. I dodged him, landing on the parapet of the balcony outside his bedroom.

"I'll be back to talk to you once you have calmed down." Marcus was furious at me for every reason, he doesn't know that the person I attacked was not his mom, so I decided to leave him be for a minute so he could calm down. But Marcus had other plans.

"NO! Come back here," He ran toward me, trying to catch me before I could fly out of there, but he was too late. I was already a few feet away from the balcony, and I didn't know he was trying to catch me; otherwise, I would have caught him before he could have fallen in the backyard.

"Marcus, are you alright?" I landed next to him in my human form, trying to make the appearance of a menacing being less threatening.

"Leave me alone," Marcus was angry at me, embarrassed at the fact that he couldn't get me.

"Marcus, I—"

"I said, leave me ALONE!"

And I did.

I disappeared out of there and back into my house. The house was empty, with no sign of Angela Carey, Dr. Octavio Ruer, or Camille Liam.

'My Queen?' I sent Angela Carey a T.P.

'I'm here.' Angela replied to my Thought Projection, sending me the location of where she was.

I disappeared inside of my Exotic Matter Sphere, reappearing inside of a cave not far from where I was.

'William,' she sent me a T.P. once a manifested inside of the icy cold cave under a mountain, here in Charon, 'I thought this place would be a better place to question our prisoner.'

Against the wall, chained from head to toes, was Camille Liam looking irritably at us.

"YOU CAN'T DO THIS TO ME!" She shouted at all of us.

"You can scream as much as you want, no one will hear you here," Dr. Ruer told her. "I am a Doctor and fully against torture, but I'll allow it this time. You almost killed the son of my dear friend Katherine. Where is SHE?"

Camille replied to Dr. Ruer's questioning by spitting on his face, to which he responded by raising his hand at her, but changed his mind before hitting her face, punching the wall next to her instead, "You're not worthy!"

'Dr. Ruer knows I am against torture as I am sure you are; however, she doesn't know that. Try to get something out of her, we need to know what she did to Katherine and if she truly is working for Mario or worse, for someone else.' Angela Carey sent me one last T.P. before disappearing out of there inside her Exotic Matter Sphere.

"Will do," I told her.

"If anything,"

"Dr. Ruer," I called him before he could press his E.M.S., "before you go, I need one more favor."

"Spill it out, Chase,"

"It's Marcus. I think he's hurt."

"Say no more, take me to the Natural. I hadn't seen him since when he first came out of his mom's womb," Dr. Ruer held his hand out, allowing his staff with two big snakes wrapped around it to manifest itself out of thin air. "Ready when you are."

To track another Porter by Thought Projection is only possible if the other Porter allows themselves to be found by sharing their exact location. However, in Marcus' case, he has always been connected with me since he and I first met on the morning of his sixteenth birthday. And now that Marcus is utterly mad at me, his location is pretty easy to find. I could very well feel his anger light-years away from here. I touched Dr. Ruer's staff, as I pressed my Exotic Matter Sphere with my free hand, disappearing out of there and to where Marcus is: the Cambridge Hospital.

"Be careful, too much anger can give you cancer, don't you know that?" I told him as soon as Dr. Ruer and I manifested in front of him in his hospital bed.

"You little piece of —"

After a semi-heated conversation, I explained to him that I was there to prove to him that I was still his friend, that the whole thing was not much more than an accident, and to show it, I brought Dr. Ruer, Porter of the Ophiuchus Constellation, the Serpent-Holder.

Dr. Octavio Ruer, who was heading to Uranus after here, healed Marcus with one of his snakes, who climbed on top of him, biting him on the exact position where his leg had broken, making Marcus fall unconscious. I stayed there till morning with Marcus, watching him sleep, just to make sure he'd be safe throughout the night.

As soon as the first ray of Sunshine hit the room, I disappeared out of there and back to the cave where Camille Liam was shackled.

"Camille Liam. I hope you slept well, given the circumstances and the chains,"

"How long are you gonna keep me here, William? Antimatter eventually will wear off, and I will be able to break free out of these shackles. You can't hold a Porter prisoner forever."

Camille was right. Antimatter was useful, but only for a few weeks. It will eventually wear off, and the shackles containing her wrists and ankles will be easy to break as if they were made out of paper.

"I do not intend to keep you here forever, Ms.

Liam. As soon as you tell me what I need to know, you'll be free to go."

"And that is...?"

"Who sent you to kill Marcus Mathias?"

"I wish I could tell you, but I won't, Willie."

"William. My name's William. You leave me no choice but to leave you here staring at the emptiness of the dark sky of Charon." I made my way out through the gate of the cave.

"William, come back. You can't leave me here. I'll starve to death."

"You and I both know that Porters are practically immortals, Camille." I locked the gates after stepping out of her eyesight.

"Yeah, but I still feel HUNGER, WILLIAM!"

"Send me a Thought Projection when you're ready to talk, I'll bring some blueberry scones." I made my way out of there, flying to the top of the mountain where I could see Pluto in the night sky from here.

Camille Liam, Wanderer Porter of the Chameleon Constellation, is a tough cookie to break. I have to find a way to break her, or even better, to find Marcus' mom, the real Katherine Mathias.

Even though Marcus and I were light-years away from each other, I could hear his conversations with his dad, who was trying to convince him to go to Venus so he could learn how to use his powers, how to ignite his Stardust whenever he needs it. But Marcus doesn't like the whole idea of being a Porter. His life has changed drastically in the last couple of Earthian months, and he was not happy about it.

'Marcus, there's no need for you to go to Venus,' I sent him a Thought Projection.

'Where are you, Will? Why don't you show yourself? FACE ME!' Marcus demanded.

'Marcus, I don't wanna fight you, I don't have much time to talk but know that you don't need to learn how to become a Porter, you are one already. A Natural Porter.' I sent him another T.P.

'You have no right to tell me what to do, not after what you did to my mom and me!'

'Listen, I gotta go, but don't forget I'll always be looking after you. I'll see you later, buddy.'

I concluded our Thought Projection conversation against his will. Marcus was thinking of going to Venus to avenge his mother; to learn how to control his powers so that he can kill me. The odds of Marcus being able to kill me are rather small, but he is a Natural after all; eventually, he will find a way to kill me if he wants.

I flew back to the bottom of the mountain, unlocking the gates of the cave where Camille is. If I want to get Marcus on my side, I have to prove to him that I didn't kill his mother.

"So, how did it go, William?"

"How do you think it went, Camille? Marcus doesn't believe me. He thinks I've killed his mother when I was saving him from you."

"Well, honey, I guess you and I both know you shouldn't have interfered with my plans, I had everything under control." Camille's tone of arrogance was almost as intolerable as the sound coming from the chains wrapped around her ankles and wrists.

"You and I both know you're not doing this on your own. Who hired you? Who are you working for?"

"I'm working for myself. I'm a Wanderer just like you, but unlike you, I don't want that stupid boy becoming the next Wonderer of Earth. His family has disgraced our reputation for way too long, William. Don't you see?"

"All I see is how much of a lunatic you are! Marcus is the Natural Porter of the Taurus Constellation, regardless of what you think. But sooner or later, you're gonna have to tell me who you're working for, Ms. Liam."

"Will, buddy, it's me, Marcus. Let me out of here so I can help you." His voice was of Marcus and even his looks. If I didn't know better, I would have been confused by the abilities of Ms. Camille Liam, Porter of the Chameleon Constellation.

"You're not the only one with the ability to mimic someone's voice, Camille." Even though she could change her looks and voice, I could also mimic sounds, and hers was the voice I've just spoken.

"Willie, come on, let me out of these chains. You know it can't hold me forever." She begged me as I turned and walked out of the dungeon.

"It's involved in Antimatter; it should hold you long enough."

"Willie—"

"WILLIAM! My name is William. I should've have killed you for real in front of Marcus when I had the chance." I stepped out of the room, locking the gate behind me. "Now, if you'll excuse me, I gotta go find the real Katherine Mathias."

'William. I swear next time I see you, I will make you pay for what you did to my mom.' I SWEAR!' That would be another T.P. from Marcus himself, sent to me just before I disappear out of that cave back to my house.

I haven't slept in a while. I decided this was the perfect time to do so.

Marcus is right now spending the weekend in Venus learning about all the Porters, including the Wonderers and Wanderers. He has been busy learning how to transform himself at will into his astrological sign, Taurus, the Bull; how to defend himself against everyone and, especially, his archenemy: Me, William Chase. At least that's what he thinks.

If only he knew that I was not his enemy but his friend. He needed time. He needed time to grieve the loss of his mom, to calm his anger. Time to truly understand who he is, who his father is, and to decide if he truly wants to become a Porter or not, the Wonderer of Earth. So, I decided to wait, to give him the time he needs.

The Sunrays here in Charon woke me up. I took a nice warm shower, picked up a pair of black pants with a dark-blue shirt, and threw them on. I went downstairs to the kitchen to grab a bite to eat and found a surprise guest drinking some coffee.

"I hope you don't mind," she said.

"Donna, what are you doing here?"

"Wow, I just brewed us some coffee, and this how you welcome your best friend?" The toaster went off as two slices of wheat bread popped out of it, hot and toasty.

"Sorry, I just wasn't expecting to see you," I replied perplexed, wondering if I had made plans with Donna Saihtam, Porter of the Virgo Constellation, the Virgin.

"Did we have any plans for today?"

"No, we didn't. But now that I am a Wonderer without a planet, that really makes me more of a Wanderer, doesn't it?" She helped herself to a slice of toast and some butter from the fridge. "How long have you had that ancient toaster? We must get you a new one that you don't have to stick your bread in. So last century..."

"You know I'm an old-fashioned kind of guy." I made my way into the kitchen.

"Yeah, I can tell by the way you— ooh never mind, you're dressed nicely. Someone has plans for today."

"No, not really, just thinking of maybe going to Earth in a bit but not sure yet,"

"Humm, you don't sound very convincing, Will, what's up? Anything to do with Marcus?" She asked casually as she sat in the chair by the kitchen table.

Donna was one of my closest friends, but I still didn't feel like sharing the whole 'Marcus Mathias Saga' with her. Something about this entire thing didn't feel right.

"Nothing really. Like I said, you just caught me off-guard," I leaned against the counter facing her. "So, how is it going? You know, finding you a planet with Queen Stars, has she found anything yet?" I poured myself some coffee, trying to change the conversation.

"Not really. I'm supposed to meet up with her in a few hours for a monthly update. She says a planet is being disclosed very soon, and she might assign me to it. But as of now, she told me to stay on Pluto till she discusses all of this with Titus Vespasian, you know the "king" of the Milky Way Galaxy."

"You know, he is actually the King of our Galaxy?"

"Yeah, yeah, yeah, not for long."

"You don't seem very excited about it?" I grabbed the other slice of toast and some grape jam.

"I am. Truly. It's just that I go there every month, we talk for hours, and nothing comes out of it, so I'm trying not to keep my hopes up. However, I did dress nicely today. Do you like it?" She twirled herself around to show me what she was wearing.

I just now noticed Donna's outfit. She had a strappy flowy red tank with a deep plunged neckline with matching sky-high high heels and body-hugging black tight jeans. Her hair was shoulder's length in its natural dark brown curls, matching her equally brown eyes. The red stood out against her skin; a tone lighter than Marcus. They could even pass as brother and sister.

"Yeah, I do. You look nice."

"Nice? I look NICE? What's up with you? I had this shirt come all the way from Dione to me, do you even know how much it costs?"

"That's not it. What I meant to say is Mariah doesn't like clothes that are too revealing, especially when you're attending court matters," I explained to her.

"I know, that's why I brought a knee-length coat to cover up." She pointed to a black leather coat with matching fur around the neck hanging in one of the hooks in the living room.

"Is that mackleadia?" I recognized the texture of her black leather jacket.

"A few centuries ago, there was an epidemic of mackleadia in Triton, so a few Porters went over there to keep it under control. A lot of clothes were made out of their skin for the people of Neptune's biggest moon, so they don't get hurt if there is ever another epidemic. Did you know that mackleadia's skin is indestructible? The only way of killing a mackleadia is from the inside out. Tough animals those bastards."

"Mackleadia's leather and fur are only allowed in Triton. How are you going to explain to the Queen how you got it, and why are you wearing it, anyway?"

"IT WAS A GIFT! Allison gave it to me. She was one of the Porters on that epidemic control team, so she was allowed to have it. It was just sitting in her closet, so she gave it to me. And I, being a great friend that I am, accepted it." She threw on her coat, showing it off. "See, don't I look good in it?"

'IS THAT ALL YOU GOT, DRAYTON? C'MON!' That was another loud and confused Thought Projection from Marcus Mathias.

"What is up with you today? Your body is here, but your mind is someplace else." Daniella's voice brought me back to the conversation. It's hard sometimes to keep a straight line of thought when Marcus is regularly sending Thought Projections in my head.

"I'm fine, really, just a lot on my mind," I responded somehow avoiding her.

"C'mon Billie-Willie. You know you can tell me, what's bothering you?"

"Listen, I'm sorry to cut this short, but I have to go." I put my plate and mug in the sink. "By the way, you know I hate when you call me that, Don."

"I know, I know, I was just messing with you. But don't go. I still have two Plutonian hours to kill."

"I have to go. I'm already late as it is." I kissed her on the cheek. "Raincheck?"

"Yeah, that's fine. I'll just go shopping on the moons of Neptune."

"Donna!"

"Don't tell Mariah. See ya later, Will." She pressed her Exotic Matter Sphere out of her belly button and disappeared out of my house.

I've been alive for over three centuries. Actually, in a couple of Earthian months from now, on November 14th, it will be my 357th birthday, and thanks to the Stardust running through my bloodstream, I still look like a twenty-five-year-old.

'I hate you, William! I HATE YOU!' And there it was, another T.P. from Marcus, reminding me how much he hated me for killing his mom. But I'm not giving up that easily. I will find a way to talk to him even if I have to fight to get him to listen to me.

The Center of Higher Education for Porters has

five campuses throughout the Solar System. The one Marcus is studying is located in Venus, on the North Pole, on the Ishtar Terra Continent, a continent roughly the size of Australia on Earth. On its eastern edges lies the grand mountain chain Maxwell Montes standing at a couple of hundred feet taller than Mount Everest, the tallest mountain on Earth, located in the Himalayas.

On the east side of Mont Maxwell, in the country of Fortuna Tessera, there is a small city named Rakhu, and there is where Marcus is right now. And there is where I appeared out of my E.M.S.

Rakhu is a small city for Venus' standards, but compared to a city on Earth, Rakhu is roughly the same size as Boston, Marcus' hometown. Here is where Kent, Roberto, Margaret among other Porters came to learn about Porters.

Unlike Boston, Rakhu has a feeling of a rural town. The houses and buildings are made out of a mixture that resembles clay. The city is very mono-chromatic with different shades of terra-cotta discerning their small structures. Besides the flare that each owner would put outside, you couldn't tell them apart.

I flew unnoticeably to this small three-story-high building where C.H.E.P. was located. I could see Marcus on an open field outside, fighting against another guy give or take a few years older than him. His skin was also pale like mine; however, his hair was yellow blond just like Jacques', and his eyes were blue, on a much lighter shade than mine.

"Don't go easy on me. I know you're a Natural and all, but I will beat you, mate," he spoke with an English accent.

"In your dreams, Drayton." Marcus' voice was that of excitement and anger infused in one, still not in the right place.

Marcus ran toward Drayton with his hands fully transformed into a bull's hooves. Drayton flew out of Marcus' punch but not out of his grip. Marcus somehow knew Drayton was going to spread his angel-like wings, so he sprung up his horns as his hind legs turned into those of a bull, making Marcus bigger and taller, striking Drayton in mid-flight. Marcus, however, didn't stop, he aimed at Drayton and started charging.

"ENOUGH!" I just now noticed Maisha Thompson, Porter of the Sculptor Constellation, who had slammed her fist on the floor transforming the orange soil under their feet into the mud. This made Marcus fall into it, turning himself back into his human form involuntarily.

"You have to learn to control yourself, Marcus," she said, coming out of under the thick green-colored tree.

"I HAD control of it," he shouted as Drayton got up to his feet, checking his head for lumps.

"Of your abilities, not of yourself. You could've seriously hurt Mr. Colton."

"It's alright, Professor. I can take it." He flew closer to Marcus, getting him out of the mud.

"I'm sorry, Dray, I don't know what got into me." Marcus apologized.

"No worries, Marks. That's why we are here, right? To learn how to control our abilities."

"That's enough training for today. Go inside, get yourselves cleaned up before supper. Ptorn's cooking is not as good as mine, but today is his turn."

They all left the orange, dusty field and went inside the building they were staying at. I sat in one of the branches of this enormous tree nearby. They were all too tired to hear or see a bluebird blending in the equally blue foliage that surrounded the houses in Venus.

Venus is the second planet from the Sun and Earth's inner neighbor. The two planets are virtually identical in size and composition, but these were two different worlds. An unbroken blanket of dense clouds permanently envelops Venus. Underneath lies a gloomy, lifeless, dry world with a scorching surface, hotter than that of any planet. Venus' landscape is dominated by volcanism.

That was the definition found by the astronomers. What they were not allowed to find out was the rivers of yellow colored water, trees of green colored trunks and blue foliage. Animals of different colors and sizes than those seen on Earth. People of six to seven-foot tall tanned by the harsh rays of the Sun, living in clay houses decorated with different types of sunflowers. A tranquil and calm place in the galaxy. Mr. Patrick Cobain, Porter of the Libra Constellation, Wonderer of Venus, achieved a very balanced civilization.

The light in one of the rooms came on. A few seconds later Drayton came into the room followed by Marcus. Drayton flew to the top bunk just like how I would do. One minute he was on his feet, the next he was landing gracefully on his bed. Clearly, learning how to fly was not an issue for him. Marcus, however, was less chirpy. His expressions were gloomy, and his eyes held an empty gaze as if he was absent from his body.

"Hurry up, mate, put some clothes on. You don't want Maisha to get mad."

"Let her wait. I'm not really looking forward to eating that garbage they call food today." Marcus grabbed a pair of shorts and put them on.

"And in less than a few hours, you'll be back on

Earth eating delicious food prepared by, what's her name again, Ms. Hors?"

"Ms. Hills. Mr. Hors is her boyfriend. How would you know? You have never met them." Marcus corrected Drayton without even making eye contact.

"Anything is better than Kyle's cooking." Drayton laughed.

I could see Marcus almost allowing himself a smile, but that idea vanished just as quickly as it came.

"ARE YOU GUYS READY YET?" Maisha Thompson screamed from downstairs. "IF YOU GUYS HADN'T SPENT UNNECESSARY THIRTY MINUTES IN THE SHOWER, I WOULD NOT HAVE TO YELL! FOOD IS GETTING COLD!"

"Let's get a go, mate," Drayton flew out of his bunk bed, tossing a t-shirt to Marcus.

"Let's." Marcus threw the shirt on.

'Time flies when you're having fun, doesn't it?' I sent a T.P. to Marcus just before he could leave the room.

"Hey, Dray, tell them I'll be right down. Your shirt is too big on me."

"Alright, mate. The green one you like is in the top drawer over there." Drayton knew he was lying. Marcus was not a good liar, but even so, he left the room.

"At least have the decency of showing your face, coward," Marcus spoke the words through his teeth.

I flew out of my branch, lading on the parapet of Marcus' window. "Better?"

"Give me one good reason not to punch you right now, William." He approached me with his eyes shining bright-white like stars.

"Wow. Are you really thinking of charging against me?"

"STAY OUT OF MY HEAD!" He shouted.

"You really gotta learn how to control your T.P.'s."

"Marks, are you okay?" Drayton ran into the room just before I could press my E.M.S. disappearing out of there, back in my living room.

VI

TIME AFTER TIME

Marcus is still furious at me. However, I have to find a way to talk to him. He needs to know that I am on his side, that the person who I'd supposedly killed was not his mother but an impostor who may or may not be working for Mario Shawyze. His mom is still out there, and I will find her, with or without his help.

'William, the Queen, and the whole Solar System are looking for you.' Angela Carey, the Queen of Moon, sent me a T.P.

'Understandably. She must also think I've murdered Katherine Mathias,' I replied, sitting down on my couch, getting some rest.

'Come clean, Will, I'm sure she'll listen to you and

absolve you of your crimes. Plus, you have Camille under your custody.'

'Camille is being held captive without a trial. Queen Mariah wouldn't approve of this either and would probably have me arrested. I have to find Katherine. Only with her, I can prove my innocence.'

'I'M EIGHTEEN? WHAT DO YOU MEAN I'M EIGHTEEN?' Marcus sent another involuntary loud T.P.

'William? Are you there? I lost you for a second.'

'Listen, it's Marcus. I have to go back to Earth. His mom is Unportable, so she has to be somewhere on Earth. I'll send you a T.P. later.'

'William, please be careful.' She sent one last T.P. before we disconnected our communication.

I pressed my Exotic Matter Sphere, appearing in my full bluebird form in one of the branches of Ms. Hills' tree in her backyard, all the way back in Cambridge, Massachusetts, United States of America, North Hemisphere, Planet Earth.

I could see Marcus by the door talking to his dad, clearly aggravated.

They couldn't see me.

Marcus left agitated to the backyard asking to be left alone. Once he was by himself, he sat under the tree, the same spot where he and I chilled a few minutes ago if you're from Pluto, like myself, or a couple of years ago if you're from Earth. Time is a very complicated thing throughout the galaxies.

"I guess nobody explained how time works for us, Porters, huh?" I landed next to him in my fully human form, with only my midnight-blue feathered wings revealing me as the Porter of Lyra Constellation, the Lyre.

"William, you—"

Marcus got up to confront me, but I stopped him before he could say anything, "Listen, I'm not your enemy like you think I am. I did not kill your mother."

"I SAW YOU, WILL. YOU KILLED HER!" Marcus raised his voice, pushing me against the tree.

"That wasn't your mother. It was a shapeshifter, Camille Liam, Porter of the Chameleon Constellation"

"YOU'RE LYING!"

I touched my Exotic Matter Sphere in my belly button, making us both disappear in it.

"WHERE AM I?" Marcus shouted once we both came out of it.

"Charon. Pluto's moon."

"WHY DID YOU BRING ME HERE?"

"I brought you here so I can prove to you that I did not kill your mother. Matter of fact, I didn't kill anyone.

"YOU—"

"STOP... shouting!" I took a deep breath. "I know you're angry at me but give me a chance to prove to you that I didn't kill your mother. Things aren't always what they seem."

"Fine! You have thirty minutes. I gotta get ready for Prom tonight."

"Prom, huh? That oughta be fun. Here in Charon, we call it Debutante Ball," I explained to him, "Who are you taking?"

"Twenty-nine minutes,"

"Earthian's or Charonian's?"

"What?"

"Listen to me, a day in Charon is over six Earthian days; therefore, five minutes there would be—"

"Is that what happened to me? When I was on Venus for three days, how long was that on Earth?"

"A day on Venus equals two-hundred-and-forty-three days on Earth. You were there for three Venusian days, seven-hundred-and-twenty-nine Earthian days."

"I was in Venus for that long?"

"Yup. Over two Earthian years, give or take a few hours."

"So, I'm eighteen now? Great! I missed my seventeenth and eighteenth birthday party," Marcus said, completely bummed out. "How come it didn't feel like that long?"

"As Porters, our bodies adapt to the planet's atmosphere, liquids, and temperature without your body noticing the difference. The same thing happens with gravity. Your body adapts to the planet's gravity allowing you to walk on it just as if would on Earth, all of that without the need for equipment. If any other human came to Venus on their own, you know, Unportables, they would die of lack of oxygen; their bodies would just take high leaps on Venus since its gravity makes your human body weight less."

"What about the humans from Venus that I saw? They look and walk just like us..."

"Humans aren't from Earth. They were brought to Earth and the other planets in the time they were finished being created by King Titus Vespasian."

"I thought Josh said that Humans were brought first to Earth, and Angela mentioned that we get Porters from Earth," Marcus highlighted.

"Correct, just not entirely. Thea was the first planet Mariah brought the humans, followed by every other planet in the Solar System a few years apart from each other. You know that time works differently on every planet. Before Mariah could bring Human Races to Earth, the whole incident with Thea happened."

"Yeah, Josh told me that Mariah went all crazy and smashed Thea against Earth,"

"Well, Mariah didn't want King Vespasian to interfere with her star system, so she destroyed Thea by smashing it against Earth," I concluded.

"How?" Marcus asked, horrified.

"You know how every Wonderer can manipulate an Element?"

"Yeah, like earth, air, wind, and fire. Go on."

"Mariah can control gravity."

"Gravity as in the gravity that is holding us in this moon, so we won't float away?" He asked, surprised.

"Yup, the same one. Mariah relinquished all gravity from Thea, allowing Earth's own gravitational force to do the rest. From there on, you know what happened; everyone in Thea got destroyed, Earth's moon was created, and Humans were brought to both, Earth and Luna."

"Luna?" Marcus asked, confused.

"The Moon is known as Luna as well, as the Sun is

also known as Sol," I explained to him.

"Where did the King bring the humans from?"

"Only King Vespasian knows."

"Can we find out? You know, go there?"

I don't know if Marcus was curious or furious about not knowing where humans come from.

"No, we can't. As Porters of the Solar System, we are not allowed to go to any other star systems. If we pass through the Kuiper Belt on the edge of the Solar System, our Stardust dissolves in our blood system, and without it, we become normal humans in the void of the Universe," I told him.

"We'd explode?"

"No. The first thing you would notice is the lack of air. You wouldn't lose consciousness right away; it might take up to fifteen seconds as your body uses up the remaining oxygen reserves from your bloodstream, and, if you don't hold your breath, you could perhaps survive for as long as two minutes without permanent injury."

"If I don't? But what if I do?"

"If you do hold your breath, the loss of external pressure would cause the oxygen inside your lungs to expand, which will rupture the lungs and release air into the circulatory system. The first thing to do if you ever find yourself suddenly expelled into the vacuum of space is exhale."

"Damn! What about planets that don't have an atmosphere? Like the Moon, for example, how come the Moon has air, sky with clouds, birds, and all different types of foliage and animals?"

"Luna, the Moon, has nothing; just rocks and craters according to your astronomers. That is because Angela Carey, the Queen of Moon, decided so. With the power of the Stardust bubble engulfing the whole Moon, Angela decides on how 'aliens' see the Moon, regardless if by any equipment, rovers, or even with their own eyes. She decided on a silver, white tone of sand and rock surrounded by craters to avoid people from Earth trying to colonize the Moon. And that also goes for every planet, body in our Solar System," I explained.

"That's pretty smart!"

Marcus doesn't have a strong Bostonian accent, but, in some words, you could tell his regionality. 'Smart' came out 'smaht'.

"Yeah, it is. But for the people of Luna and all the other Porters, you can see everything like it truly is, a beautiful, colorful, diverse Moon. Same thing when you travel to other celestial bodies like planets, moon, suns, and stars. The Earth, to other beings, is seen as a deep, ocean-blue planet surrounded by water with no continents, lands, nothing. Just water."

"Wow! What about time?"

"Time is nonexistent!"

"What do you mean?"

"Let me rephrase that, time is a constant that changes depending on where you are out there in the Solar System. Every planet, every moon, every celestial body in the Solar System has different times according to their rotation in relation to our Sun, Sol. It was created by humankind to help us differentiate the night from the day. That's all."

"So, what does that have to do with me?"

"When you were in Venus, it felt like three days because, to your mind, you were there for three days. As Porters, our minds reset itself up to adapt to its new environment, your body, however, still grows as if you were on Earth, simply because you are from Earth, so until you get your Halley Tattoo, you'll keep growing old. That's why you didn't acknowledge the years going by, but your body did, so now you're eighteen."

"Why no one told me that?"

"You said it yourself; you would only be there for three days, and we all accepted that. You were very adamant about it. Sometimes it's easy for all of us to forget about time since time doesn't really affect immortal beings like us, Porters. Here we are!" We've reached the cave under the mountain where I have Camille shackled.

"Marcus, before we go in, I just want to let you know one thing: Camille is good at what she does, so don't believe anything she says."

"Can we just get it over with? Don't you think I know the difference between my mom and a poser?"

Marcus walked into the cave with me right behind him, stopping only in front of the gate where I had Camille locked in. From there, we could see the shadow of a woman sitting on the floor with her back toward us, facing the barred window. Even though it was dark, Pluto's light shining through the window made it possible to recognize her blonde hair all disheveled.

"Marcus, don't forget—"

"Just let me in, will ya?" He said impatiently, recognizing the woman's silhouette.

I unlocked the gate, allowing ourselves in.

"Marcus? Oh my God, Marcus, is it really you?" She turned to face us. There, bounded by her chains, was Katherine Mathias sitting, in tears, reaching out to Marcus. A woman I haven't seen in a while, that, if I didn't know her myself, she would have me fooled completely.

"Mom?" Marcus rushes to her, embracing her in his arms, receiving the hug he's been longing for.

"Marcus, honey, how are you?"

"I've missed you so much," he spoke, still hugging his mom.

"Marcus, she's not your real—"

"SHUT IT, WILL!" He barked at me. "Are you okay?" He took his attention from me to his 'mom'.

"Marcus, let's go back home. Get me out of here, out of these shackles," she begged him, showing her wrists and ankles shackled by the chains.

"Hold on, let me get those out for you..."

"Marcus, NO! She's—"

"I SAID HUSH IT, WILL. I'm taking my mom home with me. We are through with you."

Marcus broke the chains off of her wrists and ankles, just as if they were made out of glass. Anti-matter could only be broken from outside in, not the other way around, making it the most resourceful material to lock Porters in.

"Oh, Marcus, thank you, now let's go home." The woman got up and hugged Marcus once more.

"Now tell me, Mom. How are you here?" From afar, I could see a bit of Stardust coming out of Marcus' eyes.

"What do you mean? HE BROUGHT ME HERE!" She pointed at me. "You were there when I was attacked and almost killed by that bird over there, and, when I woke up, I was here locked in these chains." She pointed to the remaining pieces of the chain on the floor.

"Yes, but how did you survive? I mean, how are you even alive now? Only Porters can survive outside of Earth. You're not a Porter! Or are you?"

"No, of course not, never! Marcus, none of this matter, okay? Can't you recognize your own mother?" She reached out to him, with tears in her eyes.

"You're right, I'm sorry." Marcus got up to hug his mom. She hugged him back.

"Son, what are you doing?" She asked, confused after a couple of odd minutes trying to free herself from Marcus' hold.

"You are not going anywhere!" Marcus spoke, still holding her.

"What're you talking about, son?"

"You're not my mother! What have you done with her?" He shook her firmly with his arms strong and muscular, just like that of a bull.

"You're hurting me, let me go!" She pleaded, trying effortlessly to free herself from him. "Marcus, it's me, I'm your m—"

"YOU'RE NOT MY MOTHER!" Marcus shoved Katherine against the wall.

"Hahaha, very good!" Katherine laughed, revealing her true self as Camille Liam. Her hair went from blonde to brown, wavy and no longer disheveled; her skin was still white just like Katherine's; her height was about Marcus' height; her petite figure made it easy for Marcus to keep a hold on her. If it weren't for her eyes shining bright-white like stars, you wouldn't even know she was a Porter herself.

"You're not as stupid as he makes you be."

"He who?" Marcus was face to face with Camille, still holding her against the dark gray cave wall.

"Our King, of course, who will not be happy once he finds out that your buddy there betrayed him."

"What is she talking about, Will?" Marcus turns his attention from her to me.

"Marcus, I can explain, I—"

"He didn't tell you? Ah, this oughta be interesting, but unfortunately, I have other matters to attend."

"MARCUS...!" I tried to warn him, but Camille had run out of the cave fast as the speed of sound, courtesy of the Gemini's abilities.

"What was she talking about, William? Who's this king you've betrayed?" Marcus approached me with his eyes going from green to bright-white like stars.

"Great! You just let our only hope to find your mom escape."

"You caught her once; you can catch her again. Now answer me! Who is this king she was talking about? Is it Titus?"

"She was talking about a Wanderer, Mario Shawyze, Porter of the Orion Constellation, the Hunter. He's not a king, at least not yet."

"And how come I'm just now hearing about this? Were you always working with him, this Mario Shawyze?" Marcus' whole body was shimmering with Stardust, not a good sign.

"NO! I mean, in the beginning, yes. I went to Earth to find you, to report back to Mario if you were a threat, and if so, to kill you," I explained as I took a few steps away from him, trying to gain more space between us.

"And instead, you decided to kill my MOM?" He shouted with his bull-like horns spring out of either side of his head.

"I haven't killed anyone. I just proved to you that the Katherine I attacked was not your mother, she was Camille Liam, the woman you just set free!"

"Or maybe Camille is in this with you. Maybe you did kill my mom, and Camille is covering it up."

"No, Marcus, I—"

"Is this the part where you spread your wings out in full bird form and take me to your 'king,' or are you just gonna kill me?" He grabbed me by my two arms just like he did with Camille before, with his legs transformed into the hind legs of a bull, standing at over ten feet tall, instead of his normal 5'8" height.

"Actually..."

I touched my belly button, where my Exotic Matter Sphere was and disappeared with Marcus back to Ms. Hills' backyard.

"Where did you bring me to?" Marcus shouted before even recognizing the place he was residing for the last couple of months on Earth.

"Home," I told him as he went from his bull self to his normal eighteen-year-old self. "You got a prom to attend. Don't wanna keep your date waiting."

"Marcus! There you are, *pote*[15]!" I heard Jacques, Marcus' best friend, exclaim before I pressed my E.M.S. out of there and back to my house in Charon.

Bringing Marcus back to Earth was the smart thing to do. Thirty minutes here on Charon equals over a couple of hours on Earth. Soon enough, everyone would start worrying about him. Having him vent with his friends was a good idea for now before I try to get to him again. But now I have something else to worry about: Camille Liam was free. It will only be a matter of time before she gets to Mario Shawyze and tells him about my betrayal; knowing Mario, she would surely have me killed for that. Vanishing forever without even leaving a trace of Stardust behind was not part of my plans.

I have to do something.

"S.T.A.R.S.S., connect me with Mario Shwayze."

CONNECTING WITH MARIO SHAWYZE – PLEASE, STAND BY

The familiar female computerized voice of our communication system spoke.

---

[15] *Pote:* Buddy (French)

"WILLIE, *CIAO*[16], WHAT A SURPRISE," Mario appeared in my leaving room with a rather busy background of a lot of people walking around behind him.

"I'm sorry to disturb you, my King, I see you're busy!"

"*SÌ, SÌ*[17], WILLIE, THAT'S WHAT I LIKE ABOUT YOU, YOU'RE VERY *PERCETTIVO*[18], EH? I'M MEETING WITH MARIAH AND TITUS TO DISCUSS SOME COURT MATTERS ABOUT THE GIRL DONNA SOMETHING. YOU TWO ARE *MIGLIORI AMICI*[19], NO?"

"I wouldn't say best friends, but..."

"OH, *NON IMPORTA*[20], I'LL SEE WHAT THE QUEEN HAS TO SAY. *CIAO*[21] FOR NOW, WILLIE". Mario disconnected the call.

At least I know I have some time. Donna is in an audience with Mariah, Titus, and Mario. That should take a least a couple of local hours, and from what I could see in the background, they are in Jupiter right now, which means I have to move fast.

I poured myself some yamahuie liquor.

'Where is he? We're already late to Prom as it is.'

---

[16] *Ciao:* Hi (Italian)

[17] *Sì:* Yes (Italian)

[18] *Percettivo:* Perceptive (Italian)

[19] *Migliori amici:* Best friends (Italian)

[20] *Non importa:* Doesn't matter (Italian)

[21] *Ciao:* Bye (Italian)

Marcus' T.P.'s are becoming part of my own thoughts. Not one hour passes without Marcus sending me a Thought Projection. This time, I can feel the sadness and anger he was feeling.

I took a quick shower and then grabbed a dark-blue shirt and black dress pants, with a matching suit and a navy tie. I put on my shoes, styled my hair, and disappeared out of there to Earth, not before grabbing the Silhouettes for tonight's festivities.

I could see Marcus outside of his house, actually Ms. Hills' house. He was dressed beautifully in a black tuxedo and baby blue shirt with a blue bowtie. I don't think I have ever seen him so handsome before. It is too bad that his green eyes were stained in tears. Barely noticeable, but I noticed it.

"May I escort you, Mr. Mathias?"

"William," he said, wiping the tears off his face quickly so I wouldn't notice them, "what are you doing here?"

"Taking you to Prom, silly," I climbed up the stairs to his doorstep where he was sitting.

"But, Drayton?"

"It's late. Unless you want to spend the rest of your evening waiting for him here, I suggest we leave now."

"I'm already late as it is. Dinner has probably ended by now, and we'll never make in time to the first dance, and I..."

"You talk too much." I grabbed Marcus' hand and disappeared inside of my Exotic Matter Sphere, reappearing behind his school; the same place where the

Gemini Twins tried to kidnap him not too long ago.

"We made it!" He said enthusiastically with his eyes bright-green, watching the people still pulling over in the parking lot. "Let's go!"

"Wait, hold on, Marks," I pulled him close to me. "In Charon, our Debutante Ball, the dates both wear a matching symbol off their relationship; something that reminds them both of when they met. We call it Silhouettes. So, I got us both a brooch."

"A brooch with a fish on it?"

"Koi fish is a symbol of prosperity and luck in Earthian's Japanese culture. I thought it would be very fitting since the first time we officially met was the day I rescued you from the Rowes Warf waters. Remember?" I said, stabbing the brooch through his tuxedo lapel, where usually a rose is inserted through. "Here, now, you do me."

Marcus grabbed the other brooch I gave to him with his trembling hands and pierced against my black tuxedo suit in the same location where I had placed his. The silvery, golden fish stood out against our black suits.

"Thank you for this, Will."

"Thank me after the night is over," I smiled, reaching out my hand for him to grab it. "Shall we?"

"We shall," Marcus grabbed my hand with his sweaty-cold hand as we made our way into the gymnasium at Everett High School.

We passed through a lot of people that knew who Marcus was but had no idea who I was. I don't even think they knew Marcus was seeing someone, or do they think I was Drayton? Regardless, we went straight for the punch where we said hi to Mileena and her date, Jacques, who barely even said anything to both of us. I guess out of shock for seeing me with Marcus instead of Drayton? After all, he is the one dating Marcus.

What was I doing anyway? Marcus is seeing someone else. I'm clearly not the guy for him. No matter what I do, Marcus will always see me as the guy who killed his mom; it's only a matter of minutes before he snaps and yells "Murderer" at me.

"Wanna dance?"

Marcus interrupted my train of thoughts, bringing me back to reality. I nodded, grabbing his hand, and leading him to the dance floor. My heart was pounding out of my chest. I could feel Marcus trembling too. His face had a hard to read expression. Was he enjoying himself, or was this just a way for him to keep his eyes on me? Or maybe even kill me?

"Thank you, for this," Marcus broke the ice. "I've missed all the other school's activities last couple of years and wouldn't want to miss Prom."

"You're very welcome."

I couldn't help but smile at the beautiful man Marcus was growing up to be. He will always be centuries younger than me, but once he's twenty-five, we'll basically be forever the same age. He won't age anymore, and I won't age as long as I keep renewing my Halley Tattoo.

"Are you as nervous as I am?"

"Very, Marks." I laughed. "I haven't been to a

Debutante Ball since my own."

"Were you this charming then as you are now?"

"Ha, no." I smiled awkwardly. "At my Prom, I didn't have a date. I was sitting by the bleachers sulking on the punch while the guy I had a crush on was making out with a cheerleader."

"Relatable," Marcus laughed. "Quarterback?"

"Something like that. Same over-glorified position, different sport though."

"Typical. At least now you get to have a do-over with me." I couldn't tell, but I think Marcus was flirting with me.

"Except that you have a boyfriend, or has Mr. Colton already slipped through your mind?" I reminded him.

"He's not my boyfriend, plus where was he when I needed him?"

"I'm sure somet—" Before I could finish my sentence, someone grabbed me from behind, tossing me through the air across the gymnasium: Drayton.

"ARE YOU KIDDING ME?" He shouted to either Marcus or me; I couldn't tell. I got myself back up again, with my wings sprung open inadvertently.

"DRAYTON! What the hell, man?" Marcus yelled at him.

"WHAT THE HELL? WHAT THE HELL WITH YOU, MARCUS. DID YOU FORGET HE KILLED YOUR MOTHER?" Drayton shouted at Marcus, towering over him with his horse-like hindlegs in place of his own, with his bright-white wings sprung open like mine.

"So, you're just gonna kill him?"

"If you don't have the balls to do it, I will." Drayton pushed Marcus out of the way, flying toward me.

"Listen, Drayton, I—"

"SHUT UP!" Drayton punched me back against the wall with hooves in place of his hands, thanks to the power of his own Constellation, Pegasus.

I could've avoided it. I could stop him. But should I? After all, I took his boyfriend out. Maybe I did deserve this. He kept on punching me. I could feel some blood coming out of my nose, a sign that I was not stellar. I needed to activate my Stardust, so he doesn't hurt me. Or kill me. He was punching me constantly. The music had stopped, and so did everybody in shock. I could hear Marcus yelling, saying whatever he was saying, but I couldn't make it out.

'WILLIAM, FIGHT HIM!' He sent me a Thought Projection as loud as someone yelling in my ears. And that was all I needed to hear.

I ignited my Stardust, grabbing his hooves midair before he could strike my face again. I could see my whole body turning blue, and in less than a second, my wings were completely open with my tail hovering over my head, and then, I let him have it.

A sonic boom came out of my mouth like a wave of sound, knocking Drayton out and everyone in the gymnasium. Except for Marcus, who was still standing there, with his hard to read expression.

"I'm sorry," I mouthed before disappearing inside of my Exotic Matter Sphere.

VII

There was nothing left for me to do. I had to leave Marcus to deal with his boyfriend, or whatever Drayton was to him. I poured myself a glass of yamahuie liquor, trying to ignore the pain I was feeling, not from Drayton's punch, but from the situation I was just in. Stardust had pretty much healed me fully by now, and my pain was only hurting my ego.

"Hi, Will"

Donna appeared right behind me, inside of my house. I dropped the glass of yamahuie, startled by her presence. In a swift movement, Donna unsheathed a six-foot-long sword out of thin air right under my glass, catching it just before it could've smashed on to the floor.

"Good catch,"

"Don't wanna waste good yamahuie. It's some expensive liquor you got there." She handed me the glass back without spilling a drop.

"Would you care for some?" If Donna appeared here unannounced, something's up.

"Actually, I was wondering if you wanted to go out for a drink. I think you and I need to talk." She sheathed her sword as it disappeared at her waist.

"I'm okay. Aren't you supposed to be in an audience with the Queen?"

"She dismissed me. Said that something 'came up,' whatever that is. Plus, I need to know what happened between you and Camille."

"Camille," Of course. I had forgotten about Camille. "Listen, I—"

"You should've told me. I would've helped you." She grabbed my two hands. "I am your friend, you know?"

"I think I could use that drink now," I said, confused. Was Donna not mad at me for kidnapping her friend?

"Great! Is there any place around here that has great handcrafted drinks? Ugh, don't answer that. I forgot for a second where I was. Lemme think, lemme think. Oh! I know. Let's go, Billie-Willie." She grabbed my hand and **PUFT** we disappeared inside of her Exotic Matter Sphere and appeared in a dark alley with some strange small people passing by.

"Is this...?"

"Deimos? Yes! Mars' smaller moon has a perfect

bar with handcrafted drinks made by real Marsians, you know, dwarves."

"They are not dwarves. They are little people, Donna!"

"Yes, they are. And they make the best drinks in the entire Solar System." She opened the door for us to get in. "Trust me, I know. Shall we?"

"How would you know that? Never mind. The fact that you've been a Porter for only a few decades and already know about this makes me wonder about my whole existence."

"Sway-o, Swah-yo," she replied casually. "What can I say, I'm a cool chick."

"Hold on, you two. Non-Deimos people aren't allowed in here!" This five-foot-tall muscular woman halted us before we could move in any further.

"Unless they are Porters like us, right?" Donna let her eyes shine like stars so everyone could see.

'What are you doing? You know we are not allowed to reveal ourselves to Unportables.' I sent her a Thought Projection.

"The lady is cool, what about you pretty boy, got some stars behind those eyes?" She asked as a couple more dwarves approached us.

'Show her your eyes, Will.' Donna sent me a T.P.

And so, I did.

"Alright, they are Porters, people, they're okay. Treat 'em nicely."

"What just happened?" I asked, intrigued.

"Porters are treated like royalty here. Porters come here illegally from all over the Solar System to get drunk," she told me as we approached the bar. "They keep our secret, and we keep their business going."

"This is crazy. Thanks, Donna!"

"Don't thank me yet. We still haven't talked about Camille and this whole Marcus Mathias Saga But first, hey, Teena, that's your name, right? Can you give us two Protostars?" She asked the bartender behind the bar.

"Protostars?" I asked, intrigued by the two short glasses of a neon-blue drink in front of us.

"Just shoot it up, Will," Donna said before she, herself, drank her own shot.

"Skál!" I shot the neon drink down my throat.

"Saúde!"

"You speak Portuguese?" I asked, intrigued by her strange choice of word replacement of 'cheers!'.

"And you speak Icelandic. Now that we got this out of the way, tell me. What's going on with you?"

I have known Donna for only a couple of Earth years. Here in Charon, it has only been a couple of days. She was young, inexperienced, and needed help venturing around the Solar System. Allison Prior was the one who recruited her in Pluto, a planet that Allison, Porter of the Scorpius Constellation, used to govern until the King of the Milky Way Galaxy decided on a new rule of planetary objects, reclassifying it a Dwarf Planet and no longer part of Mariah Stars' jurisdiction. Mariah, being the Queen of Solar System, had told her to sit still till she reassigns her to a new planet in our star system.

Donna and I have grown close throughout the years and, even though she is one of my best friends, I still haven't had a chance to tell her about Marcus Mathias, the supposedly Natural Porter of the Taurus Constellation, if he accepts it that is.

"You've heard of Marcus Mathias, right?"

"Sort of. Our King has mentioned his name a couple of times here and there, but he never really told me why he is so obsessed with this boy from Earth. Allison also doesn't tell me much. She says not to worry about these things and to stay out of Mario's way." Not surprised about how little Donna knows of Marcus, Mario is truly keeping this between some of his most trusted. "Why do you ask?"

"You know I know him, right?"

"Surely you know him, Mario has you keeping an eye on him in case he becomes a threat to our King," Donna ordered another round of the neon-blue drink.

"No, I mean, I do know him. I actually had a chance to get to know him, you know, talk to him," I told her.

"So, what's he like? Is he as special as everyone says?" Donna's eyes were shining with excitement.

"Oh yes, he is special," I told her as I took another shot of whatever that stiff neon-blue drink was.

"Oh, my stars!" She faced me in amusement.

"What?"

"You like him!" She smiled from ear to ear.

"What? No, it's not like that," I said embarrassedly.

"You do like him, Willie-Billie. Hey, it's okay. I'm

your friend. You can tell me anything. Trust me."

"I do trust you. It's just that Marcus, well, regardless of how I feel about him, he's with someone else."

"Oh, that happened to me before back in Pluto, I met this guy who was super sweet, nice, kind, but he just wanted to be my friend. Apparently, I was not his 'type'. Hey, maybe I could introduce you two, I think he's—"

"DONNA!" I interrupted her very enthusiastic train of thought. "A little off-track, don't you think?"

"Oh, yeah, I'm sorry. You're saying..."

"So, I do know him, and I don't think he represents any danger to Mario and his plans on taking over Mariah Stars' place as King of the Solar System." This time I ordered another round. "You gotta catch up, you know?" I pointed to her untouched drink in front of her.

"Thanks!" She took her shot. "That's great news. We should tell King Mario Shawyze about it so he can stop obsessing about your boy-toy."

"Don't call him that."

"So that explains why you had Camille in shackles a few hours ago," she told me enthusiastically.

"What?" I almost spilled out my drink. "Did she tell you that?"

"Oh yeah, she told me everything! How you brought Marcus to her so he can see his mom for one last time. You know that was really nice of you. But Camille would have done that for the two of you either way without the shackles, you know?"

"What?" I asked, uncertain about what she said.

Did Camille tell her a different story?

"It's okay, William. If you ask me, I think it's pretty sweet of you. So, when do I get to meet your new thing?"

"Listen, Marcus and I are just friends. I'm too old for him. Plus, the only reason why we are hanging around is so I can report back to Mario like he asked me to. And I will continue to do so until—"

"Until he falls for you... aww that's so cute. I better be invited to the wedding." She danced around with glee as if holding a bouquet in her hands.

"You and I both know we can't make people fall in love plus—"

"I know, I know, Marcus is not into you. I'm sorry, I just want you to find the right guy. You deserve it, after the whole fiasco with, what was his name? C.J.? T.J.? Or was it just Jay?"

"Never mind about him. Someday I'll find the right guy, just not right now. I have other things on my mind." I ordered another round of Protostars.

'FUNERAL? WE ARE NOT HAVING A FUNERAL WITHOUT A BODY!'

"I gotta go, sorry I have to disappear like this, but I'll call you later..." Marcus sent me one of his involuntary angry T.P.s about his mother's funeral.

"Hey, what about the drinks you just ordered?"

"Fine, one for the road." We both shot up the last round of neon-blue drinks. "Here are twenty Halleys, that should cover it, right?"

"Heck yeah! T.P. me later, Willie."

"Will do," I said, kissing her on the cheek before

vanishing out of there, back to my house.

The smell of cigarettes, cigars, and booze was all over my clothes so, I grabbed new pair of black slacks and a black shirt plus my sunglasses and headed out to where the funeral would be.

If there was going to be a funeral, I knew exactly where it would be held: the same place where they held the funeral for Marcus' young sister, Daniella Mathias, about ten years ago. I remember seeing Roberto's side of the family and Katherine's side of the family all dressed in black, paying their last tribute to her. Katherine was being consoled by her mother as she sobbed on her shoulders. Roberto was staring at the small, white coffin fit for a ten-year-old girl with calla-lilies and carnations all over it. His eyes were empty as if life had also left his own body. He was standing there, hoping that somehow, he would wake up from this nightmare. Marcus was only eight at the time. He was sad, standing by his father, too young to understand what was happening. That was the first time I had ever seen him. Today, however, the scene was somewhat different.

Roberto was fully dressed in black, standing there looking at the adult-sized black coffin, but unlike before, his tears were flowing down freely, making his brown eyes look green. He wasn't sobbing or even making any noise, but the tears kept coming down.

Marcus, now eighteen, was just a couple steps behind him with an angry and sad expression. A mix of anger and sadness, relief, and sorrow. His eyes bright white as if they were no longer there, instead, two stars. The same look a Porter has when they are about to strike.

I saw from afar the men lowering her coffin as everyone else was leaving the cemetery. Marcus went in a different direction alone as if to collect his thoughts, his emotions. I knew this was hard to do, but I had to talk to him. I have to prove to him that his mom is not dead, that we are going to find her.

I made my way closer to him, watching him stare blankly at the grass under a tree. I took a few more steps. I was right behind him. Marcus was too taken in his own thoughts that didn't even hear me approaching.

I took a deep breath and...

"William?" I look behind me, and to my surprise, I saw someone who I was not expecting to see me. I myself didn't even hear Marcus' father approaching us. "What are you doing here?"

"HOW DARE YOU SHOW UP HERE? THIS IS ALL YOUR FAULT!" Marcus shouted from behind me, preparing himself to charge against me, his skin luminous with Stardust all over.

"Marcus, control yourself. I'll handle this." His father spoke.

"I'LL HANDLE THIS MYSELF." He grabbed me by my two arms, throwing me on the floor. "YOU'RE NOT GONNA FIGHT? COME ON, LIGHT UP!"

"I'm not here to fight you. I came here to talk to you, to you both actually," I said, trying to control my own instincts and not ignite my Stardust.

117

"YOU HAD YOUR CHANCE." Marcus' hand became a hoof, just like that of a bull. However, a loud, long grunt followed by a short 'moo' stopped him and honestly, scared me too.

"That's enough, Marcus. I said I'll handle this. Let William go." Roberto's voice was deep and intense, a tone I haven't heard coming out of him in a long time.

Marcus was a guy again; no parts of his body were that of a bull, his skin was no longer luminous, and neither was his eyes; they were now their natural shade of green.

I flew up to my feet without even thinking, positioning myself in front of them. Marcus had taken a couple of steps back as a precaution to not charge against me. However, he was more afraid of his father than of me, obviously.

"Thanks, Roberto," I said, straightening myself.

"Your time is short, boy."

"You and I both know I am much older than you two combined, so do not call me 'boy'." This time my eyes did flinch back and forth between its natural shade of dark-blue, to white, to blue again.

"Tick-tock," Marcus emphasized his father's warning. Sometimes I forget how impatient and stubborn people ruled by Taurus can be.

"I have reason to believe Katherine might be alive," I said cautiously.

"What about what Marcus saw? Didn't he see you killing my wife?" Roberto spoke with his words behind his teeth, blocked by anger.

"I would never hurt an Unportable, Roberto. It's

against the law, and besides, death by Oblivion is something I'm trying to avoid. The woman he saw me attacking was Camille Liam," I explained.

"Camille Liam? Porter of the Chameleon Constellation?" Roberto asked. "Are you sure about this?"

"I was with Marcus just before she showed up. We were interrupted by a noise coming from the kitchen. Marcus left, thinking it was Jacques; however, I wanted to check on him for myself to make sure that Marcus was safe. I was looking out the window when I myself couldn't believe that Katherine was there. At first, I was in shock just as Marcus was, and then when she asked to talk to Marcus outside, I saw something that gave her away. She had a Sagitta in her hands when she grabbed Marcus."

"A Sagitta?" Marcus asked.

"An arrow. Gia Lia is the Porter of the Sagitta Constellation, the Arrow. Her abilities consist mainly of creating sharp arrows out of her hands, the same arrows that Josh Rogers uses. They are sort of co-dependent on each other." Roberto explained.

"Josh Rogers as in the Porter of the Sagittarius Constellation, Wonderer of Jupiter?" Marcus' classes in Venus paid off, at least the name of the Wonderers he has them down.

"That's right," I said.

"What does that have to do with my mom?" He asked a bit calmer than before.

"You see, Camille has the ability to transform herself into anyone she has ever touched before. All she has to do is think of them and boom, she becomes

119

whoever she wishes," I explained. "Katherine can't possibly hold a Sagitta on her hands, only Gia and Josh can. So, then I concluded your mom had to be Camille since she's the only one who can create replicas of all of Porters' weapons, appearances, voices, and powers, making her truly a chameleon."

"I knew if I followed you, you would lead me straight to them, Billie-Willie." I could hear but could not believe it. Her tone of voice was not of a friendly one, on the contrary, more as of a threatening one.

"What are you doing here, Donna? This is a family matter."

"If there's someone here who is not part of this family, it's you, William." She took a few steps closer to Marcus and Roberto.

"I don't understand. What does she mean, Dad?"

"What, Marcus? Don't you recognize your big sister?" Donna let her hair fall in front of her eyes, covering her face.

"It was you!" Marcus recognized her. "The girl I saw outside Ms. Hills' coffee shop on my first day at work was you!"

"Ah, you should have seen your face. You were so scared of me that you even passed out on the floor." She let out a proud laugh.

"Daniella?" Roberto's voice broke as he stared at his little girl, now all grown up.

"Oh, Daddy, wipe those tears off your eyes. Being sentimental like this was one of the reasons you failed as a Wonderer."

"How is this possible? How could you have become a Porter? A Wonderer? I saw you grow up in Pluto," I asked, astonished, wondering how my friend of many years was Marcus' long-lost sister.

"Mommy. She gave me away to Allison Prior, who took me in and taught me the way Plutonians live and speak. I couldn't use my real name so, inspired by my middle name, Donovan, I called myself Donna, as for my last name Saihtam, it's Mathias spelled backward; by the time you met me, Willie, I had already become Donna Saihtam, Porter of the Virgo Constellation, a Wonderer. Mariah Stars had assured me that I would soon have my own planet, but that's not happening anytime soon. We all know she despises people of Virgo, thanks to her tossed-into-Oblivion former best friend Regina Khales and the destruction of planet Thea. But that's a story we are all already too tired of hearing." She stopped in front of me.

"You pretended to be my friend all these years so that you could get close to Marcus?"

"William, I am your friend. But ever since I found out, you've been hanging out with my little brother, I had to keep a closer eye on you. I couldn't let you get in the way of King Mario Shawyze, and, as always, I was right."

"Daniella, sweetheart, what are you talking about? Mario is just a Wanderer, Porter of the Orion Constellation, the Hunter." Roberto took a few steps closer to her, confused by his daughter's statement.

"For now, Daddy." Her tone of voice didn't match her words. Donna was calling Roberto 'daddy' in a very diminishing way. "Once he dethrones Mariah Stars, he will be the new King of our Solar System and not that two-face, self-centered woman."

"I know I just started learning the Solar System's Laws, but I'm pretty sure that's treason followed by Oblivion."

"Not bad, little brother, stay in school. Nevertheless, I'd rather be wiped out of existence by Oblivion than to live in this Solar System ruled by the oh-so-powerful Queen Stars." I couldn't believe that the little girl I met a few years ago, grew up to become this vengeful woman. I knew Donna was on Mario's side, as was I, but the more I heard her argument, the more I wondered if I had indeed chosen the right side.

"Daniella, I—"

"DONNA! I go by Donna now, DAD!" Her eyes are now going from brown to bright-white like stars. "I knew you and Marks would get in the way, so that's why I'm here, to help William bring you back to the king."

"William?" Marcus' expression was once again full of rage.

"Donna, grab Marcus. I'll take Roberto myself."

I look at Roberto, who was still in disbelief with everything that had just happened. I flew toward him, landing myself between him and Donna; she turned around and flew toward Marcus.

I must say that my wings were pretty awesome, but there was nothing more majestic than the wings of a Virgo. In the case of Donna, her black mackleadia fur coat opened up, allowing her equally black feathered wings. Her whole body turned black, lit up with Stardust all over with only her eyes shining bright-white like stars.

She unsheathed her six-feet long sword and flew toward Marcus, who was somehow completely immobile just like a rabbit about to be snatched by an eagle. But what happened next was almost too fast for me to see.

Drayton came flying from behind Marcus in full angel mode, his white wings completely contrasting against Donna's black wings. He knocked her out, with his right hand fully turned into a horse's hoof. The element of surprise got Donna, who fell backward against a tomb's plate, shattering it in pieces.

Drayton landed in front of Marcus fully transformed into a white-winged horse.

"You're a..." Marcus' words barely came out, he was entirely shocked. "You told me you were..."

"Technically, I am a Virgo. I was born on September 3rd. I just always hated being a winged horse, so I portrayed myself as an angel, like Virgo, but as you can see, I look nothing like them," he replied, turning himself back into a twenty-year-old blue-eyed guy from London. "I'm a Wanderer, Porter of the Pegasus Constellation, the Winged-Horse."

"Maybe now you should embrace your inner Pegasus as you can clearly see Virgo is not a very nice sign," Marcus remarked.

"Now, now Marcus, you and I both know people can be equally good or bad regardless of their astrological sign," I inserted. "I know outstanding people of Virgo that are nicer than Scorpius."

"Not a very good, compelling case, William. Allison is not a very good Scorpius either," Marcus replied, remembering our last encounter with her.

"I gotta go. I'm going to take Donna, Daniella actually, with me before she wakes up and goes to her King. I'll come back once she's locked away.

"William, what took you so long?"

"Not now, Roberto. We'll talk soon." I grabbed Daniella and pressed my E.M.S. disappearing out of Earth back to Charon.

***

I reappeared back in Charon inside of the cave I had Camille locked in a few hours ago, with Donna, still somewhat unconscious. Drayton really did a number on her.

I shackled her just like I had done before with Camille. I can still see on the floor the broken shackles that Marcus took out of Camille when she made him think that she was his mom.

"Well, hello there. Fancy to meet you here." I looked behind me, and even though I shouldn't be surprised, I was.

"Camille, what a surprise!" I said, making sure Donna was firmly locked. "What brings you to this side of the Solar System?"

"You know, after I lost communication with Donna, I figured you must have knocked her out and brought her here, just like you did with me." Camille was prancing around the place as if she was about to jump at me at any time.

"Aren't you clever?" I positioned myself between her and Donna.

"Nope, you're just that predictable. Now be a good bird and hand Donna over to me."

"No, can't do. You see, just like you, Donna isn't who she claims to be. That twenty-year-old woman over there is Marcus' presumed dead sister, Daniella Mathias."

"Oh my! Even better! Imagine Mario's face when he finds out that Daniella is still alive. He's going to kill her and Alison for lying to him. He will finally recognize me as one of his royals."

Camille's eyes were shining like stars, but yet somehow, I can still see the sadness and anger of never being approved by Mario Shwayze. I have never had to gain Mario's trust. Allison spoke very highly to him about me, to my surprise, and he just took me under his wings just as if I was one of his Hounds.

"Donna has information on where her mother is. I'm pretty sure if I let her go, she'll find and kill Katherine, and I'm not gonna let that happen." I told her igniting my own Stardust, allowing my eyes going from midnight-blue to bright-white like stars.

"Of course not, or your boyfriend will get really upset with you, wouldn't he?" She mocked me, "What? Donna, or better Dani, told me everything about how much you're in love with Ma—"

I flew toward her to strike her face just before she

could finish talking, but she ran to a different spot in a blink of an eye.

"Did I hit a nerve?" She laughed at me, knowing that she did.

"Marcus and I are just friends. You two are crazy for thinking otherwise." I was trying to get some space between us so that I could advance at her. "Oh no. You are not getting away from me."

Camille was moving fast. To fight against her was like fighting against the Gemini Porters; she was using the speed of sound to hit me every second. She punched my stomach six times, followed by her elbow in my face, then in my back, making me drop to my knees. All of this in less than ten seconds.

"I thought we would have more fun. You're too slow, Willie." She ran to the other side of the cave so she could get some space between us. She ran back toward me to knock me out.

"It's WILLIAAAAAAAAAAAAAAM!" I let out a sonic screech knocking her out against the cave wall, barely conscious.

"What in Pluto is going on?" Daniella shouted from the opposite side of the cave.

"The usual. Bad guys try to overtake the good guys. Good guys win, bad guys get imprisoned. Did you sleep well?" I said, straightening myself up.

"William! GET ME OUT OF HERE! I DEMAND YOU TO GET ME OUT OF HERE!"

"Or what Daniella? What are you gonna do?" I said, making my way over her.

"You should have kept your eyes on me!"

Camille had moved from where she was to right behind me, with her skin now turned to green scales. Her arms and legs were claws just like that of a chameleon, piercing my two arms and legs. Her tail was wrapped around my neck, which tightened it up, making it hard for me to break free. As I was about to let a sonic scream out, she flipped me through the air, throwing me against the cave's dark grey wall.

"Nighty-night, Willie." She waved just before I fell unconscious.

VIII

I woke up on the floor of the cave with no one around me. Camille and Daniella, gone. I pressed my Exotic Matter Sphere and disappeared out of there, back to my house a couple of miles away. This whole situation is a mess. I can't allow it to get any worse. If they both go to Mario, it would be only a matter of time before he sends his Hounds after me, and I cannot fight them all by myself. I need help.

I took a shower, cleaned some of the wounds caused by Camille, and got dressed in my jeans and a royal purple t-shirt. I went downstairs to the kitchen to reheat some food: phaison with whipped otatop and jules berry gravy sauce on top. Jupiter's version of pheasant with mashed potatoes and cranberry gravy on top, except that phaison is a dark-purple bird when it's cooked, otatop is orange and not yellow like potatoes, and jules berries look like little limes but taste like blackberries. An explanation I was hoping to give to Marcus one of these days when I have the time to take him out to dinner in Ananke, one of Jupiter's moons.

I went back upstairs to fix my hair, brush my teeth, and put some shoes on. Now it was late in the morning in Boston and just before bedtime here for me in Charon, a perfect time for me to talk to Marcus and unavoidably to Roberto as well. We need to put our differences aside and work together. I pressed my Exotic Matter Sphere and disappeared out of my house and reappeared in Ms. Hills' backyard.

"I knew you would come," Marcus greeted me as he made his way into the backyard.

"Marcus! Listen, we have to talk. Your sister Daniella escaped and..." Suddenly, something impossible to Porters, happened to me, I started floating in mid-air as if I was out in the Universe with no gravity to keep me on the ground.

"You can stop with all those false statements, Mr. Chase." Mariah Stars spoke, walking in, right behind Marcus.

"My Queen! What's going on?" I was surprised and baffled to see the Queen here.

"Mr. Chase, you are under arrest for the murder of Katherine Donovan Mathias. Andrea, chain him down." Mariah Stars told Andrea Catena, Porter of the Andromeda Constellation, a Wanderer and Mariah's left hand, who was standing right next to her.

"But your Majesty, I have proof that Camille was the one who tried to murder him, not I. Marcus?" I looked at him, begging for support.

"I'm sorry, Will, but I don't trust you," he merely replied, somewhat angry and yet resolved. I could see his father, Roberto, inside the house with Kent and Margaret.

"William, you know I don't take murderer lightly, especially that of an Unportable. Because you have no criminal history, I'm giving you a trial and not just tossing you straight into Oblivion. Andrea!" Mariah let me down.

In a movement with her hand, Andrea threw her chains at me as if they were snakes trying to snatch my wrists, but I flew out of her range, landing right in front of the Queen.

"Mariah, please just let me explain, I—" With a hand gesture from the Queen, I was floating above the ground again at zero gravity.

"You know quite well what I can do with the power to control gravity itself, William, do not resist me." With another hand gesture from her, I fell face flat on the floor, only to be picked right back up by Andrea's chains.

"Once your time is up, you'll have time to explain yourself in front of all the Wonderers. Till then, stay put. Oh, and Marcus? Good job! You'll do great as Earth's new Wonderer. I'll see you at the trial." Mariah pressed her Exotic Matter Sphere out of there, as did Andrea Catena with me in it.

As I was expelled out of Andrea's Exotic Matter Sphere, still held by her chains, I could see in front of me a building that I've only heard about before: The Triangulum Australis Facility, T.A.F. for short.

The dark-orange clay brick triangle-shaped facility is a jail for Porters like me. Right in front of us is this high electrical fence surrounding the three-story-tall building. The fence does nothing to a Porter; it is just there to protect any Unportables to break in. Rumor has it, this whole place was built by another Porter.

Andrea pressed the old-fashioned intercom allowing the gate in front of us to open. As we passed through the patio, I could see the officers walking around with guns on their backs, protecting the oddly deserted facility. We got through the main wooden thick door with the bright-red T.A.F on top of it where a short red-haired woman in her 40's, with a tan-rusted color skin complexion, greeted us.

A step behind her was a tall man also in his 40's a younger version of what Kent Hors would have looked like, except his dark brown eyes had no love in it. Empty and dark like a starless night sky. Both were dressed in rusty red uniforms matching the building's facade.

"The Queen has asked me to keep this one locked up till she deliberates if he'll be tossed into Oblivion or not," Andrea explained to the short woman, removing the chains around my arms.

"Your powers don't work in here, so don't even try to make a move, young man," the same short lady spoke handcuffing me. "What's the crime?"

"Mr. William Chase here thinks he is above the law and thought it was a good idea to kill an Unportable. Coward! I'm sure the Queen will toss him into Oblivion," she said as they looked at me in disgust.

"Mr. Wolf, take him to his cell while I'll fill in the paperwork with Ms. Catena. I shall inform Mr. Detcha personally about this one; make sure he has a nice view since it will be his last."

"Thank you, Ms. Knox." Andrea thanked the short red-haired lady, walking out of the building.

"Come, boy!" Mr. Wolf said, grabbing me by the handcuffs.

The Triangulum Australis Facility is located at the Hephaestus Desert, in the southern hemisphere of Jupiter, Western side of the globe, pretty much where South America is on Earth, except here, there's no tropical weather, no rain forest, no beautiful tanned, happy people. Quite the contrary: T.A.F. is in the middle of nowhere with nothing or anyone around for thousands of miles. This place is at least ten times bigger than the Sahara Desert and from what I remember from my classes on C.H.E.P., it is over thirty million and six hundred thousand square miles.

From Earth, you can see what is known as the Big Red Spot, which is, in actuality, a one-thousand-mile-long storm of red and blue winds created as a defense mechanism by Adrian Boyle, Porter of Antlia Constellation, the Air-Pump. His storm surrounds the whole facility.

Inside of the building is bright-white clean with

red details here and there, a great triangle-shaped building capable of holding around one-thousand Porters. A luxury not needed since we only have about five-hundred Porters out there in our Solar System.

Inside of the triangle-shaped facility, there's an equally triangle-shaped patio where the Queen holds her audiences and, depending on the Porter's crime, decide if they will serve a sentence here, either for a few months, years, or centuries, or if they'll die tossed into Oblivion.

Oblivion is a Black Hole mechanism created by King Titus Vespasian, King of the Milky Way Galaxy. Whenever activated, it sucks the convicted Porter in, leaving any sign of existence behind, vanished for all eternity or the True Death as we know.

The cells of this facility face outward, so no one sees the place of their judgment until the day of it. Through my cubicle right now, I could see the beautiful multicolored Jupiter sky. The only real imagery that the Ruler of Jupiter, Mr. Josh Rogers, Porter of Sagittarius, allowed, was the colorful bands of sky you see when you study Jupiter in school. Jupiter has about ten different 'skies' going in every direction possible. These 'skies' are known for the people on Earth as either Belts or Zones, differentiated only by their temperatures and colors.

The Hephaestus Desert is located in South Equatorial Belt. From here, I can see right now, Metis, Adrastea, Amalthea, Thebe, and Io, some of Jupiter's moon in the sky. As time goes by, I'll get to see many more moons come and go. Hopefully, I'll get to see Jupiter's rings soon. For now, I'll just sit and wait for my trial.

"Yeoboseyo, meosjin[22]." A woman stepped out in the front of the Sun, blocking the light, allowing me to see only her silhouette and her big, beautiful, orange, voluminous hair all the down to her waistline.

"You know I don't have any powers in this cell, so I can't really understand you," I replied, annoyed at her.

"Wow, your attitude hasn't changed, has it, sexy beast?" She replied with her silky-smooth voice that can get any man or woman enamored.

"Nari? Is that you?"

"The one and only! And I'm here to rescue you," she said, dancing like she was in a Broadway musical.

"How in the world did you get in here?" I got up to my feet to meet her against the cell. Nari Anser hasn't changed in hundreds of years. Her unique look makes her quite hard to forget. Nari is from Corea, Jupiter's own version of Earth's Korea. She's the Porter of the Vulpecula Constellation, the Fox.

Her outfit was a combination of a white skirt with a matching revealing tank top. Her big orange hair was always in place, matching her equally bright-orange eyes. She looked just like a live anime character, a five-foot-seven with six-inch heel orange boot knee-high character.

"Mr. Wolf and I used to be a thing, you know?

---

[22] *Yeoboseyo, meosjin:* Hello, handsome (Korean)

From time to time I come here to chat with him, see what's going on, who are the new intakes. Guess my surprise when he told me that they had arrested William Chase, the Golden Boy! So, I had to come and see it for myself," she explained more enthusiastically than a ringmaster in a circus arena.

"I'm no Golden Boy. And he just let you in here?"

"You'd be surprised at the things you can achieve just by asking nicely." She smiled at me, displaying another pose.

"And how do you plan to get me out of here? Just by asking him 'nicely'?" I asked her less than nicely.

"William, you're just... you know what? Never mind. I am not gonna let you ruin my *Pungsu-Jiri!*" She stomped her foot on the floor.

"Your what?" I asked, confused.

"My *Feng-Shui.*"

"Huh?"

"My flow, my energy, my VIBE!" She shouted at me.

"For someone trying to break me out of jail, you're being rather loud, you know?"

"Hah, you're right! Teehee. Let's get you out of here." She laughed as she took out of her boots a key to unlock the gate.

"You had the key with you this whole time?"

"Well, of course, how else would you expect me to break you out?" She responded logically.

"Okay, now what? We can't just ask nice Mr. Wolf to let us leave, can we?" I asked, obviously mocking her.

"Of course, we can! Watch me," She strutted all the way down the corridor, where Mr. Wolf was sitting as if she was a model on a catwalk.

"*Annyeong, Misteo Neugdae!*[23] *Misteo* Chase and I are going for a walk, *eung?*[24]" She asked flirtatiously.

"Of course, Ms. Anser." Mr. Wolf smiled and blushed, opening the gate that separates us from him.

"*Jal itsuh!*[25]" She spoke as we both passed through and down the corridor in front of us.

"What did you say to him?"

"I just asked him nicely if I could take you for a walk," she said delightfully.

"I don't believe you. If I didn't know you better... wait, what about the cameras?" I asked, pointing at one of the security cameras right around the corner between the two corridors we were in.

"Already taken care of." She danced around under the camera without missing a beat.

"Already taken care of?"

We opened the door to our right and went down a couple of flights of stairs. We stopped right in front of this door, where, for the first time, Nari seemed cautious.

"Do you know where we're going?" I asked, afraid of her answer.

"No. I mean, I—"

---

[23] *Annyeong, Misteo Neugdae!:* Hi, Mister Wolf (Korean)

[24] *Eung:* Okay (Korean)

[25] *Jal itsuh:* Stay Well (Korean)

"NO? WHAT DO YOU MEAN NO?"

"Sorta, listen, *puleun sae*[26], for us to break out of here, we gotta get to the main room of this triangle and switch the main source off. That's the only we can get out of here."

"Alright, how are we gonna do that? Our powers don't work here," I asked her.

"Yours, don't; since you're registered in here but me, I'm a free fox," she smiled at me all proud, showing all her orange nine tails, matching the same color of her hair and eyes. "How do you think I was able to persuade Mr. Wolf to let us through?"

"You sneaky Fox," I smiled at her. "Alright let's do this, lead the way."

"*GAJA!*[27]" She opened the door in front of us,   revealing three white, long corridors, one in front of us, one to our left and the other one to our right.

"Which way?"

"I never thought I would say this, but we gotta go straight," she laughed.

"How long until they realize I'm gone?" Just as I finished my sentence, the alarm went off with sirens echoing everywhere, with blue-green lights flashing throughout the corridors.

"You had to ask," she gave me a look.

"Sorry,"

As we turn into a corridor on our left, we saw

---

[26] *Puleun sae:* Blue bird (Korean)

[27] *Gaja:* Let's go (Korean)

three guards in their red uniform. I'm not much of a physical fighter since I often use my vocal cords, but right now, I had to use my own two fists, and that's what I did.

"William, WATCH OUT!"

I kicked one of the guys toward Nari, who grabbed him with her tails, tossing the officer against the wall, knocking him out. She then jumped over me and grabbed the guy right in front of me with her two fox paws, throwing him out in the opposite corridor as if he was a bowling ball.

"Do you wanna take care of this one, so you know, you don't look bad?" She mocked me, pointing to the remaining guard in between us.

"Well, I could." I punched him in the face, knocking him out too. "Thanks!"

"Hurry! This way." We went on the opposite side from where the guards came and then left at the next corridor, stopping abruptly in front of a red door — a huge contrast from the overall white, silver corridor throughout the building.

"What now?" I asked her.

"The switch is inside of this door. I don't know much of it at all having never been in it. Good luck to you," she said before walking in the opposite direction from where we came from.

"Wait, wait, wait! Where are you going?"

"I'll be back before you can find the switch. Must get something that's going to help on our way out of this place. Go, William, I know my way around."

"Are you sure?" I asked, opening the door.

"I'm a fox, Will. I'm always sure." And just like that, she bolted out of the corridor on her way to whatever it is she needed to grab.

I stepped into the room, closing the red door behind me, surprised that the main switch room of this place had no lock. I took a couple more steps, and all the lights in the room came on. All that light made me block my eyes, something that would normally not happen if I had my powers.

"Mr. Chase."

A bald man in his fifties was floating with his eyes closed in the middle of a silver triangle on the floor in the middle of the bright-white room with nothing else in it.

"I'm sorry, you are?" I asked, not recognizing the skinny older man.

"I am Namu Detcha, Porter of the Triangulum Australis Constellation, The South—"

"...Southern Triangle," I finished his sentence.

"You've heard of me?" He asked for the first time opening his eyes, which were shining bright-white like stars.

"I've heard of you, rumors of you at least," I replied, looking at him curiously. "You've built this place."

"I have indeed. And you're looking for a way out of here." He landed his two feet on the floor.

"I don't think you're willing to consider my request, are you?" I asked, a bit skeptical.

"Why should I? If the Queen finds out that I've let you escape, I will be tossed into Oblivion," he spoke, walking from side to side in his triangle.

"Maybe not?" I tried, "Listen, Namu, I—"

"Mr. Detcha."

"Sorry, yes, Mr. Detcha. I have been wrongly accused of murder, a crime I did not commit. If you let me out of here, I can prove my innocence before the Queen finds me again." I pleaded with him.

"Isn't everyone always wrongly accused of a crime they didn't commit?" His voice was intensely annoying; his air of arrogance was suffocating.

"LET ME OUT OF HERE!" I shouted.

"For a Libra, you're not very balanced at all," he laughed, lifting his two legs in the air again in a sitting position as if to meditate.

"You leave me no choice!" I ran toward him to knock him out, but instead, I was the one who got knocked out after crashing into an invisible force field around him.

"Mr. Chase, I assure you nothing and no one can harm me while I'm inside of this facility," he closed his eyes in a complete statue posture.

Nari walked in, closing the door right behind her gasping for air from what I assume was a run.

"Hey, *meosjin*[28], I hate to rush things, but we really gotta go, like, now!" She leaned against the door as if hiding from someone chasing her.

"I wish we could, but I can't seem able to negotiate with him." I pointed out to Mr. Detcha floating in the middle of the room, unbothered by the two of us.

---

[28] *Meosjin:* Handsome (Korean)

141

"Is that? Oh, my Kumiho, yes, it is! Namu, *oppah, jal jinaesseo?*[29]" She strutted toward him with her fox tails swishing from side to side.

"Nari, sweetie, how you've been?" He asked all smiley, stepping out of his meditation pose to hug her.

"You guys know each other?" I asked flabbergasted.

"Oh yeah, Namu and I used to be a thing." She winked at me.

"So, you know this bird?" He asked her about me.

"Not really, he's a friend of a friend. You know how that goes. You'll never see me hanging around with the likes of him. I mean, c'mon! A fox and a lyrebird? What is a lyrebird anyways?" They both laughed mockingly.

"Hello? LYREbird in the room!" I spoke loudly to no one's avail.

"So, Namu here's the thing. I need to take him out, but I promise I'll bring him back so the Queen can toss him into Oblivion, but first, I have to give him a chance to explain himself, right? Look at him. Poor thing is so desperate." They both looked at me with a 'poor-boy' expression.

"Alright, fine. Here." Mr. Detcha put a triangle-shaped bracelet around my right wrist. "You have until one hour before your trial with the Queen. If you're not back voluntarily by then, this will create a

---

[29] *Oppah, jal jinaesseo?*: Honey, how are you? (Korean)

wormhole and bring you back here. If you try to remove it, it will also bring you back here, understand?"

"Yes, thank you, Mr. Detcha. What about my abilities?"

"You can ignite your abilities anytime you want.
Except for your Exotic Matter Sphere. That's another
matter up to Mr. Boyle." He sat back in his floating
meditation position.

"But—"

"We'll figure something once we are out of here."
Nari dragged me out of the room before I could even
finish my train of thought. *"Jeongmal gomawoyo.*[30]"

"Nari, how are we gonna get out of here?" I asked,
closing the red door behind me.

"This way." We turned right onto another long
white, silver corridor.

"There you are!"

I heard this rough, loud man's voice howling right
behind us.

"Is that a werewolf?" I asked in astonishment.

"For now, Hi Mr. Wolf!" She shouted back at him,
all giggly.

The werewolf, however, jumped and turned himself into a full big black wolf, barely fitting inside of
the corridor.

"I guess Wolfie doesn't wanna play, RUN!" Nari
warned me as we both ran down the corridor and left
on another hall with Mr. Wolf missing us by an inch.
We opened a door on our right back inside of the

---

[30] *Jeongmal gomawoyo:* Thank you so much (Korean)

stairs we once were. I went down instinctively as she went up.

"Up? I thought we are heading out and out is down." I told her.

"No, out is up, trust me." She pleaded.

"Nari, I—"

BOOM

The door busted wide open with Mr. Wolf in his werewolf form, debating if he should go up after her or downstairs after me as the three of us just standing there waiting for one of us to make a move.

In a blink of the wolf's eye, I jumped, passing above Mr. Wolf, opening my wings and flying upstairs toward Nari, grabbing her with my two hands almost getting mauled by him.

"Faster Will, we gotta go faster, he's catching up to us."

"I'm trying. How much further?"

"Next door, get this next door." She pointed to the red door coming up. We got through the door, closing it right behind us. Mr. Hugh Wolf, the werewolf, was right behind me, almost gaining strength to burst the door open.

"I can't hold him much longer," I told her.

"Just a bit longer, Will, she should be here any second now."

"She who?" I asked, even more surprised.

BOOM

The door behind us busted open, sending both of us in opposite directions, with Wolf right in the middle.

"I'm gonna KILL you!" He snarled at me.

"No, you're not."

A black-haired girl not older than fifteen, all dressed in black, appeared right behind the wolf, jumping on his back, locking arms in a chokehold around his neck. Mr. Wolf twisted himself around, trying to get ahold of her, but she was too small for him to grab. Finally, he grabbed her leg from under his own legs, dangling her in front of his large wolf face as he bared his teeth.

The girl, however, just swung herself as if to kiss him, but instead, she simply held his face with both hands; her eyes, bright-white like stars, released a jolt of electricity running down her face, through her arms and hands, electrocuting the wolf making him fall on the floor completely unconscious back in his less scary six-foot-tall self. Mr. Hugh Wolf is the Porter of the Lupus Constellation, the Wolf.

"Where is he, Yngrid?" Nari asked the little girl who landed on the floor, utterly unfazed by what just happened.

"Downstairs, where you were supposed to meet us," Yngrid told us, running back through the door Mr. Wolf had just busted, heading downstairs.

"Sorry, I wasn't sure if you count the basement as the first floor or not so I—"

"Let's go!" The girl shouted at Nari as we followed her downstairs.

"Who's she?" I asked Nari.

"Oh, that's Yngrid Hevelius, Porter of the Volta Constellation, the Battery. Yngrid, this is William—"

"William Chase, I've heard all about him, thanks to my cellmate, now listen: I can no longer go with you guys. If Alicia sees me here, she will only increase my penalty, and I don't want to risk it. Once you cross this door, you're on your own. Now get to him and get out of here. And don't forget about us." Her white skin turned blue again, with the flow of electricity coming from her eyes all down her legs as she kicked down the door, bursting it open.

"Volta? That means she's a Van—"

"Hey, guys!"

"E.J.?" Was all I could say in disbelief. Last I heard of him, E.J. was being sentenced to death. Now he is standing right across from me in his usual boots-jeans-tank-top getup, holding against the wall an enormous red-orange lynx with his Bo staff across the beast's neck avoiding being mauled off by it.

"A hand, please?" His eyes went from bright-white to brown to bright-white like stars again, followed by a bright-white smile contrasting his skin complexion, darker than Marcus, lighter than Kent.

His whole skin turned into wood as he now focused his attention back to the lynx, avoiding its gnarly, wild, big pointy teeth. Without any hesitation, I knew exactly what to do: I let out a high-pitch sonic screech, breaking all the windows around us, leaving everyone powerless and unconscious on the floor with the power of my voice except for him.

E.J. was vibrating like bamboo in a windstorm for a few seconds before returning himself to his natural skin color, woodless.

I walked past everyone completely knocked out on the floor to greet him. I could see the lynx that was trying to bite him off was the short red hair lady who received me here with Mr. Hugh Wolf when I was brought in by Andrea Catena: Ms. Alicia Knox, Porter of the Lynx Constellation.

"Hi, Willie." He looked at me with a big smile on his face, completely unaffected by my powers. "I knew you'd know what to do. Great timing, always."

He gave me a big hug. A hug of a loved one who I thought was dead, gone, someone, I never thought I would see again.

"How are you alive?" I asked him, still in amazement.

"We'll have plenty of time to catch up. Let's get Nari and get the hell out of this place before they wake up.

E.J. grabbed Nari and threw her over his shoulders without any effort, a sign that he's been working out or that she is just too light. He kicked the main doors open, but the exit wasn't as smooth as we thought.

"Stand down, Porters!" A group of about twelve heavily armed soldiers was in front of us, blocking the gates, our way out of this place.

I opened up my wings in front of E.J. and Nari as the guards started shooting at us, but unless you're a Porter, no other weapon could harm us.

"Nari, sweetheart, it's time for you to wake up, we can definitely use your help right about now." E.J. put Nari on the floor as he tried to wake her up. "Can you knock them out with your sonic screech?"

"Not all of them. In an open field, my sonic screech won't do much damage. I can try to knock some of them out with my sonic boom, though," I explained. "E.J., you gotta wake her up. If she doesn't ignite her powers, she is completely vulnerable to the shots, and she will get killed. It's only a matter of time before Alicia and Hugh wake up and come for us."

"Scream, Willie."

"What? I told you my scream would not harm them, but would definitely wake up the whole facility..." Without saying a word, E.J. just looked at me, turning his skin into wood again, and I knew what he meant. I let out a sonic screech as loud as I could. The guards dropped their weapons on the floor in an attempt to cover their ears.

"*Daeche mwoya?*[31]" Nari jumped out in her full fox form.

"Good, you're awake! Let's get out of here. Willie, make way."

I flew toward the guards, knocking them out as if they were bowling pins. E.J. followed behind me, knocking whomever I missed with his staff. Nari jumped way up high, landing right in between two guards, kicking one in the face and grabbing the other one with one of her tails, throwing him across the open field against a couple of other guards.

"THERE THEY ARE!" Alicia Knox joined the party chasing after us.

---

[31] *Daeche mwoya?:* What the hell? (Korean)

"Guys, let's get out of here." With one jump, Nari went up and over the fences, landing on the other side. "Let's go!"

"Be right there, babydoll!" E.J. pointed his staff toward the fences, allowing it to grow as he prepared to stick it on the floor, jumping over the fences just like a professional pole vaulter, landing flawlessly on the other side of the fence.

"Willie, you're up, man." He smiled at me from the other side of the fence.

I jumped and opened up my wings to fly to the other side, but something grabbed hold of my leg, dragging me all the way down to the floor. It was Ms. Knox in her half woman, half lynx shape.

"You're not going anywhere!" She said, holding me down.

I let out a sonic boom knocking her completely across the field, landing against the facility's main doors.

"Willie, let's go!" E.J. shouted from the other side.

I flew up high again and over the fences, but I couldn't land. A strong gust of wind got ahold of me, lifting me back up in the air along with Nari and E.J.

"What's up?" I asked, looking around me.

"He's up!" Nari pointed up to the sky. "Adrian Boyle, Porter of the Antlia Constellation, the Air-Pump. The Wanderer responsible for the Big Red Spot Storm defense mechanism of the Triangulum Australis Facility."

A mini-tornado surrounded this guy with a white skin complexion, orange-blond hair, with drapes around him for clothes with his hands stretched over us with his eyes bright-white like stars, fully ignited.

"You're not going anywhere!" He shouted at us.

"I beg to differ, Mr. Boyle." Mr. Detcha spoke, stepping out in the field. "I allowed him to leave. Until the time of his deliberation, that is..."

"But Mr. Detcha, the Queen—"

"The Queen needs to know nothing about this. He'll be back one way or another an hour before his trial. Till then, he's free to go." He gestured to him to lower me back on the floor, but instead, he just let us three free of his wind, allowing gravity to do its part by pulling us hard against the orange soil.

"Thank you, Mr. Detcha I—"

"Thank me later, Will, once you have proved me your innocence. Till then, stay away from the Queen, or she will toss us all into Oblivion. Now go, your time is running out."

"Daedanhi gamsahabnida, Misteo Detcha[32]." Nari waved and smiled at Mr. Detcha as we all walked out of there.

"Rendezvous point?" E.J. smiled at Nari, stretching out his hand.

"Rendezvous point." She smiled back at him, reaching for his hand and grabbing hold of her own Exotic Matter Sphere.

"Guys, wait, wait, wait." I interceded before they could disappear out of here. "Did you forget I don't

---

[32] *Daedanhi gamsahabnida, Misteo Detcha:* Thank you very much Mister Detcha (Korean)

know where the rendezvous point is?"

"Just like old times, Willie." E.J. stretched out his free hand as I grabbed his hand, disappearing inside Nari's Exotic Matter Sphere.

IX

"Where are we?" I asked once we reappeared at the rendezvous point, not recognizing my surroundings.

"Triton! Neptune's most beautiful and biggest moon. E.J. and I-whoa—" Before she could finish her sentence, Nari fell on her knees.

"Hey, baby, are you okay?" E.J. kneeled next to her.

"Porters are only supposed to take one person at the time inside their Exotic Matter Sphere; taking both of with you with me pushed my powers over the limit. I need to lie down for a minute." She closed her eyes as E.J. leaned her against a purple rock nearby.

"We will be close." E.J. kissed her forehead.

"So, you and Nari, huh?" I asked curiously.

"Yes, me and Nari," E.J. replied, walking away from us both up a cliff nearby. I followed.

"What's wrong?"

"Don't do this, Willie?" He stopped facing the green river passing under the cliff.

"Do what? Can I not ask—"

"Ask what? Ask how am I dating her? A woman? Did you forget you are the one who left me for that Brazilian guy, what's his name, Bobby?"

"That's not what I meant." I sat close to him with my feet dangling over the edge. "Are you happy?"

"Very!" He sat next to me with a smile that comes after you remember the person you love, the person you're in love with, loves you back.

"Then I am happy for you." I smiled back at him, putting my arms around his shoulders. "What you and I had was beautiful. I truly thought you were the one for me for a very long time."

"Until you met him," E.J. interrupted me.

"Roberto. His name's Roberto," I told him.

"You two didn't work out, I take."

"Nope!" I got up to my feet, turning my back to him, looking at Nari, sleeping soundlessly at the bottom of the cliff.

"Listen, Willie, it's not your fault. Sometimes relationships don't work out. Look at Nari and me. We are completely different people, and somehow we work." He made his way next to me.

"That's easy for you two, you both like guys and girls, meanwhile, I only..."

"Roberto doesn't like guys, huh?"

"No. He only has eyes for the love of his life, Mrs. Katherine Mathias. She is—"

"Katherine Mathias?" He interrupted me, surprised.

"Yeah, why? Do you know her?" I asked, astonished by the fact that he seemed to know her.

"Of course. She's the mother of Marcus Mathias, the Natural. Every Porter has heard of him. Wait, didn't you murder her?"

"No! You know I couldn't possibly murder anyone. It's not in my nature. Camille impersonated her, and she's the one I'd supposedly killed. Now I have to find Marcus and convince him that I didn't kill her and that his mother may be very well alive."

"That's awesome. I can't wait to meet him," he said enthusiastically.

"Of course, you can't," I said, much less enthusiastic.

"What? Are you not even curious to meet him?" E.J. asked, eager for my response.

"Well, I" Walked back to the edge of the cliff again.

"By Neptune, you do know him!" He exclaimed gleefully.

"William likes Roberto, Roberto likes Katherine, Roberto, and Katherine get married and have a baby. And boom here comes Marcus Mathias."

"Mr. William Chase, how did you get yourself in that situation?"

"Working for Mario. He sent me to spy on the kid and even kill him if he was a threat to his plans on becoming the new king of the Solar System. Then I went to meet him and—"

"You fell for him too! You dirty bird. You couldn't get with the father, so now you're going for the son." E.J.'s laugh echoed everywhere.

"I didn't know this was gonna happen. When Roberto got married, I left them two alone to be happy. I made a promise never to be a part of his life again, so I've—"

"Been living in Charon ever since. Completely isolated." He finished my sentence.

"Am I that predictable, huh?"

"I was with you for a couple of hundred years. I think I know you," he smiled. "Wait, does Roberto or Marcus know of this?"

"Does she know about us?" I gesture to Nari, still sleeping by the purple rock.

"Who do you think had the idea of breaking you out? She couldn't wait to see you again," he responded, all smitten by her.

"I've never told Marcus about this. I don't think he likes me in the same way. Plus, I'm too busy trying to find his mother,"

"I think I can help you with that." E.J.'s excitement was all over his face.

"What do you mean?" I looked at him.

"There's someone I know, Jessica. She is a Vanisher too; if she's alive, she can help us find anyone alive in the Solar System."

"If she's alive?" I asked, less hopeful.

"Well, Vanishers are hidden everywhere. Last I

heard of her she was in Neptune. But that was before the stripping of powers by the Queen."

"Alright then, what are we waiting for?"

"Well, there's one more thing." He walked around me, leaning on his Bo staff as if he was an elderly man. "I will only help you find Marcus' mom if you tell him how you feel."

"Nope! Not going to happen. Look how well that turned out with his father."

"That was hundreds of years ago." He danced around me. "Give love a try. Remember when you asked me out in that little bar in one of Saturn's moon?"

"Pasiphae moon, in a stinky old bar where only Saturnians teenagers hang around with fake I.D.'s! I remember clearly."

"If you hadn't approached me by the Skewers table, I wouldn't even know." He reminisced.

"I hate that game. I was just trying to impress you." I laughed.

"And it worked! All because you took a chance on me, on love."

"And look how we turned out, I dumped you over a guy I just met, your girlfriend is right down there completely passed out and you, my ex-boyfriend, are giving me advice on how to get the new guy I like. Aren't we messed up?"

"Not at all. The years you and I had together were beautiful, and we were in love with each other, but then, things didn't work out, and it's okay. It was magical for that period of time, and I will always cherish that memory, but sometimes people grow apart and fall for other people, and thanks to you, I found the love of my life. If you hadn't have dumped me, I would have never gone out on a date with Nari. So, thank you, Willie. Thank you for dumping me." He opened his arms, embracing me like he did many times before.

"I'm still not telling Marcus."

"Fine. You won't tell Marcus, and I won't tell you about Katherine. See ya next Halley."

And just like that, E.J. dove backward into the cliff, just as if he were diving in a pool, except that there wasn't a pool, just a long, narrowed river in between the purple rocks that compose the cliff we were on.

"E.J.!" I shouted as I dove right after him, with my midnight-blue wings sprung open.

I flew as fast as I could to get to him. I know E.J. couldn't die if he ignited his Stardust, but he had to ignite it; otherwise, he'd die. And because he's a Vanisher, he would not be back next Halley.

"ELIJAH, IGNITE YOUR POWERS!" I shouted. "There are too many rocks around us; I can't fly fast enough to grab you."

"Are you going tell Marcus?"

"Elijah, you're a Vanisher! If you don't ignite your powers, you won't come back next Halley."

"Oh, well. I guess my life is in your hands, huh?"

"Really?"

"Yes, really. Are you going to tell him or not? Eventually, I will hit rock bottom and will be bye-bye, Elijah."

"Fine, fine. I WILL TELL HIM! Ignite your abilities!" I shouted, getting close to him and the ground.

"There you go."

E.J.'s eyes went from brown to bright-white; his skin turned into wood. His Bo staff appeared out of thin air again, attaching itself between two rock walls, stopping E.J. from crashing on to the floor. He dangled around it a couple of times and, after a somersault, landing perfectly on the floor with his arms wide open with a proud smile, just like a gymnast after performing daring acrobatic number waiting for the judge's score.

"You know, it's because of stunts like this that you and I didn't work out." I landed next to him, gasping for air.

"Yeah, right. You always liked to live dangerously. Or did Marcus turn you into a p—"

"GUYS!" Nari screamed from the top of the cliff. "Are you having fun without me?"

"Hey, babe! Come join us." Nari appeared out of her Exotic Matter Sphere right between the both of us.

"Feeling better?" E.J. planted a light kiss on her lips.

"Better now," she replied. "What are you two doing down here, came down for a swim?"

"Actually, guess who William is looking for?" E.J. asked her, knowing that she already knew the answer.

"You're going after Marcus' mom, aren't you?" Nari asked excitedly.

"Elijah thinks if we can find Jessica, we can find her."

"He's right. If what I heard from her is true, she can find anyone," Nari confirmed.

"So, how do we find her?"

"Well, remember Pablo? I think he might know where she's hiding. But I'm not sure if he's running his business anymore. I have never been to Neptune before."

"You've never been to Neptune before?" Nari asked, surprised by her boyfriend's statement. "Honey, we gotta take you out more often,"

"GUYS!"

"Sorry, Will," Nari continued, "I haven't been there in centuries but, if Pablo is still running his business, we'll certainly find him."

"Then it's settled, let's go find this Pablo guy so he can help us find Jessica who then can help us find Marcus' mom," I told them. "It's such a long shot, isn't?"

"Yes, it is, but we are not going to give up. Mariah will not toss you in Oblivion." Nari danced down the river margins. "Alright let's get this mission going, but first, let's go to my place. I need a shower and a change of clothes. Plus, I'm starving like Marvin."

"Ditto, oh, and please don't say his name."

"Sorry," she kissed him, "who's hungry?"

"I AM!" Elijah and I shouted together.

"Ugh, you guys are too *gwiyeowo!*[33]"

---

[33] *Gwiyeowo:* Cute (Korean)

We walked down a few miles contouring the green water river known as Ulueb, according to Nari, who was telling me all the peculiarities of Triton. You would think that after being alive for over a three-hundred years, I would have had a chance to visit Neptune's biggest moon, right? But no, instead, I have lived most of my life on Earth, Saturn, Pluto, and Charon. I've also been to a few moons here and there but not enough to say I know them.

The dark green river composed our surroundings, the different shades of purple in the soil, and rocks all around us just like the different shades of grey rocks on Earth. A few birds were flying above us, not close enough for me to make out their shapes or color.

Neptune could be seen floating above us in its magnificent splendor with its royal-blue color decorating the light-yellow sky of Neptune. Triton and Neptune are much closer to each other than Earth, and the Moon are to themselves, making a very majestic spectacle to observe at the night sky that was now setting on Triton.

We are in Hulia, Triton's most prominent city. The city is located in one of the three countries on this moon, Jamelluwee. The other two are Thyaghoul, situated in the northern hemisphere, and Wulle-Oht in the southern hemisphere.

Jamelluwee is a very diverse country, quite similar to Brazil, with its tropical temperatures never getting too hot or too cold for Triton's standards. It is also very ancient, but yet quite advanced as if Earth's

Japan had merged with Brazil in a thousand years from now for Earth's standards.

Hulia was a big city full of skyscrapers. Its vibrant purple color dominated everywhere, thanks to its equally fertile purple soils. Shades of green, blue, and red were also accent colors throughout the city. Grey was a standard color, too, and was used mostly in essential buildings, just like white was on Earth.

The streets reminded me of the streets of Mumbai, in Earth's India, except here they have banners flying vertically everywhere to denominate buildings, stores, or street name all in color coordination in relation to its representation. For all I've noticed, official buildings had purple banners in white letters, regular buildings had grey flags in purple colored letters, street banners were green in red letters. Business banners were all various colors and sizes to differentiate their business. The alphabet here was nothing like the one known to Earthians, and the letters looked like Egyptian's hieroglyphs infused with the Greek alphabet.

People were bumping into us from every direction, just as they did in every big metropolis on Earth and some other planets. Their ethnicities were diverse, with people of every race, color, height, body, and outfits, showing that, regardless of their unity as a striving city, every single person kept their culture. This made it quite easy for a white-skinned, blue-haired guy like me to blend in with a black, tall, toned, black-haired guy and a petite, white, Asian girl with big orange hair.

"My place is just around the corner." Nari pointed to a seven-story-high building that was literally around the corner from us.

When we got to the building, a short four-foot-high green guy opened the door for us right after recognizing Ms. Anser, as he calls her.

"Thank you, Mr. Loobardhu, how's your evening so far?" She smiled at him, tapping his head, a gesture that he genuinely seemed to enjoy.

"I thought Marsians were not allowed outside of Mars?" I questioned, amused by the little guy's dark-green skin color.

"Good to see you haven't lost your sense of humor, Willie!" She laughed back at me, pressing the elevator button on the wall.

I looked at E.J., who mouthed 'Marsians are not green.' To which I replied with a typical 'I didn't know' raising my shoulders and eyebrows as we were entering the elevator.

As the door closed behind us, Nari pressed her finger against a scanner on the right side of the elevator, where a number-pad would be on most elevators on Earth.

"Which. Floor. Ms. Anser?" A computerized male voice came from inside the scanner box, pronouncing word by word.

"Seventh, please." Her voice would always come out as a happy tune, emphasizing even more her 'anime' look.

Once we got to the seventh floor, the door opened, allowing us out. We took a right and down the hall, on the right, was her apartment — number 54378.

"Fifty-four-thousand, three-hundred-and-seventy-eight. How?" I asked.

"This building is located on Berkshiis Street, number 543. Floor number seven, eighth apartment, Silly-Willy." The door unlocked open right after Nari pressed all the numbers into the door, allowing us in.

"Ulijib-e on geos-eul hwan-yeonghabnida![34]*"* Nari shouted with her arms wide open in a welcoming pose.

The apartment's layout was a bit different from the designs on Earth. We stepped right in the living room with couches and sofas spread around. To the left was a balcony overlooking the whole city; across from the leaving room was a door leading to Nari's and E.J.'s bedroom. The next room adjacent to the living room was the kitchen. It was like a wide corridor with appliances on both sides of the wall, quite small for American standards but very functional. At the end of the corridor's shaped kitchen was the dining room with a six-sided black glass table in the middle of the room with mismatching chairs on each end, in different heights and colors. From the dining room, there were two doors, one leading to the bathroom connecting to the living room, and the second door leading to bedroom number two, where I would be staying.

Nari and E.J. finished showing me their place as

---

[34] *Ulijib-e on geos-eul hwan-yeonghabnida:* Welcome to my home (Korean)

we set in this winter garden-like room connecting both bedrooms. The room has a glass ceiling, floor, and wall showcasing the beautiful night view of the city, with individual lounge chairs in it with a triangle-shaped table in the middle of it. I sat down on this midnight-blue chair next to the glass wall, with E.J. sitting across from me in a red chair, followed by Nari sitting on his lap.

"So, what do you think of the place?" Nari asked excitedly.

"I think it's incredible. The place has breathtaking views from the bedrooms, and this room, what a great idea to have a glass room adjacent from the building itself, so it feels like we are floating out in the open. Surreal!" I complimented her.

"Yeah, that was quite a pricey acquisition..." E.J. commented, regretful about the adjacent room, "but if it makes her happy, it makes me happy," They shared a quick kiss on the lips.

"I'm gonna fix us something to eat. Are you okay with herckyrus, Willie?" Nari asked me.

"Sure, of course. Please, don't go crazy with dinner, I'm okay with whatever, really. I'm not that picky when it comes to food."

"It's no trouble at all. Herckyrus takes no time at all to prepare." Nari stepped out of the room toward the kitchen. "Let me know if you need a drink or two. I have a bottle of evol that I've been saving for a special occasion."

"Thanks, babe," E.J. shouted just before Nari could make her way out, shifting his attention to me.

"You have no idea what herckyrus is, do you?"

"Nope, I do know what evol is, though. Does it count?" I laughed.

"It does, Willie, it does." He joined in the laughter.

I usually don't let anyone call me Willie, and E.J. is the reason why. When we first met, he never liked my name, William, a name that, according to him, was for people way older than I am. Regardless of my intent to explain to him that old people were once young, he decided to call me Willie, and that's how he's been addressing me ever since.

After he and I broke apart, I decided only to be addressed by Will, since every time I heard the name Willie, I thought of Elijah Jones, Porter of the Malus Constellation, the Mast, a Vanisher. It was also a reminder of a big mistake I made by leaving him for Roberto Mathias. Only to find out that Roberto is straight, husband to Katherine Mathias, father of Donna Saihtam, Porter of the Virgo Constellation, A.K.A. Daniella Mathias, the long-lost thought dead sister of the guy I was crushing hard right now, Marcus Mathias, the Natural Porter of the Taurus Constellation.

What a novella!

Was I making the same mistake again? Was I falling for a straight guy again? One thing is for sure, Marcus doesn't like me in that way. Because of him, I am now a prisoner of the Triangulum Australis Facility, commonly known as the T.A.F., which that reminds me I have to find Marcus' mom, who is thought dead, killed by yours truly.

"Willie? Hey, Triton to Willie, do you copy?" E.J.'s voice brought me back from my train of thought.

"Sorry, I spaced out for a minute. What's up?"

"Hey, if you're freaking out about trying hercky-rus, I can assure you it tastes just like chicken," E.J. joked.

"No, I'm fine. I'm sure it will be great. Thanks, buddy."

"Buddy, huh? That bad? Are you okay, you know, with Nari and me? You don't still have feelings for me, do you?"

"Oh no, no, I mean, you'll always have a special place in my heart but—"

"You're in love with someone else. Again." He finished my sentence.

"Yes, I mean no. I don't know. It's too soon to tell, plus all that's on my mind right now is finding Katherine Mathias so I can prove my innocence before the Queen and avoid being tossed into Oblivion." I showed him the triangle bracelet on my right wrist.

"I think I can help you with that. I don't know where she is, but I'm sure one of the other Vanishers can help us out. Nari and I can bring you there first thing tomorrow."

"Other Vanishers? How's this possible? How are you even alive, E.J.?"

"What do you mean? Was I supposed to be dead?" He laughed.

"You're a Vanisher. Vanishers, as the name implies, were Porters who had their Constellation vanished from the skies by the King of our Galaxy himself," I told him.

"Willie, Vanishers have figured out a way of cheating death and are still keeping their powers," he began. "When you last saw me, the Queen had gathered the rest of the Formers and me to have our Stardust removed from our bloodstream. However, a lot of us were against, including the Porter who was removing our powers himself, Mr. Marvin Byron, Porter of the Hirudo Constellation, the Leech. He asked me and every single Former before removing our Stardust if we wanted it gone or not, those who denied, he let them keep it by removing most of the Stardust, leaving just enough for them to use their powers minus the Exotic Matter Sphere and the ability to send Thought Projections."

"You mean to tell me that all the Formers are alive?" I asked him bewilderedly.

"Most of us, yes, a few of us died in the process; others like Charles Koan decided to go to his home and live the rest of his life peacefully till he finally passes away last year in Uranus."

"Yes, he was the Porter of the Robur Carolinum Constellation, the Oak," I remembered. "Who else is alive?"

"You've met our little girl, Yngrid Hevelius, Porter of the Volta Constellation, the Battery." He reminded me of the black-haired teenage girl who electrocuted Hugh Wolf, Porter of the Lupus Constellation, the Wolf.

"Your little girl?" I asked, confused.

"No, not like that. We're still Porters, can't have kids. Yngrid is our inside ally. She produces energy to keep the Triangulum Australis Facility open, and in exchange, they don't remove her Stardust tattoo." E.J. explained.

"This way, she can still have her powers and live forever as a human-battery for Mr. Namu Detcha. Is that any better than withering away?"

"She knows the rest of the Vanishers will find a way to free her from that prison." E.J. got up to his feet and faced the outside through the glass wall, leaning on the handrail there.

"She knew the risks," he continued, "and even though we haven't found a way to get her out of there, we figured that once you knew that we are all still alive, you'll help us out. To remain alive."

I got up, also leaning against the handrail with my back toward the city. "And how did you figure that?"

"Because, as you said a few minutes ago, I still have a special place in your heart."

E.J. and I didn't work out not because we didn't find each other attractive but only because of a stupid mistake I made by leaving him for Roberto, a man who indeed never led me on. But a heart in love is as helpless as a skydiver without a parachute; no matter how much it struggles, it eventually crashes, leaving nothing but pain afterward.

Now seeing him here, examining his brown eyes naturally shining so brightly, ornamenting his wide white smile, even so, more in contrast with his dark brown skin complexion, illuminated by the colorful neon lights of the big city of Hulia makes me wonder if I had let go of him too soon. Would we still be together if I hadn't fallen for Roberto? Or would he have dumped me once he met Nari?

"Should I open the bottle of evol?" Nari made her way into the room, dancing around as always.

"YES!" E.J. shouted, "Tonight is a special occasion!" He joined her in the dance.

"And what occasion is this?" I asked laughingly at both of them.

"Dear William Chase, today is the day we broke you out of jail, we're going to prove your innocence, bring the Vanishers out of hiding and then..." Elijah smiled, pulling me in the dance with them.

"And then...?" I asked coyly.

"We will get you your guy, Mr. Marcus Mathias to make him your husband, of course."

"Husband?" I asked, surprised both at the idea of me having a husband and that this 'husband' would be Marcus. He hates me.

Nari left the room almost immediately to bring in the bottle of evol. Evol is a dark-blue fruit from northern Pluto used for the fabrication of liquor, something somewhat similar to wine on Earth, except our vino is naturally blue colored. The variation of its color comes from how much fruit they used in the process; the lighter the color, the lighter the flavor and intoxication level. The dark-colored evol that we are drinking right now is midnight-blue, matching the natural color of my eyes, making this drink a bit heavier and bold in flavor, perfect for sipping in the autumn weather of Hulia right about now.

I finally had a taste of herckyrus: a sizeable red plumage bird with a body like that of a turkey, with a large red, black and white w-shape tail, with a long neck similar to that on a goose, but thicker, leading to a beautiful ornamented head full of matching feathers everywhere, just like those costumes from the Carnival in Brazil. A description very well given by Nari while she was slicing down the bird in front of me.

"I mean, I have never been to Rio de Janeiro, but that's what I heard from E.J." She concluded the descriptions.

"E.J. is right! I've never seen this bird in person, but the happy people of Rio dance around with big colorful ornaments in their heads during the Carnival, leaving pretty much the rest of the body uncovered."

"Sounds like a fun place to visit, right, honey?" Nari kissed E.J. on the cheek.

"Willie, what did you think of it?" E.J. asked in amusement anxious to hear my opinion on the exotic bird after having the first bite.

"I usually don't eat birds, but this is pretty good. Just like chicken." We all laughed together.

"You don't eat birds?" Nari asked, truly surprised by my statement.

"Would you eat a fox?"

"If it's well seasoned..." She smiled at me.

"That's my girl!" E.J. smiled at her, grabbing one of the drumsticks out of the four-legged roasted bird.

After too many glasses of evol and many plates of food and dessert, I excused myself to the guest room where I was staying for the night. I took a shower and changed into a pair of shorts E.J. had lent me. I looked out the window. It was way past bedtime here in Hulia. People were still out and about, but not as many as earlier. I saw a couple getting out of a bar completely drunk. The guy was a bit taller than the girl, holding her with his arms around her waist, trying to keep balance with every step they'd take. Finally, they both collapsed on the floor, side by side followed by their loud, embarrassing laugh. They exchanged looks, and he kissed her passionately, to which she responds with equal passion.

I realized I have never been that drunk. I had never experienced that in almost three-hundred years of existence. Even before I'd become Porter of the Lyra Constellation, I had never experienced alcoholic beverages like that. Of course, I had the usual couple of beers here and there but nothing more than a 'buzz'. As a Porter, it is even harder to get that feeling. Evol is a wine-like beverage just like many other alcoholic beverages I've had before, but because of Stardust running in our bloodstream, the 'buzz' feeling is over in less than an hour.

Don't get me wrong, I don't want to be a drunk, but I'd like to feel like that one day. Being out of the bar with a guy that I like in my arms and not really worrying about this whole Porter thing. For the first time in a long time, I feel ready to be free again from these responsibilities, prepared to settle with someone I care about, someone like...

Before I could even finish my train of thought, I was there. Outside of Marcus' room at Margaret Hills' home. I leaned against the parapet where I many times before came to see him. Now, he's just lying there, sleeping so soundlessly just like in a scripted movie. It was almost Sunrise here on Earth.

I know it's creepy to just appear like this at someone's house unexpectedly, but as Porter, boundaries are not really our strong suit since all of us can go anywhere we please in all of the Solar System. I knew I was not supposed to be here; however, I needed to see him, to make sure that he's been taking care, protected, safe from all this madness, especially from Mario Shawyze and his Hounds, from his sister Daniella, and from whoever else is trying to get to him.

I have lost my mind.

I appeared back in the room I was staying in E.J.'s and Nari's place.

Stalking Marcus Mathias for his safety was an excuse I'd been telling myself just to get close to him, only to be able to talk to him and it's truly absurd. Marcus is much younger than me, and for all I know, he might not ever correspond to my feelings. He's the reason why I am wearing a Triangulum Australis Facility bracelet right now, a reminder that if I don't prove myself innocent, I will be tossed into Oblivion by the Queen herself, Mariah Stars.

I got to get some sleep. Tomorrow is a big day! We will move one step closer to find Marcus' mom and get me out of my true death. I will then regret to my ordinary, uneventful life in the farthest corner of the Solar System, my place at Pluto's moon, Charon.

If only I could sleep...

'Will...'

Maybe I do have a chance after all. Marcus' Thought Projection for the first time in a while, was not of anger, not of fury, but that of concern. I usually would appear back to see him, but for now, it is best if he thinks that I'm still contained at T.A.F., at least till I can tell him something more concrete about his mother's whereabouts.

Knowing that his feelings of anger for me are changing, may not even be there anymore, was a really good thing. Maybe if I play my cards right, I could have Marcus back in my life again, even if just as a friend.

X

The rays of the Sun woke me. I could see beautiful Neptune in the sky and some of the other moons as well. The city was awake for a while, with people running around getting to work, driving small cars and motorized bicycles in every direction. Hulia is a magnificent city, indeed.

KNOCK-KNOCK

"Come in."

"Good, you're finally up. Breakfast is ready. Put on some clothes and join us. It's thirty past nine already." E.J. spoke by the door with his body halfway in the room, halfway out.

"I'll be right there, Elijah."

"Oh, and Willie, good morning." He smiled before

closing the door behind him.

I put on the same clothes I was wearing yesterday. I guess we could go by my place later in the day before we go after Marcus' mom, but since I'm supposed to be locked in, it's better to keep a low profile. So, reappearing at my house might not be the best of ideas, especially if Donna, Daniella actually, is there waiting for me.

I stepped out of the room into the dining room, where breakfast was being served.

"*Joeun achimieyo*[35], William. Did you sleep well?" Nari asked as soon as I entered the room.

"Yes, I did, Nari, thank you so much. You shouldn't worry much about breakfast,"

"Oh, I didn't do anything too fancy. I know you're still quite fond of Earth's food, so I hope I did it right with some scrambled eggs and baked pig." She said proudly, putting a whole oven-roasted pork on the table.

"I think ham got lost in translation." E.J. joined in the conversation, steeping in the room with a plate of toasts.

"This is great! Thank you, Nari!"

"Pull up a chair, while I go grab the zuiue juice. They don't have any orange juice on this moon, but at least it's the same color." She left the room to grab the strange juice.

"We don't have many guests here," E.J. commented, laughing a bit, sitting across from me, on the

---

[35] *Joeun achimieyo:* Good morning (Korean)

other side of the table.

"I heard that." Nari walked back in the room with an eggplant-shaped jar filled with an orange liquid just like orange juice. "Elijah is right. We don't entertain much, but we do love having people over." She set the jar right in the middle of the table, sitting at the head of the table between us. *"Mani deuseyo[36]!"*

KNOCK-KNOCK

"Are we expecting company?" I asked, helping myself to a slice of the roasted pork.

"Not that I'm aware of. Elijah?" Nari got to her feet to get to the door, but E.J. stopped her.

"I'll get it," Elijah made a gesture for us two to stay quiet as he went from the dining room into the kitchen, leading back to the leaving room toward the door. "Who's this?"

"Canes Venatici Organization. Open up, Elijah! We have reason to believe you're sheltering a fugitive," a man responded from the other side of the door, banging it loudly.

Elijah's skin went from his normal dark complexion to rustic wood, with his Bo staff appearing out of thin air into his both hands.

"GO!" He mouthed at us with his black eyes now shining bright-white like stars.

"Willie, get the food and go to your place. E.J. and I will stall them for a bit." Nari scooped some scrambled eggs onto my plate, as her eyes went from orange to bright-white like stars.

---

[36] *Mani deuseyo:* Enjoy your meal (Korean)

"What's the C.V.O. doing here?" I asked, letting my eyes shine as well.

"Doesn't matter, just go. Oh, and don't forget your zuiue juice." She gave me a glass filled with the orange-colored drink. Nari was almost in her full fox form, with her pointed ears and nine tails out.

BANG

The sound of a door being busted was the last I heard before disappearing inside of my Exotic Matter Sphere back in my house.

My time was running out.

I sat at my empty dining room table, staring out the window, eating Nari's delicious breakfast. It is nighttime here in Charon. Pluto is majestically out in the sky in its full splendor. Just like the Full Moon on Earth, but unlike the Moon, which is only seen in its silvery color from Earth, Pluto is seen in its brownish, red color in the sky with white and light-blue tones here and there as if to accentuate those earthy colors. A complete contrast of its rocky, icy moon that I reside in, Charon.

I finished my breakfast, put the dishes in the sink, and went upstairs for a quick shower and a change of clothes; if the C.V.O. is after me, it would only be a matter of minutes before they trace me back to my house. I have to do something.

Not sure if this was the best idea, but I had to try. I appeared in Marcus' room, all the way on Earth, at Ms. Hills' place. If we are going after his mom, I have to bring him with me. It's the only way to convince him and the Queen that I had nothing to do with his mother's disappearance.

"G'mornin', mate," Drayton walked into the room, laying down on the bed. "If you're looking for Marcus, you're out of luck."

"What are you doing here?" I asked somewhat surprised and infuriated at the same time seeing Drayton without his shirt lying on Marcus' bed comfortably.

"Me? Well, I have been staying here for a while now, since when we came back from Venus. The question is, what are you doing here, prisoner?"

"You..."

"Whoa, put those eyes out. Marcus should be back soon, why don't you get comfortable here with me while we wait for him, Birdie." He lightly tapped on the bed on an empty spot right next to him, unbuttoning his jeans.

"William!" Marcus' voice echoed in the room in a mixture of anger and surprise.

"Oh, here he is. Marcus, babe, perfect timing as always." Drayton smiled all excitely from ear to ear.

"Button up, 'babe' and leave us alone, will ya?" Marcus held the door open, waiting for him to go.

"You guys are no fun! I'll be Sunbathing on the roof if you need me." Drayton disappeared inside his E.S.M., leaving nothing but a trace of Stardust on the bed.

"You and Drayton are really a thing, huh?"

"What's it to ya? If I didn't know you better, I'd think you're jealous." Marcus opened the French doors of his room, stepping out to the balcony. "What are you doing here? I thought I had you locked away."

"You didn't, the Queen did. And I am still locked away." I showed him the triangle bracelet on my right arm. "At least until Mariah decides to toss me or not into Oblivion."

"Knowing you, you'd probably escape out of Oblivion too," he responded sarcastically.

"Unless you know a way to reattach matter back together, I think it's pretty safe to say that there's no escaping Oblivion. They don't call it the true death for nothing." I joined him in the balcony, sitting on the parapet.

"Why are you here? Came to ask forgiveness before being executed?"

"Is there a heart beating inside of that chest of yours, or is it all shallow?"

"Remind me again why I should feel any compassion for the man responsible for the disappearance, even the death of my mother, William?" Marcus' anger was back again with his bright-white eyes taking the place of its natural green eyes.

"That's why I'm here. I know where your mother is, and I want you to come with me."

"You're lying to me. You probably have Camille Liam disguised as my mother again to convince me you no longer need to be tossed into Oblivion. Could you really have gone this low just get yourself free, Will?" Marcus walked out of the balcony back into his room, sitting on the edge of the bed, waiting for me to answer.

"Marcus, I—"

'Willie, where are you?' Nari's Thought Projection interrupted our conversation.

"Nari," I spoke out loud, *'on Earth, Ms. Hills' home.'* I sent her a T.P. of my own.

"Who's Nari?" Marcus asked, evidently unaware of the Thought Projection conversation that had just happened. Before I had the chance to explain to Marcus what was going on, Nari and E.J. appeared right next to me on the balcony.

"Marcus, I'd like to you to meet Nari Anser, Porter of the Vulpecula Constellation, the Fox; and Elijah Jones, Porter of the Malus Constellation, the Mast. Guys, this is Marcus Mathias, the Natural Porter of the Taurus Constellation, the Bull."

Marcus made his way toward E.J., "You're a Vanisher." Marcus stared at him with a hard to read expression as if he was analyzing the world map.

"Call me E.J.," Elijah stretched out his hand for Marcus to shake it.

"You're hanging around with criminals now?" Marcus completely ignored E.J.'s hand, confronting me with his eyes bright-white like stars again.

"Who are you calling criminal, buddy?" E.J.'s eyes were threatening, but they were still its natural brown color.

"Vanishers are supposed to be, well, vanished. It is illegal for you to have powers still." Marcus was not backing down, on the contrary, he was somewhat close to E.J.'s face. Too close.

"Wanna put your money where your mouth is, Natural?" E.J.'s eyes were now bright-white like stars with his Bo staff appearing on his right hand stretching out to Marcus' chin, touching it very lightly.

"Boys, boys, boys! So much testosterone in one room. Put those eyes away, and we have important matters to deal with." Nari, who was on my left, passed in front of me, stopping between Marcus and E.J., grabbing Elijah by his hand leading him into the room. "Let's not forget the Hounds are after you, Will."

"How did it go with the C.V.O.?" I followed them both inside the room.

"C.V.O.?" Marcus asked after me, joining us in the room.

"Canes Venatici Organization. The F.B.I. of the Solar System," E.J. replied to him as he made himself comfortable on a chair nearby. "For someone who knows about Vanishers, I'm surprised you haven't heard of them."

"Drayton mentioned about Vanishers once before while we were training on Venus," Marcus replied, not so cheerfully to E.J.'s sarcastic comment.

"I'm sorry, who's Drayton?" Nari asked him.

"I am!" Drayton flew down from the roof landing on the balcony with his white long feathered wings spread open, still shirtless, in his jeans and barefoot. "Drayton Colton, Porter of the Virgo Constellation, the Virgin; and Marcus' lover."

"And a compulsive liar," Marcus interceded.

"Am I not your lover?" He threw his arm around Marcus, putting his wings away.

"You're Porter of the P—"

"Pegasus Constellation." Nari finished Marcus' sentence. "I can smell a horse a mile away." She dangled her nine orange tails from side to side, matching her equally orange eyes, to my delight.

"Foxy Fox. Smart. I like you. If Marcus and I weren't a thing..."

"Still wouldn't happen, horse." She made her way next to E.J. sitting in the armchair, putting her arm around him.

"This can't get any more awkward. Marcus, I need you to come with us. They know where your mom is." I approached him, trying to get him to focus his attention on the issue that really matters.

"Do you really know where my mom is?" He faced E.J. for the first time without any anger in his voice, with hope instead.

"Not all of us wanted to give our powers away and die; those who decided to disobey Mariah Stars' orders and live 'illegally', as you've put it, have kept hidden locations all around the Solar System. I have a friend whom I haven't seen in a while who can tell me everything that happens in the System."

"Does he know where my mother is?"

"She knows everything!" E.J. smiled at Nari, who smiled back at him.

"So, what do you say, Marks? Are you ready to go with us on one last adventure?" I asked him.

"Sure!"

"You will?" Nari and E.J. got up to their feet in excitement.

"I will. If Drayton comes along." Marcus' condition made E.J. and Nari sit down again less excited as Drayton jumped with joy, shouting a very enthusiastic "Yes!"

"And one more thing..."

"Hey son, I got your T.P." Marcus' dad Roberto Mathias walked into the room.

I was wrong. Things could get more awkward.

"He's coming along." Marcus gestured to his dad, who had just stepped into the room.

"William, what are you doing here? And who are those people?"

I hadn't spoken to Roberto since he and Katherine started dating years ago, way before Marcus and Daniella were even born. I'm not counting the brief time we exchanged a few words on his wife's pseudo-funeral before Daniella crashed the party revealing to everyone that she was well alive living as Donna Saihtam, Porter of the Virgo Constellation.

"Mr. Mathias, hi, I'm Nari Anser, Porter of the Vulpecula Constellation. This is Elijah Jones, my boyfriend, Porter of the Mast Constellation, and yes, a Vanisher."

"How's that possible?" Roberto asked, intrigued, examining Elijah up and down.

"Can we not do this right now? I'm really on a time frame over here." I looked at him with my eyes now entirely white, not because I was angry but because I was nervous, anxious. I was not expecting any of this to happen right now.

"We are doing this now, William. You and my father have unfinished business, and I deserve to know why," Marcus imposed. "How am I supposed to believe you when you keep hiding things from me, from us?"

"It is not as simple as you think, Marcus, there are other parties involved in this, and we are running out of time," I told them.

"Marcus, whatever you decide, you have to decide soon, the Hounds are after us, and they should be getting here soon."

"The Hounds, E.J.? I thought the C.V.O. was after me?" This is the first time I hear about the Hounds.

"That's what we came here to tell you, Mario has sent the Hounds after you. They were the ones who broke into my apartment, not the C.V.O." Nari explained.

"What do you mean? I heard them saying they were with the Canes Venatici Organization before I disappeared out of there."

"They did say it, Willie, however, when I open the door, it was the Hounds."

"The Hounds?" Marcus asked, more confused than before.

"Mario Shwayze, Porter of the Orion Constellation, the Hunter, has two other Porters working for him; Canis Major, the Greater Dog and Canis Minor, the Lesser Dog. They are commonly known as the Hounds. This is not good. We must move fast. Marcus?" I looked at him, pleading him to trust me this my time.

"I'm not going without my dad. He's a Porter just like the rest of us, and he can help find my mom if she truly is alive."

"Marcus, I am, son. However, I think it is best for you to go with them. I'll stay here to hold them, giving me time to explain everything that's going on to Margaret and Kent. We'll join you as soon as we lay down a plan."

"Alright, I'll go. But not before explaining to Jacques what's going on. He, Mileena, and Jena were not very happy last time that I left. They didn't see me for two years. Meanwhile, you two better work things out, whatever this is," Marcus stepped out of the room, heading downstairs to Lulu's Coffee Shop, where Jacques works.

"Thank you for convincing him to tag along, Roberto, I truly think this time we can find your wife. With the Vanishers alive, we have a huge advantage on our side." I approached Marcus' father for a one-on-one conversation.

"How are they alive?"

"Long story short, Marvin Byron never fully removed all the Stardust out of the Vanishers, at least not to those who sent him a T.P. begging him not to do it. Those who didn't, he removed it," I explained.

"Marvin Byron, Porter of the Hirudo Constellation, the Leech?" Roberto confirmed with me.

"The one and only. It wasn't until Nari and E.J. broke me out of jail that I found out a lot of the Vanishers were still alive." I looked at both of them who were in some heated debate with Drayton.

"Are you two okay? Last I heard you two had called it quits."

"Yeah, we are. Elijah was a big part of my life then as my boyfriend, and now he is back again as a friend. Nari is a great girl! She's perfect for him."

"I don't know how you do it. I don't know if I could become best friends with any of my exes."

"You'd be surprised about all the things a heart can handle."

"Do you really think she's alive? My Katherine?" He asked, all hopeful.

"Yes, I do, and now that I know Jessica is alive, she'll be able to help us find her."

"Why didn't you tell me?"

"I would have, but I was just recently made aware of the Vanishers myself," I explained to him, confused by his question.

"Why didn't you tell me you had feelings for him?"

"Excuse me?" I responded automatically.

"William, you like him, don't you?" Roberto asked unexpectedly. "You like my son, Marcus,"

"Roberto, I don't know what you mean, I—"

"You look at him the same way you used to look at me," Roberto stopped for a second to look at me, a second that felt more like an eternity.

"You knew?"

"Of course, I knew. I was hoping you would've come to talk to me. Why didn't you ever tell me?"

"I wanted to, but by the time I took the courage to break up with Elijah and tell you, you were already married and expecting your baby girl. It wouldn't matter."

"Not in my relationship with Katherine, I love her. I'm the luckiest man on Earth to have found such a beautiful woman, but Willie, you were my best friend. The guy I could always count on a battlefield, even if it were just on training sections with Kent." We both laughed. "You were my buddy, meu *parceiro[37],*" Roberto and I stepped out to the balcony.

"I know. I'm sorry, *parceiro,* you truly are a great friend. Typical Taurus." We both laughed, remembering our great time as friends back then.

"I would have loved for you to be there as my friend through it all: Daniella's birth, Marcus' birth. The wedding, the moment we lost Dani, and even now when we had to bury another empty casket, this time for my wife, Will. You didn't have to run away."

"Roberto, I... I'm not sure what to say." I was doing everything that I could to keep my tears from falling, but I guess by doing that, I also lost my ability to communicate appropriately.

"Come here..." Roberto hugged as if to keep me from falling apart. "Promise me you'll keep him safe?"

"Of course, I will," I assured him.

"Is everyone ready?" Marcus walked back into the room.

"YES!" I shouted to Marcus, making my way back in the room, not before Roberto held hold of my arm.

"William, I don't like that Drayton guy. My son deserves better, do you understand me?" I nodded in

---

[37] *Parceiro:* Partner (Portuguese)

agreement walking back in the room with my mouth as dry as the Hephaestus Desert.

"What's going on?" Marcus asked us both suspiciously.

"Nothing, just giving William final instructions before you leave," Roberto told him.

"You guys are weird, but whatever it is, I'm glad you two have it worked out."

"Are you ready?" I asked him.

"Alright, let's do it. If this ends up being a waste of time, it's your funeral anyway. When do we leave?" Marcus asked everyone in the room.

"As soon as horse there puts on a shirt and some shoes," Nari barked at Drayton, who simply replied by blowing her a kiss. "Hurry up, before I change my mind,"

"I'm still going, right?" Drayton joined in the conversation.

"Sure, why not, we could use an extra shooting target in case we get ambushed." E.J. sarcastically commented.

"Ha ha ha, you're funny, man." Drayton playfully punched him on the shoulder as Elijah walked away. "He is joking, right?"

"Of course, he is," I told him sarcastically for my own amusement.

"How did it go with Mr. Mathias?" Nari asked, all smiles.

"It went well, actually," I smiled. "But I better not screw this one with Marcus."

"You won't." Nari kissed me on the cheek.

"Alright, are you guys ready?" E.J. shouted it.

PUFT

Before anyone could reply, a cloud of Stardust manifested in the middle of the room, revealing two men right in the middle of it.

"Are we interrupting something?" One of them spoke.

"WHO ARE YOU?" Marcus demanded of them.

"Marcus Mathias, the Natural Porter of the Taurus Constellation. I'm Ezra Sirius, Porter of the Canis Major Constellation, the Greater Dog. This guy over here," Ezra pointed to his left, "is Isahul Blahq, Porter of the Canis Minor Constellation, the Lesser Dog. We are the King's Hounds,"

Both Hounds were dressed in black, except for the shirts; Ezra's was a blood-red shirt while Isahul's was army-green. Isahul was also wearing a black jacket where Ezra was not, pretty much showcasing his biceps. Ezra is a very tall and slightly muscular man, a big contrast to Isahul's physique. Isahul stands the same height as me, with the same equally toned body as mine; however, with Ezra towering over him, it is easy to see who's Greater and who's Lesser.

"Midnight," Isahul spoke for the first time, revealing a quiet, mysterious voice, completely the opposite of the deep, loud voice of Ezra. "Call me, Midnight."

"And we are here to take you, Mr. Natural, to our King, Mario Shwayze." Ezra moved precisely closer to Marcus, revealing his big white canine smile while his eyes went from its natural black color to bright-white

"And you too, traitor." Midnight stepped closer to me with his eyes still green, without any sign of Stardust in it.

"NEVEEEEEEEEEERRRRRRRRR!" I let out a sonic screech knocking everyone out of their feet, except E.J., who's naturally immune to my powers, and apparently, Mr. Sirius, who was barely bothered by it.

'Get Elijah and go to my place.' I sent out a T.P. to Nari.

"Stupid bird," he mumbled under his breath, his skin was now all covered in black fur, his hands now showcased his claws just like those of a wolf. He ran toward me, growling, displaying his teeth just like a rabid dog foaming in his mouth.

I slid under his legs, avoiding his bite by inches, landing right in front of Marcus, who was still somewhat immobilized on the floor by my screech.

"Let's?" I stretched out my hand to Marcus, who quickly looked around to Drayton, who was just now getting up.

"GO!" He shouted.

Marcus reached out to my hand. I grabbed him and pressed my Exotic Sphere Matter, disappearing out of there and back to my place in Charon.

"You can let go now," I told him once we rematerialized in my living room.

Located at the top of a hill, my house in Charon has a very similar layout to those on Earth. When someone walks in the house, it leads straight to the living room, connected with the dining room adjacent to the kitchen. Upstairs is my master bedroom suite, and in the basement is a guest bedroom, bathroom, and a workout area, equivalent to a gym on Earth. The living room, where we are standing now, is surrounded by high ceiling windows as is in my bedroom so that we can see Pluto and its remaining four moons bright, up in the sky above the city of Luxiel, in Serrait.

"Drayton! We gotta go back for Drayton," he shouted desperately in a mix of fear and anger.

"Nari did." Elijah came into the room with a glass of water in his hand.

"We gotta go back, we gotta help her," Marcus pleaded with us.

PUFT

"Hi, guys." Nari materialized a few feet closer to us, caught by E.J. before falling from exhaustion, letting the glass of water fall on the floor, shattering everywhere.

"Nari, babe, are you okay?" E.J. laid her down on the couch.

"Drayton, where is he?" Marcus ran toward her.

"Gone!" Nari spoke, struggling to let the words out. "I went back there right after dropping off Elijah here, and I must just have missed you, for when I got there, I could still see the spot where your Stardust was,"

"And...?" Marcus asked impatiently.

"And they... they had him," Nari started crying. "It all happened so fast, Ezra grabbed him by his neck laughing and smiled at me, disappearing out of there. I tried to get to him, but Midnight kicked me out of the way, knocking me out against the wall. I collected the last of my energy and came back here." Nari fell unconscious out of exhaustion.

"No! NO! We have to do something! We gotta go find him!"

"Where, Marcus? We don't know where they took him," I told him, trying to comfort him.

"To Mario Shwayze, let's go after him!" He got to his feet.

"Marcus, my powers barely affected Ezra; we can't fight him. Imagine facing him, along with Isahul and Mario himself. We would never win."

"We have to try," he said a bit defeatedly.

"Marcus, Mario isn't playing around," Elijah joined in, "we don't even know how many people are on his side. We need a plan, and we need allies. We need to regroup and figure out a way to defeat him.

MR. CHASE, MARIO SHWAYZE WANTS TO CONNECT

The Service of Telecommunications Around Representatives of Sun Systems, S.T.A.R.S.S., as we call it, interrupted our conversation.

"Message," I commanded it.

"WILLIE, *CIAO, COME STAI?*[38] I WAS HOPING TO TALK TO YOU ABOUT YOUR NEW ADVENTURES WITH, WHAT'S HIS NAME, UH? OH, SÍ, SÍ, MARCUS, THE *NATURALE*[39]. WELL IF YOU SEE HIM, LET HIM

---

[38] *Ciao, come stai:* Hi, how are you (Italian)

[39] *Naturale:* Natural (Italian)

KNOW THAT I HAVE HIS PONY. DON'T WORRY; HE'S SAFE FOR NOW ON MY STABLE. IF I DON'T SEE MARCUS BEFORE YOUR TRIAL WITH THE QUEEN, I'LL KILL HIM RIGHT AFTER YOUR DEATH. SUCH A SHAME, I HAD SUCH HIGH EXPEC- TATIONS FOR YOU, WILLIE. ANYWAY, LET'S SORT THIS THING OUT, MAYBE WE CAMN GO BACK TO BE FRIENDS AGAIN. *CIAO[40]*, FOR NOW," Mario's ho- logram message disconnected.

"Ugh, that son of a—"

"Whoa there, Porter, no need for such language," E.J. interrupted him. "At least now we know Dray- ton's safe."

"Elijah is right. He's waiting for us to come to him, so that buys us some time." I sat on a chair nearby.

"So, when are we leaving?" Marcus asked, excited, and impatient.

"One thing at a time, Marks, first we gotta go find your mom so that I'm not tossed into Oblivion by the Queen. My time is running low."

"My mother? Again, with this whole thing with my mother. She's probably dead. Even if you didn't kill her, someone else already might have just to in- criminate you."

"Then, I'm dead. And I'm not resting until I found out the truth." I got out of my chair and went to a win- dow nearby, staring out at the night sky with Pluto shinning right above us.

"What if Mario has her?" Marcus asked us both.

---

[40] *Ciao:* Bye (Italian)

"I've been working with Mario, and as far as he and everyone else in the Solar System are concerned, she's dead. Thanks to me," I told him, leaning against the window facing the living room again. "Whoever has your mom did this on their own."

"Why don't we rest for a bit. Nari is exhausted, and honestly, I could use a little rest too." E.J. got up from the couch and stopped between Marcus and me.

"Well, I can't possibly go to sleep right now, I've only been up for a couple of hours. It was still morning when we left Earth." Marcus went to the window where I was leaning against not long ago.

"How about you two go for a walk while I keep an eye on Nari?" Elijah suggested. "I'll have her send a Thought Projection once she's up and ready to go." He sat down by her side, caressing her hair.

"Alright, lead the way," Marcus said, with a sarcastic tone of courtesy on his voice.

"Right this way," I opened the glass door as high as the windows and stepped out to the hill with Pluto right on top of us.

"Do you really trust him?" He asked once we stopped by a bench nearby in the only street on top of the hill. Marcus sat on it. I sat where people usually lean against it.

"Of course, I do. We used to date."

"You and Nari used to date?" Marcus looked at me, puzzled, sitting on the bench next to me.

"No, me and Elijah," I told him with my heart pounding out of my chest.

"You and Elijah used to date? I didn't see that

coming." Marcus let out a semi-laughter, leaning back on the bench.

"What?" I asked nervously.

"It's just that Elijah is so deeply in love with Nari that I could never picture him with anyone else."

"Love is a very complicated thing, Marcus." I jumped off the bench and walked a few steps away from him.

"What's bothering you?" He got up to his feet but stayed by the bench. "Your heart is beating its way out of your chest."

I glanced back at him, amazed.

"Heightened senses, remember?" He said behind a corky smile.

"It's nothing; I'm just worried about your mom, that's all," I lied.

"We will find her; we will be able to prove your innocence." He came closer to me.

"Do you believe me now?" I asked, astonished by his statement.

"I can tell that you're not lying through your heartbeat. It's something I'm still learning how to do." Marcus was really close to me now. "So, you and Elijah, huh?"

"That was centuries ago."

"Earthian's or Charon's?" He joked. "Who now owns Mr. Willie's heart?" Marcus put his hand where my heart is.

"Will Marcus, not Willie." Marcus was inches away from me.

"Nari, Elijah, even my dad calls you Willie. Why

can't I?"

"Marcus, you're..."

'I'm up and ready to go. Are you guys ready?' Nari's Thought Projection completely took me by surprise, making me almost fall backward. I grabbed Marcus' hand and ignited my Exotic Matter Sphere, reappearing back in my living room.

"Yes, we are," I said as soon as we materialized, "I'm just gonna head upstairs for a minute. Be right back."

"You okay?" Elijah asked as I was going up the staircase.

"Yeah, yeah. I'm just gonna take a quick shower, be right down."

XI

ZENY/ZANY

It was daytime in Neptune. A complete contrast to the dark night that was a few instants ago on the moon of Pluto, Charon.

We materialized on a beach. The translucent pink waves were crashing up and down by the shore, a few miles from where we were, but you could clearly see the pink ocean all over the horizon, incandescent by the reflection of its thirteen or so moons. We could see Neptune's faint rings above us, as well as some of Neptune's moons up in different locations throughout the sky.

"Oh, there!" Nari pointed to the sky in the direction of the biggest moon, "That's Triton, the moon where E.J. and I live," she told Marcus very excitedly.

"I miss home already."

"I miss it too, babe," E.J. grabbed her by the hands and kissed her on the forehead.

"Have they just started dating?" Marcus asked me, curiously.

"No, they've been together for at least one-hundred Earth years." I smiled at his curious comment.

"Humph," Was all he said.

"What?" I asked as we both started walking on the dark-blue colored sand.

"Nothing. They are so in love it's uncomfortable sometimes to watch."

"Not as uncomfortable as you and Drayton interact with each other," I replied quicker than I should have, without thinking.

"Ouch!" He sarcastically commented.

"What's up with you two anyway? Are you guys a 'thing' as Drayton called it?" I didn't mean to ask, but I had to know.

"Yup, you can call it a 'thing'." Marcus said, giving little thought about his relationship with Drayton.

"If you're not happy with him, then why are you together?"

"We are not together. Drayton and I sleep together sometimes, but more often than not, we spend time hanging out just as friends. What happened between us on Venus was in the heat of the moment, and that was it."

"I'm sorry to hear that," I sincerely apologized to him, "no one should be in a relationship where they are not fully happy with one another."

"It's alright; he wants to party and have fun, and I," Marcus stopped to think for a minute. "I don't even know what I want. In my mind, I'm still sixteen trying to hold on to my normal life before you, and all this madness walked into my life.

"Ouch!" Now it was my turn. Marcus' words sometimes can be very hurtful; he may not mean it, but he's an honest Taurus with maybe some Sagittarius in him.

"I didn't mean to offend you. It's just that—"

"I walked into your life and BAM. Your life got turned upside down. I understand."

"Thanks." Marcus looked to see if Nari and E.J. were still walking behind us. "I'm sorry about your situation, too, you know, with E.J., my dad... are you okay?"

For a moment I couldn't answer. Not because I didn't know the answer but only because this is the first time that I can remember Marcus showing sympathy toward me. He seemed to care genuinely. And with that, I answered with a smile on my face: "Couldn't be happier."

Marcus and I had a short but meaningful conversation where I told him about my dynamics with Nari and E.J., how we have had our good times in the past and how he, pretty much coming back to life to me, is now one of my best friends again, alongside with Nari, who up till the moment that she broke me out of the Triangulum Australis Facility, I hadn't seen in centuries either. I guess being heartbroken really messes with your mind, with your trust, with how you interact with people, and even with a sense of time, especially for Porters since time is practically nonexistent.

Alongside the beach was a small two-way road with pebbles as crystal clear as if they were made of glass.

"Do you know where we're going?" Marcus asked once we switched from the royal-blue colored sand to the crystal glass pebbles road.

"No idea. I have never been here."

"At this beach or in Neptune?" He asked, curiously.

"I've been to Neptune before, you know, in Florida." I laughed.

"Wait, you can literally travel between planets, and you don't?"

"After the whole thing with E.J., I mostly kept to myself between Charon and Pluto," I explained to him.

"What about before, while you were dating Elijah, you've never traveled?"

"I've been to Jupiter to see the Queen a few times, I've been to the Moon, some other moons here and there, but mostly stayed on Earth. Being born in the little town of Heitt Hjarta, in the heart of Ís-Land, Pluto, I haven't really known much of Earth, since Elijah has been there many times, he'd show me around."

"So, you're an alien?" Marcus asked to my laughter.

"To you, yes; to me, you're the alien." Now was my

turn to make him laugh.

"Hey guys, we should go down this way." Nari, for the first time in a while, joined back in the conversation. "This is the way to the city of Komorebi."

We took a left turn and made our way down the hill. There, we could see the small city of Komorebi that Nari was talking about. The city was in all earthy colors, with houses built out of woods and bamboos; light-colored tapestry was attached every whereas if were floating. The whole town had a vibe of a very tranquil isolated beach resort in Hawai'i. Women were walking around everywhere in earthy, light clothes with sandals and hats made very stylishly out of straw.

"Oh, how I love this city!" Nari exclaimed very excitedly as we walked through the dusty streets.

"Uh guys, where are the guys?" Marcus asked, noticing the lack of men around us.

"Holdover there," a short white woman with white short wavy hair dyed in a light shade of purple, dressed in a forest-green jumpsuit and brown boots with matching belt spoke, behind us, with a deep, authoritarian voice. On her left chest was a brown badge with a shield on it with the initials K.P.D., Komorebi Police Department. "I don't know how you guys made all the way out here from Zany, but I am bringing you right back to your nation."

"Officer, what appears to be the problem? My friends and I were just walking around, how's that a crime?" Marcus questioned as she handcuffed us.

"Listen, mister, I'm not sure if you're trying to be

funny or if you think I'm stupid; either way, unless you have identifications proving that you are all women, you'll have to come with me right now. Now get in," she pushed us into the carriage nearby.

"Wait, wait, wait a second, I know you," Nari said, analyzing the full-figured woman before she could have tossed Marcus inside the carriage.

"Of course, you do, I'm the Captain Chief of the Komorebi Police Department."

"No, that's not it," Nari stared at her very hard, trying to ignite her memory.

"That's not it? Who do you think I am, Santa Claus?" She finally tossed Marcus inside the carriage.

"YES!" She shouted it very enthusiastically. "I mean, you're not working with Santa Claus anymore, you're his sister Ms. Hannah Klaus."

"Huh?" The officer stared at her blankly as she was about to toss Elijah in the carriage too. "Who are you?"

"It's me, Nari Anser. That guy you're about to toss in your carriage is my boyfriend Elijah, this is my friend William, and the smaller one in the carriage is Marcus Mathias. You should really be careful with him, he's a Natural,"

"Oh, I'm so sorry." She let go of Elijah. "Nari, oh my goodness, I hadn't seen you since when you were what? Eighteen? Fresh and out of your training. How's life as a Porter treating ya?"

"Yes, well, I'm a few hundred years older now," she laughed, helping Marcus out of the carriage.

"What's going on?" Marcus asked, more confused

than ever.

"This is Hannah Klaus, Porter of the Auriga Constellation, the Charioteer." Nari introduced her to us.

"Actually, it's Mrs. Kringle. My brother Nicholas took over the Constellation as a wedding gift, so Kriss and I could get married." She chuckled with her face slightly blushed. "But dear, what were you thinking about bringing males to Zeny? You know they aren't allowed in our nation."

"Right, The Great Gender Division." Nari tapped her head lightly as if she'd just remembered something vital. "Ms. Klaus, sorry, Mrs. Kringle, I have always come here to hang out with a few of my girlfriends when I used to be single. I haven't been here in so long that I've totally forgotten the Zohun Nation is now divided into two Nations, Zeny, the female nation, and Zany, the male nation. You know quite well I don't see gender."

"I heard of that. I wish the people of Neptune saw hu-man beings the way you do; hurry now back in the carriage, I have already spent too much time talking to you. I have to bring you to the Zany Nation." Mrs. Kringle removed our handcuffs as we jumped back in the carriage.

"So, Nari, what business brings you to Zeny, particularly the city of Komorebi?" She said, pulling out the carriage on the road.

"We are looking for Mr. Pablo Nuñéz." Nari said enthusiastically, "Is his club still around?"

"Looking for fun times, aren't we?" She laughed loudly, joined by Nari's high pitch laughter, while all the rest of us just stared at each other, completely clueless of what they were talking about. "Yes, it is. However, Mr. Nuñéz's place is on the other side of Neptune."

"I'm well aware. I always get confused with, which is the male nation, and which is the female nation. Zeny and Zany sound rather similar." Nari explained.

"Indeed, they do," Mrs. Kringle agreed.

We rode down the road for a couple of hours talking about the most casual things, unrelated to Porters, Wonderers, Wanderers, and especially Vanishers. Technically, Elijah is still a fugitive, along with all the other remaining Vanishers.

"Alright, kids, this is as far as I'm allowed to go." Mrs. Kringle pulled over the carriage on the side of the road. "About a mile from here is the border to the Zany Nation; there, my brother will be able to escort you in."

"Thanks, Mrs. Kringles, and say hi to Mr. Kringles, we'll be back for Hanukah!" Nari thanked her as we all stepped out of the carriage.

We headed down to the crystal-clear pebble road toward the east. We could see an enormous iron-built wall with electrical wires contouring the top of it with guards dressed in dark red uniform patrolling around.

"So, I just want to double-check on one thing," Marcus asked as we began walking. "Was that really, Mrs. Claus?"

"Yup, she used to be Mrs. Klaus with a K, when

she was Porter of the Auriga Constellation; now she's married to Kriss Kringle. I heard rumors about her brother Nicholas Klaus taking over for her once she fell in love with Kriss, but never truly had confirmed it up until now. Too bad I missed their wedding, I heard it was a beautiful winter wedding, everyone was there," Nari spoke as if seeing the gallant event with her own eyes.

"Including Rudolph, the Red-Nosed Reindeer?" Marcus asked laughingly, but she didn't understand his reference between the Most Famous Reindeer of All and the Father of Christmas.

"You shouldn't joke about a serious matter, Mr. Mathias," Nari replied to him in a less pleasant voice, to everyone's surprise.

"How are we gonna get through this?" Elijah pointed out as we approach closer and closer to the wall, "Even I can't jump that high."

"Elijah is right," I concorded. "I could try to fly us all over the wall, but it could be too risky, one of the guards could see us."

"I could break a hole through the wall," Marcus suggested.

"Yes, you could, and Stardust would regenerate everything back as it was, just like on Earth; however, Nicholas, Hannah, and all the other Porters here could see us and call the C.V.O. As you know, we are trying to keep a low profile," I reminded Marcus, who was a bit disappointed for not being able to break through things as he enjoys it very much.

"Wait, what if we were to teleport to the other

side?" Nari suggested.

"That could actually work, but do we know where we are going? None of us have been to Zeny, to use our Exotic Matter Sphere. We have to know where we're going or have an anchor there, another Porter. To appear at a place, we don't know, it is like stepping in a dark room and not being sure where you're going to land," Elijah warned us.

"You know what? I'm just gonna break a hole through it." Marcus transformed himself into a big white bull and charged against the wall before any of us could stop him.

BOOM

"Come on. We gotta move fast if we don't want to be seen," Elijah said, running after Marcus through the hole.

"Stop right there!" An officer stepped right in front of Marcus and Elijah, blinding them and us with his flashlight.

"How can you see us?" I asked in astonishment since all of us had Stardust running in our system, "Unless..."

"I'm a Porter like yourselves." He revealed his eyes, bright-white like stars.

"Oh, my Kumiho!" Nari ran through the hole and hugged the officer. "I haven't seen you in over a century!"

"It's been over two centuries, Nari!" He hugged her back, dropping the flashlight.

"What's going on?" Marcus asked, confused.

"They used to be a thing," I answered that question.

"Yes, we did," Nari spoke excitedly, "guys, this is Rudolph Skye, Porter of the Tarandus Constellation, the Reindeer."

Rudolph removed his dark-red helmet, showing off his face, letting his light brown bangs fall to his eyes to which he just moved behind his ears.

"You're Rudolph?" Marcus asked him in amusement.

"I'm sorry, do we know each other?" Rudolph looked at Marcus as if trying to remember him.

"No, we don't." Marcus walked toward him, stretching out his hands. "I'm Marcus Mathias."

"Porter of?" Rudolph reached out his hand as well in a handshake.

"He's the Natural Porter of the Taurus Constellation," I replied, approaching them as well, followed by Elijah.

"A Natural Porter from Earth, nice!" Rudolph tapped Marcus on his shoulders. "I haven't seen an Earthian in so long. But tell me what brings you guys to Zany?"

"We are here looking for Mr. Pablo Nuñéz. I was hoping you could help us find him,"

"Looking for a fun ol' time, aren't we? I dig."

"Oh, nothing like that, you see, my boyfriend Elijah—"

"Your boyfriend?" Rudolph asked, looking around, trying to figure out which one of us was Nari's boyfriend.

"Oh, my Kumiho, how rude of me!" Nari ran effortlessly next to E.J. who was just standing there next to me, "this is Elijah Jones, Porter of—"

"The Malus Constellation," Rudolph walked fast, toward him, shaking his hand with both hands enthusiastically, "you are part of the great Argo Navis Constellation, what an honor to meet you."

"Former Argo Navis Constellation, now I'm just a Vanisher like yourself," E.J. spoke with an undertone of defeat.

"Such a humble warrior, now I know why Nari is smitten by you. And who are you, Midnight-Blue Eyed Guy?" Rudolph let go of E.J.'s hand and reach out to mine.

"William," Marcus shouted, walking between us. "William Chase, Porter of the Lyra Constellation." Marcus for the first time ever introduced me, very proudly.

"Mr. Chase, very nice to meet you," Rudolph smiled at me, noticing the awkward moment between us. "It is quite refreshing meeting you, guys. A couple of interstellar couples traveling through the Solar System."

"Oh, William and I... we are not a..., I mean, we are just... huh, friends... yeah, just friends." Marcus was somewhat embarrassed by Rudolph's statement, moving from next to me to Nari.

"Right," Rudolph replied, smiling. "The conversation is good, but we have to get you somewhere else. I can't keep holding a Stardust Dome."

"Where do you suggest? None of us have ever

been to Zany, and Nari cannot be seen either," I asked as we ran through the empty dark field on the other side of the wall.

"I'm way ahead of you, Wanderer. He should be here in a few minutes now."

"He who?" Marcus asked him as we all looked at him waiting for a response.

A loud motor noise came from the dark dunes nearby; the sand around us was dark and muddy, a mix of dark-blue snow and brown earth.

"Oh, there he is. Right on the dot." Rudolph ignites his Stardust as the rest of us did.

We looked at a dune nearby and saw a dark red motorized type of snowmobile rushing our way. The driver was dressed in a dark red coat with a snowy white scarf and a long equally white beard. His head was covered with a mildly pointed red hat. He roughly stopped the sleigh next to us, splashing mud everywhere. We all jumped in it, barely making in time before taking off.

"Hiya kids, I heard you guys need a lift," he said without moving out of the snowmobile.

"Come on, guys, jump in," Rudolph told us as he jumped in the automobile himself. The vehicle didn't have any tires, it looked and felt just like a sleigh, except for the fact that it was motorized with a steering wheel, and red lights under it.

"Running from the law, kids?" The driver asked somewhat smiling.

"They are looking for Pablo Nuñéz," Rudolph told him.

"Looking for fun times, huh?"

"Nothing like that, we are hoping he can help us find Jessica—" The driver pressed the breaks so harshly, making us all almost fall out of the sleigh, interrupting Nari's sentence.

"Jessica?" He replied in a mixture of anger and surprised with his icy, baby-blue eyes piercing through every single one of us. "Porter of the Atelier Typographique?"

"The one and only," Nari responded excitedly. "Do you know where she is?"

"She's dead! She's been dead for centuries along with some of the other Vanishers." He looked back to the road as if looking for someone all the way down in the darkness.

"Listen, uh?" I asked, "You are?"

"Wanderer Nicholas Klauss, Porter of the Auriga Constellation, the Charioteer. Sorry, introductions aren't my forte."

"That's a first," Marcus replied, remembering how every Porter he knows always had a flair for introductions.

BOOM

An explosion right next to us shook us all.

"What was that?" Nari looked around to see what was happening.

"The C.V.O. is right behind us." Rudolph jumped out of the sleigh mobile. "Take them, Nick, I'll buy us some time."

"Rudolph. Don't do anything stupid, son," he supplicated as Rudolph ran into the night after the C.V.O.

with his antlers sprouted out above his head.

"I'll be fine. GO!" He shouted in between explosions nearing in on us.

Nicholas drove forward in the middle of the darkness with only the red light under his snowmobile illuminating the way.

"How can you see in this darkness, even I can't see that far," Nari asked, trying to see through the black night.

"I can't. I just know the way by heart."

BOOM

Another explosion hit right behind us missing us by inches, making the sleigh spiral out of control, tipping it sideways, with the red light under it spotlighting right where Rudolph was, revealing his location. Rudolph was on fours wholly transformed in a reindeer, much larger than your typical reindeer that is.

Before any of us could react, Rudolph jumped over the tilted side of the automobile, putting it back in its upward position with his antlers.

"Release the reins," Rudolph told Nicholas, who was still recuperating from the accident.

"Rudolph, don't."

"C'mon, old man, I can smell the dogs behind us." Rudolph was on his hindlegs, fully towering over us, a threatening sight to see if he was not on our side.

Nicholas, against his will, pressed a button releasing a pair of reins in front of his snowmobile. Rudolph, half man, half reindeer, wrapped them around his waist and shoulders.

"Buckle up," he told us.

Rudolph took out of his pocket a dark red pouch. He put his nose in it and inhaled quite deeply, to which Nicholas sighed in defeat.

"Let's do this," Rudolph said in a cheerful voice, wiping the excess glittering dust out of it. With one blink, his big brown reindeer nose turned bright-red as if a flashlight was inside of it, illuminating up to a mile in front of us.

We could now hear packs of dogs running behind us, with loud barks coming from every angle.

"Run, Rudolph, run," Nicholas shouted out at him.

Rudolph ran faster and faster, probably even faster than the snowmobile was running before. The dogs were now behind us with less than a mile to reach us, and we could see the dark fur moving right behind us.

"RUDOLPH!"

"Almost there."

"I'll buy us some time." I got up and faced the dogs, letting out a sonic boom, knocking some dogs out of the way, but there were hundreds behind us; my power is pretty much useless out in the open.

"STOP THAT!" Rudolph yelled, "You almost knocked me out too, you know sound waves echoes?"

"Sorry," I apologized, not realizing that we were running through a valley. With mountains all around us, my sonic boom echoes in every direction.

"Rudolph, they are getting to us." We could see the big black Dogs near us with their eyes bright-white like stars, and frightful smile on their mouth.

"Almost... THERE!" Rudolph jumped and then we

were flying above a cliff, the same cliff where the majority of the dogs fell in, turning into Stardust.

"WHOA!" Nari exclaimed as we were all absorbed in the magical, full of lights view of the Zany Nation.

The Zany Nation was dark, full of skyscrapers everywhere, one competing with the other on height and style, with lights of all different lengths and colors, contouring them. Gigantic billboard screens were everywhere throughout the city, promoting all sorts of products in a foreign language. This enormous metropolis was well alive. From up here, we could see men rushing to their destinations in every direction, cars soaring above the magnetic streets no more than a couple of feet above the ground, new vehicles with a 1950's Earthian vibe to them — a distinct take on the 'old' interpolating with the 'new'.

"Rudolph, take us down before your abilities run out," Nicholas advised him.

"Lighten up, Nick, this is the first time these kids are seeing the majestic Zany Nation." Rudolph took us up twirling around the highest building around.

"What do you mean 'before his abilities run out?'" Marcus wondered.

"Rudolph is the Porter of the Tarandus Constellation, the Reindeer; as you all know, reindeers can't fly, or at least that's what we thought. Many centuries ago, Jessica and I used to live in the small city of old Luduabi, Oksoing, Northwest hemisphere of Neptune. At the time, males and females used to live all over the planet, just like Earth and many other planets in our Solar System. After I was asked to become the next Porter of the Auriga Constellation, the Charioteer, Jessica became very saddened by the idea of never having any kids. One day she would grow old and die while I was forever young. I told her that I wouldn't take the position for more than one Halley and—"

"One Halley?" Marcus interrupted him.

"Unlike you, Mr. Natural, all of us have to renew our Stardust Tattoos with Comet Halley's dust in it in order to keep our powers and not grow old. But everyone's Halley Cycle is different based on the Comet's trajectory on their home planet. For example, my cycle will end in another forty Neptune's years from now, where Marcus', being from Earth, would take about eighty years from cycle to cycle until he has to renew his Tattoo," Nicholas explained to him.

"But I don't have a Tattoo," Marcus said, somewhat ashamed of it.

"Naturally. As a Natural, you were born with Stardust in your bloodstream. As the years go by, the amount of Stardust will increase just like your hormones in your teen years. A human becomes an adult by the age of twenty-five and becomes fully developed; so, will you. With Stardust running through your body naturally, you don't need to get a Tattoo to manifest your powers. It never ceases to amaze me the extent of it. A blessing or a curse?" Mr. Klauss stared out in the open again to see where Rudolph was taking us.

"What about him?" Nari brought Nicholas back from his train of thought.

"As the years went by, Jessica became older than me, and bitterness took over her once happy, beautiful soul. She would spend most of the days out and about doing God knows what. Between my job and taking care of Wanderers' business, I lost her. I came home one day to find her gone, with only a note saying that she couldn't do this anymore. I searched for her everywhere throughout Neptune without any luck."

"And then he found me," Mr. Klauss continued as Rudolph was approaching a small building nearby, preparing to land. "I let go of my powers, I grew old, The Great Gender Division happened, I got kicked out of my place and thrown in the city of Azuhiawl. Without anywhere to go, the streets became my home, my friend, and so did kwi'irty."

"I hate to interrupt you again..." Marcus began.

"Equivalent of vodka on Earth," I told him.

"Rudolph found me on the streets unconscious. He took pity on me and brought me to his place, afraid I was going to die of hypothermia; little did he know I was just drunk." I could see a tear falling bashfully running down his rosy cheek. "Months went by, and Rudolph nursed me back to life. He said I looked just like his deceased old man. At the time, I was too heartbroken to feel anything but pity about myself. Rudolph was also battling his own demons with Stardust."

"How did he get a hold of it?" Elijah joined in the conversation.

"I'll never tell," Rudolph answered proudly with a

quirked smile on his face. "We are here!"

We landed on a rooftop terrace of a thirty-story-high building; a house compared to all the other sky-scraper buildings around us.

"Thank you for sheltering us, Mr. Klauss. We wouldn't have made it without your help." I thanked him as all of us stepped out of the sleigh shaped snowmobile.

"Call me Nick, thank him, he's who saved us," Mr. Klauss gestured to Rudolph as we unwrapped the reins from around his shoulders and waist.

"Tell me, Rudolph, how did you do that? I didn't think reindeers could fly, and yet you did."

"Listen, Willie, I—"

"William. Please, call me William." Only those close to me can call me that.

"Right, William, I inhaled Stardust, okay? I'm not proud of it, but I did it. I do it only when needed or when I want to fly away. I mean, look around you. This nation is full of buildings ready to be explored. Everyone who's someone lives at least fifty stories from the floor, and only the low, miserable people live down there." Rudolph flew out up at least another ten stories. "Yes, my nose glows red as a side effect, but I don't care, it's actually rather helpful in these dark nights of Nep—"

Rudolph let out a gasp as his nose stopped glowing, fading back into his human nose.

"NO!" Nicholas shouted next to me.

Rudolph tried to fly back down to the rooftop but came to a halt abruptly as if something had got a hold of him. He then started having convulsions, spelling out Stardust everywhere.

"Somebody, please go get him. FAST!" Mr. Klauss pleaded with one of us.

"I GOT THIS!" Nari, half transformed into a fox, jumped effortlessly to where Rudolph was, but just before she could get to him, a massive ball of Stardust exploded out of his body knocking Nari a few feet away across the sky, making both Nari and Rudolph free fall to their death.

"E.J. go grab her, I'll get the kid," I told him as we both jumped out of the rooftop after our designated targets.

I ignited my Stardust but not my wings; I let my body dive toward the floor after Rudolph. I could see Elijah also free falling with his Bo staff behind his back with his black eyes now turned white with the power of Stardust running through his body. My target was getting closer to the ground as I was getting closer to him. I let out a wave of sound weak enough so it wouldn't harm him, but strong enough to bounce back from the ground back up, slowing down his speed just enough so I could grab him.

And I did.

I disappeared midair about a few feet above the ground with him inside of my Exotic Matter Sphere, reappearing right under Nari freefalling above me with E.J. a few feet closer to her. This time I let out a sonic boom. Its effect is significant to push people away from me just like I did with the dogs chasing after us earlier. In this case, it shot Nari back up, facilitating Elijah to grab her and smoothening their fall. Elijah gracefully landed next to us using his Bo staff just like an athlete.

"You okay?"

"Thanks to you, Willie," Elijah replied as we both smiled at each other with Nari and Rudolph regaining their consciousness.

"We should get back upstairs and out of the streets before we get hit by a car," I suggested.

"Nari, sweetie, are you okay?" Elijah put her back on the floor as Nari was looking around gathering her surroundings.

"Yeah," she replied, still dazed.

"Can you teleport E.J. back to the terrace?" I asked her, holding on to Rudolph who was still coming and going out of consciousness.

"I can try," she replied weakly.

"Listen, can you teleport just yourself?" Elijah suggested.

"Yeah, I—"

PUFT - she was gone.

"Give me your hand. I can teleport us three back up to the terrace," I reached out my hand to him.

"No, you'll exhaust yourself, bring Rudolph up and have Marcus come to pick me up." Elijah sat down on the sidewalk.

"Actually, how about if we fly?" I suggested.

"You can't fly the three of us up there. The building is thirty stories high."

"Come on, you know I can carry you; I've done it a million times and Rudolph is about my weight."

"Alright, I'll grab the boy, you take us there."

PUFT - Marcus appeared right behind us.

"Hi, guys,"

"What are you doing here?" I asked him.

"I couldn't have you two have all the glory," he laughed. "I'll take Rudolph back up, and you grab Donatello over there." Marcus grabbed Rudolph out of my arms and disappeared inside his Exotic Matter Sphere.

"Who's Donatello?" Elijah asked, confused, not getting Marcus' reference.

"I'll tell you later,"

PUFT

XII

SHOWTIME

The first thing I saw once I teleported back to the rooftop terrace was Nicholas Klauss laying Nari down on a cherry-colored lounge chair nearby. She was still unconscious, weakened by Rudolph's blast, using her last energy to teleport herself back up here.

"Thank the stars you're okay," he said, noticing us back with Rudolph, who was still unconscious.

"That was a close one," Elijah said, sitting down across from Nari.

"What happened to Rudolph? I have never seen anything like this before," Marcus asked, intrigued, lying Rudolph down on a lounge chair opposite from where Nari was.

"When inhaled, Stardust runs for a very brief moment, not lasting more than a half-hour or so. Once its effect wears out, the user expels all of Stardust out of their system, becoming human again until his Stardust Tattoo ignites itself up and runs throughout his bloodstream, allowing their power to be back on again."

"Exactly what happens to us when we go inside our Exotic Matter Sphere," I inserted after Nick's comment. "We need time to recuperate before teleporting again,"

"Yes and no," Nick continued, "when you go inside your Exotic Matter Sphere, it takes less than an ounce of Stardust for you to manifest from one place to another, taking no less than a couple seconds for your body to replace; however, you'll never run out of Stardust in your body. The process exhausts each Wonderer or Wanderer differently. As a rule, no one is capable of teleporting more than four times in a row, and that's not counting the carrying of another person with them."

"What about Vanishers like Elijah and Rudolph?" Marcus asked curiously.

"Unlike you, Natural, we need an Exotic Matter Sphere to teleport from place to place. Ours was removed from us once the Queen stripped us from our titles," Elijah answered, helping Nari to a sitting position, who was beginning to regain her consciousness.

"We went from Formers to Vanishers just like that," Rudolph said, to everyone's surprise, not realizing he was awake. "I hate what she did to us, to all of US," he shouted.

"Rudolph, son, lay back down, you're still too

224

weak," Nicholas rushed to him as a father goes to aid his son.

"I'M FINE!" Rudolph shouted back at him as if Nicholas was trying to hurt him.

"As you can see, besides losing his powers, he also loses his temper. It just keeps getting worse every time he uses."

"NO, IT DOESN'T." It was definitely a contrast from the upbeat, jovial Rudolph that we met not too long ago, to this angry guy in front of us laying against the lounge chair. "Stop this nonsense, old man, I'm not your son." He fell unconscious again.

We all just stood there awkwardly in silence as Nicholas Klauss sat next to him, covering him up with a throw that was nearby.

"I'm sure he didn't mean that." Nari got up and kissed the old man on the cheek.

"That is sweet of you." He got up to his feet and walked near the parapet overlooking the Nation of Zany. "I can't help but blame myself for it. You see, when I lost Jessica, I became a burden to him; my days and nights became a blur infused in one. There were times I would pass out in the middle of the living room downstairs for days, not getting up even to shower or to eat. Rudolph would get tired from time to time, and then, one day, I was lying there, and a bright-red light illuminated the whole room, waking me up. I looked around, trying to find where the blinding light was coming from. Then, I heard a knock coming from outside the window. It was Rudolph. He was in flying outside of the window semi turned into his reindeer shape. I'd recognize those antlers anywhere."

"Must have been a sight to see," Nari commented to everyone's surprise.

"Oh, yes, it was. Rudolph, the Red-Nosed Reindeer, couldn't contain himself and started flying all over the Nation, not caring if any other human saw him. I mean, who would believe if they saw or heard of a flying reindeer?" Nicholas finished his story. "I'm sorry you had to see him like this, he truly is a great guy, a son I never had."

"You have nothing to apologize for," I approached him, "but I'm afraid I'm on a time frame." I showed him my triangle bracelet.

"You've been imprisoned? I heard of your stellar reputation. You aren't capable of killing your own food if you had to."

"You're very kind, Nick, that's why I'm here. Your sister told me you know where to find Pablo Nuñéz. Do you know where he is?" I asked, hopefully.

"Mr. Chase, you didn't come all the way here just for a fun time with Mr. Nuñéz, did ya?"

"It's not like that," Nari interjected. "Pablo has information that can help us prove Will's innocence."

"So, you can help us?" Marcus joined in the conversation.

"I think I can. I, personally, have never met Mr. Nuñéz myself, but I know where his club is," Mr. Klauss told us.

"His club?" Marcus asked, surprised. "I don't think I can go in. I don't have a fake I.D."

"I.D.?" Nari asked, confused.

"On Earth, they carry their identification on a card inside their wallets. I.D. stands for identification." I explained to everyone around us.

"Wait, they carry their identification on a card, like a plastic card instead of inside their wrist?" Elijah asked, confused, "Why?"

"It's just the way they do things on Earth," I told them, "you know they are not as evolved as the rest of the Solar System,"

"I still don't know why you spend so much time on that planet with so many other planets much better than Earth," Nari injected.

"Even Saturn's moons have a better lifestyle than Earth." Elijah joined in.

"I know, but—"

"GUYS!" Marcus interrupted us loudly. "Earthian in the room." He pointed to himself to remind us that he is from Earth.

"At least you're a Natural," Nicholas joked as everyone laughed but Marcus.

"Focus! The club? Me, a minor?" Marcus asked again.

"Marcus, you're a Natural, and just like the rest of us, age no longer exists to you, you're free to go as you please throughout this Solar System; all you have to do is show your beautiful eyes to them. Your Porter's eyes, that is, not that your green eyes aren't beautiful," Nari explained prancing around him.

"You, however," Mr. Klauss began, "need a disguise. We're gonna have to put you in male clothes."

"Bummer," Nari began sadly. "I really wanted to show off my new boots around town. BUT I also do like dressing up like a guy from time to time so, sign me up," she said gleefully.

"You know I love you, right?" Elijah planted a kiss on her cherry-colored lips.

"Alright, let's go downstairs, grab some of Rudolph's clothes for Nari, and I'll drive you there." Mr. Klauss lead the way downstairs.

"What about him?" Marcus pointed out that Rudolph was still unconscious.

"He'll be fine, Marcus, it's not like he can catch a cold," Nari told him, pretty much dragging Marcus downstairs with us.

"Please, make yourself comfortable while I'll take these boots out and grab her some clothes."

The stairs landed in the living room, where a couple of brown couches were laid out in opposite directions; a fireplace was next to one of the lounges. A magnificent ceiling to floor window was the focal point between both couches, with dark red curtains framing both sides matching the tapestry in the middle of the living room. The only bedroom in the house is where Nicholas sleeps. A small closet in the living room had all of Rudolph's clothes. The kitchen was on the opposite side of the bedroom, too small to have a dinner table in it.

"Here," Mr. Klauss walked back in the living room with a long black trench coat on his hands, "it might not be your style, but it serves its purpose. All you need is a hat, which should be here somewhere, and we are all set."

"Thank you for doing this; we appreciate your help."

"Thank me after we find what you're looking for, Mr. Chase. Now let's go, time's a-wasting."

We followed Nicholas Klauss out to the elevator in the hall and down to the lobby. The open, grey marble decorated lobby was a complete contrast in comparison to the apartment we were in a couple of minutes ago. Glass doors and windows everywhere displaying equally high class, expensive buildings all around us, a typical metropolis.

"Where's your car?" Elijah asked once we stepped outside to the same spot we were when we rescued Nari and Rudolph from his own blast.

"It's right here." Nicholas Klauss waved to an empty parking spot, and a black S.U.V. materialized out of nowhere.

"WOW, that's a neat trick, Mr. Klauss. Cloaking device?" E.J. asked excitedly.

"I'm afraid not, Mr. Jones. As Porter of the Auriga Constellation, I can manifest any automobile I want, as long as I'm around it, so will it be," he explained as we all got in the car.

"Why aren't we flying then?" Marcus asked, impatiently as always.

"We could, Mr. Mathias, but the place we are going is not, well, how can I put this? Not well seen by the High Society of Males in this Nation."

We drove off to a busy street with black S.U.V.'s everywhere, intercalated by different types of sports cars, just like on Earth; except here, the vehicles floated above ground at three-feet high. It didn't take us more than ten minutes to reach the destination.

"We are here," Mr. Klauss said as we stopped in front of a dark alley with barely any lights in it.

"Is this the place?" Nari asked, analyzing the one single back door that seemed to connect to a kitchen of a restaurant in the streets of New York City.

"Yes, it is, now you three go, and Nari and I will be out here to keep a lookout. If the C.V.O. comes by, we'll handle them."

Marcus, Elijah, and I jumped out of the car.

"Guys, I have a bad feeling about this," Marcus said as he looked up and down at the door as if trying to see through it.

"Just follow my lead. I'll T.P. you through it all," I assured him.

"HAVE FUN, BABE," Nari shouted from inside the car to Elijah, who blew her a kiss.

"Let me go in first." Elijah stepped in front of us, knocking at the door. "You two clearly have never done anything like this before,"

The door opened, and a man as big as a door and thick as the doorway stood there. He makes Kent Hors look scrawny next to him.

"What's your business?" The thick-muscled man spoke one word coming out of each of his three mouths.

"Entertainment," Elijah spoke excitedly.

"I need to see some identification. Wrists, please."

"How about these?" E.J. let his eyes shine bright-white like stars.

"What about you two back there, wrists or eyes?" He spoke, alternating his words between each of his three mouths.

"Eyes, they will show their eyes, right guys?" Elijah told us.

And we did.

The place was so dark that we lit the doorman as if we had flashlights on us, revealing his dark purple skin and eyes.

"Alright, alright, put those away. You can blind the whole damned Neptune with those," he said, allowing us in.

He opened the second door behind him, where a couple of different guys were, all with three mouths and purple colored skin and eyes. He made a signal to them, and they allowed us in. A red silk curtain was opened, revealing us the fantastic place.

The place was enormous, set up just like the Roman's Colosseum with rows full of men on round tables all the way around, twenty stories deep. Between each row was another row of exotic female dancers. And I do mean exotic. Females with all different types of bodies: some enormous, some large, some big, some medium, some curvaceous, some petite, some tiny and some teeny like a small breed dog. Women with two heads, two long necks, four legs, six arms, with horns, with tails, with paws, with furs in every single color imaginable in the universe. It's like the Colosseum gone Vegas.

In the middle of it, all was the "arena." A huge

dance floor with a catwalk stage interloping in every direction with females dancing semi-nude collecting money from the intoxicated crowd full of males. Males who, like the females, were also all different shades, sizes, and different body types looking for a fun evening.

"Can I get you guys anything to drink?" A blonde-haired woman looking just like a regular woman from Earth, wearing nothing but a glittering-silver bikini and high heels, asked us.

"No, thanks, we're fine," I told her.

"Listen, I don't know if you know this, but male dancers' night is on Tuesdays and Thursdays, it's not too late to get a refund, just talk to Big Mike at the door and—"

"We are looking for Pablo Nuñéz, Ms.?" Elijah interrupted her.

"Krystal..."

"Of course, it is. Now Krystal, could you get him for me?"

"Even if I wanted to, I couldn't. Mr. Nuñéz is about to perform. If I were you, I'd get a nice spot by the table over there, and if you're lucky, he'll stop by to handout autographs," she explained, pointing to a table three rows down.

"Thanks, Krystal, grab us three porters while you're at it, please?" E.J. shouted as she cursed him in a foreign language.

PEOPLE OF THE ZANY NATION, HERE IS THE MOMENT EVERYONE'S BEEN WAITING. PLEASE WELCOME THE QUEEN OF THE NIGHT, THE HOTTEST FEMALE OF THE NUÑÉZ BOÎTE, THE ENTERTAINER OF THIS EVENING, OWNER OF EVERYTHING YOU TOUCH, PAVHOA

A male's voice echoed through the speakers of the entire place as it went dark as the crowd went wild with roars, cheers, whistles, and applause.

Under a single focal light, a woman wearing a bright-purple sequined dress rose from under the stage, taking center stage as the upbeat song begun playing as the crowd erupted in cheers again.

"Here are your beers! Three kaskos, please," Krystal put the beers down on the table.

"I thought you said Pablo was performing?" I asked her as I handed the money.

"That is Mr. Nuñéz." She took money out of my hand with a slightly irritated face. "Great, Porter's money! Now I have to exchange this, next time, please bring our Zany's currency!"

"I don't think she was happy with that," Elijah told me.

"She'll be once she exchanges that cash and realizes that I over tipped her," I told him, focusing my attention back to Pavhoa.

As the upbeat music went on, Pavhoa made her way through the crowded dance floor and up the rows of where the men were, collecting money as she went along, dancing for them, and joking with the crowd, lip-syncing through the song.

"Do you have any Halleys left?" Elijah asked me to my surprise.

"Yeah, why? We just got our beers. I doubt—"

"Just give me a couple of Halleys, Willie," E.J. demanded. "I only have Tritos, Triton's currency."

"Alright, but you owe me seven Halleys,"

"Fine, fine, you'll thank me for this. Watch and learn, boys."

Elijah waved the money in the air as Pavhoa was dancing a couple of rows under us.

"Pavhoa, come here, gorgeous. PAVHOA!" He shouted, trying to get her attention.

Halley is Porter's currency accepted throughout the Solar System in places that deal with Porters, usually only on certain moons, but if Pavhoa was indeed Mr. Pablo Nuñéz than he'd surely recognize the silvery money.

"PAVHOA!" He shouted one more time, waving the money side to side as if he was holding a small flag.

Her eyes caught a glimpse of it, and she gracefully jumped two rows of people to exactly where we were for the crowd's amusement. She stared at her bright, rainbow-colored eyes between the three of us. She then blinked, revealing her eyes, bright-white like stars, just as Elijah's were. And then, with a wave of her hand, the music stopped.

She grabbed the money quickly, hiding out of sight and faced the crowd. She rose her hand and ripped off her purple dressing revealing a glittering-green leotard. The crowd roared with excitement as she jumped out of our row to seventeen rows down toward the floor, spreading magnificent rainbow-colored wings and a peacock tail, more significant than any peacock I've ever seen. The wings were at least ten feet long from tip to tip, and the tail had to be twice as much. The music kicked back in as the crowd went crazy with roars; money was being thrown at her from every balcony of the place.

Pavhoa landed gracefully in the center of the stage, hiding her wings and tail, looking just a typical show dancer, letting her curly brown hair out of a bun, flowing all the way down her waist as she exited the stage under the loud cheers and applause of the crowd.

"That was something else!" Marcus spoke for the first time since being in this place.

"You three, with me, NOW!" Big Mike was back, speaking every word out of his three mouths. "Boss wants to see you."

The three of us got up and followed him all the way down the rows till we hit the stage that was filled with dancers again. We went around the stage, through a door and down a tunnel, where we stopped in front of a red door with a gold star on it.

"Boss, I brought you the Porters," he shouted from the outside.

"Oh, *bueno,*[41]" we heard a male voice coming from

---

[41] *Bueno:* Nice (Spanish)

inside as the door swung open, *"entre, por favor,*[42]*"*

We stepped into the room and saw a much different person inside wearing the same glittering-green leotard. A man in his forties, slim but toned figure, with short black hair and tanned skin complexion, just like those of tropical places on Earth.

"You must be wondering how a woman like that can look like a man like me?" He asked with a very thick accent. "Makeup, darlings, makeup, and Stardust."

"Stardust?" Marcus asked him.

"Allow me to introduce myself. My name is Pablo Nuñéz, Porter of the Pavo Constellation, the Peacock. And who might you three be?" He asked, hiding behind a French obfuscated panel as he switched clothes.

"This is William Chase, Porter of the Lyra Constellation, the Lyre; to my left is Marcus Mathias, Natural Porter of the Taurus Constellation, the Bull. And I am Elijah Jones, Porter of the Malus Constellation the—"

"The Mast, a Vanisher," He stepped out in the open again, sporting a dashing black suit with a purple shirt under. "I remember meeting you before, Mr. Jones, your skin tone is quasi-unforgettable."

"WOW!" Marcus let out an involuntary sigh.

"Mr. Natural, was this your first show?" Pablo asked Marcus, analyzing him and down.

"Marcus has never seen anything like this. He just recently became a Porter and—"

---

[42] *Entre, por favor:* Come in, please (Spanish)

"No need to get all protective, Mr. Chase, I'm not looking to date your man, I got my own. Plenty for that matter," he laughed.

"Oh no, it's not like that," Marcus began, "we are just friends. William and I are just good friends."

"*Si, claro*[43]," Pablo looked Marcus up and down and back to me while I was trying to not think about the awkward situation. "What about you, *Papi*[44], are you looking for some fun tonight?" He asked E.J., who was comfortably sitting on a chair nearby.

"Me? Oh no, my beautiful girl is waiting for me outside, but thanks for the offer. I'm flattered, handsome."

"A girl, huh? My oh my how you've changed." He analyzed Elijah up and down, sitting on a chair next to him, fixing himself in front of the mirror framed with bright-white light bulbs. "If you're not looking for some fun, then why are you here?"

"Pablo, we are looking for a woman on this side of Neptune, and you are the only one who knows of all the women working illegally on this place," Elijah told him.

"True. But tell me, who's this woman you seek desperately? Susan?" He suggested laughing.

"Susan? Who's Susan? We are looking for Jessica, Porter of the Atelier Typographique, the—"

---

[43] *Si, claro:* Yeah, sure (Spanish)

[44] *Papi:* Daddy (Spanish)

"DEAD! Dead, dead, dead, dead! *MUERTA*[45]! Just like the rest of the Vanishers. Or most of them, anyway," he said, giving Elijah a dirty look. "Now out, out, out, I've already wasted too much of my time on you, a time I'll never get back."

"But Pablo, we have reasons to believe she's alive. She—" I started.

"They lied to you. Now get out of here and go slap the faces of the people who lied to you and made you waste your time, and most importantly," he opened the door, "MINE! Now go!"

Pablo pushed us out of the room, closing the door right behind us.

"Come back on Tuesdays or Thursdays; I'm sure you'll have a fabulous time. *Adiós*[46]!" We heard him speak sing-songy from the other side of the door.

"Oh, there they are," Nari appeared around the corner with a woman right behind her.

"Nari!" I exclaimed, surprised to see her here in her full feminine clothes without the trench coat and the hat. "What are you doing here?"

"Guys, you're not going to believe this. I was outside keeping a lookout when I saw this person dressed in a black coverup approaching the club, and I knew right there and then that it had to be her. I mean, the disguise was on point, but her legs gave her away," she said excitedly.

---

[45] *Muerta:* Dead (Spanish)

[46] *Adiós:* Goodbye (Spanish)

"Hi, I'm Elijah Jones, Porter of the—" Elijah introduced himself only to have the tall, dark skin woman interrupt him mid-sentence.

"Porter of the Malus Constellation. A Vanisher just like myself." she shook E.J.'s hand. "You're quite popular among the Vanishers, you know?"

"I'm sorry, you are...?" Marcus jumped in the conversation.

"My name is Vanezzza Ninaè, Porter of the Vespa Constellation, the Wasp," she introduced herself with the same tone of authority as any other Porter would, "and if I'm right, you're Marcus Mathias, the Natural Porter of the Taurus Constellation?"

"Yeah, how did you know?" Marcus changed his tone from that of an inquisitor to a distrusted one.

"Wonderers have not stopped talking about you since the murder of your mother by one of the Wanderers," Vanezzza switched her gaze from Marcus to me, "which, by the bracelet on your wrist, leads me to believe you're William Chase, Porter of the Lyra Constellation."

"That would be me."

Vanezzza was dressed like one of the showgirls, with a silver sequined leotard and high stiletto heels with an enormous hairdo adding at least a couple of extra feet to her height. A look that didn't match her walk or persona. Something was off about this 'showgirl'.

"How can a Vanisher like yourself know so much about us? As far as I'm concerned, Vanishers are supposed to be hidden, and here you are, working as a showgirl in one of the most high-profile clubs in all of the Solar System."

"Illegally, Mr. Chase. This whole place is a distraction to all of the Porters, local aliens, and humans alike. The only reason why it is still running is that as soon as every Unportable leaves this place, they won't remember a thing. Plus, a girl gotta make a living."

"Am I missing something here, Nari?" I asked, still confused about why she thought it would be a good idea to reveal ourselves to Vanezzza.

"Ugh, let's get you guys out of here before Pablo has Big Mike remove us from his club."

Vanezzza led the way in the opposite direction we came from. We took a few turns, and she opened a door leading to the dance floor. She looked at the bartender who nodded at her with all her three heads at the same time, gesturing to a round booth in the corner.

"Go take five, Salisa," Vanezzza told the green-skinned woman dancing on top of the table, who gladly stepped out, chewing gum, playing with her blue hair, flashing her miniskirt to the guys at the bar, and causing some cheers from the rowdy crowd.

"Nari here told me you're looking for Jessica, right?" Vanezzza began us as we sat in the booth.

"What?" Nari asked us in reply to our judgmental look.

"Let me guess; you guys were a thing?" I asked.

"I wish," she told us all regretfully, as if not wanting to remember something.

"It's cute that you still think that the only way for people to be affectionate with each other is to have sex with them," Vanezzza told us. "It's a weakness I don't have, for I am not attracted sexually to anyone."

"I know," Nari got up to her feet. "I'm gonna go get us some beers. Does anyone have cash? Never mind, I'm sure a handsome Plutonian will be more than willing to pay for me."

"Did she forget I'm here?" Elijah asked, perplexed by Nari's remarks.

"You and I both know she is madly in love with you, she just needs some space," I assured him. "As you were saying?"

"Right," Vanezzza continued, "I know where she is."

"You do? So, what are we waiting for? Take us there." Marcus jumped out of his seat in excitement.

"It's not that easy. For us to get to Jessica, we have to find a hidden door under the main stage. That's all I know."

"Alright, so where's this door?" Marcus asked impatiently.

"HIDDEN!" Nari sat back down in the booth we were in with a giant bowl of an orange and green clear colored drink with five straws in it, with a floating red, pink animal that looks like a hybrid between a garden snake and butterfly. "Weren't you paying attention?"

"What's this?" Elijah asked with a disgusted face.

"Trubahuba. A local specialty drink. Don't worry, its venom it's harmless to humans," she explained, taking a sip.

"If Jessica is in this building, why is everyone saying she's dead?"

"She's clearly hiding something of very high value, Mr. Chase."

"Vanezzza is right," I took a sip out of the weird-looking drink. "Whoa, that packs a punch."

"Yeah, it's very citrusy." Nari laughed about my reaction to the orange and green drink.

"Oh, looky here, our little Porters made a friend. Vanezzza, aren't you supposed to be on top of the table shaking your eeffocty-colored body?" Pablo joined in the conversation alongside Big Mike and somebody who could very well be called Bigger Mike. "You know a lot of people pay good money just to touch your beautiful smooth *piel*,⁴⁷"

"Eeffocty?" Marcus asked, uncertain if he heard it right.

"Another fruit unimaginative people use to describe skin color like mine, Marcus." Vanezza explained, "It's my day off today, Mr. Nuñéz."

"Then I hope you won't mind showing our less than welcome guests the way out, would you?"

"Mr. Nuñéz, I was hoping to—"

"To leave, Ms. Ninaè?" Pablo leaned over in the booth. "You know I hate to cause a scene, but I will if I have to." He blinked his dark-green eyes showing his star-like eyes.

"YOU—" Marcus got up to his feet, igniting his

---

⁴⁷ *Piel:* Skin (Spanish)

own eyes.

"You've been very kind to us, Mr. Nuñéz," I pulled Marcus back down. "We appreciate your time, and I'm truly sorry if we overstayed our welcome."

"William, what—"

"Let's go, Marcus. Guys?" I looked at them as I made my way out of the booth following one of the Mikes.

"There, see, there's always a smart one in the group," Pablo laughed mockingly. "Take 'em out, boys. I have a closing number to perform. Can't be dealing with this nonsense right now."

"Oh, Pablo?"

"Yes, Mr. Chase?"

"Obviously, I won't be able to see you're closing number, so will you indulge me?"

"Oh, Mr. Chase, I guess you did come for a good time, *lindo*[48], but I gotta keep my secrets. After all, I can't let people know I'm flying down from the ceiling all the way to the main stage. That'll ruin the surprise. You know the best-hidden secrets are kept above us." He winked at us as we made his way inside the door we had just come out of it half an hour ago.

"Really?" Marcus asked as we made our way up the rows to the exit door, followed by both Mikes.

"What was that all about? We could have taken them out," Marcus shouted once Big Mike and Bigger Mike shut the door behind us.

"Yes, we could have, but we would never find out

---

[48] *Lindo:* Handsome (Spanish)

where Jessica is," I told him, stepping close to the car where Mr. Klauss was.

"And how in the world did you find that out by asking about his closing number?" Marcus imposed.

"Marcus, you haven't been around many divas in your life, if there's one thing they can't resist is a big opening or closing number. Hold on." I grabbed Marcus and flew all the way up the building. It didn't take much for the others to follow with Nari jumping from building to building climbing her way up, as did E.J., jumping with his Bo staff just as fast as Nari could jump. Vanezzza was flying right behind us with her four wasp wings sprung open.

"Good thinking," Vanezzza told me as we all landed on top of the highest building in the Zany Nation.

"I figured Pablo wouldn't have her hidden beneath a club but at the top of the building where his club is."

"So, now what? We'll just break our way in?" Marcus ignited his Stardust. "Where should I knock?" He looked around the floor for a spot to make a hole.

"Through the chimney, of course" Rudolph appeared right in front of us with his antlers out, and his nose bright-red illuminating the whole rooftop.

"What are you doing here?" I asked, baffled by the fact that Rudolph was flying again.

"I got to the car just as you all took off, and, against Nicholas' advice, I decided to fly up here." He landed between us, losing his antlers but not his red reindeer nose. "I thought you guys would be happy to see me."

"We are, except now we have to worry about you, exploding at any minute," Nari said, somewhat still annoyed about the last time he exploded and knocked her out almost to her death.

"Listen, I'm sorry about last time. If we move fast, we'll be out of there before I explode." Rudolph ran toward the chimney and jumped right in. By the way he did it, you could tell he had done it before.

"Let's just hope she's not roasting chestnuts." Nari jumped right behind him.

"Marcus, stay stellar at all times," I told him as Elijah jumped in the chimney.

"Stay stellar?" He asked me, confused with my terminology.

"Keep your powers running through your veins all the time; even though you're a Natural, you can still die. You haven't got your Halley Tattoo yet. You may not need your Stardust Tattoo to ignite your powers, but without the Halley Tattoo, if you die, you won't come back, so stay stellar at no matter what," I explained to him.

"You guys coming or not?" Vanezzza jumped in the chimney.

"We'll be right behind you," I told her as Marcus jumped in the chimney.

I jumped right behind him, landing in the middle of a candlelit library. The place had large windows all around with high ceilings and bookshelves framing each window and every empty inch of the wall. All around us, there were couches, sofas, and lounge chairs of every size and color. In the far corner of the magnificent place was a small desk with nothing but a notepad and a peacock feather next to small black squid ink vase.

"Is anyone here?" I asked as we all dusted off the fume from the chimney.

"Oh yes, there is." All the lights in the room went on, pretty much blinding us all. "What are you doing here?"

"Jessica Klauss?" Rudolph asked as he approached the blonde-haired woman near the desk in the far corner.

XIII

DO YOU SEE WHAT I SEE?

The woman was of short height, light skin complexion, and wearing simple clothes: a blue blouse and a knee-high skirt and black ballerina shoes. Her blonde hair was up in a bun with a few threads here and there. Her big, brown eyes were hidden behind a square shape black glasses. She could not be older than twenty-five.

"Actually, it's just Jessica now, my dear Rudolph." She removed her spectacles. "Why didn't you knock? If I knew I was going to have visitors, I would have prepared us some hybacea tea."

"We're sorry to drop in like this, literally, but we're in a rush." Rudolph stepped closer to her holding her two hands. "We thought you were dead, how is this possible?"

"You're not the only Vanisher who didn't want your powers stripped, son." She hugged him tightly. "How is he?"

"After you left, he became a man of drinking habit. He could never believe the woman he loved had left him. Why did you leave?"

"Oh Rudolph, I couldn't grow old while you two stayed the same. I tried to build a life of my own, by myself, even tried a relationship again, but that didn't last, my heart was still prisoner of Nick. It wasn't until I ran into Allison Prior, you know, the Porter of the Scorpius Constellation, Wonderer of Pluto, that I even gave a thought about becoming a Porter myself. By the time I went back to tell you, you both had left. I was told he had stopped renewing his Halley Tattoo and was now an old man, living in a remote place on Earth. Devastated by my own doing, I succumbed to my books, my readings, and my archives. I asked Pablo for a place to stay hidden from the eyes of any Porter while I dealt with my own heartbreak," Jessica's words came out while she was fighting back the tears.

"Why didn't you tell him, us, that you're alive and well? He looked for you in every house on every planet."

"Oh yes, I heard about your games with him, getting into people's houses through the chimney," she laughed, "what were you thinking? You guys could've got caught,"

"And we did. It all began as a search party for you,

but on one cold winter night, we got caught. The guy screamed 'thieves; somebody help us!' Startled and scared, Nicholas decided to do completely the opposite and gave the man all the money he had in his pocket. The guy, marveled by Nicholas' kindness, thanked him so much, calling him a saint and all. Every year since, on the same date, 'Saint Nick' and I would visit the houses of every poor person, leaving money, toys, clothes and whatever we could carry in a big red sack. Some planets would leave us cookies and milk. Gosh, I miss Earth,"

"Rudolph, how exactly did you manage all of this? There's no way you could teleport yourself into every single house; you two would exhaust yourselves." Jessica put her spectacles back on.

"Well..." Rudolph lifted himself, floating in the middle of the place with his nose bright-red.

"Oh no, tell me this isn't—"

"Stardust? Yes, it is." Rudolph landed back again on the floor. "Listen, I know you don't approve of it, neither does Nick, but I love it. There's no better feeling in the world, any world for that matter than to fly, fly way up high in the clouds between the stars, the moons, anywhere I want, ***COUGH-COUGH***"

"You're alright?" Jessica rushed to him as he grabbed hold of himself, leaning against the desk.

"Yeah, I'm good." Rudolph straightened himself up, shaking off a weird cough. "Which that reminds me, Jessica, I'd like you to meet a group of friends. Actually, besides Nari, I just met them."

Rudolph made his way back to the middle of the library, where we were as Jessica followed him with curious eyes on who these people may be.

"I'm—"

"No introductions needed, Mr. Mathias," Jessica interrupted Marcus before he could finish his sentence. "I've seen each and every one of you in the pages of my books. Matter of fact, you and every single Porter, living or dead."

"Can you see my mother?" Marcus got up to his feet, anxiously.

"Right to the point, just like your dad. I like that."

"I'm sorry, Jessica, Marcus, and I have been looking for his mother for a while now. If we don't find her and prove my innocence, I'll be tossed into Oblivion by the Queen herself," I explained.

"Let me see what I can do. Marcus, give me your hands," Jessica instructed, reaching for Marcus' hands with palms facing up, "and think about your mother."

She closed her eyes, and the whole room got dark again, with only the lights of the candles spread randomly around the room. She opened them up again, revealing her Porter's bright-white like stars eyes.

"Oh, yes, I know her. Very resilient, strong, beautiful woman." Jessica let go of Marcus' hand and glanced around the bookshelves all around us without moving one inch. "Wish you guys would've come in sooner to avoid all of this mess you've put yourselves into."

"We would have, but it wasn't till long ago that I just found out the Vanishers were still alive."

"It's okay, Mr. Chase, everything has its own time even if time itself is variable," she let out a soft, quick laugh. "Oh, there it is..."

With a hand gesture, one of the books that was on a top shelf, to the right of the fireplace, we had just popped out of flew on its own, glistening with a silver light around it, as if made out of Stardust. The book stopped a couple of feet away from us in midair. The pages opened and shuffled vigorously as if a mad person was looking for something desperately, except no one was touching the book. And then, it stopped.

"Is this your mother?" With another hand gesture, the page popped out of the book and became life-size with a picture of Marcus' mom floating in the middle of the room.

"Yes, that's it. That is her!" Marcus rushed toward the floating page as if trying to hold his mom. "Is she alive?"

"Let me see..." She closed her eyes again for a second as if trying to remember where she left something of importance. "Yes! She is alive, barely, actually. Oh, I'm sorry, dear." Jessica's eyes were open again, but this time without her Stardust in them, revealing their true, blue color, holding back tears.

"Where IS SHE?" Marcus shouted at her, making her and the whole room jump. Scared, she retrieved a couple of feet away from him into Rudolph's arms, as if looking for a shoulder to cry on.

"MARCUS!" I shouted at him, pulling him back. "I'm sorry about him. He has a hard time controlling his temper."

"Mr. Chase, she's with the River," Jessica said, drying her eyes, with a terrified look on her face.

I stared at her blankly and whispered, "The River?" Now I know why she was crying; she wasn't scared of Marcus, she was scared for Marcus' mom.

"She's in a river? What river?" Marcus' voice was trembling in a mix of anger and fear.

"Not in a river but with the River, more precisely with Wanderer Ralphel L'Acuah, Porter of the Eridanus Constellation, the River," I explained to him.

"Okay, so how do we get to him?" Elijah joined in the conversation.

"Guys, I sense something,"

Before Nari could finish her sentence, a whirlpool of Stardust manifested itself in the middle of the library, with a man stepping out of it. With another hand gesture, Jessica made all the books on the shelves disappear before the man could finish manifesting himself in the room.

"Oh, what I surprise to find you here after all these years, Ms. Jessica... Klauss? Don't matter, thanks to my friend Vanezzza Ninaè, I have now found you, and together we'll find all the other Vanishers. It's time to end what the Queen couldn't."

Vanezzza got up to meet the man who was dressed in a dark-blue suit, almost black, with a lighter shade of blue shirt underneath it, contrasting his white skin and matching his equally dark-blue eyes and sleek black hair.

"Adam Ford, what's the meaning of this?" I asked, recognizing his tone of authority.

"Mr. Chase, you may know me merely as Adam Ford, Porter of the Pisces Constellation, Wonderer of Neptune, and as such, I'm the ruler, the emperor of the Zany Nation, and you will respect me as such."

"What do you want with us?" Marcus' eyes shifted from their standard shade of green to bright-white like stars.

"Oh, I heard about your temper, Mr. Mathias?" Adam smirked at him completely unafraid of Marcus' threat. "I want nothing to do with you, Natural. This is between the Vanishers and me. By the power invested in me, I will take them back to the Queen, and with the help of Jessica, we'll be able to find all of the others."

"I'll never help you." Jessica got in between Adam and me.

"It's fine. I'll just keep him to myself then." Adam touched a device on his wrist, and a projection of Nicholas Klauss wrapped in chains took the center of the room.

"NO!" Rudolph shouted at the sight of his beloved friend/father, completely helpless. "Just take me instead, leave him along,"

"Oh, I am taking you in, but my interest is in her. With her help, I'll find all the rest of you and eliminate the Vanishers scum."

"How could you? You're one of us." Rudolph's eyes were bright-white like stars, but you could still see the anger toward Vanezzza, who was standing there next to her emperor.

"I'm tired of this life. I'm ready to let go of my powers and live the rest of it in one of the moons of Jupiter. My time is up, and I'm okay with it," she told the room.

"But mine is not, you dirty piece of—"

"IT'S OKAY," Jessica shouted at Rudolph before he could charge against Vanezzza, "I'll go with him. I'm sure once I meet with the Queen, she'll understand, and we'll recognize us as Formers again, she is a fair queen after all."

"Like hell, you will!"

Rudolph charged against Vanezzza, who was caught off guard, allowing him to shove her against the wall, with his right arm choking her.

"Get off me, you filthy animal" Vanezzza tossed him quickly with not two, but four arms across the other side of the room. She flew on top of him with a needle sword in her hand pointed down to his throat, just like a fencing sword fighter.

"GUYS!" He looked at me, and I remember that look on his face. I looked at Nari, who already had sprinted toward Elijah, who had no idea what was going on as neither did Marcus.

'Stay stellar.' I sent Marcus a Thought Projection and ran toward Jessica, who was still gazing at Nicholas' projection as if waiting for him to jump out of it and hug her.

Rudolph let his nose shine bright-red, temporarily blinding Vanezzza, a trick she was not expecting.

He then grabbed her and flew all the way up toward the high ceiling of the library, and...

BOOM

Rudolph exploded just right after I could disappear out of there with Jessica inside of my Exotic Matter Sphere to a rooftop nearby.

"You're okay?" I asked Jessica once we were safe.

"Yeah, it's been so long since I've been inside of an Exotic Matter Sphere," she said, checking herself to see if any parts were missing.

"WILLIAM!" Nari shouted from behind us, dangling from the building across from us with Elijah in her hands.

"ARE YOU OKAY?" I shouted at them.

"RUDOLPH!"

The power of the explosion propelled Rudolph a few hundred feet above the building, and he was now free-falling unconsciously, and so was Vanezzza.

"Stay here. I'll be right back," I told Jessica before flying off the building toward Rudolph, who was getting closer and closer to hitting the destroyed top part of the building where the library once was.

I rushed as fast as my wings would allow, grabbing him in an instant. I looked down, and Vanezzza was still free-falling, and much closer to the ground.

"NARI!"

Nari jumped off of the rooftop where she and Elijah were, disappearing inside her own Exotic Matter Sphere, manifesting herself right on top of the destroyed building, preparing herself to catch Vanezzza.

As she grew closer, Nari transformed herself into

her full nine-tails orange fox form, pushing her whole body against the floor to jump and catch Vanezzza.

As Porters, our bodies weigh more than the average human being by at least twenty pounds in our natural human form. Once we transform into our Constellation, our body weight can increase a few hundred pounds, even tons, depending on the size of the Porter's Constellation. In the case of Nari, she weighs about four hundred and something pounds in her full fox form, making the now damaged structure under her give in a few stories down, swallowing her inside of a hole, and Vanezzza not much longer afterward.

"NARI!" Elijah screamed in desperation once he saw what happened.

"No need to shout, I'm right here, *jagiya*[49]." Nari appeared right behind him.

"Oh, baby, are you okay?" He hugged her passionately.

"I couldn't get to her in time, she's..." Nari couldn't finish her words. Instead, tears took the place of them.

Elijah looked at me from across the building as I was landing on the rooftop where I had left Jessica not long ago. I shook my head, letting him know that Vanezzza was gone.

"Is she dead?"

"I think so. She was still unconscious when she fell in the hole," I told Jessica as I laid Rudolph, who

---

[49] *Jagiya:* Sweetie (Korean)

was now slowly coming back to his senses, down.

"What happened, did we kill them?" He asked with a smile on his face.

"Vanezzza was a Vanisher like yourselves; and as such, she lacks the Exotic Matter Sphere in her body, making it impossible for her to create her own wormhole and dematerialize out of any situation. If she had gained her consciousness back, she wouldn't be hurt by fall. Instead, she could easily fly out of any danger just by igniting her Stardust and staying stellar. However, since Nari says she saw her body unconscious, she probably never gained her conscious back, dying the true death. May she find peace among the stars." I explained. "We should get going before Adam Ford returns."

"No, you go," Jessica told me, "Nicholas is in chains because of me. Rudolph and I will go after him. The rest of you go after Marcus' mom. You know where to find her."

"MARCUS!" I looked around and saw no sign of him.

'Nari, can you see Marcus?' I sent her a T.P.

'No, I can't see him anywhere, wait. Is that him?'

I flew to where she was pointing and saw Marcus unconscious on the rooftop of a much lower building around us.

"MARCUS!" I shouted as I landed next to him. "Marcus, talk to me, are you okay?"

"Yes, Willie, yes," he replied, still on the floor with his eyes shut, "is it okay for me to call you Willie now, right?"

"Yes, it is." I usually only let people who I trust or love to call me Willie. I think it's safe enough to say Marcus and I was beyond that. I pulled him over my shoulders and flew back to the rooftop, where I had left Jessica and Rudolph.

"Marcus, I'm sorry, are you okay, buddy?" Rudolph helped me put him down once I'd landed back.

"It's alright. That was pretty badass what you did back there, man," Marcus replied, somewhat smiling as he sat back up.

"A feat that could have killed us all, Mr. Skye," Jessica reprehended him.

"But, it didn't." He smiled graciously at her, just like a son jokingly playing with his mother.

"Let's go home," I told them. "Marcus, are you okay to bring Rudolph back to his place?"

"Yeah, let's do it," Marcus got up to his feet, stretching out his hand toward Rudolph. "Are you ready, buddy?"

"Let's do this!" Rudolph grabbed Marcus' hand in a very brotherly way. I wouldn't be surprised if they have a secret handshake by now.

'Rudolph's place.' I sent Nari a Thought Projection.

"C'mon, let's go home," I hugged Jessica as we all teleported our way back to Rudolph's place.

Jessica and I reappeared back at Rudolph's apartment after everyone else, and, to my surprise, everyone was quiet. And that's when I noticed something wrong: two' somethings wrong' to be precise.

"Hello there, birdie. Did you miss us?" Two dogs almost as tall as the ceiling were in the middle of the room. It didn't take me more than a few seconds to recognize them. The smaller black dog, standing at over six-foot-tall, was undoubtedly the Doberman Isahul "Midnight" Blahq, Porter of the Canis Minor Constellation. Under his paws were Marcus and Rudolph, being crushed against the floor. Nari and Elijah were under the bigger dog's paws, the dark-grey Pitbull Ezra Sirius, Porter of the Canis Major Constellation.

"Uh-uh, don't think of hitting one note, Chase, or your friends are Chow-Mein if you know what I mean," the bigger dog told me as soon as I thought about opening my mouth to let out a sonic blast.

However, a blast came in the room, not from my voice but the large window behind them. Five men entirely in black swung in through the window with cables and weapons on them just like the F.B.I. or the Interpol on Earth would have done. Four of them turned into large brown dogs with a big black spot on their back. Their legs and tails were white stained along with their faces, except around their eyes. Instead, a brown spot was around both eyes as if they were wearing a superhero mask. A contrast from the black they were all spotting before transforming themselves into the greatest hunting dogs know to men, the American Foxhounds.

'Don't move,' the guy in the middle of the dogfight sent me a T.P. He was wearing a black helmet similar to a biker, so I couldn't tell what he looked like. Two dogs went for the smaller dog as the other two dogs went for the bigger dog, while the man in the middle

stayed in front of the window, pointing his gun at me.

The Foxhounds were not biting the bigger dogs. They were smaller than them but definitely more agile. You could see Ezra and Isahul trying to get a hold of them, but they were moving all around them in unison and precision in a very well-choreographed dance, switching back and forth between their human selves and dog selves. Eventually, the four Foxhounds synchronized a backflip kick in a circle with Ezra and Isahul right in the middle, colliding them both against each other, forcing them going from their dog selves to their human versions. Two of the Foxhounds stayed in their dog form growling at their faces, while the other two were back in their full soldiers' form dressed in black with their guns pointing at the Hounds' faces.

"Don't move, or I'll shot one Stardust bullet straight to your brains and then..." he lifted his visor, "see ya next Halley."

"You son of a—"

"Yes, I am, Mr. Sirius. And by order of the Queen herself, I'm taking you both in." The other two soldiers handcuffed both of them. "Don't even try breaking out of it, it's involved in Antimatter," he told them as the soldiers, all back in their human forms, escorted them out of the apartment.

"Is everyone okay?" He put his gun away.

But nobody said a thing.

"Forgive me. I haven't introduced myself. I'm Jonathan Asterion, Porter of the Canes Venatici Constellation, the Hunting Dogs." He removed his helmet showing his white skin complexion with brown hair and eyes. The guy was not older than twenty-five. "I'm with the Canes Venatici Organization, also known as the C.V.O."

"You're with the C.V.O.? You're here to take me in, then?" I asked him, still astounded by what just have happened.

"No, he's here because I called him," Jessica told us.

"I came as soon as I received your signal, Jessica. Are you okay?" Jonathan checked on her.

"What's going on?" Elijah asked, confused just as the rest of us were.

"After the whole incident of Rudolph exploding in my library, William, Rudolph, and I discussed how Will is going to look for Marcus' mom with the rest of you. Rudolph and I will stay behind and look for Nicholas Klauss," Jessica explained. "So, I called in reinforcements, my friend Jonathan Asterion, who just happens to work with the C.V.O., the F.B.I. of the Solar System, the Interpol of it all."

"But you can't send T.P.'s."

"I know, Mr. Chase, that's why I sent him a text message by cell phone while you were rescuing Marcus on top of the other building."

"Alright, so when are we leaving?" Jonathan asked all excitedly as if a little kid was heading out to an amusement park.

"You guys, I'm not sure, but the rest of us are leaving as soon as everyone is feeling better and ready to go," I told Mr. Asterion.

"Can we rest for a minute? We just had a pretty eventful night. I'm beat, man." Marcus sat down on the couch, cleaning out the pieces of glasses.

"I'm with Marcus, Willie. I need a minute as well." Nari approached me as Elijah joined Marcus on the couch.

"Tell you what, why doesn't everybody relax for a minute while I make something for us to eat? Rudolph, help me in the kitchen, love?"

"Yes, of course. Guys, turn on the T.V., make yourselves comfortable. I'll be right back with some roasted trabullium."

"Trabu-what?" Marcus asked as I sat next to him.

"Trabullium," Nari replied, salivating just by the thought of said dish, "It's a local fish similar to flounder on Earth, Marcus."

"Except its color is blue instead of white. It's a bit more flavorful, more of a bigger fish, but yeah, it's a bit similar to flounder." Jonathan sat on the opposite couch across from us.

"And how would you know? Have you ever been to Earth?" Nari asked in an instigating tone.

"But of course. I have been to every village, every city, every county, every country, every nation of every world and moon in the Solar System," he said proudly, "if you want, I can tell you about it, Ms.?"

"Anser, Nari Anser. Porter of the Vulpecula Constellation, the Fo—"

"The Fox, of course. Tell me, how many tails do you have? Five? Seven?" He asked curiously with a big smile on his face.

"Nine! And for your information, I truly dislike dogs." Nari leaned on the other side of the couch next to Elijah.

"It's too bad cause I love foxes, especially the female kind," he said gleefully, showing his perfect white teeth.

"Down doggie, this fox's taken." Elijah joined the conversation, jealously.

"Oh, I'm truly sorry, Mr.?"

"Elijah Jones, Porter of the Malus Constellation, the Mast."

"The most popular Vanisher. I mean not as popular as Rudolph, but I heard of your fighting skills, especially on the sea. You're a great sailor!" Jonathan complimented him, making him blush a tiny bit under his dark skin. "And who you might be, younger one?"

"Marcus Mathias, Porter of the Taurus Constellation, the Bull," Marcus told him less excitedly than Elijah did.

"You're Marcus Mathias? The Marcus Mathias? I can't believe this." He got up excitedly. "First time meeting a Natural. Dude, you gotta own it: 'I'm Marcus Mathias NATURAL Porter of the Taurus Constellation, THE Bull'." Jonathan introduced himself as if he was indeed Marcus, imitating even his Bostonian accent.

"Oh man, this is awesome!" He sat back down again, gaining his breath back again out of excitement. "And you? Who are you?" He sat forward on the edge of the couch, waiting for my response, and, as you guessed, excitedly.

"I'm William Chase, Porter of the Lyra Constellation, the Lyre," I told him proudly.

"Oh!" He laid back again, disappointed with my response. "You're like a harp or something?"

"Like a lyrebird. I can replicate any sound I hear," I told him.

"Any sound?"

"Any sound," I responded in his own voice.

"That's a neat trick," Jonathan said less enthusiastically.

"Don't let that fool ya. William can send sonic booms that can knock you out miles across the field, mister," Marcus told him, proud of me.

"IT WAS YOU! I thought I'd recognized you from somewhere. You guys were running away from me in a snowmobile or something."

"Yup, that was us," Nari told him. "You tried but couldn't catch us,"

"Well, I was just doing my job; after all, you did break a hole through the border wall."

"Sorry," Marcus apologized.

"No harm done, plus that wall should be destroyed anyway."

"Guys, food is ready." Rudolph walked in the room with three plates in his hands, followed by Jessica, who also had three plates in her hands.

"I was looking for a dining room table but, I guess we no longer have one." Jessica laughed a bit, looking around the glasses shattered everywhere.

"We actually never had one," Rudolph explained apologetically.

"It's quite alright. We'll manage, right, guys?" Jonathan chirped.

"Right," we all said in unison, much less cheerfully, though.

"Uh, everything looks delicious, but what is this?" Marcus said as soon as Rudolph handled him a plate.

"Oh, I got this one," Jonathan said, excitedly again. "Marcus, my dear Natural, in front of you, you have a dish very typical of the Norwest region of Neptune. It's called Trabullium Jux. A piece of trabullium fish served over a type of grain very similar to Earth's rice for its consistency, shape, and size, except for its color. Rice on Earth is brown. Ours is black and juicy inside. The Jux sauce is made out of the fish bones dissolved completely into a creamy consistency, seasoned differently in every part of the globe. In this case, it's seasoned with local herbs. The natural green color comes from the fish bones itself. Trabullim is a big fish with blue color flesh, with emerald-green bones, skin, and scales."

"Very good! Please dig in, everybody," Jessica invited us to eat.

Marcus was still conspicuous about it, but eventually, he gave it a try and quite enjoyed himself. After we finished our meal, Rudolph and Jonathan went to do the dishes while Jessica went for a shower. Elijah, Nari, Marcus, and I helped clean the living room, throwing the shattered glasses away.

"So, do you really think my mom is in this river?" Marcus asked me while we were finishing up with the shards.

"Yeah, I do. Jessica is really good at keeping tracks on every Porter ever," I explained to him, putting the last pieces of shard in the trash barrel.

"I don't know. Jessica seems a bit odd at times."

"Marcus, Jessica has Autism. While that might be perceived as a bad thing on Earth, all over the Solar System, it isn't. Yes, she has extra chromosomes in her body, but that doesn't make her less intelligent, ignorance does. It's like saying that someone is less smart than you when they are speaking in a foreign language with an accent."

"That's not what I meant. When I saw my mother in the kitchen after her disappearance, she was acting a bit odd herself. Not until William proved to me that the woman I saw was actually Camille Liam impersonating my mom." Marcus explained himself. "I guess I'm just projecting."

"Hey, I told you we are going to find her. Now thanks to you, I truly have to find her. Otherwise, bye-bye, birdie." I told him.

"Sorry about that, Will."

"Are you guys done?" Rudolph joined all four of us in the living room. "It's almost time to head out. Time is ticking Mr. Chase."

"Rudolph is right. We should get going."

"Just a minute, William." Jessica stepped into the room dressed in combat gear. "I'd like to thank you for everything, and I hope you'll find Marcus' mom."

"Thank you, Jessica. I'm the one who's thankful, and I believe I speak for everyone when I say the food was delicious."

"Yup! This was my first time having it, but I can't wait to have it again," Marcus told her all smiley.

"Honey, are you okay? I never had a chance to have a son biologically. Rudolph is the closest thing to a son I ever had, but I can tell you one thing, you are all your mom is thinking about. A mother may lie, hide, or try to pretend she doesn't care for her babies, but she does. There's not one hour that goes by that she's not thinking of you. Go get her, Marcus."

"Thanks, Jessica. It means a lot to me." Marcus hugged her fondly.

"Jessica where are you going dressed like that, girl?" Nari asked her, checking out her getup.

"After my man. I'm ready for my mission, are you guys ready for yours?"

"Yeah, let's go, but first-" Jonathan grabbed his helmet nearby and retook the center of the room. "I promised you backup, so let me call you back up."

Jonathan howled very loudly in the middle of the room, transitioning from a howl to a low growl; his brown eyes were bright white like stars again. He let out a short single bark, and as he did it, another "Jonathan" came from behind him in the same position the first Jonathan was. He barked again, and another "Jonathan" showed up on his opposite side. All three Jonathans howled one last time, as their eyes went from white to brown again.

"Alright, Jessica, Rudolph, two of us are going with you, while I," one of the Jonathans in the middle spoke, "I'm all yours, Mr. Chase. You're ready?"

"Let's do this," I told him.

We all stood side by side with each one of us touching the other's shoulders with one hand and the Exotic Matter Sphere with another.

"Uranus, here go!"

XIV

NOT SO FAST

It was daytime in Uranus when we manifested ourselves in the middle of an orange, tall grass field. We could see on the horizon, Uranus' faint rings and some of its moons.

"Whoa, I feel weird." Marcus stopped with both of his arms open wide as if trying to regain his balance.

"Uranus' poles are tilted sideways, a drastic change from Earth's and Neptune's poles," I explained to him. "Once you get your Halley Tattoo, you'll adapt quickly to new places when you teleport yourself to them."

"You guys don't feel anything at all?" Marcus looked around to see if anyone was somewhat imbalanced like him.

"Nope!" Jonathan told him, "But we should get going."

"Do you know where we're going?" I asked him.

"Yes, of course. We're going to the Nru Palace to see the King of Uranus."

"You mean Ben Cruise?" I asked him, surprised to hear about a King on Uranus.

"Listen, Willie, we—"

"William!" I corrected Jonathan.

"Right, William, if we are here looking for Ralphel L'Acuah, Porter of the Eridanus Constellation, then I suggest we'll talk to the King first. He should know where he is."

"What if he's working with Mario Shwayze?" Nari asked him.

"I don't think that's a possibility. I've never seen or heard Mario speak of him before," I told them, trying to remember if indeed Mario has ever spoken of Ben.

"I think we should see where he stands anyway, plus it—"

BEEP-BEEP

"That's weird."

"What's that on your wrist blinking, Jonathan," I pointed out to the weird device on his wrist.

"Shhhh, hold on," Jonathan pressed a button on his wrist, and a hologram of Mario popped up in the middle of the tall grass fields.

CARO SIGNORI[50] ASTERION, IT HAS COME TO MY ATTENTION THAT TWO OF MY PERSONAL BODY-GUARDS, MR. EZRA SIRIUS, AND MR. ISA-HUL BLAQ, WERE ARRESTED BY ONE OF YOUR DOGS AND I'M NOT HAPPY ABOUT IT. IT IS ALSO MY UNDERSTANDING THAT YOU'RE HELPING MR. MATHIAS AND HIS FRIENDS TO FIND HIS MOM. ALLORA[51], TO ME, NON-IMPORTA CAZZO[52] WHAT YOU'RE DOING WITH MARCUS. I DON'T CARE ABOUT THE KID. I JUST WANT HIM AND ALL OF YOU TO STAY OUT OF MY WAY, CAPISCI[53]? TELL MARCUS I ALREADY FED HIS HORSE SOME HAY. CIAO[54], FOR NOW

The hologram finished with Mario tossing a bunch of hay on Drayton, who was tied down with ropes.

"DRAYTON!" Marcus shouted at the sight of his boyfriend.

"Do you know him?" Jonathan asked him curiously.

"Yeah he's my... he's a... my—"

"He's Marcus' friend," I finished Marcus' sentence knowing that he would never be able to say the word

---

[50] *Caro Signori:* Dear Mister (Italian)

[51] *Allora:* Now (Italian)

[52] *Non importa cazzo:* I don't give a damn (Italian)

[53] *Capisci:* Understand (Italian)

[54] *Ciao:* Bye (Italian)

boyfriend out loud.

"Interesting, I thought you and he were 'friends'," Jonathan pointed out to Marcus and me, *non-importa*, like Mario said, let's get to it."

"Wait, wait, wait, wait." Marcus grabbed Jonathan's arm before he could take another step. "We're simply not gonna do anything about it? We're just gonna leave Drayton like that?"

"First off, I'm your friend and am here to help but do not touch me like that ever again, I'm still a law enforcement officer, and you will respect me as such." Jonathan removed his arm from Marcus' hold.

"Secondly, Drayton is tied up yes, but he is safe. Mario is waiting for William's time to be up, so once he's back in his cell, he can come after you himself. Lastly, do you honestly think it's a wise choice to teleport ourselves to the middle of that mansion that he calls castle and start a war without backup, Mr. Mathias?"

"No, but you can multiply yourself, can't you?"

"Surely as I'm here now talking to you, I'm also in various other places, including Jupiter, where Mario and the Queen resides. So, let's go get allies before we go to war."

Every single one of us stayed quiet throughout the way to the Palace, which didn't take more than a half-hour of walking among the tall orange grass. We stopped once a river came in touch with the field. In the horizon, we saw the beautiful icy-blue castle, which was not as tall as Angela's Pearl Castle on the Moon, but much broader in a square shape.

"How do we get all of us there?"

"Nari, baby, leave it to me. You guys rest for a minute, and I'll be right back." Elijah went on his way as the rest of us sat under a tree nearby.

"I'm gonna find us some berries. I think I see a bush over there of sweet berries." Nari went in the opposite direction.

"Nari, I'll join you. I can help you sniff out the poisonous ones." Jonathan went after her.

"You're okay?" I asked Marcus once he sat down next to me.

"I guess. I mean, Drayton and I are complicated, but still, the guy likes me in his own way, you know?"

"You can say that again," I laughed, joined in by Marcus' laugh as well.

"I know he and I are not going to live happily ever after, but we still have to save him, right?" Marcus got up to his feet and started pacing around.

"We will, once we find your mom, we'll go right after him. I promise you, okay?" I got up trying to calm Marcus down.

"Thank you for doing this. I'm really sorry I got you in this situation with the Queen."

"Thank me, once we are all safe, Marks."

"Hey, guys, what do you think?" E.J. was back again, holding a bunch of wood interlaced by rope to each other. "Do you think this raft is big enough for all of us?"

"If not, William can fly over," Marcus mocked me as he walked toward Elijah.

"Actually, even though you're joking, Mr. Mathias,

that's not a bad idea," I told them. "This way I can keep a bird's eye view while the four of you cross the river."

"Alright, so, guys, I didn't find any berries, only this stupid dog that keeps following me everywhere I go. Are you strayed?"

"To be strayed is to move away aimlessly from the right course. I know exactly where I am and where I'm going," Jonathan said gleefully.

"His cheerfulness is gonna kill me someday!" Nari said, approaching E.J., "What about you, babe, got what you're looking for?"

"Yeah, I built us a raft." He showed her the wooden raft.

"I adore you, know that? Now let's go," Nari said excitedly as we moved closer to the water.

"I'll see you on the other side." I took off, flying above the river looking for any sign of danger from land, air, or water.

Uranus is a magnificent place. Its baby-blue sky is just as beautiful as Earth's, if not more attractive, for its shade of blue had a light lavender nuance to it. Umbriel and Ariel, two of the twenty-something moons that orbit around the planet, were right above the Nru Castle, with the brightest and biggest moon Titania on the far right, surrounded by a couple of smaller moons. Down by the horizon was Oberon on a moonset. On the opposite side, near the Sun, was the waxing crescent smaller moon, Miranda, the moon where I once got my Stardust Tattoo.

Even though it was daytime, you could still see

the light silver spheres in the sky. I looked down at the river and saw Nari, Jonathan, and Marcus sitting down on the raft already on the river, and Elijah using his Bo staff like a paddle to take the raft across the river toward the castle.

I flew closer to the icy-blue castle to admire its architecture, but a scream from the river brought my attention back to the raft. A guy with silver-blue scales in place of skin was flying in and out of the water above the raft.

I was too far from them to send a sonic blast, so I flew as fast as I could, but the fish-looking guy was already attacking them. Elijah was using his Bo staff to hit him out of the raft with no luck. Marcus had no room to charge against him, and honestly, the guy was too fast and slippery for him to catch.

"Nari, get E.J. to the shore. Marcus, Jonathan, GO!" I shouted as I got closer to the raft. The silver-blue fish guy flew back up to meet me in the air before I could land on the raft.

He came straight for me without even blinking, and then I let him have it: "Heeeaaaahh," I let out a sonic blast knocking him back in the water.

"Is everybody okay?" I shouted at everyone still on the raft.

"Yeah, thanks to—" Before E.J. could finish his sentence, the flying fish guy had sprung from under the water smashing against the raft, sending every-one to the sea.

I flew toward him, but a wave rose in between him and me, with a woman on top of it, making the both of us stop mid-flight abruptly. She then rose her hands and started to sing a very melodic song, similar to that of an ambulance but subtle, sweet even, almost like a hum.

"Ooooh-ohhhh-ooooh-ohhhh-ooooh-ohhhh."

The woman had long wavy blonde hair worn out almost like a dress. Her breasts were bare, but the hair kept her modest. Her lips were bright-pink as was the makeup around the eyes, which were bright-white like stars just like all of ours were right now. Instantaneously, I felt nauseous, seasick even, losing my balance and falling from the sky along with the flying fish guy. Just before I hit the water, I saw her diving from the top of the wave down to the river, and I'm not sure if I saw things, but the woman had two silver-green fish-like tails instead of legs.

I woke up on land, with Marcus slightly slapping my face.

"Hey. I'm alright," I told him, getting myself back up in sitting position. "Please don't tell me this was our first kiss, and I was unconscious."

"Wait, what? I mean, you're—"

"Chill, Marcus, I'm just joking," I told him as I got myself fully up, and so did Marcus.

"Guys, he's awake!" Nari shouted once she saw me standing again.

"Welcome back, buddy," Jonathan waved from afar, talking to this woman, the same woman that was on top of the wave, still fully naked with only her hair covering her body.

"William, come here, I'd like you to meet our heroine," Elijah spoke as I approached them.

"Heroine? As far as I remember, she knocked me out too."

"Mr. William Chase, I'm Ghaeily Uhayves, Porter of the Siren Constellation." She extended out her hand, with her bright-green eyes now in place where her white stars-like eyes were. "It's an honor to meet you,"

"I'm sorry. Did I miss something?" I asked, confused.

"Allow me to explain. Noah Atlas, Porter of the Volans Constellation, the Flying-Fish attacked you. I came up to the shore to see if the threat would affect the underwater world population. I usually don't interfere with his business since he's pretty good on keeping the underwater world safe; however, when I spotted Elijah Jones, I knew I had to interfere. After all, he's a Vanisher like myself and a very honorable man."

"What was it that you did that made you so well recognized in the Vanisher community?" I asked E.J., surprised to know that every Vanisher we meet knows about him.

"He also told me why you're here, and I think King Cruise will be able to help you," she concluded as I looked at him, stunned by him trusting her with our mission.

"Don't blame him. I can be quite persuasive." She let out a big, wide, white smile.

"Isn't she pretty?" Jonathan spoke very enamored by her.

"Yeah, she is," Elijah replied to him, with the same enamored look.

"What happened to, what's his name, Noah?" I asked them, looking around for the flying-fish guy.

"Oh, he's gone. Flew, swam back to whatever he came from." Nari approached with Marcus. "She's so pretty."

"Even you, Nari? Please don't tell me you see her like that as well, Marcus?"

"Nope, I'm actually glad that I'm not the only one who's not enamored by her."

"I have that effect on people. People who are attracted to the female sex that is." Ghaeily passed between the two drooling men and stopped in front of Marcus and me. "Clearly, that does not affect you. That's refreshing."

"Well, it's not like I don't find you attractive, it's just that, I, well me, you know—"

"Everybody knows, Marcus. Are you ready to go see the King or not?" She asked the crowd.

"YES!" Nari, Elijah, and Jonathan shouted excitedly.

"Oh boy, how far are we from the Nru Castle?" I asked.

"William, don't be silly, the Castle is right behind you."

I looked behind me for the first time, noticing the beautiful icy-blue castle less than a mile away from us.

"Alright, we've come this far, let's do it!"

I started our journey heading up the trail be-tween two large purple trees with orange leaves, the green path that leads the way to the castle.

"What's that?" Marcus pointed to a red bird sit-ting on a branch nearby who, in turn, flew off, turned into a fish, and dove in the water.

"If only I knew," I told him, completely unsure of what we had just seen.

We got by the gates of the castle, where no one was there to be seen. I even wondered if this castle was the right castle.

"Alright, so there's no one here to greet or open the gates for us. How do we get in?" I asked Ghaeily as I looked around, trying to find someone there.

"I got this."

Nari squatted almost in a full sitting position with her nine fuzzy orange tails wiggling from side to side, just like a fox when ready to strike, and then in one jump she reached all the way up the gates, but an in-visible force field knocked her back down, almost un-conscious. Elijah caught her before she could hit the floor.

"You could've just sent a T.P. to our king, you know?" A woman came down the steps of the main doors wearing a green dress with sleek brunette hair all the way down her waist, wearing sandals. Her skin tone was similar to Marcus' skin, olive tone.

"I'm sorry to disturb you, we are here to see King Cruise," Ghaeily shouted from the other side of the gates.

"I know who you are. Mr. Atlas warned us about

your presence." She opened the gates.

"Warn you? I can guarantee you we mean no harm," I told her.

"Come, the king has agreed to see you." She gestured for us to step inside the gate.

As I stepped in through the gate, a tingling sensation went over my body from head to toes. I stopped and looked at Marcus, who seemed to have felt the same thing.

"Hey, what happened to my staff?" Elijah asked as he tried to manifest his Bo staff.

"My tails are gone too," Nari asked afflicted, looking for the first time like a real girl.

"Your powers won't work inside of the Nru Castle, thanks to me," she told us.

"What about your guns?" I asked Jonathan, who was still walking around in his full combat gear.

"These are very real. No powers needed to handle these babies." Jonathan displayed his guns with a big, proud smile.

"Your human weapons won't work on us anyway, Mr. Asterion." The woman guided us back through the main doors into a big vast open room adorned with six high columns.

"So, you've heard of me?" Jonathan asked her with a confident smile.

"Unlike your friends, your profile isn't quite low, especially since you're head of the C.V.O., Mr. Asterion,"

"Call me Jonathan, Miss?"

"Umma Troya, Porter of the Urna Constellation.

Aquarius' Urn," she introduced herself.

"A Vanisher like me," Elijah told her.

"You're a Vanisher?"

"Yeah, he's Elijah Jones, Porter of the Mallus Constellation, the Mast," Ghaeily injected surprise that she hasn't heard from him. "I'm Ghaeily Uhayves, the Siren, a Vanisher as well,"

"Impossible! I was told all the other Vanishers were extinguished," she looked at us in disbelief.

"Don't feel bad, I was only made aware of their existence not too long ago," I told her.

"There you are. I wonder what took you so long to bring them in." A man dressed in navy clothes with a long fury cape with black hair and eyes in a very light skin complexion walked in the room, followed by another man, with short, sleek blue hair in a light-orange shirt and pants, wearing no shoes. "Mr. Atlas was kind enough to warn me about your visit."

"Your Majesty," Umma Troya bowed as King Cruise walked in the room, as so did all the rest of us.

"Your Majesty, I can assure you we represent you no harm. On the contrary, we are here to ask for your help," I explained to him.

"I'll be the judge of that Mr. Chase," Ben Cruise gestured for us to get up again. "Now please, if you'll be so kind, tell me why shouldn't I send a Thought Projection right now to Queen Stars? After all, you're about to be trialed on the count of murdering the mother of Dogie over there, who honestly, if I may ask, what are you doing with your mother's mur-derer, Mr. Mathias?"

"I'm no Dogie, you—"

"MARCUS!" I shouted at Marcus, trying to control his anger.

"So, the rumors are true. You do have a temper problem, Mr. Natural. It will be quite handy in the Final War," he spoke loudly, seating on his throne in the middle of the vast room surrounded by empty armors.

"That's what we are here about," I began. "We were told that Ralphel L'Acuah, Porter of—"

"Eridanus? Are you looking for the ever-flowing river? Good luck with that! Mr. L'Acuah is always on the move just like the entrance of his river, now if you'll excuse me, I—"

"King Cruise, please, I need to find my mom. He's the only one who knows where she is," Marcus pleaded.

"Mr. Mathias, does the Queen know you're here? Does she know about the possibility of the woman that you sent William to jail for, and eventually get him tossed into Oblivion, is alive? Is this some sort of game you're playing? I suggest you leave the kingdom of Uranus altogether and let us, the adults, deal with his crime. I do not want to be associated with this. Now leave."

"But Ben—"

"I'M A KING!" Ben Cruise shouted at Marcus. "Ms. Troya, do what you do best and get these kids out of my sight!"

Ben Cruise flew, without any apparatus or wings, to the higher level of the overlooking balcony, as did

Noah Atlas, who used his fish-like wings to land next to his king.

Umma Troya raised both of her arms, and a gigantic wave surrounded us, leaving nowhere to go. We all instinctively tried to use our powers, but nothing came out. Jonathan got one of his guns and shot at her, missing by a couple of inches. Astounded by his action, Umma let her arms down, and so did the wave. The place filled up quickly with water, drowning us in a matter of seconds.

Ben Cruise was standing there unaffected by the water, as was Noah Atlas. Both of them looking down at us, watching us gasp for air, a feeling that as a Porter, we never had to worry about before. Umma Troya, who was still in the middle of the room, rotated one arm above her head, controlling the water in the same direction as her hand.

Then, with another gesture of hers, the floor underneath us opened into a hole, swallowing us all in just like a sinkhole. We tried to swim upwards to the surface to grasp some air without any success, except for Ghaeily Uhayves. Being the Porter of the Siren Constellation, she is naturally a good swimmer. Instead of swimming up to the surface to grasp some air, she swam straight into the sinkhole to everyone's surprise.

It didn't take long for us to be drained in it. The sinkhole led us to a tube, just like a water slide. If it weren't for the fact that we were all trying desperately to grasp for air every chance we got, it would have been a fun ride.

Without any warning, we got dropped out of the tube onto a river in the front of the Nru Castle, the same river where Noah attacked us not too long ago.

Once in the water, indistinctly, we all tried to swim back to the surface, but a rapid took hold of us unexpectedly, dragging us to the bottom of the river instead. Then, just before we could hit the bottom of the river, we fell right out of the water onto land, dry sand just like that on a beach.

"What just happened?" I looked around surprised, checking if everyone was okay.

"I happened!" We looked up and saw a terrifying thing: Ghaeily's head was floating midair with her body transformed back into a two-tailed siren in the water. "You're on the bottom of the river, the entrance to Eridanus River. I couldn't bring you here before because Noah was protecting it for Ralphel. With him back in the castle, I was able to guide you here."

"How are you doing this?" I asked, still amused by what we were all seeing.

"I'm not doing anything. Ralphel's power is to create flowing water, rivers if he likes. This is where my river ends and his begins. His river connects to my river, my home. If he is hiding anything, this is the place. The only dry place in this whole river," she explained to us, still swimming above us with only her head on our side of the bubble. "Now go before Noah returns."

"You're not coming with us?" Jonathan asked.

"I'm afraid not. If I'm not here when Noah is back, he might get suspicious. I'll distract him. Oh, and guys," she said just before leaving, "whatever you do, don't run into Ralphel. He can literally fill this whole place with water, drowning you for good. Even I wouldn't be able to save you in time."

"Thanks for the warning," I thanked her a bit weary before she swam away back up the river.

"Well, that was not even a bit scary," said Nari sarcastically.

"She's right though. So far, none of the Wonderers are on our side. It's good to assume that no else is. At least until we prove that Marcus' mom is well and alive, and my name is clean in front of the Queen's court."

"William is right. We shouldn't trust anyone else until we get this story resolved," Jonathan joined in. "Let's get going through before anyone finds us here."

"You know the weird part of this? If my mom is truly here, how is she able to breathe? To exist in a place outside of Earth is impossible for any Unportable." Marcus asked curiously as we made our way inside the cave in front of us.

"Stardust water," E.J. replied to him, "it's what we give to young Porters in training before they get their Stardust Tattoo. It allows them to have the power of their Constellation and practice it before they become real Porters, something you never had to go through since you have Stardust flowing in your body naturally."

"Guys, it's too dark in here, can't see much."

"I apologize, Elijah, I realize you're the only Porter here without heightened senses." Jonathan re-moved a flashlight from his utility belt, illuminating the whole cave.

The cave was mostly made out of corals and incandescent shells that seem to switch colors depending on the intensity of the light. The coral-co-lored sand made everything look like a magical place.

"So, this is an impasse," Nari mentioned after we reached a bifurcation.

"Not so much," Jonathan began, "Marcus and William go to the left, Nari and E.J. or Elijah, whatever you call yourself, take the right cave."

"What about you?" I asked him.

"I'm going with both of you, actually."

Jonathan put his two knuckles against each other, letting out two small, short barks, and two more Jona-thans appeared on either side of him, sporting the same black combat outfit with the C.V.O. logo on their right arms and a J. Asterion name tag on their left chest, wearing the same black biker helmet with a dog symbol in the back of it.

"What about the third 'you'," Marcus asked, con-fused just like the rest of us.

"The 'third me' or simply me, will be here keeping a lookout. If anyone comes this way, the other ones will know and so will you. Giving you time to teleport out of here." Jonathan stood there in guard between both caves, shutting down his visor.

"Alright, let's do this," I told them, as Nari, Elijah, and one of Jonathan's copies went with them to the right as Marcus, the other Jonathan copy, and I went to the left cave.

The cave was a bit narrower than before, barely allowing us to walk side by side. Jonathan had his flashlight out, still illuminating the way, even though all three of us have heightened senses just like those of the animals we bear the Constellations of. Then, without any warning, the narrow cave ended on an open dome, a bigger cave without the seashell's decorations. The sand from coral became dull-green as if made out of algae. The whole place suddenly had a gloomy vibe.

"What is this place?" Marcus asked, looking around.

"Hello? Is anyone out there?"

Marcus and I looked at each other, and he ran toward where the voice was coming from. A square hole in the wall on the opposite side of the dome we had just walked in.

"Mom? Is that you?" Marcus looked through the tiny hole, barely able to put his hand through.

"Marcus, son, is it really you?" She reached for his hand as Jonathan and I stayed right behind Marcus.

"Yes, Mom. It is really me." Marcus' tears fell out of his eyes bashfully.

"Oh, son, if you're here, that means you're a Porter too. I failed you. I let them take you in all of this madness. No, no, no!" Marcus' mom fell in despair, crying, and sobbing on the other side of the wall.

"Mom, no, don't cry. We're gonna get you out of here." Marcus stepped away from the cage, with his eyes bright-white like stars, his skin glistening with

Stardust. Without thinking, he punched a hole through the wall. He looked at his hands, looked at us, and before we could even say anything, Marcus was in his full bull form. "Mom, stay back, I'm breaking in."

"Marcus, wait," Jonathan warned him too late. Marcus had already charged against the wall, breaking a large hole through it, allowing himself inside his mother's jail.

"Mom! Mom, I'm here, okay? Everything is going to be okay. I'm gonna take you home." Marcus was kneeling by his mom, who was on the floor completely covered in dust and rumbles from the impact.

"You could've killed her," Jonathan said as the two of us helped Marcus carry out his mom.

"Or, I don't know, made enough noise to attract us here," a female voice spoke behind us from the same and only way in and out of this dome. "Look, aniki[55], is Marcus and his boyfriend,"

"And the C.V.O." Jonathan grabbed out his shotgun and started shooting at the Gemini Twins, who dispersed quickly on either side, stopping right in front of us, punching Jonathan right on the face.

"Bad doggie," Lynne told him, once he was on his knees, after her brother's punch, "and you're not going anywhere." Lynne grabbed Marcus' mom out of his arms, swiftly throwing her back in her cell.

"Leave her alone!" Marcus shouted at her.

"Listen, Dogie, I understand you may see this as us being the bad guys, but truly we are the good guys.

---

[55] *Aneki:* Sis (Japanese)

She has not been a good mother to you," Lee, Lynne's brother joined in the conversation, "now, Mr. Natural, let's take you to the king where he can show you that what we're saying is true."

"NEVER!" Marcus stomped on the floor, and the whole cave shook, making the twins drop their hold. "William!"

"I got this." Marcus already had his hand on his ears as well as his mom's. I let out a high sonic screech, knocking the Gemini Twins against the wall.

"Damn, Willie, you cracked my visor." Jonathan got himself up, tossing out his helmet.

"Jonathan I'm sorry about your helmet, now let's go before they get up."

"Or her." Marcus' mom was passed out on the floor, unconscious. "I guess your screech got to her too. How come the three of us are still standing?"

"That's simple, Marcus. My clothes and my weapons are infused with Stardust, making it pretty much Porter-proof, except for my visor, which is purely made of glass. You, however, are standing up simply because Porters' powers are harmless to those who they love," Jonathan explained very casually to Marcus, trying to revive his mom.

"She's not waking up, so..." Jonathan threw Marcus' mom above his shoulders as if he was wearing her like a scarf.

"Let's go." He rushed out of the door as if not carrying a one-hundred-and-eighty-pound woman around his shoulders. But before Jonathan got to the door, he let out a scream and fell backward as if knocked out by an invisible foe.

"What happened?" Marcus asked, looking around to see if the Gemini Twins were up and running, but they were still unconscious against the muddy wall of the cave.

"It's Jonathan. He's killed." Jonathan let out a sigh of pain.

"What do you mean, you're killed? What happened?" I asked him, helping him up to his feet.

"Not me, one of my copies. When one of us dies, all the other ones feel it, too," he explained it to us.

"Wait, a copy? But I thought you were the copy."

"Marcus," he stopped groaning in pain for a second, "we've been alive and duplicating ourselves for so long that we no longer know who's the original and who's the copy."

"Did you see who killed you?"

"No. It hit me faster than I could have seen, even smell them, William."

"Them? You think it was more than one?"

"Two, to be precise." Lynne and Leen Yang, the Gemini Twins, were in the entrance of the cave. "Shouldn't have sent copies to do an original's job, sister, a problem you can understand, Mr. Asterion." Suddenly Lee and Lynne's copies, who were still knocked out on the floor, dissolved into Stardust.

"I hate you two so much." Marcus went charging against them, but Lynne moved in the speed of thought, and in a blink of an eye was standing right next to Marcus' mom.

"One more step, Natural, and bye-bye, mommy.

This time you'll truly become a Dogie,"

"I'm still not dead, you know?" Jonathan pulled out his gun and pointed at Lynne's direction.

"Even *SWISH* the *SWISH* mighty *SWISH* C. *SWISH* V. *SWISH* O. *SWISH* isn't *SWISH* fast *SWISH* enough *SWISH* to stop us." With every word spoken, Lee Yang had pushed Marcus, Jonathan, and I against the wall, tying us against each other before he could even finish his sentence, giving us no time to react, pointing Jonathan's gun to my face. "Not one sound, otherwise, bye-bye, birdie."

"You guys talk to effing much." Nari appeared in her half-woman, half-fox self with her pointy orange ears and nine tails waving side to side, kicking Lynne against the wall. "Babe?"

"Say no more." Elijah, who came in through the entrance, knocked Lee with his Bo staff against his head, making him fall unconscious as well.

"It's good to see you got this with me." Jonathan walked in the cave toward the other Jonathan. "Hey."

"It's been a long time since we have felt one of us dying, huh, brother?" They embraced each other in a hug that was both painful and sad to see. A pain that only them two were capable of feeling, completely alien to us. "We should get going before Ralphel L'Acuah shows up and sinks us all."

"One quick thing, though, your mom was not the only one buried here," Nari told us.

"How do you mean?" Marcus asked her.

"This is the backside of the jail where Vanishers are being held," Elijah added.

"The other side of the bifurcation is the front side of this jail. This dome is the back of it," Jonathan explained. "I'm gonna go the other way to open the locked gates while you get Marcus' mom out of here before they wake up. Just teleport to the surface."

"Jonah, see you in a few." Both Jonathans shook their hands before one of them leave the room. "Here, keep my helmet. I'll move faster as a dog anyway,"

"Alright." Jonathan put on his helmet. "Let's go, Porters,"

"This time, I'll take my mom." Marcus passed in front of us and lifted up his mom, who was coming back to her senses.

"Not so fast."

A strong, loud, deep voice of a man echoed the whole place coming from the top of the dome above us. A man wearing nothing but a surfer short, carried by a wave, was right above us.

"I'm Ralphel L'Acuah, Porter of the Eridanus Constellation, the River, and you're not going any-where!"

XV

VANISHED

Ralphel L'Acuah waved his hand before any of us could react. A wave poured from the top of the dome all the way down, filling the place with water quickly. And just as quickly as he appeared, Ralphel was gone with only a trace of Stardust in the air.

"Guys, we must get out of here," Elijah started panicking as the water began covering his feet.

"We can't yet," Marcus' mom spoke, coming back to her senses before any of us could teleport out of there in our Exotic Matter Spheres. "What about the other Vanishers locked in here?"

"She is right," Nari began, "we can't just leave them here to die."

"Then, we move fast. Everybody, stay stellar, and let's get these people out of here. Jonathan, lead the way," I told them.

"Marcus can you break a hole through your mother's cell? If my calculations are right, we should meet my other half on the other side of this wall."

"All you gotta do is ask, Jonathan." Marcus charged through the hole he had made not long ago to free his mom, back in the cell, running straight through the back wall, opening another hole big enough for all of us to get through.

"Oh hey, Marks!" Jonathan, sans helmet, greeted Marcus on the other side of the wall through the hole Marcus had just made.

"Hey, Jonathan."

"Hey!" Both Jonathans replied at the same time.

"Alright, to avoid any confusion, Jonathan with the helmet is Jonah, Jonathan without the helmet is Jonathan, okay?" Marcus imposed in a perplexed and demanding way.

"Fine by me." They both replied simultaneously again.

"Alright, Porters, let's go! The water is only getting higher." I made my way right after Marcus, with the water already by our knees.

Once all of us got through the whole Marcus had just made, we saw a hallway with jail cells on either side going in both directions.

"Is there a Vanisher is every single cell?" I asked Jonathan.

"My friends and I already freed half of the cells behind us, and now we only need to free these cells in front of us," Jonathan answered.

"What friends?" I asked him.

"Them," Jonah and Jonathan pointed to the other two Jonathans running toward us.

"Hey, guys!" They greeted us in unison.

"Marcus, to avoid confusion, you can call me J," the one on the left spoke.

"And me, J.J.," The other one on the right told him.

"Great! More Jonathans," Marcus spoke sarcastically.

"The more, the merrier," Nari joined Marcus in the sarcastic tone.

"I actually think it's a great idea," I interrupted them approving of the extra Jonathans. "We can use all the help we can get."

"We still don't have time to break through all the cells," Elijah pointed out to me.

"I can help," a voice coming from one of the cells next to us, shouted.

"How can you help?" I walked over to the cell where the voice was coming from.

"My name's Douglas Martin, Porter of the Hippocampus Constellation, the Sea-Horse," the twenty-something-year-old guy introduced himself. "Just release one of your sonic booms against the lock, that should do it."

"Step back." I leaned over the lock, held it with my hand, and let out a short sonic boom, and the lock dissolved in my hand just like sand. "How did you know that?"

"I've heard of your powers, Mr. Chase, and because of my powers, I can smell the materials used to build this place and everything around us, as long as the water touches it," he explained, stepping out of jail.

"That was cool and all, but we still don't have time to break every single lock, the water is already by our waist," Marcus told us.

"True, Mr. Natural, however, I did say I can help, so let me do what I do."

Douglas dove in the water, transforming himself fully into a sea-horse in the size of a large horse on

Earth. He swam fast up the water stream and disappeared out of view.

"Did he just run away?" Elijah asked, not believing what he just saw.

"Wait for it," J.J. spoke.

"Look!" Nari pointed out to the water where we could see the orange-green sea-horse making its way back to us.

"I told them to immerse underwater while you release a sonic blast," Douglas explained, emerging out of the water in his olive skin body with his bright-green eyes under his shoulder-length black hair.

"Will it work?" I asked him, afraid that my blast would knock everyone unconscious.

"The water should absorb most of the impact, making them feel just a small wave impact on the water, as long as they stay underwater."

"Are they ready?" I asked him.

"They are Porters. They don't need to breathe, but just like us, if they stay too long underwater, they'll lose their powers and fade away into Stardust, so I'd say yes, they're ready," He explained.

"Everybody down," I shouted just to make sure that everyone around me could get cover, including those down the corridor.

BOOOOM

I let out a loud, deep, sonic blast, destroying every single jail lock into dust.

"That was pretty awesome!" Marcus spoke right behind me.

"You were supposed to be underwater. I could have knocked you out unconscious," I reprimanded him.

"No, you couldn't," Marcus said proudly as the other ones emerged out of the water.

"We will talk about this later, Mr. Natural. Now

let's get these people out of here."

"Wait a minute, is that?" E.J. began as he saw this woman stepping out of one of the cells, "Captain Lance?" He shouted at her.

"Mr. Jones, is that you?" They both ran toward each other. "I can't believe this, you're alive!"

"And so are you!" He smiled at her.

"Errrrr," Nari was right behind him with a some-what jealous face of the long, brunette-haired woman.

"Oh, this is my girlfriend, Nari Anser, Porter of the Vulpecula Constellation, the Fox." Elijah introduced his girl to the Captain.

"You did well. You're a lucky fella, for I would have dated her myself if I wasn't already taken." She smiled at Nari, who blushed by the sound of her com-pliment. "I'm Deena Lance, Porter of the Caenus Constellation, the Captain of the Argo Navis Constel-lation,"

"There you are, babe." A blonde woman hugged Captain Lance from behind. "Sorry to interrupt, I ha-ven't seen this woman in years." They shared a kiss.

"I'm Tara Whirls, Porter of the Tarabellum Cons-tellation, the Drill, and I'm gonna get us out of here. LET'S GO!"

"Hold on. We need some help once we're out in the ocean," Captain Lance told us. "Jonathan, haven't seen you in a while, how are you?"

"I'm good, Cap. How can I be of service?" Jonah offered.

"Teleport me to the surface. I'll have a ship wait-ing for you all once you are all out of here," she asked him. "Honey, get these people and the rest of the Vanishers out of here up through the large dome, I'll be waiting for you on the surface."

"I'll see you in a few." Captain Lance and Tara shared one last kiss before Jonah teleported her out of there.

"Alright, Porters THIS WAY!" She shouted to all the remaining Vanishers so they could follow us back inside the dome.

At this point, all of us had to swim through the hole Marcus had made. It didn't take long for us and about fifteen of the Vanishers to get inside the dome.

"I need to get out of the water and against the wall," she told us once all of us were in the large, domed room.

"I can get you there, Ms. Whirls," I told her.

"Just call me Tara, we are way past the formalities, Mr.?"

"Chase, William Chase," I introduced myself. "Hold on."

I flew out of the water and grabbed her with both hands flying all the way up the dome.

"Not so high, I need to be just a few feet above the water so the other Porters can climb through," she instructed me as I flew her down closer to the water. "William, throw me against the wall."

"Excuse me?" I asked her, not sure if I heard her right.

"I need you to throw me against the wall so that I can drill us a hole through. If you don't, I'll hurt you in the process. Now THROW ME!" She demanded.

"Alright, it's your funeral." I swung her back and forth, throwing her against the wall.

She dove out of my arms into the wall, and just before hitting the wall, her whole body became some type of metal, with large razor blades all around it, spinning faster than I have ever seen someone do, making a tunnel through the wall.

"Willam, get everybody up through the hole and quick, before the water covers it, I'm gonna dig us out of here," Tara shouted before throwing herself back in the hole.

"Alright guys, you heard the lady," I shouted at the floating Porters. "If you can fly or get to the hole without any assistance, go now, the rest of you put your arms up, and I'll take you to it."

Some of the Vanishers flew through, and some of them climbed the wall into the tunnel made by Tara. It didn't take long enough for Jonathan, J.J., J., Nari, E.J., Marcus, his mom, and me left to go through.

"Alright Jonah, J.J. and J, you're up. Let's go. I told them."

"Actually, I'm Jonathan, Jonah left with the Captain," one of them replied.

"Doesn't matter, you're all the same person. Now go," Nari shouted at them.

"Geesh," they told her as they all jumped through the hole.

"Alright Nari, Elijah, you guys are next."

Nari grabbed E.J. and jumped out of the water and cannoned through the hole.

"The Mathiases come with me." I grabbed both Marcus and his mom and put them through the hole, going through myself. At this point, the water was already making its way toward the hole Tara drilled.

"I NEED EVERYONE TO MOVE FAST! GO! GO! GO!" Tara shouted through the hole, breaking her way through the crowd toward us.

"Hey, momma, I need you to do your thing for us, okay? We won't make it up there in time if the water keeps following us," Tara told Marcus' mom, who looked at us ashamedly.

"What is she talking about, Mom?" Marcus asked her, surprised to know that his mom was hiding a secret.

"You'll see. Now let's get out of this water and fast," she told him, pushing all of us forward.

"Mom, what you're doing?" Marcus asked his mom, but with no answer, instead, she went the opposite way, back to where the water was coming from. "MOM?"

She didn't look back; instead, she leaned over the water, barely touching it, turning the stream into stone. She got up again and walked toward us, passing through Marcus and me, avoiding eye contact.

"How did you do that?" Marcus pushed me out of his way. "HOW DID YOU DO THAT?" He grabbed her by the arms with his body translucent in Stardust.

"Marcus, I'm not proud of it, please not now, let's just get out of—"

"You're not her," he began. "You're NOT MY MOTHER!" Marcus shoved her against the wall completely towering over here with his skin turned fully in white fur, his horns sprouted up, just like he once did with Camille Liam in the cave I had her imprisoned.

"Did you ever get to remove the blood from the kitchen walls?" She said, barely making eye contact with her son.

"What?" Marcus stared at his mom, uncertain of what he heard.

"The fake blood that spilled out of the zombie cake for your sixteenth birthday." She now stared at him with a half-smile on her face. "Did you ever clean the blood off the kitchen walls as I told you to?"

"Mom?" He let go of his grip, letting his mom fall to her knees. "But how?"

"It's a long story that I'll happily tell you over a fresh batch of white chocolate chip, macadamia nut cookies." She smiled at him.

"Mom, I'm sorry." Marcus bent over, aiding his mom back up again. "let's get out of here."

"INCOMING!" One of the Jonathans shouted as a river of water flowed down at us, completely immersing us underwater instantaneously.

All the Porters used whatever tool they had to swim up out of the tunnel. As Porters, we can't really die, even without oxygen. However, the continued use of Stardust will tire us, eventually turning us back into humans and causing us death. At least till next Halley.

I swam back as fast as I could upstream. I could see already the end of the tunnel leading into the open sea, and just as I was losing my strength, a riptide propelled me forward, rapidly reaching the end of the tunnel along with the rest of the Porters, into an air dome.

"Are you okay?" Ghaeily Uhayves, the Siren, asked inside of the air dome, well at least her head while the rest of her two-tailed mermaid body was still swimming outside of the air dome.

"Yeah, thanks. Where's everyone?" I asked, looking around for the rest of the Porters.

"I already got most of them out with the help of the nautical Porters like myself, who have some advantage in the water field," she explained it.

"William," Marcus' mom, who was also in the air dome with me, spoke, "let's get out of here before he returns."

"He who?" Before either one of them could reply, Ralphel L'Acuah, swimming faster than anyone I have ever seen, grabbed Ghaeily from behind in a chokehold, making the air dome around us dissolve, putting us back in the open water.

Marcus' mom grabbed my hand, gesturing us to swim upward to the surface. I let go of her, gesturing that we should go back and help, but instead, she shook her head and swam away.

I swam toward Ralphel, who was still holding a struggling Ghaeily trying to free herself of his choke-hold without any success. Just then, I saw an orange-green tail wrapping itself around Ralphel's neck, letting Ghaeily sink unconscious underwater.

As fast as I could swim, I grabbed hold of her. Another riptide came my way, almost knocking me unconscious. I looked up and saw Ralphel and the sea-horse Douglas struggling in a fight.

Ralphel got a hold of Douglas, who still hadn't unwrapped his tail from Ralphel's neck. Douglas was struggling but was still holding on. Then, just as they had appeared in the murky water, a crab, as big as Ralphel himself, grabbed Ralphel's arms with its pin-cers, wrapping his other six crab legs around him, making impossible for Ralphel to free himself.

'Help...me...', he sent me a painful Thought Projec-tion, but it was too late. The crab pulled his two arms apart, breaking Ralphel in half, leaving nothing but Stardust where he once was.

"No!" I said it to myself as my body sank down to the ocean, where Ghaeily has sunk as well.

***

I woke up coughing up the water out of my lungs, regaining my consciousness with Marcus towering over me.

"Hey, Willie, are you alright?"

"Please don't tell me you had to mouth-to-mouth me back to life again, did ya?" I brought myself up, sit-ting on the orange tall grass field.

"No..., I..., we..., uhm, I got worried and..."

"Marcus, thank you." I stared at Marcus, who had his skin flushed in embarrassment.

"William, you're awake!" Elijah stretched out his hand, helping me up. "We need to talk."

"What's going on?"

"The Vanishers. Did they kill Ralphel L'Acuah?" He asked as low as he could.

"Yes, they did. May he find peace among the stars," I answered him, remembering the heartbreaking scene that I had just witnessed under the water.

"Wait, you actually saw them killing Ralphel L'Acuah?" E.J. asked me, surprised.

"I saw the large, blue-silver crab ripping him open. Porter of the Cancer Minor Constellation, if I'm not mistaken."

"Shhhh, keep your voice down," E.J. hushed me, "no one, but you witnessed Zhuir Pierns kill him. You sure about it?"

"I never saw the Porter behind it, just the full crab version of the Porter's Constellation, and as far as I know, the only blue-silver crab Vanisher out there is Zhuir Pierns."

"True, unless was Camille Liam again, Porter of the Chameleon Constellation." Marcus joined in.

"Unlikely; Camille can transform herself into any person she comes in contact with, but I doubt she would have their powers to the fullest. Even she has limitations." I explained to him.

"What do you mean no one witnessed it? Ghaeily was there, so was, what's his name? The sea-horse guy?"

"Douglas?"

"Yeah, Douglas. He was strangling Ralphel with his tail, but it wasn't long till Ralphel himself got a hold of him, and that's when the blue silver-crab appeared, and pretty quickly got a hold of Ralphel's arms, pulling them apart with its pincers, sending him to the stars." I told them.

"A lot of us saw the Stardust on the surface, but no one is talking about it. Once Ghaeily brought you to the surface, she disappeared into the water again. Killing another Porter is an Intergalactic crime resulting in incarceration," Elijah explained, "but once the annihilated Porter is back, the murderer is set free again."

"That's a fair law," Marcus spoke sarcastically.

"It is actually. Unless the Porter murders an Unportable, then he's tossed into Oblivion. The same destiny I'll meet unless we bring your mom in front of the Queen to prove my innocence," I told them, "which that reminds me, where is everybody?"

"Everyone who's not a Vanisher has been teleporting the Vanishers back to their home planet, except for Marcus, who decided to stay here with you, and I, of course, am not going anywhere till my Nari is back," Elijah explained.

"What about your mom?" I asked Marcus, looking around for Mrs. Mathias.

"She's here. She's been talking to the other. Vanishers." Marcus looked behind him, where we could see his mom talking to Jonathan and a couple of Vanishers who were still here.

"Have you two talked?"

"Not yet. She's busy with them still, and I was busy helping you back to life." Marcus took a few steps away, in the opposite direction of where his mom was.

"I'll give you two some privacy." Elijah went to meet up with Katherine, Jonathan, and the other Vanishers.

Marcus was leaning against a purple tree with orange leaves, giving him some shade under the hot summer weather of Uranus. Facing a river connecting the ocean we were both in not long ago, before the Porter of the Eridanus Constellation, Ralphel L'Acuah tried to kill us but instead got murdered by Zhuir Pierns, Porter of the Minor Cancer Constellation, a Vanisher.

"Hey, are you alright?" I asked him, leaning against the tree trunk next to him.

"Yeah, I guess," he stepped closer to the river in front of us, facing out in the horizon where we could still see the Nru Castle.

"Marcus, you and I both know you're not a good liar," I said, following him, "what's bugging you?"

"My mom." He turned around, facing me with his eyes shifting colors between their natural shade of green and to bright-white like stars. "At first, I thought she was just working. Then she just appeared out of thin air in our kitchen with her hair bleached, which I thought was only a new hairstyle, but then you came over and killed her. I grieved her, I angered you, damn, I was enraged by you. I met Drayton, Porter of the Pegasus Constellation, the Winged-Horse, who, besides being a compulsive liar, helped me control my powers so I could avenge my mother and kill you. Drayton didn't understand it, but either way, he stood by me. He believed in me and, unexpectedly, he became more than just a friend. When we went back to Earth, two years had passed by, but to me, it had only been a couple of days. Everyone was older, and so was I. Then you, William Chase, Porter of the Lyra Constellation, the Lyre, came back again, kidnapping me to Pluto."

"Charon, actually," I corrected him.

"Yeah, Charon, Pluto's moon," he remembered,

"where my mom was in chains in a cave. It didn't take much for me to figure out that the woman in front of me was an impostor. Just like the woman in the kitchen, she had her hair bleached blonde, but that wasn't my mom even though she looked and sounded just like her. She truly was an impostor, the Porter of the Chameleon Constellation, Camille Liam."

"Yes, what I've been trying to tell you. I would have never hurt your mother, Marks."

"I know, yet I still hated you. I thought you were playing mind games with me, so just I could forgive you and move on, but instead, I betrayed you. I sent a Thought Projection to the Queen of the Solar System Mariah Stars, who came and arrested you. And in less than a few Jupiter hours, she's gonna toss you into Oblivion unless we can prove your innocence."

"And now we can. You trusted me, and I was able to prove to you that your mother is alive. All we have to do is bring her back to court with us so the Queen can see she's alive. And the person that I've supposedly killed is, in fact, Camille Liam. Who's well and alive, out and about in our Solar System working for Mario Shwayze, Porter of the Orion Constellation, the Hunter," I concluded.

"Who has my so-called boyfriend locked in a stable." Marcus now faced his mom again with his back to the river. "And now, my real mom is right there with her natural unbleached brown hair, talking to your ex, Elijah Jones, Porter of the Malus Constellation, the Mast of Argo Navis. He's a great guy, you know? A great fighter."

"You haven't seen anything at all. He is an incredible fighter." E.J. was there talking to Marcus' mom and as weird as it should be, it wasn't. Elijah and I are just good friends. However, it's clear to see Marcus was feeling lonely in all of this.

"Have you talked to Drayton?"

Marcus briefly faced me again in a sort of defeated look and out to the horizon again, letting out a long sigh.

"Every chance I get," he began shyly. "He's fine, plotting against Mario, trying to find a way to get out of there. I told him we'd be on our way soon, right after your audience with the Queen."

"We will. Once I'm free out of this bracelet, out of the control of the Triangulum Australis' Porter, Mr. Namu Detcha, you, and I personally will ask for the Queen's help to free Drayton. We'll get your life back, Marks," I assured him.

"Is it true that your powers don't affect me because you love me?"

I could reply, I was going to, but Marcus stepped away from me.

"It doesn't matter," he continued, "is not like you and I can ever be, right? Why do I feel so confused? Hurt? I should be happy. We found my mom, who is a Porter like us. Is she a Wonderer? A Wanderer? A Vanisher? I don't know where to go from here. Can't we just go back to the way things were? We are too far gone into this."

"Marcus, do you trust me?" I grabbed Marcus closer to me. "Do you believe me?"

"William, I stopped believing in Santa Claus and Rudolph the Red-Nosed Reindeer when I was seven, only to be proven wrong eleven years later." He laughed, remembering Nicholas Klauss, Porter of the Auriga Constellation, the Charioteer, and Rudolph Skye, Porter of the Tarandus Constellation, the Reindeer.

"They are real, alright," I joined him in laughter.

"Let's go home, let's enjoy the last few hours we have before tomorrow's trial and take it step by step, day by day. You don't have to decide anything right now. You still have time to figure things out."

"You're right. I'm only eighteen. I do have time." He said, smiling again, walking in the direction of his mom.

"Actually, Marcus," I interceded before he could walk further, "you're almost twenty now."

"WHAT?"

"Time on Neptune and Uranus runs differently than on Earth. Remember our little conversation on Charon before bringing you to your 'mom'?" I reminded him.

"You know what? I'm not even mad. I'm not gonna worry about it." He shrugged his shoulders. "Time is pretty much nonexistent for us, Porters, right?"

"That's the spirit." I joined him, walking toward his mom. "Step by step."

"Day by day," he beamed a big smile.

"Marcus, honey, perfect timing, we need to talk." Marcus' mom met us halfway, along with Elijah, Jonathan, and two other Vanishers. "We were not the only ones locked in a jail."

"Apparently, Vanishers have been locked in jails all over our Solar System by Wanderers and Wonderers alike that feel it is their duty to lock'em up," Jonathan explained.

"What do you mean?"

"There have been rumors about Porters going rogue on their own, kidnapping Vanishers all over, but we never had any proof. At least not until now." One of the Vanishers spoke.

"I'm sorry, I don't think we have met before," Marcus interjected.

308

"My apologies, I'm Dorotheia Sonny, but you can call me Dot, I'm Porter of the Solarium Constellation, the Sundial," a brown-skinned woman in her thirties dressed in rags introduced herself to us.

"Theodore Hershey, Porter of the Telescopium Herchelii Constellation, the Reflective Telescope." The other Vanisher, a white man in his forties, stretched out his hand to Marcus, introduced himself, "we are quite aware of who you are, it was a mistake to think you'd know us, young Natural."

"I'm still getting used to all of this. It wasn't long ago that I was made aware of Vanishers and their past as Formers," Marcus explained himself.

"Don't be too harsh on yourself; we wanted to keep our existence hidden from everyone to avoid exactly what's happening right now," Theodore explained.

"Exactly, but now that we are out in the open again, we can find the others. Every single one of them," Dot complemented.

"How so? If you're thinking of Jessica, she—"

"She's not the only one capable of finding Porters, Mr. Chase," Theodore interrupted me, "with the Vanishers gone; other Porters were created for different purposes, their power was... upgraded if you will."

"I think I have an idea of who you're talking about," I told them.

"When Deena Lance asked me to teleport her out of the cave we were all in, we went to look for someone who can help us find anyone she knows, so we left to find her."

"Well, did you find her?" Marcus, being his impatient self, asked him.

"We did. And here we come, just in time," Jonathan walked through us and right in front of him, a few feet away, appeared out of their Exotic Matter

Sphere two Jonathans with Captain Lance and Tara Whirls followed by four other Porters. "Mr. Mathias, I'd like you to meet the Nautical Ark, Argo Navis."

XVI

M r. Mathias, as you know by now, my name is Deena Lance, Captain of the Argo Navis Cons-tellation, the Nautical Ark. When I heard Elijah Jones in that subterranean jail, my hopes of reconnecting with my ship grew alive in me again, for you see, E.J. is the Mast of the Argo Navis. I set out to find the rest of my ship and, thanks to you, here they are. And with their help, we'll be able to find all the Vanishers throughout the Solar System. Please allow them to in-troduce themselves."

"I'm Karina Dumont, Porter of the Carina Constel-lation, the Keel of Argo Navis," the olive-skinned woman to the right of Captain Lance spoke, wearing a brown pirate hat similar to the one Captain Lance was wearing, but a bit smaller.

"Oliver Ways here, Porter of the Puppis Constellation, the Stern of Argo Navis," the black guy with a shaved head and short beard, also dressed in pirate's clothing, introduced himself.

"Guy Paris, Porter of the Vela Constellation, the Sails of Argo Navis," the white man with black, long, sleek hair wearing some sort of a black bandana around his neck, to the left of Captain Lance, spoke.

"And I'm Lucy Wacher, Porter of the Pyxis Constellation, the Compass," the blonde-haired girl wearing a goggles device introduced herself. Unlike the rest of the crew, she was not wearing pirates' clothes. Instead, she was wearing a knee-length skirt, short brown boots, and a white embroidered blouse with her hair up in pigtails.

"I'm Elijah Jones, Porter of the Malus Constellation, the Mast of Argo Navis, but you all already knew this," E.J. introduced himself, hugging his friends with a big smile on his face. "What's up guys, I've missed you."

"We thought you were dead," Karina told him, "and by default, we would never be able to sail again,"

"As you can see, I'm very much alive." They all joined in the laughter.

"And just so everybody is on the same boat," Jonathan spoke loudly through the laughter, "I'm Jonathan Asterion, Porter of the Canes Venatici, the Hunting Dogs, also known as the Canes Venatici Organization. C.V.O., for short," all three Jonathans spoke, each one of them finishing the others' sentence introducing themselves.

"Since we are doing introductions, I'm William Chase, Porter of Lyra Constellation, the Lyre."

"I'm Marcus Mathias, Natural Porter of the Taurus Constellation, the Bull." Marcus introduced himself after me, through murmurs of the crowd by the sound of the word Natural. "And this is my mom..."

Marcus and everyone else looked at his mom, who was standing there petrified, motionless.

"Hi, my name's Katherine Mathias, Porter of the Caput Medusae Constellation, the Medusa's Head," she introduced herself, causing Marcus to gasp in disbelief that his mom was indeed a Porter as well. Not only Marcus, but everyone else gasped and, besides the sound of the ocean around us, not one other Porter made a sound.

"You're Porter of the Caput Medusae, Mrs. Mathias?" One of the Jonathans spoke as all three of them stared at her.

"..."

Mrs. Mathias didn't speak a word. She just looked at Jonathan somewhat, still ashamed of herself.

"I'm Dorotheia Sonny, Porter of the Solarium Constellation, the Sundial," Dot introduced herself, breaking the awkward icy air.

"Theodore Hershey, Porter of the Telescopium Herchelii Constellation, the Reflective Telescope,"

"Less but not least, I'm Tara Whirls, Porter of the Tarabellum Constellation, the Drill, and wife of the most beautiful Captain in all the seas across the Solar System."

Everyone joined in laughter and cheers as the two of them shared a short, passionate kiss except for Marcus, who was still looking at his mom curiously.

"Hey, guys!" Nari appeared out of her Exotic Matter Sphere next to us. "Wow, who are all these people?"

"Guys, this is my girlfriend, Nari Anser,"

"Hi, everyone. I'm Porter of the Vulpecula Constellation, the Fox," Nari introduced herself to the group, as everyone waved hi back at her, "And who might you all be?"

"No, no. No more introductions. I'll tell her everything she needs to know about you, guys," Elijah told her, among people's laughter.

"Alright, now that we know each other, how do we go at this?" Jonathan asked the large group of Porters.

"I can help," a man a bit taller than me, with his jet-black hair covering his bright-white eyes, wearing black from head to toes, appeared out of nowhere to everyone's surprise. Especially Marcus'.

"You must have lost your mind appearing here after what you did to me and my mom," Marcus shouted at Lee Yang, Porter of the Gemini Constellation, Wonderer of Mercury.

"Maybe. I just lost someone I love," Lee's voice was cracking in a mix of anger and pain, "King Shawyze killed my sister right in front of my eyes. Yes, he did kill you, *Aneki*.[56]"

---

[56] *Aneki:* Sis (Japanese)

Lee seemed to have been speaking to us as well as someone else next to him that none of us could see.

"She'll be back next Halley," I reminded him.

"No, she won't. You don't understand. She's dead! Dead for real. Dead. I saw her body turning ice cold in front of me. The most terrifying thing ever. I'm sorry, Sis. I should've protected you. I should've stopped him, somehow. But he was too fast. I didn't think it was possible to murder one of our kind. But he found a way. He somehow found a way to kill us."

Lee was having a conversation with us, and with someone else that wasn't there. He'd switch his gaze back and forth to us and to a particular empty location next to him. His movements were fast and slow at the same time, and Mario was having difficulties controlling his actions. His words, his eyes were flickering back and forth between their natural shade of black to bright-white like stars as if he was having a glitch.

"What do you mean, he found a way? Porters can't be killed. Unless..." Jonathan stopped mid-sentence.

"Unless what?" Marcus asked him.

"Unless he found a way to expel the Stardust out of our bodies, but that's impossible," Jonathan explained, "not even Marvin could suck all of our Stardust out of the bloodstream."

"Apparently not anymore. I saw it with my two Wonderer eyes. I told you, they were not going to believe us, *Aneki*, not after what we did with Katherine Mathias. If only I, we, could apologize to her, oh wait," before anyone of us could blink, he was already in front of Marcus' mom, "you're here. I'm sorry. We're sorry. We didn't have a choice. Mario knew that if we took you, your son would come after him, and he, himself, would kill him for good. The plan was to take you two to him, but my sister, I, no, I made the mistake of bringing Jacques along, thinking that he was the Natural. So, I'm sorry, I really am, we really are." Lee sincerely, with teary eyes, apologized to Katherine, who didn't know what to do.

"Why is Mario obsessed with my son?" Katherine asked firmly but with compassion in her voice.

"Your son? Your son, oh." He moved again from one spot to another in the blink of an eye, in the speed of sound, stopping in front of Marcus. "Marcus Mathias, the Marcus Mathias, Natural Porter of the Taurus Constellation, rightful Wonderer of Earth by birth. Mario is in the process of reshaping the Solar System, revamping the way Queen Mariah Stars rules the Solar System."

"Yes, but our Queen is simply following what King Titus Vespasian tells her to do," Nari interjected in defense of Mariah Stars.

"Or is she? According to Mario, she doesn't report everything she does to the King of Milky Way Galaxy, only what she deems necessary. I know, I'll get to it, Sis. Mario thinks that once he takes her place, he can, what were his exact words? Oh yeah, thanks, he wants to make the Solar System great again," Lee explained. "He thinks that with Marcus Mathias on his side, a Natural, he'll be unstoppable, undefeatable."

"I would never help him!" Marcus spoke between his teeth in anger and disgust.

"I know. We know. I remember when we came to ask you to come with us, but the Cattle stepped in and took you from us, Dogie, we—"

"DON'T CALL ME DOGIE!" Marcus' eyes were bright-white like stars.

"I guess you have a point, you're no longer a Dogie since you now have found your mom," Lee spoke apologetically. "Sorry, I, we, took her from you. The idea behind it was to bring you both to King Shawyze so we could show you two what he has planned for the Solar System. He never meant to separate you two. No, I know, Sis. We failed him. Them. And we paid the price. Yes, he sent her instead, that scorpion lady, Allison. Yes, Ms. Prior. And he left us there, in that jail. Looking after those delinquents, the Vanishers. Breakers of the Law."

"How would you feel if you were told you could no longer use your powers? That you'd have to give your Stardust away and not be able to run as fast as you can? To eventually die?" Elijah joined in the conversation with an infuriating tone.

"I didn't think about that," Lee began. "As a Wonderer, I always thought of myself as untouchable, unkillable, immortal until when I decide to die."

"A choice that was taken away from us," Captain Lance injected firmly.

"You're right. And that's the reason why King Shawyze wants to dethrone her. To make sure all of us live under the same law, including the Vanishers,"

"Wait, didn't you say your king just killed your sister?" I asked him.

"Yes, he did. To teach us a lesson, he said. To gain respect in front of the others. To teach us not to fail him again."

"I guess you're trading one tyrant for another, aren't ya?" Katherine asked him.

"Hum, the irony," he laughed. "No system is perfect. While I, we, don't agree with everything he says, we agree with most of his policies; and honestly, I feel like half of the problems we are having right now are all thanks to Mariah Stars. If she had not taken away the powers of all Vanishers, none of this would be happening."

"What do you want?" Jonathan asked him. "Tell me, why shouldn't I report you right now to the Queen?"

"Jonathan, don't play me for stupid. We all know that everything that one of your copies know, all the other copies know at the same time. It would be stupid of me, us, to think that she already doesn't know what has happened here." Lee moved around, speaking every word in different locations in front of every Jonathan without even realizing he was moving around, stopping right in front of one of them. "So, tell your Queen that I'm here to help you find and free all the other Vanishers kidnapped by outlaw Porters."

"Ha! And we are dumb enough to believe in you," Marcus shouted at him from across the field.

"Fine. You, right there, little girl with the goggles, you can find anyone, right?" Lee moved from in front of Jonathan to right in front of Marcus, stopping right in front of Lucy Wacher. All before finishing his sentence.

"Lucy. Name's Lucy, and yes, I can find anyone I want, but I'm not helping you."

"Isabella Ochio, Porter of the Uranoscopus Constellation, the Star-Gazer. Look for her."

"Leave my wife out of this," Theodore shouted at him from across the field.

"Mr. Hershey, I'm just trying to prove a point." Lee moved again, stopping with his bright eyes in front of him. "Do you know where she is?"

Mr. Hershey didn't say a word; he just shook his head while looking at Lucy, who was waiting for his answer.

"I didn't think so." Lee moved again. "Do what it is that you do, Ms. Wacher."

Lucy Wacher's eyes went from their natural shades of brown to bright-white like stars, even though you could barely see them behind her big goggles. Then, one side of her goggles became a mini screen, displaying an old lady in chains, barely conscious. "Is that her?" she asked.

"Oh, my dear Bella, what have they done to you?" Mr. Hershey dropped to his knees, gazing tearfully at his wife through Lucy's goggles. "Can you take me to there to her?"

"Not exactly. I can get us closer to her location, but we'll still need to look for her once we're there."

"I can help you with that," Lee spoke excitedly with a big smile on his face. "Lucy's powers only get you closer to her, but based on her location, I have an idea where they've been hiding her. And by the looks of it, who the Wanderers are. And if I'm right, you can use any help you can get."

"Mr. Yang, why should we take you with us; we can very well find all the other Vanishers without your help."

"I know where most of the Porters working for King Shawyze keep their Vanishers locked up." Lee moved from in front of Lucy to right in front of me. "Besides, I'm the only Wonderer on your side. If everything goes well, I can get other Wonderers to help us convince the Queen to release you. And find Marcus' boyfriend, Mr. Colton."

"You know where Drayton is?" Marcus asked him as he moved from in front of me to right in front of Marcus.

"Of course, I do. We do, Mr. Natural," he grimed at him.

"I still don't trust you," Elijah told him.

"And you shouldn't, as a matter of fact." Lee moved again. "Jonathan, here, handcuff me. Without my powers, I can cause you no harm and no longer can communicate with anybody, including the King himself, even if I want to." Lee put his two arms forward so Jonathan could handcuff him.

Jonathan looked at me as if asking for approval, to which I just nodded. He did then put his handcuffs around Lee's wrists.

"I don't know what kind of sick game you're playing, but I swear if you're planning a trap, I will maul your head off myself," Jonathan told him threateningly.

"I hope you like sushi." Lee smiled at him. "Whoa, what a relief. I'm at peace. I hear nothing again. The voice is gone, she's gone. I can think and act for myself again. Thank you for this. I will not betray you. She's making me go crazy. Her voice is always speaking in my head. I don't know how it happened; when she died, her voice took over my mind. It's like two people are living inside my head. *Arigatou gozaimashita,*[57] Mr. Asterion."

"You're welcome," Jonathan replied, a bit confused.

"Mr. Yang, what exactly happened?" I asked him now that he seemed normal again.

"Mr. Chase, it's nice to see you again," Lee began. "When my sister, may she find peace among the stars, and I went for Marcus, we took Katherine and Jacques. However, that was a mistake. Once we realized we took the wrong kid, we left him by the Rowes Wharf, knowing that you were staying there. We knew you couldn't resist saving the kid, so we used him as a bait to attract Marcus, and it worked. The following morning, we ran into the three of you closer to Marcus' high school. In hopes to convince Marcus to come with us willingly, but the Cattle interfered, defending their calf. Where did you go from there, William?"

"Taking care of private matters," I responded,

---

[57] *Arigatou gozaimashita:* Thank you (Japanese)

avoiding the question.

"It was actually a good thing you were not there. We didn't want to get you involved in all of this, so we left once we realized that our Natural already had powers and was much stronger than we thought." Lee walked between us in normal human speed again, somewhat relieved he no longer had his powers, stopping in front of Marcus. "When we came back for you again in the library, we found you with your friend Mileena, and again we were interrupted, this time by Mr. Chase over there. By the way, thanks for putting us to sleep and not blasting your sonic boom against us. That would've hurt."

"At the time, I still considered myself one of you," I told them.

"That's when we realized you had feelings for the boy. He was the last to fall asleep." Lee looked at me and back to Marcus again, but just like me, he didn't show any reaction after Lee's statement. "And that was the last drop. After failing yet again to capture you, Mr. Mathias, King Mario Shawyze confined us to guard Mrs. Mathias' cell, and if one of us were to fail, he'd kill both of us."

"And yet he only killed your sister," Marcus reminded him.

"He wanted me to see what would happen to me and to anyone who'll disobey him, so he kept me alive, for now, at least."

"Please, enlighten me again, why are you still working for him?" One of the Jonathans close to Marcus interrogated him.

"Mr. Shawyze may have some different methods, maybe even unorthodox methods, but we need new leadership, a new monarchy to take over the Solar System. And even though my sister had to pay the highest price, it was worth it. No more coming back from the stars every Halley. Now, if you commit a crime, you're done for good. Just like the rest of the planets in the System, no more privileges to Porters, we'll be all treated equally, and that's why I want to help you find the Vanishers who have been kidnapped unfairly by these law-breakers."

"We're not killing anyone," I told him.

"Too late for that, isn't it?"

He was right. We had already killed someone, two, actually. Ralphel L'Acuah, Porter of the Eridanus Constellation, the River, and the Porter of the Vespa Constellation, Vanezzza Ninaè.

"Even if that's the case, we'll need a boat to get to Ms. Ochio, she's in the middle of the Gyhull Ocean," Lucy Wache broke the momentarily awkward silence

"That won't be a problem; we do have a ship," Captain Lance told her with a big smile on her face as if she's been waiting for this moment. "Porters, it's been a while, but I think we can still bring Argo Navis back to life."

"Aye, aye, Captain," was the only pirate's expression any of us have heard up till now from all the so-called Pirates of the Argo Navis.

Karina Dumont ran toward the river in front of us. As she got closer to the water, she made a surfboard appear out of thin air just before landing in the water. When she did, she began swirling around herself, as fast as she could, making all of us feel dizzy, lose our balance, and fall down to our knees.

Karina, who was right in the center of her whirlpool, disappeared for a moment out of sight. As we regained our balance, she rose from the vortex with her surfboard, which was much, much larger than before, in the size of a ship.

"Sorry about that," she apologized unapologetically. "Mr. Ways?"

"Say no more." Oliver Ways jumped to the middle of the board, landing gracefully next to Karina Dumont, both still with their eyes shining bright-white like stars. "Hold on."

Oliver walked to the edge of the board as if he was going to dive, but instead, he opened his arms wide and twirled around himself once quite slowly, and just like that, none of us could move. We could still roll our eyes, but we couldn't move our bodies at all. Just as if we had turned into statues. Statues were what was raised all around the board. The stern was being built all around the ship. Wooden structures were being raised everywhere, making Karina's board take the shape of a boat.

"Make way, Mr. Ways, I'm going in." Elijah, who was gleaming from ear to ear, ran with his Bo staff toward the water, piercing the floor just before getting to the water, catapulting himself onto the ship. But even before his feet landed on the ship, Elijah stabbed his Bo staff right in the middle of it, letting go of his staff as it became one big mast. He then did it two more times in the front and the back of the ship. "Mr. Paris, she's all yours."

"Hold on tight, kids." Guy Paris ran toward the ship and jumped so high he landed on top of the tallest mast, right in the center of the boat. He then dove all the way down with a large white linen cape, connecting the tip of the pole all the way down, making a beautiful sail. Before his feet could touch the ship, Mr. Paris opened a small cape and glided his way back up to the second tallest mast and again to the last and shorter mast in the back of the ship, all the while without touching the floor. Guy used his cape as wings, surfing the air just like a flying-squirrel would; even though he couldn't fly, you would think he did. "Captain?"

Captain Lance approached the ship, and a walking board appeared under her feet, connecting the shore with the boat. As she made her way to the ship, all the remaining parts that were missing to complete the ship appeared out of thin air, leaving for last the wheel, where she gracefully landed her hands as she has done many times before as Captain of the Argo Navis.

"All aboard!" She shouted, gesturing to all of us to get in the ship as Jonathan, Lee, myself, Marcus, Jonah, Katherine, Jonah, Lucy, Dorotheia, Theodore, Tara, and J.J. made our way up inside the sizeable iconic ship.

"Welcome to Argo Navis, the Nautical Ark. While you're in here, I'm your Captain, and you'll follow my rules, my commands for the safety of this ship and my crew. We have a couple of hours before getting to the Gyhull Ocean. Tara will escort you to the cabin where those of you who want to, can rest. The rest of you, stay out of my way. Jonathan, may I see one of you for a minute?"

"Right'way, Cap." All three Jonathans answered with a slight mockery pirate accent, but only one of them moved forward, up the deck where the Captain was.

XVII

For the first time in a while, it was good just to relax even if for only a couple of hours. Uranus is a planet four times bigger than Earth in diameter; however, you could fit over sixty-three Earths inside of it.

The Sretaw Continent, the only continent on the planet, is the size of Mercury, a planet three times smaller than Earth and fifteen times smaller than Uranus, divided by the salty-water River of Zhulu, which connects to the Phiyiah Ocean in the west and the Gyhull Ocean in the north. The Gyhull Ocean, where we are right now, is pretty similar to the ones on Earth, with dark-blue salty water, unlike the Phiyiah Ocean, which is blood red and not as salty.

Uranus has a total of ten oceans, including the

Gyhull blue ocean in the north, the green ocean Dayon in the northeast, the gray ocean in the northwest, Wtei, Ceo, the white smallest ocean in the east, along with the pink ocean, Eioua. In the west, we have the red ocean Phiyiah and the orange ocean Hhol. The yellow ocean, M'Ven, is located in the southwest, opposite the purple ocean in the southeast Ny'ah. In the south, we have the black ocean Khoni, the biggest ocean of them all.

Under every ocean, there is a nation, a country, or a city, under the same name. The skin color of every person is related to the color of the ocean they live under. For instance, we are on the Gyhull Ocean right now, where the ocean is blue, and so are its people.

Uranus, just like Venus, rotates from East to West, but unlike Venus, it turns on its side, which is the reason why Marcus was a little woozy once we teleported to Uranus.

Looking from Earth, Uranus is seen as a baby-blue planet. You can barely see its rings or its moons; moons that are right now in the baby-blue sky. Uranus has a collection of twenty-seven satellites, and since it is now daytime here, we can see about ten of them in the sky. A magnificent scenario which Marcus Mathias is witnessing for the first time here with me, in the beautiful pirate ship of Argo Navis.

"It's beautiful, isn't it?" I asked him once he and I were by ourselves in the back of the ship, looking out to the beautiful blue sea.

"It is," Marcus replied, staring out to the horizon. "What moon is that? The biggest one rising above the water?"

"That's Ariel. Not the biggest moon, but the biggest one right now in the sky. If you look to your right, you'll see Titania, Uranus' biggest moon."

"How many moons are out there?" Marcus asked, looking around the sky.

"About twenty-seven. Of course, due to the Sunlight, you can only see about ten or eleven of them. If you look to the left, you'll see Miranda, the moon where most of all the Porters and I get our Stardust Tattoos, and where Victor Tool, Wanderer of the Pictor Constellation, the Painter's Easel, resides."

"Do you have any family?" Marcus asked, catching me off guard.

"What?" I answered, not because I didn't hear him, but I wanted to make sure I understood him right.

"Family. Do you still have any family?"

"I do, I did actually. All the family members that I once knew have already passed away," I explained. "Certainly, there are a lot of Chases out there, but I've never met them."

"How so?"

"Marcus, when I became a Porter, I told my family I was studying abroad. I had six brothers and three sisters. My mom and dad didn't care much, they were happy for me, but truly they were happy that they had one less person to worry about."

"Where are you from? Like, where were you born?"

"I was born in Pluto, in a little town called Out'el."

"What is it like?"

"Just like every small town from all over the planets in the Solar System, everyone knows everyone." I laughed.

"And you decided just one day to get up and go?"

"In the southeast of Pluto, there is this country named Phaal. There, in the city of Out'el, my family ran a diamond mining business for many generations before I was even born. One day, walking home by myself from work, I ran into my mentor Luke Horace, Porter of the Hercules Constellation, the Hero. He was somewhat lost and asked me where he could get a beer. I gave him directions to a bar nearby, and he offered to buy me a beer in gratitude. I, who had not ever had a beer up until that moment, accepted it."

"You had never had a beer before?"

"I was seventeen, Marcus, where I'm from, you're not allowed to have beers till you turn twenty."

"You guys have it easy. On Earth, we are not allowed to have beers before twenty-one," Marcus told me.

"In the U.S., you mean. In some other countries, the age limit for drinking is different." I told him. "After a few too many beers, Luke was telling me all about his adventure on Earth; about becoming a Porter and how this was his first time on Pluto, thanks to a woman he was talking to, or seeing, or maybe wanted to. I can't quite remember."

"And he was just telling you all this Porter business out loud like that?"

"Well, he knew once he was gone, I would forget about it, thanks to his Stardust Dome."

"Is that what's called?" He asked me curiously. "Up until now, I have only referred to it as a bubble."

"You need to get your tattoo. Stardust has not fully manifested in your body yet. Once you get your tattoo, you'll remember everything you've learned so far. And for everything else you're yet to learn, you will at C.H.E.P., Mr. Mathias," I explained it to him.

"After noticing my enthusiasm," I continued, "about his story, Mr. Horace asked if I'd like to become a Porter myself. I accepted. Of course, I ran home to grab some of my stuff and left with him to Jupiter for one of the C.H.E.P.'s facilities, and that's how I became a Porter."

"And did you ever go back to see your family?"

"I did, but it was rather late. Just like you, when I went back home, many years had passed, and most of my brothers and sisters were already dead. The only one I had a chance to talk to, was my oldest sister, Larissa, who, besides the old age, remembered me very well. She told me how mom had died young of dementia; how that drove my dad away to drinking, causing his death not long after of alcohol poisoning. My brothers fought against each other to see who was going to keep the family business. My sisters had moved away to different parts of the planet. It turns out I was the one to which my family left everything. I sold the business and moved to Charon, into that house I brought you to before."

"I'm sorry, I didn't know," Marcus apologized.

"About what? That was centuries ago, way before you were born. I just feel bad I couldn't say goodbye."

"I know how you feel. I felt like that when my sister disappeared, same with my mom. I couldn't fathom the idea of never seeing them again."

"And now your mom is here, and your sister is—ugh." An electrical surge ran all over my body, making me shiver for a couple of seconds.

"Did you feel that too?" Marcus asked me as the rest of the Porters joined us in the stern of the ship.

"We all did," Jonathan answered him. "It felt like a part of us left our bodies, exactly how I felt once the Gemini Porters killed one of my copies."

KABOOM

An explosion erupted in the middle of the ocean, not too far from us.

"What was that?"

"I'm not sure, Marcus, but it's coming from that way," Jonathan pointed out to the explosion in the middle of the ocean, not too far from us.

"He's here!" Lee shouted. "He's in the middle of that explosion."

"Who do you mean?" Captain Lance inquired.

"King Mario Shawyze is here. This is exactly how I felt when he killed my sister Lynne Yang, may she find peace among the stars. This electrical pulse all over my body for three long seconds."

"Are you sure, Mr. Yang?"

"Am I sure, Jonathan? AM I SURE?" Lee spoke loudly, shouting at the wind. "I have never once felt pain like this before, an irreversible loss. The day I lost my sister, the day I lost a part of me. I WILL NEVER FORGET. So, yes, Jonathan, call for back up, tell the Queen, tell everyone the King is here because I AM SURE!"

"We are more than capable of handling one stray Porter, and we will," Captain Lance stated. "Porters, hold on, we are going underwater. This is not a submarine, so hold your breath and try not to die on me today. Onward and below we go!"

The ship moved forward toward where the explosion came from as if the ship has got a life of its own, obeying the Captain's command.

'Stay stellar,' I sent Marcus, whose green eyes turned bright-white like stars, a T.P.

"Jonathan, release me." Lee approached him, demanding him to release his handcuffs.

"Yeah, right!"

"Jonathan, I need my powers to breath underwater, or I will die," he begged.

"You better hold your breath," Jonathan told him, as we were getting close to the descend spot.

"JONATHAN, MAN, it's deep down there, I can't hold my breath for more than five minutes," Lee begged again as the ship start to descend, and water was rushing in. "JONATHAN!"

"Fine, but you know the deal, anything funny, and I'll have you for dinner." Jonathan released Lee's handcuffs just in time for him to hold on to something before the water could take him away.

Argo Navis was now completely immersed underwater. All the Porters were holding on any way they could so the current wouldn't take them into the open ocean. The dark-blue water made it almost impossible to see at first. However, Mr. Hershey raised one of his hands toward the surface, and a ray of Sunlight made its way toward him. With his other arm, he directed the Sunlight from above the ship to in front of it, working just like a refractor, like a huge spotlight, giving the vessel a much-needed high beam, like those on a submarine.

We descended for at least thirty minutes before the ship came to a complete haul. An anchor fell down on its own, dropping at least thirty feet below. Once it reached the bottom, the anchor pulled us down, closer and closer to the bottom of the Gyhull Ocean. Suddenly something curious happened. All the water we were immersed in, stayed up as we got closer and closer to the bottom, just as if we were being raised from the water, but the water stayed above us and the sand under us.

"What's happening?"

"Remember when Ghaeily Uhayves brought us all the way down to the bottom of the River Zhulu, and there was a dome of air all around us, Marcus? This is the same thing. Ben Cruise and Umma Troya constructed these air domes and tunnels connecting every ocean, for all the people of Uranus to come and go as they please."

"Oh wow, a world with no borders. Wish something like this would happen on Earth."

"Yup, and even though they can go wherever they want, they usually stay within their culture, their color," Jonathan complemented.

"Alright, Porters, it's up to you now to find out what caused that explosion," the Captain spoke. "The rest of the Argo Navis Porters and I can't leave the ship without dismembering it. Go on, and if you need back up, just send a T.P. through Jonathan."

"Hey, I'm more than a walkie-talkie between Porters," Jonathan interceded. "However, she's right. I'll stay here with them, while another me will go with you to check out the site of the explosion."

"Fair enough. Jonathan, Nari, Marcus, and I will go. The rest of you stay here."

"William, I'd like to go too."

"Mrs. Mathias, I don't think it's a great idea,"

"Katherine, William, call me Katherine. I can be of great help."

"Mom, we just got you back, I can't lose you again," Marcus told her before I had a chance to say anything.

"One more reason we should stick together, son."

"Huh? Oh, you were talking to Marcus," Jonathan jumped in the conversation playfully. "We gotta get going, so what's the verdict?"

"Alright, let's do it," Marcus told us as the five of us jumped out of the ship, onto the soft, light-blue land. "But you stay close to me."

"Do you smell this?" Nari asked once she barely touched the floor.

"Yes, I do, Foxy," Jonathan answered her, "it's sulfur dioxide coming straight from that direction."

"Jonathan, I can't see anything or smell anything,"

Katherine told him.

"The smell will grow stronger as we get closer to the location. About the darkness..." Jonathan turned on the flashlight from his utility belt, illuminating the way before us, with Nari right behind him, followed by Katherine, Marcus, and myself.

"Is that a house?" Marcus pointed out.

"Where?" I was looking around but couldn't see at first the small cottage house in the middle of nowhere all by itself. "I think it is. There, Jonathan,"

Jonathan pointed the flashlight to the left side where the tiny house was.

"Oh gosh, what's the smell?"

"The smell Nari and I were talking about, Marcus, sulfur dioxide."

"And for those of us who don't speak science?" Marcus asked again.

"You know that smell when somebody strikes up a matchstick and blows it away? That's the same smell, much more intensified, as if the matchstick was the size of a large tree."

"Is it possible?" Marcus asked, more confused than curious.

"As a Porter, you should know by now that everything is possible." This time, Marcus' mom was the one who responded to him.

We approached the house, and all the windows and the front door were gone as if they were blown out of it.

"Something is wrong," Katherine interrupted us before we could get closer to the house.

"What is it?" Jonathan asked.

"I can sense heat, and this heat I'm sensing is astronomical. This amount of heat cannot possibly be coming from the body of a child," Katherine's eyes were bright-white; her hair, however, was flimsy in dark shades of green.

"Stay here," Jonathan told her, before stepping in through the front door, "by the stars..."

"What is it, Jonny?" I asked as the rest of us came right after him through the door.

A brown-skinned boy, not older than seven years old, was sitting down naked in the middle of the living room. All the surroundings were still ablaze or burnt. His body was still smoking as if he, himself, was on fire not long ago.

"Aaaaaaaaaaaaahhhhhhh!" Nari let out a horrific scream from behind us, making every single one of us jump. "What's that, is he, she, is it still alive? What's THAT?"

I walked toward her and saw in the corner lying down on the floor, a vision that will forever be encrusted in my brain. An old person withered away just like raisins with a large long pointed beak in the place of the mouth. One of the arms was stretched out while the other arm was gone, with a large feathery wing in its place. Both legs were gone; in their place were two long bird legs, completely unaligned with the body. The whole body was white as if has been frozen out, except for the eyes, which were gone from its sockets, with bright, liquid silver streaming down from them.

"HE WAS HERE!" Lee, who had appeared right behind us, shouted in a mix of anger, fear, and excitement. "I told you, he was here, this is exactly what he did to my sister, to my Lynne, and now he did it to Mr. Kandrasi,"

"Was he a Vanisher?" Nari asked.

"No, Mr. Krandasi was a Wanderer, Porter of the Grus Constellation, the Crane, caretaker of that little boy right there, Mr. Mohammed Nixx, Porter of the Phoenix Constellation."

"Is he real?" Marcus asked, amused by the stillness of the boy, getting closer to analyze him curiously.

"Of course, he is real, Mr. Mathias, every legend you heard about on Earth, every curse, every folklore, vampires, werewolves, witches, all of them are real, based on Porters that you don't yet know. Well, except for the Minotaur, which I'm sure you're aware of?" But Marcus didn't say anything; instead, he just looked at Lee, confused, and lost. "Oh, never mind. Let's just get out of here,"

"What about him?" Marcus asked about the kid in the middle of the leaving room who hasn't moved at all.

"What about him?" Lee asked Marcus.

"We can't just leave him here; he's just a kid."

"DON'T TOUCH HIM!" But Lee was a little too late. Marcus reached out to touch the kid's head and almost got himself burned.

"How is this possible? I thought Porters couldn't get hurt?"

"We can't Mr. Mathias, only when other Porters inflict us, and that Porter right there has the power to light himself on fire in almost subatomic power, destroying your home-city of Boston if he wants before you could blink. So, when you ask me about the boy, I say leave the boy. We already have too much on our plate as it is." Lee ran out of the house just as fast as he went in, in a blink of an eye.

"He's right, you know?" The boy spoke for the first time.

"Mohammed, are you okay? What happened here?" Jonathan approached him, kneeling next to him.

"If you know who I am, then you know I go by Blaze." The kid got up to his feet. "I'm not sure. I was in the cradle when three men walked in laughing and speaking with accents I haven't heard before. Mr. Krandasi, got in an argument with them, yelling, screaming no, no, no, and finally, he let go a cry for help, but they were too fast. I felt an electrical surge of energy all over my body, and I couldn't help but feel anything but sadness. Since I was just a baby, I cried. I cried and screamed so loud that the men came for me too, but once they touched me, I lit up and exploded, setting this whole place on fire."

"Where are they now? Did you see who they were?" Jonathan asked him, clearly passing the information to other Jonathans.

"I don't know. When I woke up, they were gone, and my dad was like that. I didn't think it was possible to kill a Porter,"

"Someone found a way to kill us, Mr. Nixx." Jonathan got up, looking around the house for evidence. "Let's get you out of here. I'll take you to the Queen myself; she will want to hear this from you."

"Jonathan, give him a minute, he's just a kid." Katherine grabbed a pair of shorts and an oversized t-shirt that was laying around and gave it to him. "I'll take him home. There are a few of Marcus' old clothes that I can give to him."

"Mom, there are no more of Marcus' old clothes, not even a house for us to go back to. Ever since you left, we—"

"Your dad moved you out to Margaret's house, didn't he?"

"Yes, he did," Marcus told her.

"This can't be good," Jonathan interrupted Marcus and Katherine's conversation. "It's a video message from Mario,"

"Put it through," Marcus told him, to which Jonathan just looked at me and pressed a button on his wrist device, allowing a life-size hologram of Mario Shawyze to appear in the middle of the destroyed living room.

CIAO, JONNY, COME STAI? I AM VERY DISAPPOINTED. IT CAME TO MY ATTENTION THAT ONE OF YOUR VANISHERS KILLED ONE OF MY WANDERERS SO I, BEING THE FAIR KING I AM, KILLED MR. KRANDASI. YOU MUST BE WONDERING WHY HIM, HE'S NOT EVEN A VANISHER HIMSELF. IF I AM BEING HONEST, HE WAS IN MY WAY. I WAS LOOKING FOR YOU THERE IN URANUS, AND HE

WOULDN'T TELL ME WHERE YOU WERE. I FI-
GURED THE OLD MAN WAS PROBABLY TELLING
THE TRUTH, BUT I ALSO KNEW HE WAS HIDING
SOMETHING OF GREAT VALUE TO ME. SO, I ASKED
HIM NICELY ABOUT IT, BUT HE STILL WOULDN'T
GIVE IT TO ME, RESULTING IN THE HORRIBLE
FATE YOU SEE WITH YOUR OWN TWO EYES. I
WAS SO CLOSE TO GETTING IT BUT MR. NIXX'S
EXPLOSIVE TEMPERAMENT INTERRUPTED ME;
LUCKILY, I LEFT IN TIME. REST ASSURED THERE
WON'T BE A NEXT TIME. NEXT TIME I SEE HIM, IT
WILL BE THE LAST THING HE'LL SEE. FOR GOOD!
OH, AND I ALMOST FORGOT, TELL MR. MATHIAS
HAPPY TWENTIETH BIRTHDAY. AND AS A GIFT,
I'LL LET MR. COLTON LIVE ONE MORE DAY. *CIAO,
FOR NOW*

"That was him, the man that was here. I can never forget his arrogance and that stupid accent of his," Blaze told us right after Mario's hologram message.

"For a seven-year-old, you have a mouth on you, don't ya?" Marcus told him to everyone's surprise.

"I'm older than your Earth, mister. Just because I look seven doesn't mean I am. I'm actually eight. You should know Porters are practically immortal."

"Were, Blaze, we were immortals. Clearly not anymore," Nari interrupted him. "What do you think Mario was here looking for?"

"Whatever it is, it's probably burnt by now," Katherine said, looking around at all the burnt furniture.

"We should get out of here. I keep getting the shivers."

"Marcus, right?" Mohammed asked. "Before we go, is it okay if we have a funeral? It doesn't have to be much, but I don't want to leave him here like this. Mr. Krandasi was like a father to me."

"Yes, of course, go get yourself cleaned up, while we take care of this," Marcus told him to everyone's awe.

"That's very nice of you, son," Katherine told Marcus once Mohammed left the room.

"I didn't have a chance to have a funeral when you were thought to be dead. There was a funeral, but we didn't have a body. I didn't have a chance to say good-bye. If I can help someone to have a decent funeral, I will," Marcus said, stepping outside of the house, "and I think I found the perfect spot for it."

Jonathan told the other Jonathan to join in the funeral, as so did Theodore Hershey, Dorotheia Sonny, Lucy Wacher, and Tara Ways, who was representing the whole Argo Navis crew. The crew, in addition to Jonathan number three, stayed behind protecting the Ark.

Both Jonathans and Nari helped dig a grave in less than five minutes, a perk when the three of them are natural diggers. Marcus and his mom were gathering some flowers to decorate the place while I helped Mr. Hershey lay out some reflective mirrors. Lucy and Dot were inside, gathering around all types of snacks they could find.

Mohammed walked outside, fully dressed in black, including his turban, covering his hairless head, followed by Tara Ways.

"This would have made him happy," he told us as he approached the grave.

"We wrapped him in a blanket we found since there's no coffin," Nari told him once he saw the body inside of the grave.

"It's perfect. Thank you, guys. Can I please have everyone's attention?" Mohammed faced the crowd of Porters closing on him. "Dot, do you mind?"

"Not at all," Dot sent a ray of Sunshine reflecting through Mr. Hershey's mirrors, making the whole place lit up just as if the Sun was bright up in the sky.

"Thank you," Mohammed continued, "I'd like to say a few words. For those of you who don't know me, my name is Mohammed Nixx, Porter of the Phoenix Constellation, a Wanderer. When I turned eighteen, just like many of you here, I began my training as a Porter. I was and still am the only Phoenix, and because of that, training me was not an easy thing. When I am in my bird shape, I am happy. I am free. However, when frightened, scared, or angry, I can catch on fire. It took my trainer, Mr. Krandasi, years of training to adjust to all different types of fire, going from the coolest red one, passing through the orange, yellow, blue, and all the way up to the hottest fire, the white fire. A fire that no other Porter was ever able to produce."

"When I finally got the hang of it, Mr. Krandasi brought me back home to see my parents. I am from a big city in the heart of the Sun called Zaqo. My parents knew about my training, about me becoming the Phoenix, and they couldn't wait to see me in my full form. In a grand spectacle, I showed them. They roared, clapped, and cheered for me as I flew around Zaqo, but my oldest brother wasn't happy; he was jealous of me and called me a freak of nature. Said I should have learned how to become a Steamer instead, how to make balloons, how to contribute to the city of Zaqo. Our argument got out of control, and I didn't even realize when I lit up on fire. It didn't take long for me to go from red to white, exploding like a Supernova, killing my parents, my brother, and destroying the whole city of Zaqo."

"When I woke up, I was twenty-eight years old. Everything was burnt to the ground around me, including the city and everyone in it, except for Mr. Krandasi, who had gone inside his Exotic Matter Sphere and back after the destruction. And all he could say was, "I'm sorry' even though it was not his fault."

"Porters, as powerful as they are, were afraid of me and started spreading rumors that I could explode anywhere, anytime without any warning. But that was not true, and Mr. Krandasi knew. Mr. Kandrasi took me literally under his wing. He sold his house in the middle of the beautiful purple city of Ny'ah and bought this small cottage we could live in, away from any civilization."

"He was selfless, a dedicated man, a Wanderer who gave up on everything just to look after me, especially when I'd exploded and come back again as a baby, as a toddler, or as an ancient. Through all the stages of my never-ending life, he was there. And now it's my turn to say, I'm sorry. I'm sorry I wasn't old enough to protect you. I'm sorry that you had to die. I'm sorry you'll never know how much you meant to me, how much I'll miss you, Dad."

Tears were free-falling from his and most of the Porters' eyes around us, including myself. Mohammed then bent forward, touching the blanket, setting it on fire almost instantaneously.

"May he find peace among the stars."

"May he find peace among the stars," all of us said right after him.

"Now, I'd like to ask you all to leave. I'll be right after you once I burn this place to the ground," Mohammed said to everyone's disbelief.

"What do you mean?"

"Jonathan, Mario came here looking for something; whatever it was, my dad believed was worth dying for. While I have no idea what it is, I'll burn everything so that he can never find it when he inevitably comes back."

"Alright, you heard the boy, off to Argo Navis," Jonathan told us. "Don't take long, Blaze, you'll never know when he'll be back."

"I'm betting on him showing up," Blaze responded with his eyes turning bright-white like stars.

All the Porters and I made our way back to the Argo Navis ship in less than ten minutes. It wasn't until we were all aboard the ship, that we saw a massive ball of fire coming from the direction where the house was.

"Where is he?"

"There, Captain," Lucy pointed out to something flying toward us.

Mohammed was flying with a backpack in his hand, wearing his funeral clothes, with his bright-red wing with multicolored feathers as was his long feathery red tail, a tail similar to a peacock's but with fewer feathers just like that of a lyrebird.

"Do I have permission to land on your boat, Captain?"

"Call my ship a boat again, and you'll stay stranded here in nothingness, Mr. Nixx."

"My apologies." Blaze landed on the boat next to all of us. "Ready when you are."

"Hold on to something; we are going up. Release the anchor."

Even though Captain Lance gave the orders, no one moved except the anchor who unanchored itself as if it was alive, passing above the ship toward the ocean above us. Once the anchor touched the water, we could feel the ship being dragged up again toward the blue sea, immersing us all in it little by little, and, in less than thirty minutes, we were all back in the surface of the Gyhull Ocean.

XVIII

It was dusk when we reached the surface again. Everyone was pretty much keeping a low profile, barely speaking to one another, still thinking about what everyone had witnessed.

"Listen, I know you just came back from a funeral that you didn't even know you were attending, but I have an idea. Marcus," Mohammed addressed him, who was between Katherine and me. "I know today was not the day you were hoping it would be, but I think I can help."

"Mohammed, I'm not sure I know what you mean," Marcus looked at me, confused. I reciprocated the look.

"Jonathan, show him,"

Jonathan touched his wrist device, and a hologram video of his father, Roberto Mathias, appeared in the middle of the ship.

"HAPPY BIRTHDAY, *FILHO!*[58]" Roberto spoke. **"ANOTHER BIRTHDAY WE'RE SPENDING APART FROM EACH OTHER."**

"DAD!" Marcus shouted loud of happiness.

"I'M RIGHT HERE, SON!"

"Wait, you can hear me?" Marcus asked, confused, staring at Jonathan.

"OF COURSE, I CAN. THIS IS A LIVE CONVERSATION, JUST LIKE A CELL PHONE."

"I miss you so much."

"I MISS YOU TOO, AND FOR A MINUTE I ALMOST TELEPORTED MYSELF OUT THERE TO URANUS, BUT I WOULDN'T HAVE BEEN ABLE TO GIVE YOU YOUR SURPRISE," Roberto smiled broadly at the projection. **"GUYS?"**

"HAPPY BIRTHDAY, MARCUS!" Jena, Mileena, and Jacques joined in the projection.

"Guys. Oh, wow! I wish I were there with you."

"NO SWEAT *POTE*,[59] WE ARE AWARE OF WHAT'S GOING ON. YOUR BUDDY JONATHAN HERE, TOLD US," Jacques said.

"HI, GUYS," Jonathan greeted us from the other side of the projection.

"How many of you are there?"

---

[58] *Filho:* Son (Portuguese)

[59] *Pote:* Buddy (French)

"Marcus, not now, focus on the moment," The Jonathan next to me, replied to him.

"MARK, WHEN YOU'RE BACK, WE ARE CELEBRATING ALL FOUR BIRTHDAYS WE SPENT APART, OKAY?" Jacques told him. **"OH, YEAH, THIS TIME, WE ARE GETTING YOU DIFFERENT GIFTS, RIGHT, *MA BELLE*?**[60]**"**

"YOUR ARE NEVER GONNA LET THAT GO, ARE YOU?" Mileena was dragged in the conversation by Jacques' arms embracing her. **"ANYWAYS, MARKS, HAVE A GREAT BIRTHDAY, AND HOPEFULLY, WE'LL SEE YOU SOON, BUDDY."**

"Thanks, guys. You're the best!"

"MARCUS, I HOPE YOU HAVE AN INCREDIBLE DAY," Jena hopped in the projection. **"I CAN'T WAIT FOR YOU TO MEET SAM."**

"Oh, you're dating too?" Marcus asked her excitedly. "I'll be home soon as I can, Jena, take care and tell Sam I said hi."

"HEY, SON, BEFORE WE DISCONNECT, CAN I SEE HER?"

"She's right here, Dad." Marcus stepped out of the projector, allowing Jonathan to focus on his mom.

"YOU'RE ALIVE!" Roberto breathed a sigh of relief once he saw her in the projection.

"You're not getting rid of me that easily," she laughed coyly.

"YOU KNOW, YOU'RE—"

"A LIAR!"

---

[60] *Ma belle:* My beauty (French)

In a swift movement, we saw a woman hovering around the ship, landing right in between Marcus and me.

"She's a big-time liar, isn't that right, Mommy?" Nobody could believe what they saw, Donna Saihtam, Porter of the Virgo Constellation dressed entirely in black, in her mackledia fur coat. "What? Don't recognize your own daughter?"

"Dani?" Katherine barely let any words out, completely surprised by the apparition of her dead daughter.

"I go by Donna," Daniella pushed her out of the way so she could face her dad in the hologram. "Hi, Daddy, it wouldn't be a family reunion without your precious little daughter, would it?"

"DANI, I—"

"Bye, Daddy," Daniella unsheathed her sword into Jonathan's device, removing it completely, disconnecting the call. "I'll deal with him later."

"WHAT DO YOU WANT?"

"Oh, little brother, you were always so cute when you're angry, but this time I'm here for her." Daniella swung her sword from Marcus' neck to her mother's heart. "Mommy, dearest, the biggest liar of them all. The one who gave me away to Allison Prior, who took me all the way to Pluto! PLUTO of all the planets. I was in the coldest, farthest planet in the Solar System."

"Don't be such a drama queen, Daniella. Porters don't get affected by natural weather."

"You would know, Mommy, you are a Porter after

all." Daniella moved from Katherine to in front of Marcus. "Do you really think you can trust her?"

"ENOUGH!"

"Oh, William, I forgot about how powerful your voice can get. Too bad you can't kill anyone with it."

"Wanna bet?" I got in between her and her brother.

"Maybe some other time, but you're right," Daniella flew out of my reach, hovering above the ship, "I am done talking. This story is getting too long, like a Stephen King book, and I have important matters to attend so, Marcus, I have a proposition to make. You come with me, and I'll prove to you that King Shawyze is only looking after all the Porters is our Solar System, and in addition, you get your boy toy back, and, mommy and daddy can go back home and live their meaningless lives just like they've been doing for centuries."

"And if I refuse?"

"I thought you might say that, so since today is your birthday..."

PUFT

Drayton appeared right next to her, flapping his white wings still wearing nothing but his jeans, landing right in front of Marcus.

"DRAYTON!" Marcus rushed to hug his boyfriend. "Are you okay? Did they hurt you?"

"At first, yeah, but after Daniella and I spoke, I realized she wasn't wrong. King Shawyze isn't the bad guy, after all, he's actually pretty funny."

"Drayton, the guy just murdered a Porter for fun,"

I told him.

"I know, I was there, along with Daniella. Truth be told, the old cuckoo had it coming."

"Do you hear yourself?" Marcus asked him.

"Listen, babe, the laws are about to change, and all of us will be free again, able to travel between worlds and moons throughout the Solar System. ALL OF US, Wanderers, Wonderers, Vanishers, every single Porter," Drayton spoke to the whole ship like a politician as everyone was listening to him carefully trying to decide for themselves if they agree or not with him.

"Drayton, honey, let's go." Daniella flew out of the ship. "We have other matters to attend to with the King himself, and they have bigger fish to deal with."

PUFT

Daniella disappeared inside of her Exotic Matter Sphere, leaving nothing but Stardust in the air.

"If you change your mind, just send me a T.P., and I'll come for you."

PUFT

This time was Drayton's turn to disappear inside his E.M.S.

"Are you okay?" I asked once I realized Marcus didn't move an inch.

"I guess." Marcus went to help his mom back to her feet. "Are you alright?"

"I'm alright. Thanks, son."

"I wonder what she meant by that," I asked everyone around us.

"I think I have an idea. Look!" Jonathan pointed

out a strange figure under the water approaching us faster than a submarine.

"Argo Navis, to your spots, stay there, and keep the Ark together for as long as you can. Ms. Wacher you come with me, we gotta keep you hidden," Captain Lance told them as Guy Paris, Karina Dumont, Oliver Ways, and Elijah Jones disappeared out of sight into their respective hidden place, leaving Lee Yang, Tara Whirls, Theodore Hershey, Dorotheia Sonny, Mohammed Nixx, Nari Anser, Katherine Mathias, Marcus Mathias, myself, and all three Jonathans on deck.

"Hello, Porters," a woman, climbing onto the boat with tentacles in place of her arms and legs, spoke. "King Mario sends his regards."

"Send this to Mario for me!" Jonathan shot her multiple times with his gun, to which she deflected it with one of her tentacles.

"Is that all you got?" The shot tentacle dissolved itself into Stardust, allowing a brand-new tentacle to grow, replacing the one lost. The mysterious woman then stretched one of her limbs, grabbing Jonathan and suffocating him in midair.

"Let him go," the other Jonathans shouted as they both opened fire at her at the same time.

"Stupid dogs." She threw Jonathan against both Jonathans, striking them out of the ship.

Marcus, filled with rage, charged against her, but she dodged him quite gracefully, making him crash against the stern.

"Marcus!" Katherine ran to Marcus' aid but got

caught on the way by one of her tentacles.

"You're not going anywhere," the woman said.

However, Katherine touched the tentacle, and the whole thing petrified, making the woman scream in pain, detaching her arm before Katherine could turn the giant octopus-woman into stone.

"You'll pay for this." The woman was about to reach out to grab Marcus' mom again, but I didn't let her.

BOOOOM

I let out a sonic boom at her, knocking her completely out of the ship.

"That was pretty awesome!" Blaze raved.

"Thanks, I just hope that was enough to keep her away," I pondered.

"Let's celebrate this win." Captain Lance stepped out in the open as the boat reconstructed itself the shattered parts.

"Who was that?" Nari asked, joining in.

"That, my friend, was Arielle Hyllus, Porter of the Cetus Constellation, the Sea—"

"MONSTER!" Lee interrupted Jonathan, shouting from the top of his lungs at the sight of the fifty-foot-tall creature that was rising from the water right in front of the ship, running from side to side, until finally disappearing inside his Exotic Matter Sphere.

"Coward!" Nari exclaimed, "I guess you've only upset her."

The beast let one of her tentacles fall down across the ship, splitting it in half, with Marcus, Katherine, Nari, and two Jonathans on one side, and myself, the

remaining Jonathan, Theodore, Dorotheia, Mohammed, and Tara at the front of the ship.

All three Jonathans started shooting at her. I took
to the sky, alternating between my sonic screeches
and sonic booms, and Blaze, who was flying around
her, switched his normal red-colored feathers to
bright-blue in seconds, releasing fire out from his
wings.

Arielle, the Sea-Monster, turned to us and spat
squid ink at myself and Mohammed, making us blind,
falling toward the boat. She then turned to the opposite side and smashed the part of the ship where
Marcus was, sinking it.

"NO!" Dot screamed as she released a high beam
of Sunshine at the beast, making her yell in pain,
disappearing right in front of us.

"WILLIAM!" Mohammed shouted in despair. "I'm
flying blind. I can't see anything!"

"I'm coming for you, buddy." I couldn't see much
either; only one of my eyes was free of the poison.

As I was getting closer to him, I crashed into an
invisible rubbery, sluggish, cold, wet wall, knocking
me back a few feet, followed by a burst of laughter,
revealing a big octopus right in front of me.

"Great, she can turn invisible too."

She then knocked Blaze out of the skies. Got ahold
of one side of the ship, squeezing it till it shattered in
pieces, subsequently into Stardust. All the Porters
were now in the open water, other than me. I was still
flying with one eye.

I let out one last sonic boom, as loud as I could,

which knocked her over a few feet, but she merely smashed me with one of her tentacles out of the sky, free-falling unconscious to the Gyhull Ocean.

***

I regained my consciousness while being dragged by an enormous brown, white, black Foxhound, Mr. Jonathan Asterion, in his full dog form.

'Good, you're up,' he said in a T.P. since his three-foot-long muzzle was dragging me through the ocean toward the shore, *'can you swim?'*

"Yeah, yeah," I told him as he let go of me. "What happened?"

"I'm not sure. Everybody got scattered miles away from each other, when I woke up, I only found you," Jonathan spoke, transforming himself back into his human form. "One of the other Jonathans is with E.J. and the rest of the Argo Navis crew."

"What about everybody else?"

"I'm not sure. I haven't heard back from the other Jonathan or anyone else."

"I'll send a T.P. out to them once we are out of the water."

"Hey guys," Ghaeily showed up right behind us. "Sorry, I'm late for the party. I tried to get here as fast as I could."

"Ghaeily, how did you find us here?" Jonathan asked, surprised at the sight of the blonde-haired mermaid in front of him. "Not that I'm complaining. Gosh, you're so pretty!"

"The explosion, I saw it, and I knew it wasn't a normal explosion. Imagine my surprise when I got here and found you fighting with that beast."

"Whatever happened to her?" I asked.

"It's unclear. After smashing the ship into pieces, she disappeared inside of her Exotic Matter Sphere."

"Where's everybody else?" Jonathan asked, apparently concerned about the rest of the group.

"Don't know. I know the Argo Navis have a rendezvous point they always teleport back to if something happens; I'm pretty sure they took Elijah, Tara, and Captain Lance with them as well."

"What about the rest?"

"You two are the only ones I could find so far, William,"

'William, help me!'

"I just got T.P. from Lucy asking for help," I told them.

"Where is she?" Jonathan asked, looking around.

"THERE!" Ghaeily pointed out to a glaring spot in the ocean not far from us. "I'll take us there."

A strong current of water came from under us, taking all three of us five miles east from our location in a matter of seconds, stopping right in front of a small block of ice with Lucy semi-conscious on top of it.

"Lucy, are you alright?" Jonathan climbed on top of the ice block, followed by Ghaeily and me.

"Yeah, I guess," she said, sitting up. "How did I get here?"

"We were hoping you could tell us that?" I told

her.

"There's no ice in the Ghaeily Ocean. Why is there a block of ice right here in the middle of nowhere?"

Unexpectedly, something jumped out of the water landing right in front of us: a gigantic, green-blue toad.

"Hold right there, Toad," Jonathan shouted, pointing out his gun to the oversized frog.

"Whoa, whoa, I'm one of the good guys," the toad replied, transforming himself back into a guy with different tones of green in his hair, eyes, and skin, dressed in nothing but a blue swim trunk.

"I'll be the judge of that," Jonathan informed him unconvincingly.

"I just saved her life," the green-skinned guy pointed to Lucy, who was still sitting on the ice."

"Wait, I know you," Ghaeily interrupted the conversation. "You're Litho Bathes, Porter of the Bufo Constellation, the Toad, a Vanisher just like me."

"Yes, that would be me and who you might be, beautiful lady?" Litho stretched out his hand, greeting Ghaeily.

"I'm Ghaeily Uhayves, Porter of the Siren Constellation. These are my friends, William Chase, Porter of the Lyra Constellation; that's Jonathan Asterion with the gun, Porter of the Canes Venatici, he's with the C.V.O., you can put the gun away, Jonny," Ghaeily told him as put his gun back in its holster carefully. "The girl you saved is Lucy Wacher, Porter of the Pyxis Constellation, the Compass."

"Nice meeting you guys. Tell me how you guys

ended up all the way over here in the middle of the Dayon Ocean?"

"Wait, what? I thought this was the Gyhull Ocean?" I asked him, surprised.

"Nope, if you look close enough, the water around us is as green as everyone else in this land. Including me," Litho told us. "What planet are you from?"

"They are from all over the Solar System, but I'm from here," Ghaeily told him, fixing her big long yellow hair out of her face.

"From here? But you have no color!" He exclaimed surprisingly, staring at her. "You're just like them."

"I'm from the M'Ven Ocean," Ghaeily spoke embarrassedly as she switched her skin color from pale to bright-yellow. "A little Stardust trick."

"Why would you ever hide your color?" Litho's bright-green eyes looked deep into Ghaeily's yellow eyes. "You're beautiful just the way the stars made you."

"Thanks!" Ghaeily said, awkwardly with her yellow skin flushed red.

'WILLIAM!' Marcus sent me a T.P.

"Hold on, it's Marcus," I told them. *'Are you safe?'*

'Yeah, I'm with Nari, but we can't teleport out of here.'

'On my way.'

"Is he okay?" Ghaeily asked,

"He is actually not too far from us." I looked around as if trying to find him.

"He's back at Mohammed's house, Will."

I look at Lucy. Her goggles were showing Marcus and Nari in front of the destroyed, burnt-down house.

"How are they there? There's no water; oh wait, never mind," Jonathan told us. "So, when are we leaving?"

"Now. Are you ready?"

"Wait, we can't teleport ourselves over there, the currents and the air domes make it almost impossible, thanks to Mr. Cruise," Ghaeily explained to us before I could press my Exotic Matter Sphere.

"I can help," Litho offered. "If you know the coordinates, I can take you there?"

"How so?"

"Watch this, Jonny." Litho raised his hands above water, and a blast of ice made its way into the ocean, creating a tube slide all the way down. "Last Porter in, is a falling star." Litho jumped straight through the hole.

"What you're waiting for?" Ghaeily went in, right after him.

"Should we?"

"Why not, Jonny? Lucy, lead the way." Lucy jumped in, as did I, followed by Jonathan.

We took a few turns, up and around, just like in a water slide, free-falling for about fifteen minutes all the way down to the bottom of the ocean.

Once we got out of the ice-slide, we were inside of an air tunnel, just like the one before when we found Mohammed, except that this time, the water above us was a dark-green, algae tone.

"Alright, now that everyone is down here, which

way?" Litho asked Lucy once Jonathan came out from the ice tube slide.

"We go North back to the Gyhull Ocean," Lucy told us as she confirmed Marcus' location through her goggles. "Marcus should be a couple of miles away from us."

True to her words, less than a couple of miles away, we found Marcus and Nari sitting down in front of Mohammed's house. Or what were the remainders of it.

"Took you long enough," Marcus greeted us once he saw us.

"I miss you too, buddy," I told him, greeting him with a smile on my face.

"Is that you, Litho?" Nari jumped out of excitement, hugging Litho as soon as she recognized the green-skinned man.

"You guys know each other?" Jonathan asked, entirely taken by surprise.

"Heck yeah, Litho and I used to be a thing," she said happily. "I haven't seen you in centuries, how you've been, still dating that human?"

"Oh no, we broke up a century ago, I'm single now," he told her. "Still with Elijah?"

"Yup, I'm marrying him one of these days. Talking about that, where is he?"

"He's with the Argo Navis crew at their rendezvous location. Once we find Katherine, we'll go for him," Jonathan explained. "How did you guys end up here?"

"Don't know. When I woke up, Nari was still unconscious, and we were both here," Marcus explained.

"That's weird." Jonathan was looking around for any clues. "Lucy, can you find me?"

"Not really, you are one person in different locations all over the Solar System. It's almost impossible to pinpoint a location of just one of you," she explained.

"What about my mom?" Marcus asked, hopeful.

"I tried, but just like Theo, Dot, and Mohammed, nothing came up."

"What do you mean, nothing came up?" Nari intrigued.

"They are either unconscious or..."

Lucy didn't have to finish her sentence for us to understand precisely what she meant. For being a little girl, she was really calm in this situation.

"Wait a minute." Jonathan picked up something from the floor. "I was here."

"Yeah, we all were not long ago," Marcus told him.

"No, I mean, one of my other copies was here and left this," Jonathan showed a name tag, the same as the one he was wearing under his C.V.O. batch where it says J. Asterion.

"What do you think it means?" I asked him.

"It means that he was low in Stardust on his system, with just enough to keep him alive. He was almost fully human, too weak to send out a T.P. He must have left this as proof he was here." Jonathan put the name tag in his pocket. "I'm going after him!"

Jonathan transformed himself into his Foxhound shape and ran through the pathway right in front of us.

"GO! We'll catch up," Ghaeily told us as she and Lucy stayed behind. I flew after him, with Marcus running in his bull shape along with Nari in her fox shape after me, followed by frogman Litho.

Suddenly, Jonathan came to a halt.

"What is it?" I asked him, looking around for anything suspicious.

"Humans."

We all got out of the way as a happy family of blue Gyhullians passed by utterly unaware of our presence, thanks to Jonathan's Stardust Dome revolving all of us.

"Humans? But they are blue?" Marcus asked, confused.

"Marcus, you really gotta go to school to understand the types of humans and humanoids in the Solar System, now le-ugh," Jonathan's words were cut short as he fell backward on the floor in pain, transforming himself back to his human shape.

"What happened?" Nari came to his aid.

"My head. I'm dead, the other me that is. We are too late."

"Did you see who did it?" Marcus asked him.

"No, I must have been unconscious since neither one of us was expecting it."

"Are you okay?" I asked him, helping him back to his feet.

"Yeah, I just need a minute." Jonathan wiped out

a tear out of his eye.

"Lucy, listen to me, do you know where Argo Navis is?" I kneeled close to Lucy, grabbing her two hands.

"Yeah, I do,"

"Take Ghaeily and teleport yourselves out of here, you won't go far and probably still are gonna have to swim back up to the surface, but I'm sure between the two of you, you'll make it there safe."

"But we can help," she pleaded.

"Yes, and we need all the help we can get. Get the Argo Navis' crew so they can help us here. We don't know who we are facing inside of that cave, but whoever they are, they are not playing around, and Ghaeily is a Vanisher. If she dies, she's done for good. Litho, you should go with them."

"No way. I have never backed out of a fight before, and today is not the day."

"Alright, he made his choice, but you have no choice, can you please do this for me?"

"Alright, but we'll be back before you know it."

"I'm counting on it. Now go!"

Lucy Wacher grabbed the hand of Ghaeily Uhayves and pressed her Exotic Matter Sphere, disappearing out of there with nothing but Stardust left in the air.

"How are you feeling?" I checked on Jonathan, who was still somewhat pale.

"I wish I had the strength to multiply myself right now, but I think I can manage."

"I think you're right! Whatever it is that's in there;

we got this. You got the best team with you, right, Nari?"

"Right, Marcus. We are gonna kick some butt!"

"Now, I know you guys don't know me at all, but as a Vanisher, it is my duty to help other Porters in need, especially other Vanishers."

"And we appreciate you for this, Mr. Bathes. Now, if everybody is ready, let's find Theo, Dot, and whomever else they have with them," I told them as we entered the cave right in front of us.

The cave was dark and quiet, with the sound of water drops echoing everywhere. Since all of us see quite well in the dark, Jonathan kept his flashlight in his belt to avoid calling any attention to us.

It didn't take long for us to reach the end of the cave, in an enormous dome, just like the one we found Marcus' mom and the other Vanishers.

"There's no one here!" Marcus told us, looking around, as so did we.

"Look, up there." Jonathan took out his flashlight and pointed to the top part of the dome where eight Porters were glued against the dark-purple wall in some sort of black slime.

"Are they alive?"

"I'm just about to check, Nari." I flew up what must have been about fifty feet off the floor, checking the first person I saw: an older lady I recognized from Lucy's goggles, Isabella Ochio. She and the others were unconscious. I looked around to see who they were, but I couldn't identify them all except for Mohammed, who was three spots down from me.

I flew toward him and tried to free him, but nothing was working, not even my sharp claws. I finally let out a small sonic boom, dissolving the black gooey stuff off his face waking him up.

"William, how are you? How did you?"

"Shhh, Blaze, I'm gonna get you out of here."

I flew back away from him to let out a stronger sonic boom in hopes of dissolving the rest of the stuff off his body.

'*She's right behind you.*' Mohammed sent me a T.P., making me turn to see what he meant, but I saw nothing.

I could feel the presence of something dark around us but couldn't see anything. Then, before I could even finish examining my surroundings, something knocked me out of the air, crashing against the other side of the wall, briefly losing my consciousness.

"They told me you would be back to try to save them, but I didn't think you were this stupid, but I guess I was wrong. You are!"

Arielle Hyllus, Porter of the Cetus Constellation, was there looking like freaking Ursula with her lower body as that of an octopus while her upper body was that of a woman fully dressed in black.

"Mario will be pleased to know I have all of you here, especially you, Mr. Natural." Arielle moved slow but precise, just like a snake.

"LET ME OUT OF HERE!" Blaze shouted at her.

"SHUT UP, BOY!" she raised one of her tentacles and shot the same black gooey stuff, covering his mouth. "Adults are talking."

"LEAVE HIM ALONE!" Marcus, being the short-tempered Taurus he was, charged against her, but she grabbed him quickly with one of her tentacles throwing him up the cave wall against the other Porters.

"I can't wait to report you to the Queen," Jonathan told her as he cautiously approached, growling at her.

"Oh, but you won't, Mr. Asterion, at least not this copy."

BANG

I could see it but not believe it: Daniella Mathias and Drayton Colton, walked in the cave right behind Mario Shawyze, who had just shot Jonathan, leaving nothing but Stardust right before my eyes.

"Not one sound, Mr. Chase, or you'll be next," Mario spoke, pointing his gun at me.

XIX

DEAL OR NO DEAL?

N ari's screams echoed throughout the cave, almost as loud as one of my own screeches, minus the destroying impact, obviously.

"Don't worry. There are more copies of Mr. Asterion in the Solar System than all of the Porters combined. There's no getting rid of him, just like roaches," Mario told us as he approached the center of the dome.

"Ms. Saihtam, Mr. Colton, keep an eye on Mr. Bathe, Ms. Anser, and especially Mr. Chase while I deal with the rest of these Porters, sí[61]?"

---

[61] *Sí:* Yes (Italian)

Daniella unsheathed her sword and pointed to my neck. Drayton had his hands and feet transformed into the hooves of a horse, letting us know that he was ready to fight us if needed.

"*Alora,*[62] Ms. Hyllus, bring to me Mr. Sixx and Mr. Chan, *per favore*[63], uh?"

Arielle walked up the walls of the cave, grabbing two Porters out of their gooey cocoon, dropping both in front of Mario.

"Mr. Chan, Mr. Sixx, please get up. We have some crucial matters to discuss with both of you." Both Porters got up to their feet, as Mario had the weird weapon on his hand pointing out to them. "Now tell me, who had the idea of capturing Vanishers on their own?"

"Me, sir," one of them spoke proudly.

"Mr. Chan, and why would that be?"

"Mr. Shwayze, these Vanishers were supposed to have their powers drained out of them centuries ago and died out, but yet they found a way of living illegally, and I simply won't have it, sir." Mr. Chan's words were filled with hate against the Vanishers still hanging up against the wall.

"Mr. Chan, remind us again who you are." Mario's theatricality was just like that of a T.V. talk show host.

"I'm Robert Chan, Porter of the Octans Constellation, the Octant," he spoke loud and clear.

---

[62] *Alora:* Now (Italian)

[63] *Per favore:* Please (Italian)

"And you, Mr. Sixx?"

The other Porter got up to his feet, introducing himself: "I'm Xian Sixx, Porter of the Sextans Constellation, the Sextant."

"Mr. Sixx, how do you feel about Mr. Chan's procedure?" Mario asked him as if he were in a courtroom, at the amazement of his colleagues, dangling his gun from side to side.

"Robert and I have been friends for a while now; he's like a brother to me. Logically when he asked me to help him, I didn't think it was the right thing to do, but he is right; these Vanishers are breaking the Universal Law."

"Actually, they aren't. Those are Solar System's Laws implemented by the Queen Mariah Stars," Mr. Shawyze clarified. "So, you're telling me that even though you disagreed with Mr. Chan's methods, you still helped him with it?"

"Yeah, as I said, he's like a brother to me."

"Thank you, Mr. Sixx." Mario, who was walking around in circles, stopped and pointed the gun to Robert, saying: "Any last words, Mr. Chan?"

"What do you mean, last words? I thought you hated these space trash as I do," he pleaded, confused.

"No, I don't, Mr. Chan. These, as you put it, 'space trash' are Porters just like the rest of us who got denied their right to live freely like the rest of the Porters just because somebody decided it was their time to go."

BANG

Mario Shawyze released one single shot straight to Mr. Sixx's chest, catching all of us off guard.

"Mr. Shwayze?" Xian fell to his knees, feeling the silver liquid slipping through his fingers as he tried to keep it in fruitlessly.

"If there's one thing that I hate more than an outlaw, it is a coward. Mr. Chan, while stupid, had a motive, a passion, a desire to implement the laws. However, you, Mr. Sixx, may you find peace among the stars."

We all stood there watching what had just happened in disbelief. Xian's body was expelling liquid Stardust out of his wound, his nose, eyes, mouth, and ears. His natural red skin complexion turned silver. His body withered away just like raisins, the same way Mr. Krandasi's body was left.

BANG

Mario shot again, this time across Robert's forehead, making him fall backward with the impact. "I hate outlaws. If they couldn't be trusted on an old system, they certainly can't be trusted under my newly implemented system."

"So, what does that make you?" I shouted at him, feeling the electrical surge all over my body, and again shortly after, once both bodies were utterly dried out.

"Mr. Chase, I'm not an outlaw. I'm implementing new laws, something that your queen should've done years ago. An ideal you used to share with the rest of us. What happened?" Mario stopped in front of me while Drayton removed the bodies out of the way, throwing them against the cave wall. "Was it Marcus, Will? Was it your love for him that made you switch sides? Arielle, dear, bring the rest of the Porters down."

"All of them?" Arielle asked a bit skeptical.

"ALL OF THEM!" He shouted at Arielle, making her move as fast as a squid out of water could, letting all the Porters fall to the floor.

"Porters, before you even think about doing anything stupid, take a look around you." Mario pointed out to the Robert and Xian whose bodies were withered out, drenched in silver blood, liquid Stardust.

"WHAT DID YOU DO?" Marcus shouted, wiping the gooey stuff out of his face.

"Same I'll do to you if you don't control that temper of yours, Mr. Mathias," Mario replied calmly but threateningly. "Now, where was I? Oh yes, Mr. Chase, honestly, I think you can do so much better. Whatever happened between you and Mr. Jones? He is a much better fit for you. Tall, strong, and v—"

"What do you want from me?" Marcus spoke the words between his teeth with his eyes bright-white like stars.

"YOU? Hahahahaha," Mario let his laughter echo throughout the whole cave. "I want you to understand that you have a great opportunity here by allying yourself with us, just like your sister and your boyfriend. Or is it ex? I can't keep up with these kids."

"In what world did you think that I would ever side with you? You're a lunatic."

"No, I'm not from Luna. That is a very archaic term, Marcus." Mario looked at him in amusement, pleasantly surprised by Marcus' choice of words. "Listen, *vitello*[64], you're much too young to understand the politics of the Solar System. That's why I would like to invite you to come with me to my place. I can teach you all you need to know about our Solar System and how I'll change it for a much better, fairer, inclusive System."

"And if I refuse?"

"I'll kill you just like I will do with everyone else in this room."

'NOW!' Blaze sent me a T.P. just before he broke loose. He flew up with his bright-red wings across the cave, knocking Arielle to the floor. "Damn, I hate that woman."

At the same time, Marcus transformed himself into his bull shape, charging against Mario, who was caught by surprise, crashing him against the wall.

Daniella, in a moment of distraction, let her guard down along with her sword, the perfect opportunity I needed to release a high sonic screech, which threw her against the other side of the cave.

Drayton flew to the other side of the cave to help his king up, along with Daniella and Arielle.

Nari and Litho were now free to join the other Vanishers, Dorotheia, and Theodore, who was holding Isabella Ochio's hand.

"Well, I must say this was a fun surprise." Mario

---

[64] *Vitello:* Veal (Italian)

began readjusting himself. "However, it's safe to say that you're outnumbered."

"Not from where I stand," I told him as Dot, Theo, Isa, and Litho stood behind me ready to fight, along with Marcus and Mohammed.

"You're willing to fight for them? Look there against the wall, those Vanishers, completely afraid. So afraid that they are incapable of choosing a side. Cowardly sitting on the sidelines of an inevitable war."

"Or they just don't want to fight," Nari told him.

"Ovviamente no, bella mia[65]*,* who would fight in a losing battle?" Mario let out frightful laughter. "Oh, here they come."

Zhuir Pierns, Porter of the Cancer Minor Constellation, walked in with piercers instead of hands holding Ghaeily Uhayves, who was trying to free herself out of his grip with her two tails flapping everywhere. They were followed by the Porter of the Hippocampus Constellation, Douglas Martin, the Sea-Horse, who was also wearing a proud smile on his face.

Zhuir tossed Ghaeily on the floor right in front of Mario, entirely back in her human form with her blonde yellow hair covering her equally yellow naked body.

"Grazie[66]*,* Zhuir, you always do a phenomenal job. Wish I had found you earlier when I needed a certain

---

[65] *Ovviamente no, bella mia:* Obviously not, my pretty (Italian)

[66] *Grazie:* Thank you (Italian)

Natural brought to me." He laughed, staring at Marcus, who didn't like his comment whatsoever. "The funny thing is, I never even heard your voice. I don't even know if you're a man or a woman."

Zhuir didn't say anything, just stood there expressionless with a black cloth covering the nose and mouth, just like that of a ninja, with concealed hands, dressed in black and navy blue.

"Ms. Uhayves, nice to meet you finally. I heard you were the only one who saw Zhuir Pierns kill Ralphel L'Acuah. Well, you and Mr. Chase, but I'll get to him later."

"I didn't see anything. I was unconscious," she replied to him, still on the floor, hurting from her previous battle.

"Is that so?" Mario looked at Douglas, who shook his head in disagreement. "Our friend here seems to disagree with you, Ms. Uhayves."

"She's telling the truth," I shouted at him. "I was there. Ms. Uhayves was unconscious when Zhuir attacked Ralphel."

"No need to shout, Mr. Chase, I'm not going to kill your friend, on the contrary, I'm here to congratulate her." Mario helped Ghaeily up. "Thanks to her distracting that imbecile, my guys here were able to kill him."

"That doesn't make any sense. Mr. L'Acuah was holding all those Vanishers against their will, along with my mom. Why would you want him killed?"

"Mr. Natural, sorry it's a little awkward to call you Mr. Mathias without thinking of your dad," Mario continued. "I never asked Mr. L'Acuah, or anybody for that matter, to keep your mom locked in that cave. That was all Mr. Lee Yang and his sister Lynne Yang who planned all of this on their own, along with Mr. L'Acuah. That's why I killed her in front of Mr. Yang before he could flee. I couldn't find Mr. L'Acuah in his ever-changing river, so I had Mr. Pierns find him and kill him for me."

"That's bull," Marcus cursed him.

"Such a handsome man with such a potty mouth, your parents would be so disappointed." Mario walked around in circles around the cave with his weird shotgun on his hand, not losing sight of any of us. "You see, your mom, Mrs. Mathias, is essential to us. She's been doing an amazing job for us, keeping you out of Porter's business. That was until I found out you were a Natural. I invited her and you for a cup of joyve, but your mom wasn't very keen on letting you close to me, so I sent the Twins to bring you and her in just to talk but, let's just say they didn't execute my orders right. Don't ever send Wonderers to do a Natural's job."

"You're a Natural?" I asked unbelievably.

"Mr. Chase and all of those here who have been alive for centuries of years tell me, how long have I been alive? What planet am I from? Am I even from the Solar System?"

No one spoke a word.

"Of course not! I was there along with Mariah Stars, her father, Alfred Stars, and the King of our Milky Way Galaxy, Titus Vespasian, when our Solar

System was created, and he gave it all to her. TO HER!" Mario shouted so that everyone in the cave could hear him. "He never saw my potential. He didn't think I could rule the System, now look around you. Your king and queen have us divided into categories, Wonderers, Wanderers, Formers now Vanishers. THIS IS ABSURD! Aren't we all PORTERS?!"

Mario looked down and took a deep breath, trying to remain calm.

"I told you, the only thing that I hate more than an outlaw is a coward," Mario pointed his gun to the three Vanishers against the wall cowardly curled up on the floor, "May you find peace among the stars."

KABOOM

The whole ceiling above us exploded, raining stones, rocks, pebbles, and debris all over us, scattering every single one of us all over the cave.

"Am I too late?" Jonathan, with at least ten more Jonathans, came down jumping in the cave with guns in their hands pointing at everyone. "I'm Jonathan Asterion with the C.V.O., and, by the Queen's order, you're going with me."

"I doubt that." Mario gave one look to Daniella, who stabbed the floor with her sword. Instantaneously, the whole cave floor became quicksand, making it impossible for any one of us to move.

BANG-BANG

Jonathan, who also had his feet trapped, fired shots against Daniella, who got hit on the chest, falling backward without her sword or any of her abilities, restoring the floor to its original consistency, setting us free again.

Knowing I wouldn't have another chance, I flew toward Mario, smashing against him, shoving his face against the wet, muddy, cold, cave wall.

"Is this the best you got, Willie?" He spoke the words muffled by the wall. "Did you forget who I am? The training I have? The ABILITIES I HAVE?"

Speaking like a real hunter, he flipped out of my grip, tossing me against the floor with one hand, opening fire against all the Jonathans and whoever was in the path of his shotgun, leaving nothing but Stardust rain everywhere.

"Now, you. "The gun which he pointed at the Jo-nathans disappeared, allowing him to grab a weird-looking gun holstered on his belt, the same gun he killed Xian Sixx and Robert Chan. He pointed it at my face, and I knew that if he'd fired it, I wouldn't come back from it.

"NOT HIM, YOU SON OF A—" Marcus, fully transformed in his white bull self, crashed against Mario, piercing his bullhorns across his chest, hanging him against the wall.

"Oh, that was a good move. Even for a *vitello* like yourself," he spoke the words spitting silver liquid out of his mouth. "But you should've aimed for my heart."

BANG

Mario shot Marcus in his chest, making him transform himself back into his original human self, a sign that Mario didn't shoot him with his weird gun, but a

379

regular fire gun, just like the one Jonathan had.

"Next time, it won't be a Porter bullet, but an Antimatter bullet. It'll kill you for good. Even you, Mr. Natural." Mario pushed Marcus out of the way and made his way toward me. "We're not finished,"

"Yes, we are," Marcus told him, spitting Stardust out of his mouth. "You want me, take me."

"This is a turn of events, Mr. Natural." Mario turned his way to Marcus, who was still on the floor. "You're willing to sacrifice yourself just to save that Wanderer?"

"Just kill me already and leave them be."

"Your wish is my command, Mr. Natural." Mario gave Marcus a bow out of mockery. "Drayton, come and grab your lover and let's get out of here. Daniella, leave no one alive."

Mario disappeared inside of his Exotic Matter Sphere, as Drayton flew to capture Marcus, who was now struggling to not go with him, but without his powers, Marcus looked like a helpless deer fighting against the secure grip of a lion; in this case, a winged horse.

"William," Marcus spoke hopelessly, just before disappearing inside Drayton's Exotic Matter Sphere.

Daniella looked at me, and before she could do any harm, I let out a high screech sonic boom, knocking everyone around me unconscious.

Every single one of them.

XX

AFTERMATH

"Are you sure he's here?"

"I'd recognize his powers anywhere in the Solar System," I heard E.J. reply to the familiar voice of Tara Whirls.

"By the stars, are they all...?"

"No, Ms. Whirls, they are just unconscious," I told them, still sitting on my knees after my legs had given up either for the effect of my sonic boom or for my sense of defeat. Either way, it doesn't matter. I lost the battle. I lost Marcus.

"Tara, let's gather our Porters, while Elijah gathers our hero, shall we?"

"Sure thing, Jonny."

Jonathan and Tara looked around for any Porter that was on our side. Tara was unsure of who they all were exactly, but thanks to Jonathan being able to know everything that happens at the exact same time as the rest of his copies, he knew who was who.

"Hey, are you okay?" Elijah squatted in front of me, concerned about my well-being.

"I lost, E.J. Mario took Marcus with him. I just..." I couldn't finish my sentence before my tears could betray me and fall freely down my cheeks.

Elijah hugged me tightly, which he hadn't done in centuries. "We will get him back, Willie. No matter how far they went, we will find him and bring him home."

"What am I gonna tell his mom? I promised Roberto I'd keep him safe. I failed him. I failed both of them."

"No, you didn't, okay? William, look at me." Elijah lifted my chin up, making me look at him. "You saved all of these people, all of these Vanishers here. We will find Marcus, but first, let's gather our friends and get out of here."

"We have to move fast before Mario's squad wakes up," Jonathan told us from across the room, helping a couple of other Jonathans up.

"Too late, we already have," Daniella shouted at us, threateningly.

"Not now, Ms. Saihtam," Arielle's tentacle wrapped around Daniella before she could make true to her threats. "You're not strong enough to fight. We should regroup with our King to figure out our next move."

They both disappeared inside of Arielle's Exotic

Matter Sphere, leaving nothing but a trace of Stardust in the air, as all of the Porters around us were coming back to their senses.

"What about these two?" Tara pointed out to Zhuir Pierns and Douglas Martin, who were both cornered by her and Mohammed.

"I'll take care of them myself." Two of the Jonathans handcuffed them both as another Jonathan kept a gun pointed at them. "The Queen will be happy to deal with them."

Both Jonathans disappeared inside of their own E.M.S. taking along Zhuir and Douglas, leaving the usual trace of Stardust behind.

"Now that it is just us." Nari approached Elijah and me. "Are you okay?"

"How can I be okay?" I got up along with Elijah, who was still squatting next to me. "Where do I go from here? This is it. We lost. End of story."

"William, this is not the end of the story; this is the end of this chapter. Let's close the chapter and focus on the next one."

"Jonathan is right, Will. Look around you. There are over fifteen Porters here. Vanishers and Wanderers alike who all need our help, your help, Willie."

"Yeah, but five of them are all Jonathans, so there are only about nine of us?"

"HEY!" All five Jonathans replied simultaneously to my stupid remark.

"Indeed, what about Captain Lance and the rest of the Argo Navis crew?"

"Nari, you're such a smart girl."

"Thanks," Nari replied with a small, quick smile to Jonathan, "but I still don't like you."

"Guys, as much as I'd love to hear the rest of this soap opera, we got some serious issues in our hands right now," Mohammed spoke from across the dome. He was kneeling next to three other Porters unbeknownst to the rest of us.

"What's going on, Blaze?" Nari asked Mohammed as all the rest of us made our way to them.

"It's Franklin," a woman with short brown hair, no older than twenty-five, responded as she sat next to the male body putting his head on his lap. "He's not waking up."

"Is he a?"

"A Vanisher? Yes, Mr. Bathes. Franklin Walsh is Porter of the Quadrans Muralis Constellation, the Mural Quadrant," Jonathan explained to Litho, who had joined us along with the rest of the Porters.

"Jonathan, can you take him to get some treatment, maybe some Stardust Water?"

"There's no way to transport out of here inside of the Exotic Matter Sphere without having to do at least three or four stops before I could get him out of this planet or bring somebody here for him," Jonathan replied to Ghaeily, explaining to the crowd of Porters. "I'm afraid we are running out of time."

"He is such a brave man! I can't believe he got caught in this crossfire," the other unidentified Vanisher remarked.

"I told him to stay behind me, but he couldn't. He

had to..." But words couldn't come out; instead, tears and sobs took their place.

"Kin, you know it is not your fault. Franklin had a big heart and couldn't just sit still." The short brown-haired woman sat on the floor, holding Franklin's head, tried to comfort her friend.

"Would you two stop talking, I'm trying to die in peace here," the dying man spoke with a breathy voice.

"Franklin, you're awake!"

"If it weren't for you and Kin talking, I would have been already among the stars."

"Oh, stop this nonsense. You're going to get better. We will help you." Kin joined his friends, kneeling next to them.

"Didn't you hear the C.V.O. telling you, I'm a goner, Kin?" The man tried to sit up but didn't have the strength to do so. "Listen to me, you two. I've lived a long life, and I'm ready to go. I wasn't planning on dying, but I wasn't stellar when the bullet hit me, and, being a Vanisher, you know I won't be coming back."

"Franklin, don't—"

"Stop, Lusk. I have only so much Stardust left in my blood, and I need to tell you this." Franklin grabbed Lusk's hand, looking straight into her eyes, with his eyes flickering between their natural shade of brown and bright-white like stars. "You are the most amazing woman I have ever met. I wish I had more time with you to show you how much you mean to me, but the Universe has other plans for us. Now, Ms. Lusk Khones, Porter of the Pantella Constellation, the Limpet, will you promise me to live the rest of your life to the fullest after I'm gone?"

"I will, but why don't you just—"

"Mr. Kin En-Yu, Porter of the Gryphites Constellation, the Clam, you are now responsible for my girl, okay? You two have always been the best of friends, and now, more than ever, I—" Mr. Walsh tried to speak but had to cough silver blood out of his mouth.

"Honey, let us take care of you." Lusk wiped Franklin's mouth with a ripped rag from her clothes.

"I will always love you, my seashell." Franklin looked at her with his eyes no longer flickering; instead, they remained bright-white like stars. His body began shining with glittering spots here and there, dissolving little by little in the air. He let out one last breath, falling unconscious. Finally dead.

"May he find peace among the stars."

"May he find peace among the stars." All the other Porters repeated after Jonathan, over Ms. Khones' sobs, who was being consoled by her friend, Mr. En-Yu.

"THE SKY IS FALLING!" We were all still so moved by Mr. Franklin Walsh's death that we didn't even see somebody else manifesting behind us. "THE SKY IS FALLING!"

"Mr. Yang, what are you talking about?" Jonathan asked Lee Yang, Porter of the Gemini Constellation, the Twins, who were flickering from one side to another without even realizing.

"The sky, this dome, the whole cave is coming

down. I saw. We saw it. Right, *Aneki?* Mario. No, Cruise, Ben Cruise. And what's her name? Troya, Umma Troya. NOT NOW, Sis. I WILL help them. They are collapsing. No. The dome above us is collapsing. Troya did it. Cruise told her to. He's allied to Mario."

"What is he talking about, Jonathan?"

"If he's indeed telling the truth, dear William, the air tunnel around this dome is dissipating, allowing the blue-water to crash down upon us. The pressure would be so high that it would collapse this whole dome on us, killing us instantaneously."

"I AM telling the truth." Lee moved from side to side, stopping right in front of Ms. Khones, "You, you can save us all. They won't listen to us, to me. Do that thing you do. That cone-like shell. PLEASE! I need them alive. WE need them alive to—"

But the sky did indeed fall. In this case, the whole dome came crashing down on us, and just before the stones could crash us, they hit an invisible shield.

"You gotta move fast. I can't keep holding it," Lusk shouted, standing up with both of her arms stretched above her head, where a pointy cone revolved around us.

"We can't teleport out of here. There's a field around this dome, making it impossible for us to pass through, thanks to Ms. Troya and her special abilities."

"How do you know this, Jonny?"

"Look around you, Nari. One less Jonathan for you."

"Oh, I'm sorry I—"

"GUYS!" Lusk shouted, struggling to keep the ceiling together.

"I have an idea." Kin jumped, and before his feet could touch the ground again, his whole body was revolved in a shell, as if he had been swallowed whole by a rectangular shape clam. "Mr. Bathe, if you could follow me, make sure that the earth around me doesn't collapse after a pass through. I will make a tunnel for us to get through till we reach the next air tunnel so we can get out of here."

"Lead the way, Mr. En-Yu," Litho replied with his body now transformed in a frog-like human.

"Stay stellar, Porters." Kin dove in the floor right above us, with Litho right behind him, freezing up a tunnel for all of us to get through.

One of the Jonathans jumped right behind them while another Jonathan was guiding the line, followed by Ghaeily Uhayves, Theodore Hershey, Isabella Occhio, and Dorotheia Sonny. Then another Jonathan followed them with a flashlight illuminating the way, followed by Lee Yang, Tara Whirls, Mohammed Nixx, Nari Anser, and Elijah Jones. There were only two other Jonathans behind, along with myself and Lusk Khones, who was on her knees holding the ceiling together.

"Lusk, LET'S GO!" I shouted as one of the Jonathans was dragging me into the hole.

"I'm staying..." She told me with tears falling down her eyes. "I'm joining Franklin among the stars."

"NO!" I shouted, clawing myself on the floor with

every strength I had, avoiding Jonathan to drag me in. "I'm not gonna let you do this on your own."

"She's not alone." The remaining Jonathan kicked me inside of the hole just before the ceiling came down upon them, blocking the way back to the now-collapsed dome.

"NO!" Jonathan and I shouted together. "Why did you do that? We could have saved her."

"William, I admire your heart. And trust me when I tell you, there's no way we could've saved her." Jonathan collapsed on the floor, right in front of me.

To see Jonathan like that was a reminder that he feels every single pain, every single death all his copies feel too. In less than thirty minutes, Jonathan has experienced more deaths than anyone will in all of their lifetimes.

"Jonathan, I'm sorry. Are you okay?"

"I'm uncomfortably getting used to dying. A feeling I haven't felt since before all this madness began." Jonathan got up to his feet, wiping away tears from his eyes. "Let's keep moving. Their sacrifice won't be in vain."

"You're right. We still have Porters right here, right now, and scattered throughout the Solar System who need us. We have—"

BEEP-BEEP

The triangle-shaped bracelet on my right wrist beeped and began shinning like a dying star. A reminder that my time will be over soon.

"We have to run, Willie."

Jonathan and I ran through the icy tunnel, impervious to the cold, trying to catch with the rest of the other Porters who were ahead of us by miles. No more than fifteen minutes later, we caught up to them outside of the tunnel created by Kin En-Yu and Litho Bathes.

"It took you guys long enough," Nari greeted us once we were outside of the tunnel. "Now, we just gotta wait for Jonathan number four and Ms. Lusk Khones."

"Nari, I'm afraid Ms. Khones decided to join Mr. Walsh among the stars," one of the Jonathans right behind her, replied. "And now you got one less Jonathan to annoy you."

The three Jonathans hugged each other. No words were spoken. There was no need to talk when you could feel each other's exact feelings and thoughts.

None of us spoke.

We stayed in silence, giving them the time they needed to grieve the loss of another member of the C.V.O., the Canis Venatici Organization.

"They're here," one of the Jonathans spoke after what has been an eternity. "I had Jonathan take Elijah back to the surface so they could bring the Ark back, and, here they are."

An anchor fell down above us, hooking itself in the blue sand, with Jonathan attached to it.

"And Jonathan number three is back," Nari said excitedly, to everyone's surprise.

"Hello, Porters. Make way for the Argo Navis." Jonathan number three jumped out of the anchor, gesturing for everyone to move aside as the anchor started pulling down the Ark.

It didn't take more than five minutes for the ship to land on the bottom of the Gyhull Ocean. All of us hopped on board and headed straight back up the blue ocean to the surface.

"William?" The moment I was not looking forward to had finally arrived. Marcus' mom, Katherine Mathias, approached me.

"Katherine, I'm sorry. I did everything I could, but I wasn't good enough. I couldn't save Marcus from Mario, and now—"

"Shhhh." She hugged me tightly for a brief moment. When she let go of me, she looked straight into my eyes and said: "I know you did everything in your power to save him. Your love for him is strong. Stronger than my own even. So, thank you for looking after him when I couldn't, when I wasn't there, available for him."

We both shared a few tears before either one of us could say anything, until finally: "Now, William, tell me. How are we getting our boy back?"

"Katherine, I'm not sure if I know what you mean. My bracelet is twinkling as a warning that my time is up. Soon enough, Mr. Detcha will have me teleported back to the Triangulum Australis Facility. I'm as good as Obliviated right now."

"Not if I have a saying in this." She looked around for the closest Jonathan. "Ready for our next mission?

"I'm not sure what you mean, but you can count on me," Jonathan nodded in agreement.

"To be fair, I don't even know what you mean either, Katherine." I looked at her completely unsure of what she had in mind.

"Jonathan, let's bring these people back home. Once you are done, come and see me. We're going back to Earth."

"Yes, ma'am." Jonathan agreed with her but didn't move; instead, the other two Jonathans onboard did.

"What's going on?" E.J. and Nari joined us in the conversation not long after, "We heard Jonathan bringing Theo and Isabella back to their home. Are both Jonathans bringing everyone home?"

"Yes, Elijah. This adventure is over. It is time to bring everyone home, and we'll take it from here."

"Katherine, with all due respect, this 'adventure' as you put it is far from over," E.J. interceded. "William is about to be taken in and maybe even tossed into Oblivion by the Queen. Mario Shwayze took Marcus, and no one knows what he plans to do with him. And that's not even talking about all these rogue Porters taking among themselves to exterminate Vanishers like myself. So, no! This adventure is not over; as a matter of fact, it has just begun."

"E.J., I agree with you, but we cannot ask much more of you to join us in this. As you said, you're a Vanisher, and if something were to happen to you, I wouldn't be able to live with myself," I told him.

"What are you talking about? No one is asking me anything. I'm telling you. As a Vanisher, I will see the end of this even if I have to die to make sure no other Vanishers have to, besides, aren't you a Vanisher yourself?"

"Yes, I am. But this is my son we are talking about. I can't risk your lives as well," Katherine told him.

"Or ours for that matter," Mohammed and Lee joined in the conversation.

"No, no, just no," Katherine told both of them.

"Why not? Is it because I'm a child?"

"Yes, Blaze. I mean, I know you're not a child, but your body is. I can't risk having you—"

"What, dead? You know that every time I die, I come back older and stronger, right?" Mohammed circled around her. "Plus, I have nowhere else to go, or no one for that matter."

"You'll stay with me in my house until this is all over with, okay?" Katherine squatted next to him. "But there's no way I'm letting you tag along, Mr. Yang?"

"Why not? Because I'm mentally unstable?"

"You're not mentally unstable; you're grieving the loss of your sister. I feel you should take some time out to rest, to grieve her properly, to—"

"To sit on the sidelines while Mario goes around on a killing spree? No, thanks. None of us knows what he truly has in mind. None of us is safe. We heard what he did with Xian Sixx and Robert Chan, killing them cold-blooded. They were Wanderers."

"I hate to break this up, but we're still out-numbered," Nari reminded us.

"I can take care of that," One of the Jonathans joined in on our conversation too.

"As helpful as you both are, Jonathan, they would see you coming a mile away," Katherine told the crowd of Porters. "I was thinking of bringing new Porters along the way."

"Katherine, are you sure? Do you think they are ready?" One of the Jonathans asked her concernedly.

"You, yourself, told me that they have already mastered key elements to attack and defend themselves. I think it's time we talk to them."

"Okay, can somebody fill the rest of the group on what's going on?" Nari shouted, somewhat aggravated.

"After the Sea Monster, Arielle Hyllus attacked us, I was brought up with Jonathan to the Argo Navis' rendezvous meeting point. There, Jonathan and I spoke to my dear husband, Roberto, and explained to him everything that was going on. Jacques, Mileena, and Jena were brought up to speed on everything that has been happening to Marcus and where he has been for the past few Earthian years. Jacques was never the same after that incident, and now, he and his girlfriend want to join in the fight to help bring his best friend home. Oh, and Jena is just going for fun," Katherine explained to all of us.

"You're telling me that Jena, Mileena, and Jacques are now Porters as well?"

"They haven't got their tattoos yet, but they've been training, Willie?"

"Training by who, Jona-argh—" I couldn't finish my sentence. My bracelet lit up, hurting my wrist and my stomach.

"William?"

"He's okay, Elijah. His bracelet is activating his Exotic Matter Sphere to teleport him back to the T.A.F." Jonathan explained to him.

"Listen, take a deep breath, and we'll see you soon, okay?" E.J. assured me.

"You're damn right we will. I will break out of that place again if I have to," Nari told me, but I could barely make any sound around me.

Everything was getting brighter and brighter. My ears couldn't hear anything but a high-pitched noise. I couldn't formulate any thought, just let out a sonic screech before disappearing involuntarily inside of my Exotic Matter Sphere.

I woke up back in my cell, inside of the Triangulum Australis Facility.

"You're finally up," Mr. Hugh Wolf told me from the other side of the cell. "In less than an hour, I'll be back to take you to the Queen. She's anxious to talk to you."

Hugh walked out with laughter echoing through the empty icy corridors of the Facility. I just hope there's enough time for Katherine to come and set me free.

'I will see you soon, Will,' Marcus sent me a T.P.

EPILOGUE

“ A re you two ready?”
"*Oui, ma belle,*[67]" I replied to the most beautiful woman in the world and my girlfriend, Mileena Watson. "Are you ready, *mon amie*[68] Jena?”

“I'm gonna kick your butt, Jacques,”

“Alright. Get ready. Stay Stellar. FIGHT!”

Every weekend for the past year or so, Mileena, Jena, and I get together at Ms. Margaret Hills' and Mr. Kent Hors' place to fight against each other under the surveillance of Roberto Mathias and our new friend and mentor Jonathan Asterion. However, neither one of them was here now. They had stepped out for a few minutes, leaving Mileena in charge.

---

[67] *Oui, ma belle:* Yes, my pretty, (French)

[68] *Mon amie:* My friend (French)

Mileena is a natural leader, thanks to her being born under the Constellation of Virgo. Jena, the woman I'm fighting against, is younger than me by a couple of years, but don't let that fool you. Jena Alvis is the smartest person I have ever met.

Jena was born in October, making her a Libra. Or at least that's what I thought. After drinking Stardust Water, Jena's body became full of feathers, to her despair. It took a little while and a lot of training to figure out Jena is a Wanderer, Porter of the Aquilla Constellation, the Eagle.

In this fight, Jena and I can test our abilities against each other, and whoever wins, fights Mileena, the Virgo. That should be an easy task for me. Ruled by Sagittarius, I started our fight by shooting an arrow from my bow drawn out of thin air.

Jena swirled midair, avoiding my arrow with close to no effort, soaring up to sky faster than my eyes could see. Just when I thought she had given up, Jena plunged toward me, aiming her beak and talons menacingly at me.

I shot as many arrows I could at her, but she dodged them all without slowing her speed; in fact, I think she was approaching me faster. Then just as she was right above me, I aimed at her. I waited till she was closer so I wouldn't miss it. She got closer and closer, and, right in midair, less than a few feet away, I shot. But she was gone.

I looked around the sky, and she was nowhere to be found.

"Looking for me?" I felt her tapping my shoulder.

I turned around instinctively, and ***POW*** Jena landed a left punch on my right eye, making me fall backward and land on the soft grass of Ms. Hills' yard.

"JACQUES!" Mileena shouted, coming to check on me. "Are you hurt?"

"Only my ego, ouch."

"Sorry, I didn't mean to hurt you," Jena apologized, helping me up.

"Don't apologize," Jonathan spoke, joining us in the backyard. "He should've stayed stellar just like Mileena told him to."

"You're right." I got up to my feet, facing Jena again. "Rematch?"

"I'm afraid your rematch will have to wait," Jonathan walked in, followed by Roberto and Katherine Mathias.

"Mrs. Mathias, you're home!" Jena ran to hug her.

"You're alive!" I shouted in excitement.

"Of course, she's alive, doofus." Mileena and her sweet comments. One of the many reasons why I fell in love with her.

"I can assure you I'm pretty alive, Jacques." She smiled at all of us as three other people walked in, right behind her, including a child no older than ten years old. "I'd like you to meet three other friends of ours. Ms. Nari Anser, Porter of the Vulpecula Constellation, the Fox,"

"*An-nyeong*,[69] everybody." This chick dressed in orange high heel boots, with fuzzy, big orange hair,

---

[69] *An-nyeong:* Hi (Korean)

greeted us in Korean waving her hand from side to side.

"Next is her boyfriend, Porter of the Mallus Constellation, the Mast, Elijah Jones," Jonathan introduced,

"Call me E.J., kids," the tall black dude with pronounced muscles, replied. His muscles were just as big as mine.

"You're a Vanisher?" Jena asked in amazement.

"You truly are the smart one, aren't you?" E.J. smiled at her.

"And I'm Mohammed Nixx, Porter of the Phoenix Constellation, but you can call me Blaze," the child dressed in black including his turban, introduced himself, *"namaste,[70]"*

"You're a Porter too? But you're only a child?" Mileena asked, almost sorrowful.

"I can assure you I'm much older than all of you combined."

"Where's Marcus?" I asked, looking around for him.

"Jacques, remember when you and I sat down to discuss your future on becoming a Porter and bringing Jena and Mileena into this?"

"Yes, Mr. Mathias, I remember. I told you I didn't want to be oblivious of everything that is going on with my best friend, that I want to be there for him in case he needs me. Us, for that matter,"

"Well, this is the moment. Marcus needs you. He

---

[70] *Namaste:* Greetings (Hindi)

needs all of us right now. Marcus got taken by Mario Shwayze, and it's up to us to rescue him," Jonathan inserted.

"Alright, let's go!" I told them. "Where is he?"

"Jupiter. But first, we gotta rescue William out of the hands of the Queen; otherwise, he'll be tossed into Oblivion," E.J. told us.

"We cannot let that happen," Jena spoke. "If William dies, we may lose Marcus for good. God knows I'd be devastated if anything happens to Sam."

"Thankfully, you don't have to worry about her, Jena. She's completely unaware of all of this for now," Roberto reminded her. "And you're right. Regardless of their relationship, we must save William. He may not be Marcus' boyfriend yet, but he's been a friend of mine for many years."

"And he's innocent," Mrs. Mathias emphasized. "After all, his crime was killing me, and, as we have already established, I'm very much alive."

"Do you really think we are ready for this?" Mileena asked Jonathan, unsure of his request.

"Mileena, you've been training for over a year now. This is for what you've been training for," Jonathan assured her. "So, let's go save Will and Marcus."

"He's right, babe," I told her. "We can do this,"

"Is everybody ready?" Jonathan asked us. "William's audience is about to start."

"Let's do this, beautiful people. Let's bring our golden couple back home," I told everybody around us.

"Do they know they are dating?" E.J. asked Nari

loudly so all of us could hear.

"They might not be dating, Mr. Jones, but we all know there'll be a wedding at the end of this saga," Mrs. Mathias told him in all smiles at the thought of her son getting married.

"Alright, Porters. Remember, training is over. This time is for real," Jonathan began. "We are on a mission, remember to communicate through Thought Projections, and above all, don't forget always to stay stellar. Right, Mr. DüMicahellis?"

"Hey, it was just that one time."

"Sometimes, all it takes is one time, and then, see ya next Halley," Jonny reminded us. "Porters, press your Exotic Matter Spheres, and to Jupiter, we go."

ACKNOWLEDGEMENTS

*I cannot believe this is book II!
Thank you again for the never-ending support of my
family and my friends, old and new.
Porter: William Chase, Book II
wouldn't exist without your support. Thank you!
Special thanks to my sister Marcela Miranda for
designing the cover so beautifully. To Daniel Bandeira
for taking my picture over and over again for the back-
cover, and to Jonathan Hanson for editing this book
for me, God knows I couldn't do it on my own.*

Thank You,

-N.M. Bobok

Made in the USA
Middletown, DE
05 November 2019